This was her betrothed!
He was the man of her dreams!
In truth, he was here!

She'd heard him laugh, a black-velvet ripple, sweet as the honey of the southlands, and felt something deep within her move, open. She'd looked wildly about, and her heart was like an arrow hurtling through space. Then eye met eye. A spark leaped in the meeting, and the newcomer had laughed no more. He gazed at her with...recognition, it might be, for she had felt it, too.

This is the one!

Brenna swallowed hard. There had never been any other like this man. She could not suppress a heated sensation welling deep inside. His hand, heavy on her shoulder, seemed to have the strength of iron. She wanted to tuck herself closer against that strength...and yet she did not know why...!

* * *

Ironheart
Harlequin Historical #580—October 2001

Praise for Emily French's previous works

Bogus Bride
"An exciting, realistic, steamy romantic adventure."
—*Rendezvous*

The Wedding Bargain
"The story is packed with continuous excitement
and such marvelous characters,
you'll be sorry to reach the end."
—*Rendezvous*

Illusion
"...witty and fast paced...just enough mystery
to keep you guessing."
—*Affaire de Coeur*

IRONHEART
EMILY FRENCH

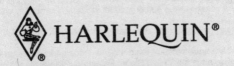

HARLEQUIN®

**TORONTO • NEW YORK • LONDON
AMSTERDAM • PARIS • SYDNEY • HAMBURG
STOCKHOLM • ATHENS • TOKYO • MILAN • MADRID
PRAGUE • WARSAW • BUDAPEST • AUCKLAND**

ISBN 0-373-29180-9

IRONHEART

Printed in U.S.A.

Please address questions and book requests to:
Harlequin Reader Service
U.S.: 3010 Walden Ave., P.O. Box 1325, Buffalo, NY 14269
Canadian: P.O. Box 609, Fort Erie, Ont. L2A 5X3

To Emily Ninnis, travel agent *par excellence*.

"He, who the sword of heaven will bear
Should be as holy as severe."
—William Shakespeare, *Measure for Measure*

Prologue

Northern Marches, Wales, 1188

The night was dark and full of menace. Leon shivered, struggling to stay awake. It was the joining point of the night. The hour of beginnings and endings. It was an unholy hour to be out of bed; the black watch before cockcrow when men most often died, and demons walked.

"Are you a knight?"

A thin little reedy sound it was, echoing somewhere from the right. At first Leon thought he had imagined it, for there was something about old piles of stone like this that accumulated shadows and odd sounds, creaks and sighs of wind.

Then it came again, eerie, alien, disembodied, drifting across the battlement, a voice soft as reeds twisting in the wind.

"Are you a knight?"

The point of his sword lifted a little.

It was an intrigue. It must be. Soon it would be dawn— the hour for murder and mayhem. He exhaled softly. It was comforting that the gray of his cowl and cloak bled into the gray of the battlements, leaving no shape for the eye to catch. There was only the shine of captured light from his naked blade as he waited, listening.

Glancing over his shoulder, Leon saw no movement, suspicious or otherwise, but his back prickled as if several thousand insects crawled up and down it. He swallowed hard.

It took courage to ask calmly, "Who is this?"

Silence.

It was some rotten trick. None had played such since he was nine years old and he'd dared the raven in the hayloft that the other pages refused to face. It had known better than to meddle with him, and fled with a great rustling of straw and a clap of wings.

"Is anyone there?" he asked the shadowed air and held his breath waiting for an answer.

Nothing changed. No voice responded. No figure appeared from the doorway. He swallowed loudly. No harm was near. A very little light came up from below, not enough to light the steps. If any spirits dream-danced there, none spoke.

He gave that some thought, then cleared his throat. He had been speaking French; he shifted to Latin. Nothing. *"Who?"* he demanded in Anglo-Saxon, and last of all, with fading hope, the old Gaelic of his childhood.

"I am here."

That rocked him on his heels. The voice came from behind him now, the same voice, as if it were stalking him. He spun around, hands out, at hearing a light skipping step from the direction of the parapet. Closer, came the high piping tone of a child.

"I said, Are you a knight?"

Leon stared a moment, heart thumping. Shadows shifted and took substance. A glimmer. It was a girl, a highborn little girl in a white night rail, but lace dragged about one ankle and her lips and hands were muddied. She tilted her head to one side, studying him.

"No," he said, to humor her while he tried to think. The girl had a pixie face, and the dark, shining hair that bounced about her shoulders was black as only an elf's can be. But she looked real, a babe scarce weaned. There was no magic.

There was nothing to fear. Her gaze remained steady. He felt heat flare in his ears, so he added, "When I am a man I will be."

A frown touched her brow, as if he had said something curious. "Is that not the way of things?" she said, edging closer, as though they already shared one secret, and might share another, in time.

Leon blinked. How could a little girl speak with such knowledge? Except for the druids, adults were jealous of their secrets and did not share them with children. Was she a druid's daughter?

Had he been enchanted? He clenched his hand to drive the thought away and touched the rough stonework. It felt real enough, down to the grit of old mortar.

I won't let her see she has me uneasy, he told himself firmly. I won't let her trick me. He took the chance. It took real effort, but he kept his voice steady.

"Are you a witch?"

"Do I look like one?"

"I've only seen one, face-to-face. At least I think it was a witch. You don't look like her. But how should I know?"

"Well, now that I see you close up, you don't look like a knight, either. You're tall, but you look like a boy."

The small doubt held him still, but that was only his good sense that said girls were not safe wandering at cockcrow alone. There were all manner of unwholesome things that haunted the night. And this one feared no harm from them—that seemed evident, whatever her reason.

He thrust his sword in its scabbard. "You're distracting me from my duty. What are you doing here?"

"I've come to watch."

"To watch what?"

Her shoulders jerked slightly. "I wanted to see Father—they told me he's going away with the prince," she said fiercely, a dimpled dragon flashing fire and smoke. Her little jaw set. Her eyes were alive with thoughts. "I had to get up early and run away from Nurse, 'n' here I am."

He started to walk. She pranced along beside him.

"The battlements are out of bounds. How did you get here?" he asked, with deep notes of iron grating on one another in his voice. "And more to the point, why?"

"I couldn't go downstairs because of the guards, and I didn't want to climb out a garderobe shaft 'cause they smell so awful, 'n' I came up here instead." She moved closer, scowling. "I tried to get up there." She pointed into space out a crenel. "But I'm not big enough. But you're here, so you can—"

Leon flinched, and said, between closed teeth, "Forget it."

He paused at a buttressed arch and turned to look into the vast hollow before them. From this angle, no lights shone, not even faint ones. It was black as a cave. Only the immensity of air, palpable as a beast, betrayed the cavernous gulf beyond.

Fear clenched his heart with an icy grip. How had he gotten into this? He grasped the merlon with one hand, to keep from shaking, and felt sandstone crumble under his fingers. He pulled back by instinct.

"Flamed rotted-out pile of—" He caught back a swearword.

She turned her head and looked at him. Then slowly she began to smile, her eyes anxious, but her grin growing wider. She was contemplating mischief, he was sure of it.

"Are you afraid?"

"Of course not! I have an arm of steel and a heart of iron!"

"*Oo-oh,* how wonderful. Are heroes always so strong?"

"Of course."

Leon sweated. Heroes are always strong, and they never run away, he told himself. And that was a worry. *He* was scared and breathless.

"You're bigger than me." A sudden pale glance, starlit. She smiled. "Can you see over the top?"

He nodded foolishly, and again she laughed. He thought

that perhaps he had never heard a lovelier sound. "Of course."

"Well?"

He was more than a little unnerved. Breath came short, in shameful panic. At the same time, his heart leaped into his throat and stayed there. Does she know? He cast her a sideways glance. A dimple winked in her cheek, but she stood there, dark eyes wide, full of faith and innocence; real, and not an illusion. It was surely the weakness that was the illusion—

Leon snapped into focus with a shudder. "Disabuse yourself of such notions. 'Tis not yet dawn." He was arguing with himself more than with her. He turned to face her, feeling his face flush. "There will be naught to see," he said, surprising himself with his vehemence.

"Oh," she said wistfully, as if dashed in her expectations. However, she was not demolished, for she stared at him with bright blackberry eyes, and went on. "I was rather looking forward to—well, this grand occasion…the wonder and excitement…it's dull in the nursery… I have to make up my own adventures—" she talked rapidly as if to ward off his saying anything "—being a boy, of course, you don't have to make up little pictures in your head of what it'll be like when you're all grow'd up."

"I never said I didn't dream, but the future is clouded, and there's no way to foretell or change it."

"Nonsense! Close your eyes. Tight. Imagine for yourself what it'll be like when you're a knight."

Leon shrugged, stunned by this abrupt assault and uneasy about its possible consequences, but did as he was bid, his hand resting lightly, prudently, on the sword hilt.

A searing flash burned his eyes. The sharp crack of lightning—or deadly magic—barked beyond the castle walls, then bugles blared and he felt the pounding of heavy hooves through the ground.

It was a trap! Nay, it was sorcery, and everyone knew sorcery was an evil used by heathens of old. For all he knew, it was a trick to distract him from his watch. It wouldn't have been the first time a child was used as bait in a trap. What can I do? he asked himself. His brain recoiled from the prospect of being the agent of assault, or worse, by failing his duty...

"No!" he protested with more determination than he felt. But the enchantment held him fast. There was no choice but to go with it.

Combat surrounded him, fire and smoke and the clamor of battle in all directions as far as he could see and hear. His helmet was gone and he could feel the gashes in his steel chain mail. His skin was torn in many places and blood covered his body. Flames spouted from the siege wagons, and some tents had caught fire. Rain kept the wagons from becoming an inferno, but the unburned canvas kept the rain from extinguishing the fire.

Then he saw the banner, the rampant lions outlined in gold against the bright red field, now trampled in the earth, torn by sword and dyed almost black in the blood of the young soldiers who followed it. He couldn't tell whether it was rain or blood running into his eyes, but his vision blurred to nothing.

Caer Llion! Where are you?

He flinched suddenly at the touch of a slender hand and turned to see a small figure standing before him. This one was not armored like the knights, nor tall nor broad enough to be a soldier. This was no manly fighter, but a woman!

"You are hurt," she said. A deep cowled hood shaded her face, and her elfin features seemed to glow and fade in the reflected light of the flames.

"The battle is lost," he whispered fiercely, straining to control his disbelief. He gasped for breath.

"You and your men fought well."

"And died well. I must claim vengeance."

"You'll get no vengeance riding alone into that nest." The girl-woman took his arm and began to lead him away, *though there was no way to tell which way to go. "And you, my golden knight, you have a destiny to fulfil. Hold on to me and you will live to fight again. I will protect you."*

He nodded his head, confused. How did this woman think she could do such a thing? He peered into the shadows of her still-raised hood. She let the hood slip back far enough for their eyes to meet clearly. Her eyes were brown, soft and deep, and he felt lost in them, lost in wondering what he had not seen.

The question seemed quite unimportant as his eyes saw more and more shadowy forms appearing, only to flee in all directions and be followed by great waves of horsemen and their riders. There were no individuals—only bodies, armed and unarmed, eager to slay and keep on slaying.

He squinted, not quite seeing their faces, and always the riders passed the two figures without seeing them. He heard the screams of men caught by lance or mace or hoof, but he felt the soft protection of magic, invisibility created by the girl-woman that now cloaked him.

A damp wind swirled around him, and he felt a slight chill. The air smelled of masonry. His reason told him he was on the battlements, but his irrational self said he must have tripped for a minute, then leaped forward a full decade or more.

"What is it? What did you see?"

Leon opened his eyes. He blinked and the vision was gone. The inky blackness of the night was giving way to a softer gray. Had the vision been an image of reality?

"Nothing much, and nothing certain," he answered, turning on his heels, but the muscles in his legs trembled despite his determination to stand firm. "Except the prince is coming, and so is bad weather."

"That's important!"

"If my knowledge of ritual is accurate, at your age, you should still be abed, and not wandering around the battlements. These are not the most friendly of parts," Leon replied, the edge of his voice as sharp as his sword.

"You try to frighten me," the girl said in a voice that sounded like music tinkling on his ears. "But I am not afraid."

He rounded on her angrily. "Are you questioning my courage?"

"Not your courage, never that. You can finish anything you start." She looked Leon squarely in the eyes as she spoke. He sought some hidden message there, some gleam of witchcraft, but instead the raven-black depths showed him she was even more uneasy than he was himself. Now all those images seemed ridiculous and absurd. Some of the tension left his body.

There was a long silence. For a long moment Leon listened to the silence that had sprung up between them because it was an unquiet silence, one rife with sizzling tension, almost a contest of wills.

Then an urgent whisper, combined with a tug of his coat, quietly, shyly, tentatively, hopefully, and smiling that innocent smile. "I want only to see Father and the others."

Leon laughed out loud. "Are you certain?"

"That's all," she affirmed, still smiling sweetly.

"How can I refuse to do a good deed?" he asked, hoping there was no tremor in his voice.

That angelic smile. "Would you...?"

He was a fool to do what a girl-child wanted him to do! Yet, her invitation was the only option he saw. Strange thing! He could see no honorable way to deny her. He dared not back out now. He did not want to go to that place—but what else might he do when he was the only one here to help her? he asked himself. It was almost as if he were no longer in command of his own body, that even had he wished to halt and turn back he could not have done so. This was where he was destined to be, what he was fated to do.

And that was magic, surely?

Rush into it and through, it's the only way to face what

you fear, he thought. Tightening his gut, he braced both hands against the wide tooth of a merlon and leaned out a crenel to see past an intervening wall buttress.

The side of the castle dropped sheer. Far down showed the footings of solid granite. Below that...

The earth and river and dark forest far, far below.

He groaned involuntarily. His palms on the merlon were slick with sweat, trembling. An icy ball of fear turned his insides to water. He wanted to go back, but forced himself to stand firm. Far away a cock crowed, calling forth the dawn. The air hung cold and wet about his face as he looked down.

It was no good. His breath rasped. His teeth danced. His sight hazed. His legs shook so violently his kneecaps drummed the stone wall. Stand here too long, and he'd pitch over the parapet like dice rattling out of a cup. Slowly, shuffling his leather boots, he crept away from the gaping space.

"What did you see? Lift me up so's I can see it, too!" Her mouth open, her face all delighted smile, she danced for the battlements rising on the western end of the parapet.

Already spooked, Leon jumped at the girl's blithe command. Deep shuddering twitched his body. Backing against the inner wall, he willed his heart to stop pounding. Surely it could only beat so fast before bursting. He blinked the night as clear as it would come. There was color in the world. It was dawn. He took deep breaths of clean, cold air.

"You'll fall," was all he could say.

She gazed solemnly up at him. Unafraid. She gave a furious shake of her head. "No I won't, 'sides, you're here to stop me."

He opened his mouth to refute but his jaw trembled. His breathing had slowed, and he mopped his brow with his sleeve. He hated being up in the battlements. He still remembered falling off the tower at Whittington. Even now, he screamed in his sleep when he recalled that day. He had been seven then. He had cried in his foster father's arms, which had embarrassed him, but his foster father had patted him on the back and hugged him the way he hugged Fulk Riven, called him his other son and assured him even grown men made mistakes and wept.

"The other end will give the best view." Indignation, combined with the fear that she might actually leap onto the crenel, made Leon stride out ahead. But she only laughed and followed him.

Walking east, he asked, elaborately casual, "Do you get giddy on heights?"

"Not the times I try," she said, skipping beside him.

He shifted his posture, suspecting mockery. He regretted bringing up the matter, but he refused to care what the witchling thought. *She* seemed absolutely fearless. So young to have such courage, he thought. He saw scratches on her arm and large muddy rips in the gown at her knees. The girl's nurse would be searching for her by now, and he almost felt sorry for the woman. She would suffer if the mother saw the child now.

"Lift me up, so's I can see over." She lifted up slender, fragile-looking arms.

The morning breeze stirred his hair and softly cooled his overheated cheeks. He became calm, and out of calmness came determination. He would not abandon his first damsel in distress. He picked her up, and set her bare feet on the seat of an arrow loop built into a buttress in the parapet.

She stood up on tiptoe, craning forward. She was mad, he was sure of it. He brought a firm hand around her waist to keep her safe, but he didn't stop her looking.

"Lean on my shoulder if you get dizzy. I'll catch you."

"I know, silly!" Steady as a rock on her perch, she rested a small hand on his shoulder and, moth-light, touched his hair. "You talk funny, but you have nice hair. Shiny."

Her voice sparkled with hints of laughter. She smelled of soap and girl and honey powder. He blinked and wriggled his leather-clad toes. "Thank you."

Leon stood perfectly still and glanced over his outstretched arm. It was just dawn; the air hung cold and foggy around him, obscured the towers, cut off the tops of gates, pooled and eddied along the courtyard outside the siege walls, and collected wood smoke in long, flat, sooty sheets.

Troops marched out of the gatehouse. He watched the glittering armor-clad company file through the dimming patches of fog, buckles clanking, pennants snapping on poles, accoutrements jumping and tingling regularly at every step in a mass musical note, muffled strangely in the sea of fog.

"Can you see the prince leading them all?"

The girl-child tossed her head to get an unruly lock of dark hair out of her eyes. "There he is! There he is!" She squealed in delight and clapped her hands.

"He must. He is the commander," Leon said briskly. He glared out the embrasure at the troops still marching past, and fretted to himself. Keith, who would be sixteen years old next Midsummer's Day, had been chosen to squire the prince. Keith, who in spite of his new length of leg and width of shoulder, could not best Leon either at mock battle or in a wrestling match.

"Aren't they grand? Where do they go?"

"Men gather here. To ride with Richard. To Palestine. To fight the Saracens."

As soon as he spoke, he regretted it, for the look on the child's face turned from joy to fear. She frowned, a little knitting of the brow. Small hands clutched at him.

"Oh. *Bad* men," she muttered. Her face crumpled. She looked so young—not a witchling now, but a frightened child.

He was quick to mend his error. "Cheer up, little girl. Your father will be home soon enough," he said lightly.

A frown. She was not to be distracted. "What if the bad men attack us while Father is away?" she said faintly. "Should we all run away very fast?"

Leon looked up at the white, frozen face. Loosing a rare and splendid smile, the one his arms-master said in a few years would melt women like wax in a furnace, he said softly, "No. My lord would stop them before they reach here."

Brave though she was, she was still a girl, and that smile held a mighty magic. She laid her hand upon his arm and squinted through black curls at him, a swift bright glance.

"I can throw rocks at them! Big rocks."

"Oh—" Leon struggled to keep from laughing. He brushed back the dark hair. "That would be most helpful."

Men marched into the fog and vanished. The air seemed unnaturally still and heavy. As an omen it made his spine turn cold. The day seemed perilous, full of portents; yet there was nothing he could put a thought around. As if—

As if he were on the brink of his own forever after—or maybe only of growing up. He had twelve summers and, with Keith's departure, was newly promoted to squire, but tall and muscular as he was, and good as he was with either sword or bow, he hadn't grown into his hands or feet yet.

The girl-child shaded her eyes, shaking her head. "I don't see them anymore."

Leon took a deep breath, drew her back from the crenel edge, tender in his grip. She studied him with grave bright eyes. "Don't you wish you could follow the prince?"

"I wish I was with him. I wish it more than you know," he told her fiercely, angry with her for asking. His voice echoing loudly in the dawn sky.

"It is not too late. If you run fast, you could catch them."

He knew that. He was also not accustomed to being made light of. "My lord isn't happy with things along the border. He wishes me to stay, be a shield-brother to his heir."

"How will you win your spurs?" she asked with just the hint of a smile.

Leon did not rise to the bait. He was a squire, past childhood, and he had seen the lordlings come and go. He thought of Keith all bruised and bloody, crying foul, and the demands of his own stubborn honor. Then he thought of make-believe things, set in the future. Images of the girl-child, now a woman, a prisoner in the place where crows gather, where the woods grow strange and twisted. Himself, helmed and mounted, sword in hand overwhelming a dragon.

No, that was too exotic.

He rebuilt the image and tried to make it something real; the girl-woman up on the battlements, dark hair aflying in the wind, laughing and holding out her arms; himself, just walking into them, and not noticing the precipice.

No, that was too incredible.

The picture changed. The name of Caer Llion had been added to those famed few that were bywords to both friend and foe, whom men would follow into the jaws of death at the wave of an arm. Iron-helmed, he sat astride a huge destrier, sword held aloft and gleaming in the bright morning sun, thundering over the desert sands, leading a band of knights, an iron-clad avalanche of destruction.

"I haven't got it all worked out yet, but one day I'll be a knight. I have to. I *must*." He used the blunt mode for conviction, for absolute duty—for oath swearing.

"You could run away and become a commoner if you wanted it enough. Father says the common women have more fun than the highborn."

"He talks too much. Knights are shields against evil. They are the only hope for pig farmers and little girls—saints preserve their stubborn necks. Nobody else will take pity on them."

"How proper. They will sing songs in your honor." A small hand crept into his, the other touched his jaw with her thumb.

"Sounds good to me."

She wound her tiny fingers through his hair. "Why not? You are brave and noble and strong. You will make a great knight."

Leon's nerves jumped, his pulse fluttered and a flush came over his skin, confusing all his thinking. She was curious. She thought he was very brave. It puzzled rather than delighted him, but it was very hard to go on being mad at someone who really believed that. He searched his mind for something clever to say in response. When nothing came to him, he settled for attempting to endow his silence with a knowing air.

She smiled prettily. Her breath was in his face, warm as a spring sunbeam. "Will you marry me when I grow up?"

Leon couldn't help feeling embarrassed. The girl was so foolish she was a woman already! He was not certain what he was supposed to say, but it wouldn't hurt to put her straight.

"You must marry a man with estates and title."

"I could never marry a man I didn't love!" she said with all the blithe confidence of a four-year-old girl.

"One day a knight will come and steal your heart." He swung her down to the parapet.

"Will you be my own special knight?" she asked straightway.

"Of course," he said grandly, flourishing a salute.

She blinked rapidly. Then she glanced upward, a piercing, anxious look. "For ever and ever?"

Leon smiled his sudden smile. His voice changed, deepened. "Henceforth, I am your forever knight." Bowing low he kissed her hand.

She slid her hand free and detached a knot of ribbon from her night rail and held it out to him. "Then I will wait, 'n' when you are all grown up, you shall come back and marry me."

"Just like that?"

She nodded her head emphatically.

Leon took the token and tousled her hair. If she were not careful, this rare blossom would grow into a thorn bush! He glanced at the dawn sky, pretending disinterest.

"All right," he conceded.

She planted her hands on her hips. There was witchcraft in her eyes. "Will you swear on it?"

Leon ground his teeth. Aggravating girl! Really, she tried his patience to distraction! He inclined his head and turned away. "I vow by sun and moon, earth and water, fire and

air. Does that satisfy you?'' he said to the free air beyond
the walls.

Behind him he heard a whisper of slippers. His back muscles went rigid.

''Nurse!'' She ran off gaily, muddy hands outstretched.
''Oh, Nurse, I could see far and far. I saw the prince ride
out!''

Leon looked around. The waiting woman lowered tight-
clenched hands and spread them, and hugged the draggled
child to her. In a deliberate, careful tone she told the child,
''You must never climb up there alone, you know.''

''Oh, I didn't. My own true knight was with me.''

''This running about has got to stop, my girl.''

''But why?'' The light voice lilted.

The nurse brushed her off mercilessly, then wrenched her
away, scolding loudly, ''It's unnatural to want to be adventuring out of doors.''

''But, Nurse, I have found my knight—only he's not a
knight yet—and he's got hair like gold!''

''One day a fine man with golden hair will ask for your
hand, then marry you, get you with strong children, a round
half dozen. But until then, little mistress, you'd best be
learning the ways of a lady.''

When she reached the doorway, the girl turned. ''Until
we meet again, may every road be smooth to your feet,''
she called in her bell-chime voice, the traditional Celtic farewell.

''And may you be safe from every harm,'' Leon managed
to reply, with more feeling than the customary response usually carried. He had forgotten to ask who her father was.
Not that he would ever see her again. The FitzWarren entourage was returning to Whittington on the morrow.

Unable to stop himself, he reached out a hand, wanting
to ask her name. She did look at him, a pale, distracted
glance, but the nurse waved him off when he'd have followed her.

He closed his eyes, just for a heartbeat. When he opened
them, they had been swallowed up in the darkness.

Chapter One

Northern Marches, Wales, 1204

"The priest is here. All we lack is the groom." Brenna heard the words as if from a great distance. They hung in the air above her head like flaming arrows, separate and solid, one after another, shooting from some unseen bow...

"He will come."

"I fear the worst." The voice drew nearer, a high sweet voice like a bird's. 'Twas her great-aunt Alice, all aflutter. "If no evil has befallen him, surely he would have arrived by now."

A creeping chill went down Brenna's back. The wind whipped her hair and her gown. But her eyes never blinked, her face never flinched, though her heart was hammering against her ribs. She said nothing, only stared fixedly over the merlon, gazing beyond the southward sweep of the battlements.

The walls fell sheer below her, stone set on stone, castle and crag set high above the green valley, field and forest rolling into the mountain bastions in the distance. In the world below, children shouted, a stallion screamed and a tuneless voice bawled a snatch from a drinking song.

The wind sighed upon the stones.

Marry. Marriage. Husband. Wife. Bed.
Children.

A great churning dread welled in her heart. She knew
nothing beyond the valley and its inhabitants and the limited
knowledge and experience acquired as a healer. The secret
tales told by the village women baffled her and yet beckoned
with promises more provocative and lurid than the vague
tutoring her aunts had imparted on the duties of a wife. She
was not certain now whether she wholly welcomed the idea
of marriage, of a husband, but it was still, all things considered, a good way to preserve the peace on the border.

He had to come! Her anxious glance went back to the
valley. The priest had come trailing in, complaining of heavy
rain, and confessing that he had mistaken an intersection of
roads and ridden an hour or more along a road before dis-
covering his error. She hoped that her groom was late for
as silly a reason, but it was making her increasingly concerned. The only other alternatives were either that he had
met foul play or that he had changed his mind.

Why? was the next obvious question, but she only
frowned for even thinking of it. Come the Sabbath she
would be wed, and she had never even met her betrothed!
The feeling of doubt and confusion at the news of her future
husband's impending arrival came laced with a dread that
she couldn't shake, a dread made up of fear for what he
might have learned…what he might have already reasoned…

She was being foolish. Don't think maybe he'll come today and maybe he won't, she told herself. Don't believe that
it's not worth keeping a lookout.

He is coming. She knew it. Yet the shadow of the gray
stone walls joined the shadow of the tower and grew long
across the courtyard. Not an hour of daylight left.

"Brenna!" Slowly she became aware of a plucking at her
sleeve. Her aunt was talking again. What was she saying?
"What of the wedding? The feast is being prepared even
now."

Brenna swallowed hard and as close to invisibly as she could. "I am not ready to abandon all hope."

"Should the preparations be halted?"

"No!" Brenna's fingers clutched the unyielding stone. Her breath left her slowly. She had not known that she was holding it. "No. Grandfather is the most indulgent of guardians, but I fear his patience is exhausted, and to halt all the preparations now would cripple his purse."

"What will you do?"

Brenna wrinkled her nose. Since childhood, she had dreamed of her perfect knight. She had built her own romance about him as she grew older. Her experience as a healer had given her a knowledge of the male anatomy, so she could even visualize in vivid detail the fascinating play of muscles across his shoulders, the rippling sinews along his broad ribs, and the taut, flat belly with its tracing of hair that she knew led downward to the manly part of him. It was at this point that her mind games always stopped for she could not totally catch the import of what lay beyond. When she thought of the future, it was of some romantic meeting with her hero.

But it had not come true...

How ridiculous, to waste time on such thoughts. Her knight was but a dream, a memory. It was no use indulging in romantic fantasies, for marriage was not a romantic business. Marriage was a shackle and no pleasure, however you looked at it. Romance belonged to the troubadours, an elaborate conceit made of flowery language, poetry and lute-twanging.

"I am forsworn, surely and irrevocably. I am betrothed to Aubrey of Leeds."

"Who has not come!"

"Have you ever asked yourself why I agreed to marry a man I have never met?"

"You don't really expect me to answer that?" her aunt replied.

Brenna shook her head.

''When I was as old as you, I had been two years a wife and nigh three seasons a mother.''

''And you didn't mind?''

''Aye, but I had not so doting a father, nor so lax a grandfather. With the coming of my woman's courses, I had perforce to put on a gown and bind up my hair and accept the husband my family had found for me. From all accounts, Aubrey is an admirable fellow…and…according to my brother, who is your guardian, I remind you, your marriage will prevent persistent suitors raiding the marches to gain an advantage over each other.''

The way Lady Alice spoke told Brenna her great-aunt considered marriage but a trifle. She shuddered. Her entire life had been spent following the dictates of authority. She was naught but a female and consequently all decisions were made for her and around her. It was unfair.

And it hurt.

It was all so terribly matter-of-fact. Chattel of one man to be chattel of another. No choice. No argument. It was as the man dictated, as the man ordered. She, the woman, meant nothing to any of them. As her grandfather, Grandy wanted a great-grandson. As Sir Edmund, he also wanted someone willing and able to keep the border barons from each other's throats, so he could spend his time plotting the stars. Aubrey was only going to marry her because of the political advantage a stronghold such as Dinas Bran would bring. The aunts wanted security in their old age, and the villagers were pleased their healer would not be leaving them.

With diminished hope, she scanned the valley once more. The road was clear enough even in the gloom. Nothing.

She drew a long sigh. She was dallying, and the day was running on. A storm was brewing. The clouds were darkening and thickening. She had to work fast. There was much to do before supper. So she controlled herself as well as she could, and twisted 'round to face her great-aunt.

''What profits me to object? I am constrained and cannot stray from Grandy's decree.''

"How long can we wait?"

"Wait for what? Grandy sees his lordship of the northern marches foundering. If the knight does not fulfil his promise by the morrow, then Grandy will find another willing to wed me."

"I can understand how sweet freedom is, Brenna, but you must wed sometime. My brother would not insist on your marrying someone who displeases you, and you must have a life of your own."

"I have a life...in my thoughts, and in my dreams. That will have to suffice."

"You were never so credulous before."

"The bride-price has been paid. The wedding feast is prepared. The priest is here. Most surely, there will be a marriage."

Follow the road, the leper said.

Trouble was, the road appeared and disappeared by turns in the uneven light of the forest. At a lichen-mottled outcrop of rock, Leon reined in and dismounted. Deso tugged at the rein, impatient, and leaves stirred and rustled under his massive hooves.

Leon walked, leading his big creamy-pale destrier along the brown, wet depths of the drifting leaves, following the ancient stonework until the trees grew so close he could no longer find the next white stone to guide him. It was like a ghost road; the only other soul he'd seen in five hours was a leper.

Shadows enveloped him. Even on a sunny day the massive trees in this region were dense enough to filter light, but this had not been a sunny day. The last hours plodding through rainy mist and mud had scarcely discomforted him, for he was already beyond weariness, his flesh chilled by the wind.

I am lost... he thought. He wished he could lie down and rest. His head throbbed, his mouth was dry and his throat burned. He kept walking, light-headed with hunger. He had given the last of his bread to the leper squatting beside an empty alms bowl at the crossroads in exchange for directions to Valle Crucis.

That had been midmorning. Now it was near nightfall. Wrong way, something said to him. He was certain of it. This was not at all where he'd intended to go. He looked back. Already the trees had closed in upon the path. He could see no more than a few lengths behind, a few lengths ahead.

I have done a foolish thing, he thought, wishing he and his escort had never been parted; and then he shook off the feeling as too much caution. Within a day of his meeting with the king's chamberlain, he'd taken his leave, gathered his men and headed for Wales, though the frosts were still too bitter for any greening of the land.

Six weeks later, appalling storm rains swelled the rivers and brooks, drowned the upland bogs and rendered the hillsides treacherous. The company had wrapped their weapons in oiled leather and themselves in heavy hooded cloaks and pressed on without pausing. Wagons bogged in roads turned to quagmires, sumpter mules sank to their haunches in mud and tempers became frayed.

Lodgings had been small and scant. His men grumbled under their breaths, laying wagers on whether Ironheart would command them to harden themselves yet further by camping in the open. It was cruelly hard, but then had come the worst blow of all. Wet fever struck down half his company. Rather than delay further, and only after much argument with his sergeant, he'd left his men at Crewe under the command of Rodney of Leyburn, while he continued on with only his squire, Thomas, to attend him.

It had seemed a good idea at the time. Now, though, he wondered if he'd been too rash. He desperately needed food and shelter for the night, for by now it was painfully obvious that the leper had not had the faintest notion of Valle Crucis.

A chill convulsed him. His brain was whirling with half-

formed thoughts. Was this a fool's mission, riding for
Wales? It was a long way to go on a hunch.

Still, he had a duty. He would deliver the relic of the Holy
Cross entrusted to him by the monks at Cluny, a perfectly
natural reason to visit the abbey—and to discover whether
the informant's reports were true or false. After that, he was
not certain. He was tired of political intrigue. Mayhap he
could resign as the king's judiciar and so buy some time, a
chance to decide what he should do next.

He could go to Dinas Bran. His heart slammed against
his ribs. It was not sane. It *was,* if one was a fool. And no
one could accuse him of that. Intemperate, perhaps. But not
a fool.

Or he could take another fork in the road. He could go to
Whittington, claim it as was his legal right. Then perhaps
he could move forward and not constantly think back toward
the lost things he remembered. Making peace with that, he
could perhaps begin to see things as vividly ahead of him,
instead of the gray space that seemed to occupy all his future...

"I think we're a long way from nowhere, don't you?"
The destrier twitched its ears at the sound of his voice, and
a rising wind whispered assent through the wet branches.

The road bent around an out-thrust knee of rock. It was
the solid ground ahead that beckoned him, and his feet were
very glad to feel that solidity under them as he left the forest
behind. He was onto a well-worn path. He glanced up the
slope, saw stones and vines through the trees, saw stone
walls and turrets, saw...

A truly wondrous sight.

Dinas Bran!

The castle enjoyed a vantage over all the valley and perhaps the plains and hills beyond, to all the distance a clear
day would afford. Like a great hog's back on top of the hill
it stood, a brooding stone pile with thick gnarled walls and
an air of neglect. Not as fine as some, but a sturdy, well-

built fortification for all that, with narrow openings in it here and there through which it might be defended.

A bell began to toll from the walls, waking echoes across the hills. Following these echoes other sounds began to reverberate from within the keep itself: dogs barking, the calling of voices one to the other, the jingling of horses. Birds rose from the tower, wheeled and drove, chattering, black specks against the lowering sky. Ravens, which gave rise to all manner of lore and legend.

Deso's nose met his shoulders and shoved. Leon gathered the reins, which he had let go slack, and remounted. "Hear that, Deso? Do they wait to pick our bones?"

A dry, distant crack of thunder cut through the gloominess of his thoughts. Ravens were not the only things threatening, it seemed. There was a bank of dark clouds piling up in the north; the kind of clouds that were laden with rain and indiscriminate in their dropping of it. A flicker of lightning ran along the edges of their contours, making them for an instant as sharp and clear as outlines cut from blackened copper.

Leon urged his mount up the steep incline, black shadow against the sullen light, for the motte and the stronghold above, a swift striding that lost not a pace. The tearing thunder-crash repeated itself a few seconds later, and just a little longer than before. The stallion snorted and shied, setting the equipment jingling and creaking. He put them to a quicker pace, and they went pell-mell up a chancy turn, over ground buried in leaves, a stretching and gathering of sinew, a flutter of mane, a streak of mire, as if that could make them safe, get them behind gates and walls.

A vast somber sound boomed out, brazen and measured, the rattle and groan of chains as the portcullis was lowered. It was not an auspicious hour to arrive unheralded and alone. Gates were secured at sundown and reopened with the dawn. Many a traveler who misjudged the timing of his arrival spent an uncomfortable night outside the walls at the mercy of robbers and worse.

"The lower gate should be open still."

The stallion shifted its weight, bowed its head, and made a quiet, disturbed sound. No doubt Deso was thinking of a warm stable, a good rubdown and some sweet oats. He himself wished desperately for a cup of ale, for a place to lie down and rest. But first he had to discover whether the postern gate remained open. He would know soon enough.

The road bent to follow a curve in the curtain wall where standing stones made an aisle leading to the gate. Here, by the towering arch of stone, a small table had been set up, in front of which stood a motley-dressed collection of beggars.

With a certain disquiet, he noted there was no watch on duty. Doubtless they kept a burly fellow or two on hand to deal with possible emergencies, but there ought to be guards posted in a hold as large this and with constant threat along the border.

Leon slid from the saddle. The stallion stood braced, head high, eyes and nostrils wide. Leon looped the reins and gave the beast a pat on the neck. It shuddered once and was still. He looked about, taking nothing for granted. With a soldier's practiced eye, he searched for irregularities.

Some distance away, four churls huddled together, talking in low voices and casting uneasy glances around. Shadows lurked and flickered about them. His brows drew hard together. No doubt he was imagining things, but he gained the impression that these ruffians were plotting some villainy. The idea intrigued him, and his spirit lightened at the prospect of a bit of action.

There was the sound of some commotion coming from the vicinity of the courtyard. A woman hurried through the postern gate. She looked about her, letting her glance rest briefly on the beggars. Despite the plain cut and drab color of her gown, he knew she was no peasant wench or waiting woman.

"Tudur?" Her voice was low and musical, with a distinctive husky tone. There was something about it that made him want to hear it again. What folly! He laughed out loud,

and surprised himself for it was not a usual thing for him.
The woman must have heard him because she swung around
and stared at him so intently that he felt both rude and careless. Her eyes held him where he was.

Leon felt his heart skipping. He wished he had come with
the clarion of trumpets, the rattle of armor and the gleam of
sword instead of by the back door and in the company of
beggars. He wanted to leap back onto Deso and race away.
He laughed again. Why he thought such foolishness was
beyond him.

A tall boy, almost as thin and angular as a spider, came
clumping out of the postern with a wooden pail that sloshed
with liquid. A flutter of murmurs rippled through the crowd.
The woman watched while the boy set the pail on the table,
then turned her gaze back to Leon, but her face was in
shadow, her features hidden. A swirl of skirts and she withdrew.

The four ragged fellows inched their way toward the open
doorway, their shadows following them like cringing dogs.
There was a pause in voices. A murmur. A tensing of the
air. A deep voice. A sudden exclamation.

A small shadow thrust forward. "Get away from there!"

"Says who?" asked a hoarse, harsh voice.

"Guards!" The sharp quick shout came from the boy
Tudur. A hairy hand wrenched the boy's head to one side.

Abruptly Leon became every inch the soldier. His heart
sped up and his hand reached for his sword hilt. Fingers
clenched and unclenched on empty air. He had let Deso
carry his sword, which he had stowed behind the saddle,
though he carried a dagger in his belt. Beneath his brown
wool cloak and leather tunic, he wore no mail, not even a
padded gambeson, naught but a linen shirt.

He'd been a fool to leave his shield and armor, even to
his helmet, at Chirk with his squire this morning, and he
was beginning to regret it. He might be strapped with ropy
muscle, tough as an oak tree and as hard to kill, for he'd
been to hell and beyond and survived. In all truth, most men

would rather not face him with or without his sword. Even so, he regretted the sacrifice of his mail. Linen and wool were poor protection against edged steel.

He had, he thought, taken a great deal on himself. He'd seen that much in his squire's eyes when they'd parted; a cool kind of reckoning he had gotten in the drill yard. Now it seemed mad to have done, and a light sweat lay on his limbs, for all that the wind was chill.

Wrenching himself free, Tudur dodged a fist, scurried past the ring of people gathered by the table, scampered across the road, and stopped, panting, in midsprint in front of Leon. The young face came up, the mouth opened and the eyes widened. The boy flinched visibly, caught himself, and drew back, the look on his face changing in an instant from surprise to confusion.

Leon sighed. His forehead ached. He realized he was scowling. He stretched his mouth into a smile.

"Are you a knight?" The boy looked afraid—not greatly so, but uneasy all the same.

Leon inclined his head to him.

A peculiar animation had come to the boy's face, a keen anticipation. "The sort that saves maidens in distress?"

No, Leon began to say. But...

"So 'tis said," were the words that tripped off his foolish tongue.

"Yes. Yes! I knew it! Some say I am daft, but I could tell straightway you were Brenna's knight!"

"I've no notion what you mean."

The boy's eyes darted from Leon's face to the postern opening, back again. "Of course. My mistake. Being daft, I get confused, so I don't—" His eyes flicked back to the postern. "You are most needed here, sir." There was tremulous expectation, as if Leon would act now, at once, in a breath.

Leon inwardly cursed. He was not usually a man given to rash acts of compassion, and, though the boy's pluck touched him, he saw no obligation to have his throat cut. Or to die for nothing because some self-righteous slip of a girl was too cocksure stupid to take heed of the curfew. He stared down his nose at the boy, who went beet-red.

"If you would give aid, good sir!" Tudur said, blinking wildly. "There may be trouble—at the gate."

Well, what the hell. Nobody else was going to play the hero, and Deso needed hay and a warm stable. Condemned now to simple workaday practicalities, Leon cast common sense to the winds. He handed the reins to Tudur, pointed silently to the open gate and stepped into the shadow of the wall, drawing his hood over his head. This action had the added benefit of concealing the greater part of his features.

He held still while Tudur led the destrier through the gate. Deso went with his ears laid flat and pricked up by turns, dancing and skipping through imagined obstacles, iron-shod hooves ringing on the gray cobbles. Ravens still circled aloft, dropped lower, as if urging him forward.

The girl came running out of the postern once more, her dark braids whipping loose from under the confining net, each with a mind of its own, her skirts aflurry, her slippered feet hardly touching the stones. This time she carried a large basket piled high with bread and meat.

"Hurry, Telyn, we are already past the hour!"

A smooth-faced youth clad in a vivid green tunic and bright yellow hose followed her, also bearing a basket. "This is foolishness. Curfew has rung. The gates should be locked!"

She gave a laugh, easy and merry. Leon caught his breath at the sweet, open sound. "Shall these poor folk go hungry because the hour grows late?" The laugh died. "Come, good people...here is some bread for you...and for you."

A vague fluting of tones rose among the group, and a voice said, "It is unsafe, Brenna. The air is charged with danger!"

The woman lifted her face, and a sudden flash of lightning bathed her features in light. There was something about the expression on her face that struck a cord within Leon; and he found himself ensnared by her face, he who did not generally pay attention to women.

His throat went tight. She reminded him of the angel in his dreams. He had never seen such perfect milky skin or such large dark eyes. She could not be considered beautiful in the strictest sense of the word, for her mouth was too large, her chin too pointed, her cheekbones too wide. But the result was somehow magical. The notion dazed him. He lost his breath and his clarity of thought both at once and stood shaking like a leaf.

She showed a smile of pearly teeth, and held out her hand, palm up. "Come, sir, there is enough for all," she said; and snared him twice over.

He hesitated. She waited.

"Come," she reiterated. Her voice was music.

Leon was thrown into a turmoil of self-awareness, caught for a moment in two flashing, dark eyes. Eyes that sat far apart above a fine, straight nose. Eyes that understood, accepted. His face burned. He could feel the cords standing out along his neck. His body knotted from throat to thigh. He must look a fool, he thought, the greenest of country bumpkins, undone by a woman.

Every part of him was drawn to her. Never had his limbs seemed so beyond his control. Every step he took seemed fraught with the potential for calamity. What if his overlong legs betrayed him? What if he tripped and fell?

Unsettled by such strange thoughts, he drew his cloak close. His feet beat out a grim refrain.

Brenna. Brenna. Brenna.

Until, finally, he stood very still, towering over her, staring down at her, sharing a look with her. For a moment there seemed a confusion in her dark eyes. Gradually he began to comprehend what he saw there: it was a reflection of his own emotions. She was shocked and trying to hide it.

Then came the thunder, rumbling, the intervals shortening between claps. Brenna shook herself, as if awakening from a trance, and held out a cup filled with milk. The smile faded to gravity. The eyes stayed upon his, dark as river water.

Fingers touched fingers. Oh, very gladly would he have touched more. He longed for a thousand things, all of them dangerous.

"My good fellow, you have enough scars to stitch a tapestry. Stand aside and I'll find some salve that lets the skin stretch—" a frown formed on her brow and she bent her head to an ailing urchin, while her cheeks suffused with color "—and that cough, child, needs an herbal tisane…that sore on your hand needs a poultice—"

Leon felt another flush heat his ears, as if he were a grass-green stripling undone by his first glimpse of a trim female ankle. He buried his nose in the offered cup, thanked her in a low voice, drank deeply, put the cup on the table and retreated a short distance.

The shadows above his head stirred, as if a gentle wind was blowing. He slitted his eyes and looked up at the sky. The ravens screamed, swirling, and vanished into the tower.

He picked up a movement out of the corner of his eye. Instantly alert, he did nothing out of the ordinary, simply allowed his eyes to track the beggars once more. One of the churls eased himself away from the wall and slid toward the postern, his hand resting lightly on his hip. But he turned back to his original position when he noticed Leon watching him.

There was trouble afoot. Deep inside Leon's mind he could feel a subtle unease. It was as if he felt, not heard, the echoes of the alarm bell clamoring across the desert air from the furtherest outpost long before the enemy has reached the gate.

The girl gave a cry of protest, which brought his head jerking up. The beggars! It seemed she was refusing their demand for a bed for the night.

"No," she said, stepping back.

The beggar scowled. "There is shelter for women and children, but not for men?"

The girl did not rise to the bait. A woman and her two children had been ushered through the postern gate into the bailey, but now the girl barred the door to the beggars with her own person. "They want herbs and potions. You have no such need. Be off with you and seek a bed at the inn in the village."

Leon stood calmly for all that his heart was racing. Four assailants or nine didn't matter to him, as long as he had his trusty dagger in his hand. That, and his own wits, skill and strength, sufficed, and he'd killed more than that in one skirmish. Armorless and alone, he was still more than a match for these churls.

Lightning flashed and edged everything in fire; the beggars, the edges of the buildings, the woman. For an instant their eyes met. Her head tilted to one side, her lips parting. He narrowed his eyes to deeper slits. She met his gaze unblinkingly, her eyes dark, staring at him strangely sharp, then she drew a long, uneven breath, as if to say, *I am the one you have been seeking, and you are the one I have sought.*

Leon had time to wonder whether his mind was going. Time to wonder about the question, but no time to find an answer. The churls inched closer, regaining his attention. Not now, Leon cautioned himself. Be still a little longer.

Five paces more.

"Give us alms and we will go in peace," said one, edging toward her. His eyes were on the purse that swung from her girdle as he rested his hand upon his hip—a subtle threat.

She was not so easily intimidated. "Do you threaten me, sir? Are you so bold? Food you have had in plenty. No more can I give you!" Her eyes were blazing hot as coals and her small hands formed tight fists at her sides.

A humming. Leon heard metal hiss and knew the sound. He cursed under his breath. Mutters rose behind him.

"He's got a sword!" somebody yelled.

People scattered, running in every direction, screaming. The rest of those who had sought food and alms moved back and away, or fled, leaving a clear space.

Now.

"I'll get help." The motley-clad youth ran past Leon, blocking his thrust. The churl made a mad lunge across the table. A lance of pain struck Leon's temple. Spots swirled in front of his eyes. His fist came down. The milk pail burst apart, sending its contents showering in all directions. The girl was sent reeling.

"One against four and I have her purse already!"

This time, Leon didn't hesitate. His hand lashed out in a blur of motion, of bone-jarring impact to wrist and elbow as his fist slammed into the assailant just below the ear. The man's eyes bulged and his head danced like that of a puppet. Leon had a momentary glimpse of the other's eyes, open wide, terror burning in them like an uncontrollable fire, before the man doubled over.

He kicked the weapon out of the man's hand as another of the churls advanced, his cudgel raised to smite him. He lunged and caught the uplifted hand. His free hand crunched across the elbow. Then he grabbed another man plunging past him, spun him around, and felt armor beneath the brown robes.

It was a poor sort of a fight. Gripping the man's arm, Leon twisted it and snapped it like a twig, grasped another attacker by the throat and flung him with contemptuous ease into the wall behind him. He planned none of his moves. They had all been drilled into him for so many years that they came automatically.

Time seemed to leap forward. There came the sound of many footsteps, all running toward them. A half dozen assorted servants and men-at-arms erupted from the postern. Hands went to swords, steel rising to the light. A roar went up.

"Get them, get them, get them!"

The four churls fled. Telyn chased after them, leading the detachment of men in full pursuit.

It was over. Done.

Leon stood with hand on hip, breathing easily. He had

not even drawn his dagger. "Are you all right?" She nodded
and he said, "In the name of all devils—why?" He jerked
his head to the baying throng. "A sentry on watch would
prevent such incident, lady."

Brenna did not move, save that her head came up. He saw
a sheen on her cheek as of light on polished, shining stone,
or firelight on water.

"I am sorry. It was mine own folly that brought it about,"
she faltered in a voice that was scarcely audible. "I should
have called for help earlier."

Leon kept his eyes on her. He had great confidence in his
wit and skill, but when it came to women, he had no confidence at all. The flick of temper faded into something else:
curiosity. She looked bedraggled, her veil askew, her thick
black braids in disarray. Her eyes were burning bright. She
was, perhaps, more shaken by the incident than she cared to
acknowledge.

"It shouldn't have happened." Memory put violent pressure on his voice. What a different ending this day could
have had! He could hardly think, his heart was hammering
so in his chest, and his insides twisted in his belly.

She drew back a little. Her lips quivered, and she shook
her head. "No one has ever threatened me before."

Leon looked levelly into her eyes and did not move.
"Such idiocy can prove fatal. Did you never think what
might be the probable result? Did you never think that you
might endanger others?" Driven by bitter memories, his
voice was still hard and unconvinced.

A wild shake of the head. "No! I am unhurt." Another
space for breath. "I suppose it was a lucky coincidence you
were on hand when those churls attacked," she said with
just the hint of a smile.

Leon felt the tightness around his mouth as his lip curled.
He had spent too many years in action, and he was not
accustomed to being made light of. Yet it was more than
that. Under the bravado, he could sense something else in

the girl. He could taste it; a nervous tension that came perilously close to fear.

"Coincidence, chance, luck. I don't believe in any of them. I keep a sharp sword." In spite of all his efforts, it was hard not to sound cynical.

She looked at him sharply. Her head was high now, her expression haughty. "You are very brave, sir. I would that all knights showed such courage. If they did, the Crusaders would have taken the Holy Land."

"Devil take that! I am one man, not the Crusader army, lady," he exclaimed.

"You were bold and confident!"

"A man of my trade lives every day of his life under threat of death," he replied with a pragmatic shrug.

"But you are valiant! With neither armor nor weapon, you sent the dogs running. You felt no fear!"

"I have nothing to lose, therefore nothing to fear," he said, too bluntly, perhaps, for she bit her lip a moment, frowning as if it were a challenge and she were searching for a proper response.

"A man who fears nothing loves nothing and, if he loves nothing, what joy is there in his life?" she asked with passionate urgency.

All his senses seemed foggy of a sudden, and his head on the edge of hurting. "I've never met a woman who speaks to me as you do," he told her.

"Even your wife?" She fixed that direct look of hers on him, challenging him.

"I have no wife."

Her scrutiny was both leisurely and thorough, taking him in as if he had been a bullock at market. Swift anger flooded through him. He felt his jaw clenching. Years of living by the sword had wrecked any comeliness he had ever possessed and any chance of winning a woman's heart.

Something changed, lifted, in the set of her mouth and eyes. Tiny facial muscles relaxed. He caught a momentary expression as she stood before him, watching him intently—

something intense and satisfied, as if it were enough to know.

"And I have no husband. Yet."

"If you did, you would be more circumspect."

Slowly the proud head bowed. She spread her hands. "It's not like that here."

"No doubt it is different in the marches," Leon agreed with a touch of irony. "I do not think it is that. You knew I would intervene, if necessary."

Her cheeks flamed, but she did not evade the charge. "Yes," she said with a directness that he guessed was characteristic of her.

There were footsteps, the ringing of swords in scabbards. The men-at-arms were returning with two of the churls, and the girl's purse. There were shouts and cheers from a tangle of servants and hangers-on. The youth had collected the baskets and was urging her within, saying it would rain soon and that Sir Edmund would be angry.

Brenna grinned up at him, her eyes bright. "Here I was wishing you away, but there was nothing I wanted more to see than you coming up that hill." She laid a slender hand on his arm. "Welcome to Dinas Bran."

Chapter Two

Could it be…was it…? Yes! He was here! He had come!

Flanked by the knight and Telyn, Brenna walked straight-backed and resolute into the courtyard, around the well and across the crowded bailey, taking no notice of the flurry of guards and flickering torchlight, the mass of shadowed faces and shocked voices. She offered not a word.

This was no time for argument or explanation. The gracious and civilized thing to do was to get her betrothed upstairs where he could bathe and prepare for the festivities. Her eyes did not even follow the guards as they bore the assailants away. She had not meant to cause any trouble by breaking the curfew, but it was done. They'd soon be in a cell for questioning, if anyone had any sense. It was up to the men now. She was too consumed by strange feelings she couldn't comprehend. Feelings that made her reel with their intensity.

This was her betrothed! He was the man of her dreams! In truth, he was here!

She'd heard him laugh, a black-velvet ripple, sweet as the honey of the southlands, and felt something deep within her move, open. She'd looked wildly about, and her heart was like an arrow hurtling through space. Then eye met eye. A spark leaped in the meeting, and the newcomer had laughed no more. He gazed at her with—recognition, it might be, for she had felt it, too.

This is the one!

It was odd, really. She'd prayed that he wouldn't let her down, that he would come. But she had an uneasiness now, about his late arrival, the peculiar look of him. There was some strangeness about him. He'd stood there, on the edge of the crowd, his hand seeming to rest on a sword hilt in the shadows, his whole aspect grim and dangerous.

Brenna swallowed hard. There had never been any other like this man. She could not suppress a heated sensation welling deep inside. His hand, heavy on her shoulder, seemed to have the strength of iron. She wanted to tuck herself closer against that strength…and yet she did not know why.

This man might be her betrothed, but he was a stranger. It just seemed impossible that he was truly the man of her dreams, she thought. And how could he so easily, so appallingly easily, become *the one?*

She had turned away so many suitors that her aunts despaired, but still her knight had not come. She had held to her dream until her grandfather had become impatient and commanded she wed. She had only consented because, with constant skirmishes to defend the border, Grandy's coffers were empty and he needed the bride-price. Besides, the amiable Aubrey of Leeds sounded more congenial a match than Keith Kil Coed!

Be honest, Brenna. This incomparable knight is something you have conjured up out of an overactive imagination—or a mad notion, brought on by the tensions of the day. She must not allow her emotions to dominate her reason.

They came up the stairs and into the keep. Light spilled over them from the torches that burned all along the wall. From the kitchens the sweet smell of roasting venison floated on the air, and there was a stir in the hall, the coming and going of servants carrying trays of cider and ale through a door to the great hall where tapestries fluttered and torches flared in drafts.

Brenna stopped and sent a page scurrying with orders to fetch her maidservant. Fingertips tapped her arm. She became aware of Telyn, hovering at her side, still clutching the baskets.

"Thank you, Telyn. You served me well this day."

The squire made a clicking with his tongue. "My lady, it would be wiser not to disturb Sir Edmund with news of this…he is at table already. Surely he will blame me for allowing you to go out unattended. No harm was done. Your purse has been recovered, and if I…"

"It is all right, Telyn. I accept full responsibility. You go eat. I will escort the knight to his chamber."

"But surely—" Telyn stopped.

"I'll be down soon. Will you please tell Grandy that Sir Aubrey has arrived and has retired to refresh himself?"

A polite murmuring. No objections. She supposed he didn't know what to say. She didn't, either, except, "Thank you, Telyn."

As she dismissed the squire, the knight swung about, swirling his gray cloak. "Deso!" he exclaimed, his voice breaking hoarse. He had said nothing up to that point, had let Brenna lead him where she willed. "Deso!"

"Is that the name of your horse? Tudur has taken the animal to the stables. The grooms will see to it." Brenna tilted her head up, regarding him sidelong. "Is it a real battle charger?"

Her tone must have betrayed something. His glance sharpened. His face was cold and still. For a heartbeat he looked like a great red stag at bay. Then his shoulders and the line of his neck relaxed.

"Yes, it is a warhorse, and a fine one, too," he said in the most ordinary of tones, but his eyes were as clear as water, with a brightness in the heart of them.

Brenna's breath shortened. His hood had flown back long since, revealing hair like hot gold. His jaw was square and rugged, his mouth bluntly carved below the jutting blade of his nose. The pale smooth marks traced across half his face like the limbs of a lightning-blasted tree bespoke of courage and mettle and the reflexes of a warrior. And the mantle of wool that swept across his shoulders emphasized their width and suggested great strength.

She swallowed hard. Her heart was thudding against her ribs. Oh, yes, he was a pleasing man, younger than she had imagined—no more than eight-and-twenty. She could do far worse than he.

So why this uneasiness?

It appeared Aubrey was no ordinary knight. For, though her betrothed knew how to defend himself, and his linen shirt was of the finest weave, and the supple leather of his tunic and boots were fastened with ornate metal toggles, he came without armor or shield. Somehow, somewhere, he had lost his armor and weapons. Understanding came. Did not a knight, unhorsed in the lists, forfeit his gear?

Did that matter? *He is here!*

"Come." Back stiff, braids swinging, she led him past the inner door that opened on the hall, up the narrow curving timber steps to the bedchambers set high in the tower of the castle, and down the corridor. At the very end, she stopped and pushed aside a beaded leather curtain.

"You may sleep here."

Her companion stumbled. His fingers tightened. The grip hurt. She drew a long, long breath and let it go. Slowly, the pressure was removed. Her muscles went slack with relief.

The room they entered was circular, with tall narrow windows all about it. A fire blazed in the hearth, and the chamber glowed in the wastefulness of an oil lamp, which shed a low, even light over a crowded table covered with sheaves of parchment and scrolls.

Brenna made her way across a floor carpeted with sweet-smelling rushes, bent, adjusted the lamp wick, and stood uncertainly, looking at him, surprised by the pounding of her heart. She pressed one hand to her chest for a moment

and it eased. Why was she so nervous? This was her betrothed!

He lingered, a shadow in the doorway. But the rugged
features were devoid of emotion. He might have been carved
from stone. And he avoided her gaze, staunchly refusing to
glance her way.

For once, the forms of hospitality deserted her. She had
kept herself from hoping. As far as she could, as far into
her childhood as she might. She'd pondered what to say to
him. She wanted to talk to him, to chatter idly, to say something to fill the silence. But now that he was here, her heart
beat with a thud of self-conscious dread, and she could only
blurt, "Are you tired?"

He shrugged. She went to him, took his arm and steered
him toward a chair as if he were a child, never mind that he
was a head taller and thrice her weight.

"A bath and a glass of mulled wine and you'll soon feel
more the thing. There are soap and herbs and clean towels
in the chest, and this is a fine feather bed."

Why had she said that? Brenna felt the heat rush to her
face. He would think her most unmaidenly, or that she could
not wait to be bedded! But he seemed not to notice her
confusion. He shrugged out of his sodden cloak, threw it
over a chair and gave a curt wave of his hand.

"It's very fancy."

In truth the chamber was plain enough, all bare wood and
aged stone. It was spacious and the furnishings were comfortable, with a faint scent of flowers. On the table beside a
pot of ink and a heap of quills lay a bowlful of rose petals,
sending up sweet fragrance like a silent blessing.

Brenna knelt and poked at the fire with an iron rod. She
looked up and up. He looked down and down. The eyes that
met hers were the shifting color of the forest. Her breath
quickened; her heart was beating so hard it hurt her throat.

"It was my father's chamber. The bed came from
France."

By which answer Brenna knew she had hit a raw nerve.

Two deep grooves appeared on his face, running from the flare of his nostrils to the corners of his suddenly grim mouth.

"I can assure you, lady, that this sacrifice is quite unnecessary. I have traveled far and am weary. A cot in a corner will suffice."

There was a sharpness in his tone that startled Brenna. He looked horrified. Her heart stilled. Had she offended him? Or did he find her unattractive? That stung her vanity a little, but not enough to cause this pain that clenched her heart.

No, it is not that, she said to herself.

It was true that men always reacted to her with admiration. It was also true it had never concerned her whether they had or not. This time she cared. For the first time in her life she felt a frank stirring of curiosity in a man, an honest awareness of him. This man reacted to the notion of using the marriage bed as if just told he had to share it with a leper.

She rose to her feet, and clutched her hands together, finding them shaking. She kept her back straight and her chin up, but she was all too painfully aware of the figure she cut. Her gown had been her mother's; it was shabby, threadbare, and covered with mud. In short, she was unkempt.

She had never believed it would come to this. How badly she wanted to make a good impression. The hospitality of Dinas Bran was well known. A visitor was sure of shelter, refreshment and ale, with meat for his hounds and oats for his horse without stint. Would she offer her betrothed any less?

Knights, it was said in the codes, had a common trait. It was honor. Privately, Brenna thought it was pride. Of which this man had an excess. If only he would catch her eye, reassure her with a curve of those generous lips, bring a glimmer of certainty surging into her heart. But no, he would only look straight ahead, his bearing contained, aloof. What was she supposed to do?

"Sir Edmund dislikes having the customs upset. He'll ask me why. What will I say?"

"That 'tis most kind, but—"

"Be not mistaken. My father no longer has use for this room. He is dead. Killed at Acre."

"Your pardon, lady. I am not at my best."

He looked feverish, but then that was to be expected; God alone knew how far he'd traveled in that damp cloak.

"In that case, I insist," she said firmly. "Besides, 'tis the custom here to give the best accommodation to our noble guests. I would not have it said that Dinas Bran lodged you meanly," she snapped, the sharper for that her cheeks had caught fire.

Leon wrapped his arms about him against the sudden coolness and looked at her. Simply looked. He had thought her magical at first sight. Now he was sure. She was indeed quite the most exquisite woman he had ever seen. Her smooth pale skin was rose-blushed. Her eyes were dark and enchantingly tilted, their brilliance set off by their fringe of long black lashes. Her fine dark brows slanted across her forehead like a raven's wing, and her hair beneath its drift of veil was black as night. Her one flaw, the chin that was a shade too pronounced, a shade too obstinate, only strengthened her beauty. Without it she would have been lovely; with it, she was breathtaking.

He leaned on the wall, scrubbing at his sweaty cheeks and chin. The chamber felt unaccountably hot. It was hard to breathe, let alone think.

What good were these doubts? he asked himself. If he were enchanted, there was little he could do. If it were naught but the fever, then a bath would cool his overheated senses. After so many days in the saddle, his clothes were so dusty, muddy and sweaty that they would probably be able to walk back to France all by themselves, and despite his attempts at washing them and himself in rivers so cold they made the teeth ache in his head, the body inside the garments wasn't much better.

All he knew for sure was that he'd never find out standing still, and the thought of hot water and soap and razors, was

a pleasant one. He felt suddenly very weary. The energy that
had driven him during his rescue mission was now taking
its toll. In short, he felt rather disheveled and somewhat
shaken. His head hurt in savage counterpoint to his heartbeat. He pressed his fingers hard into his forehead, pushed
away fatigue.

"Is it also the custom here, as it is on the Continent, for
the lady of the house to offer guests assistance in their bathing?" he asked, fearing to know.

Brenna was taken aback. For a moment, breath and sense
failed her. She lost her thread of thought, everything unrav-
eling. Was he actually suggesting she attend him? Or was
he simply making conversation? A feeling of embarrassment
arose in her, and then resentment. Why were things so con-
trary? Her wits rallied; she gathered her forces.

"If you so desire," she said in a voice that she tried to
make sound calm. Dared she do such a thing? Her grandfather did not ever allow her to help bathe their guests. It
was a chore left to the maidservants. But this was her future
husband!

"I must trust your judgment, and hope that you do not
come to regret your decision."

Brenna stared, puzzled. Filled with uncertainty, her mind
went 'round and 'round, struggled with the meaning of his
words. What was he talking about? He had paid the bride-
price. The wedding was prepared. He had come. Why was
he hesitating now? Or was he talking about what was to
happen afterward in the marriage bed? The bed he had so
summarily rejected?

"It is the least I can do, my lord."

Leon felt like a man hit by a pole-ax, still on his feet, but
reeling. He searched her face, looking for duplicity, but finding something else, something he couldn't put his finger on.
His mind screamed, Beware! But his body shrieked even
louder. A chill grew in his limbs, a slight giddiness like too
much ale. Like too much heat and too much cold. Like love.
What had put that thought into his mind?

"I fear you flatter me too much, lady. I am only a soldier, not a great lord," he found the strength to say.

Brenna's assurance foundered as she realized the significance of what he'd just said. She drew a slow breath; her first sign of temper.

"You dissemble well, sir knight. I think you are more than a simple soldier." When he opened his mouth to argue, she shook her head. "I will not bandy words with you—if you wish me to believe you only a modest soldier then so be it. I care not what your rank may be, but there is nothing common about you."

"I am glad you think so."

"What reasonable person would not?" Brenna changed tacks abruptly, fixing him with her most disconcerting stare. "I heard you were a great knight, all amiable and devout. Were the rumors wrong?"

A curl of stirred air touched Leon's cheek. The lines of his face turned icy as hill granite. A small shiver trickled down his spine like a drop of ice water, and for the merest instant the chamber seemed somehow darker than it had any reason to be. He could hear his pulse pounding in his ears. Shutters rattled, one after another. The wind howled, roared and stirred the shadows in the corners. Outside the night was alive with the hammering of rain, streaks of bouncing energy, silvered where the lightning hit it. All of it utterly foolish, of course, and just to be laughed at later, with a glass of good wine in one hand. And yet...

"How could you have heard such things?" Grabbing her wrist, as if by this gesture he could wrench the knowledge out of her. "You didn't know me at all, before this evening."

Brenna was startled at the bite in his voice. Were the rumors wrong? Her eyes looked up involuntarily into the chips of ice that were his eyes. Hers wavered the merest fraction. She rallied with a flare of Brenig temper.

"It's surprising what news comes from the court, but now

I am beginning to think it was all just exaggeration. You are wound so tight, I don't think you are amiable at all!''

He stood there, unmoving, unperturbed. A little silence passed, barely endurable, before he released her wrist and said mildly, lazily, ''You're probably right.''

Brenna felt her cheeks turn warm. This wasn't going as planned at all. Caution and guilt warred with vague, half-formed desires until, finally, duty dictated a more sensible attitude. But the itch of curiosity assailed her. More than an itch, her curiosity was a torment.

''Some said that you would not come to us, that you were bound in close friendship with the king, and that the court has need of you there. We both know that to be a false-hood...do we not?''

''You have been misinformed, my lady. The road but took some crooked turns.''

She tilted her head to one side, studying him. ''So you can be devious, too. When a man of your stature travels without his servant, one would suppose him to be—shall we say...in disguise?''

Leon thought how quick of understanding is this girl! He knew the rules of hospitality. Never ask the visitor ''From where?'' or ''Where to?'' Never ask them ''How many?'' or ''For how long?'' And most of all, never ever ask them ''When?'' In another minute she would surely guess that he was a king's man...

''Forgive my rudeness. I meant no disrespect.''

''None taken.''

''I did not realize. I thought...perhaps...'' Brenna tried to think of something to say, but no words would come. Her fluency failed her when it was her moment to speak. She could not frame a single sentence. Her cheeks blazed with the shame of it. ''You look a little the worse for wear. Were you beset upon the road?''

Leon bit down on a frown. He was certain he detected trepidation in her voice. The sparkle in her gaze, however, made him decidedly suspicious. She stood there, cool, proud, running those dark eyes over his disheveled and travel-worn figure. She wanted a bold, brave answer. He gave her one; though not perhaps the one she had expected.

"Lady," he said very softly, "I was beset by a breaker of hearts."

She looked at him, as if not understanding, or not wanting to understand. "Are you a pawn, then?" Raising a brow the merest suggestion of a degree.

"My lady," he said, and could not resist a bow, ironic mockery of her clear hesitation, "that depends upon your own intent."

This one could break your bones or your heart, Brenna warned herself. Her pulse began to quicken. Blood rushed up in her ears. Suddenly she was trembling, shivering. She bit her lip. She had to fight off the urge to touch him, to casually brush her hand against his. She had never experienced anything that made her feel like this. Her heart was beating so she felt that she could hardly be sure of controlling her voice. Surely all her senses had flown?

"Sir! I—" Brenna struggled mightily to keep her expression bland, though she was sure a spark of delight lit up her eyes. "I will feel better if you let *me* make sure you're cared for."

"Whatever the lady requests. I cannot deny her. I am resolved to please her."

That was a refuge. She snatched at it. Closer and closer then, at a careful pace. Her hand rose to his cheek. He caught it.

"No," he said.

A little silence passed, barely endurable. His eyelids flickered a fraction. A shiver traced her spine, a sensation like a touch brushing her, moth-soft.

"This offense to your person, did it go unpunished?"

"I am alive, aren't I?" His irises snapped light-sparks briefly, just a glint of cold, then control. He did not like that memory, nor the reminder.

I do not believe in coincidence.

She looked up at him from under her eyelids. All honor was in that bladed curve of nose, in those cheekbones carved fierce and high, in those brows set level over the deep eyes.

"Then that answers the question."

Her smile won free, startling as the sun at midnight, and more miraculous. Deep down inside Leon a strange feeling, almost of elation, surged—but why? Surely not because this slip of a girl showed neither sympathy nor revulsion of his ruined face? This fact alone couldn't possibly account for the new emotion ebbing and flowing within him. On the other hand—

His spare hand involuntarily went to the breast of his leather tunic, in an inner pouch of which he kept a stained knot of ribbon. It had become a treasured charm to him through the years, and he had grown almost to believe that it was a safeguard to him from the constant assaults of temptations to thoughts and deeds unworthy of a Christian knight.

He tested his courage by it. He tested it further. He released her wrist. Risked shame that a girl should trust him.

"I give you leave," he said, a little breathless.

"How generous of you."

Wordlessly, she reached out and touched his cheek softly. He felt something come alive within him, something that made him feel warm and cherished. He suddenly became aware of the delicious tension tightening his whole body. His heart jumped and started hammering. A fearful thrill ran from his chest to his groin. He had not known he could have so many needs all at once, amid such a nightmare.

Brenna touched him, because she wanted to, because she could not help herself; a brush of fingertips from his cheek to his chin, tracing the path of his scars. It was great daring. He quivered under her hand, but did not pull away. She looked up and caught his eye. A quick smile framed her lips.

"Am I transgressing?" she asked him.

In more ways than one!

"A little." Meeting her gaze, Leon struggled mightily to

keep his expression bland. *You must face that which you fear most. Confront and conquer. Know yourself first and you will overcome a legion of adversaries.* His arms-master's words, spoken to him at Whittington. A boy of twelve summers, unaware of the fate that awaited him.

Ever so slowly, her fingers progressed along their tortuous route. He kept still, hardly daring to breathe. She was close, so dizzyingly close! A painful stiffening was pressing against the confining leather of his pants, but he dared not shift to ease his position for fear his actions would be noticed.

Leon closed his eyes and inhaled sharply, allowing himself this rare moment of self-indulgence. Then, with the ease of long practice, he forced the emotional temptation back into a corner of his mind. He'd learned a long time ago that the only way to exist was to keep his feelings under rigid control, his heart hard and unyielding as iron. It was a kind of armor. After everything that had happened years ago, there was nothing left to be afraid of.

They were very close. Brenna could feel the living warmth of him, and catch the scent he bore, faint yet distinct. Musk and saddle leather and wet wool. His face was so close that she could feel his breath, so warm and soft. She hoped he would kiss her—yes, she wanted him to kiss her—and her heart beat faster as she swayed toward him, her soft breasts touching his chest. How would it feel to kiss a man?

Their lips touched. He was very beautiful and very strong, and his kiss was sweet. Swift and startling. Warm and warming. He tasted of spices. She felt his long, lean body pressed against hers, and in her secret places, unfamiliar longings began to stir.

He drew back.

Brenna only stared at him, not moving. His eyes had darkened to emerald, and he was frowning, if only slightly; his gaze gone almost to coldness. He bowed again.

"I am honored, and I hope my presence will cause you no more hardship than is necessary."

Her throat was locked. She swallowed to open a way for her voice. "It is we who are honored—no, pleased by your presence here, and all will see to your comfort. I will have a servant fetch some wine and a trencher from the kitchen—and some clean clothes."

And fled.

Two steps outside the door she came to an abrupt stop. Elen, her old nurse and present maidservant, stood there, arms akimbo, blocking the corridor.

"Merciful Mary, what means this, Brenna?"

Brenna did a little jig though she wanted to throw up her arms and yell, to leap and hop and twirl and imitate the merry dance of the minstrels, and burst into the hall shouting the glad tidings to everyone.

"Elen, the inconceivable has occurred! My knight…he has come! He's a darling, and I shall love him, I know."

Elen's face expressed disapproval of so much exuberance. "Telyn made no mention of a knight. He said it was one of the beggars who came to your aid."

"Whoever heard of a beggar with a horse? A fine horse, at that—and Elen, Aubrey's magnificent. He's exactly as I've always imagined my knight to look. Fair, powerful, self-assured. I've never seen such fearlessness, such absolute recklessness, such wild valor. I've no doubt he's all heroic virtue and unmatched goodness."

Elen narrowed her eyes. "You sound utterly smitten."

Besotted, more like, Brenna thought. Every part of her had been drawn to him. Her shoulder still prickled where his hand rested. Her lips tingled from the cool fire of his touch. She laughed lightly.

"He has all the traits of a hero—and his face is that of a warrior—such lovely eyes—all silvery-green and shining like a pigeon's breast. And his shoulders are the broadest I've ever seen. Then again, mayhap 'tis his golden hair. You don't see much hair that color around here."

"Upon my soul, Brenna, you are wit-wandering."

"Not so."

"No one ought to indulge in passion, it distorts everything."

"There are passions—and *passions*."

"You might as well know that Kil Coed has sent word that he comes not only to propose a new and strong alliance with Dinas Bran, but that it would be his great pleasure to seal that covenant by wedding with you."

Brenna stared at Elen grimly and let out an impatient breath. "The arrival of my betrothed and our marriage on the Sabbath should halt any ambitions held by another suitor! Assuming, of course, that this isn't all a joke...?"

"I wish I had told you sooner, but I did not want to burden you until I was sure."

A wild resentment filled Brenna. "We have taken Aubrey's coin. I am honor-bound to wed him."

"Keith Kil Coed is magnificent—and he's Welsh."

"I will not marry him!" It was a whisper, lest she scream it.

"You may have no choice. Since winter loosed its hold, he has begun to gather an army. The Lady Agnita says Sir Edmund suspects he will move against us, thinking to forge an alliance, and use our strength to advance west to Gwynedd."

"I am betrothed to Aubrey of Leeds!"

"Betrothals can be nullified."

"Not on the very eve of the nuptials!"

"No more dispute now. Sir Edmund has the right to decide your fate. He is in a foul mood because of this latest folly. He will be angrier if you are not at table. Go and put on your blue gown, and be nice to him, and you may find his anger only hot air."

"Even if Grandy is about to renege on the deal and have me wed that upstart Keith Kil Coed, my knight has come, as if conjured here by magic. It is a good omen."

"Don't say that! The walls have ears," Elen whispered, making the sign of the cross on brow and chest. "And there are always servants and menials of some sort to carry tales of witchcraft and druidry.''

"Old lies and old spite. How can anyone credit a word of it?"

"Be careful! I can't prevent hostile ears from attending to some ill-spoken words—I would not have you skinned for a witch or burnt at the stake."

A flood of fondness washed through Brenna. Elen's hair might be mostly gray, and she might be moving a bit stiffly on winter mornings, but she was always so indulgent, so tolerant, not at all stiff and proper. She was also very superstitious.

"You are trying to make my blood run cold, Elen. Well, I am not so easily frightened."

"Nevertheless, such talk is dangerous," Elen said in a low voice. "I've seen you grow up, Brenna. You run, jump, indulge in all manner of masculine pursuits, speak four tongues and even read. 'Tis not expected of a woman, and disturbs the natural order of things."

Brenna bit her lip to keep from laughing. "I can also sew a fine stitch, spin wool, bake bread, grow herbs, tend the sick and sing to the bees."

"It is magic. Which is why they call you a she-devil."

"Nonsense. The bees like my singing and make honey in appreciation. I use no magic, else I would make that upstart Kil Coed weak, turn his muscles to pudding. Instead he bends an iron axle over his knee as if it were wet bread dough."

Low and thick, Elen said, "Don't give them any more substance to talk about!"

"What does it matter?"

"It matters," Elen said harshly. "I'm just trying to protect your reputation. I know you say I gossip too much, but I worry—"

"Dear Elen, you have always been worried about me, haven't you? I remember when I was a child you were always in a flutter for fear I should fall down and hurt myself.

Well, sometimes there have been reason in your fears, but no more. My knight's presence is enough, and his strength and golden voice. I need no more.''

From now on her whole life would be dedicated to him. Yes, that's what they'd do—walk through the years together. As if provoked a little by this resolve, thunder boomed out above the towers, making her jump. A door shut downstairs, echoing.

''It seems unreal, but I will wed Aubrey of Leeds on the Sabbath, Elen. From that moment, I will behave like a saint, that I promise you.''

Chapter Three

Leon set his weapon belt on the bench nearest the bed, thinking how unexpected this all was, lodging in the room that had been Brenig's own in his youth. He hoped he was wrong, but he did not take for granted all that he could.

Wales was a savage and rebellious place, with great mountains and strange customs. Odd things happened, and law was a matter of local option. Beyond the Dee the land turned primitive, towns and villages growing fewer, hill and forest rising toward the western mountains. The rumors were dark here, tales of marauders upon the roads, villages sacked and burned.

He sat down on the edge of the bed and tugged off his boots. Suspicions had begun to move about inside his mind, causing swirls and ripples of unease like the movements of something large and ominous lurking beneath the surface of deep water. Had not the king but lately revoked the title of Lord of the Northern Marches, throwing this western realm into turmoil and confusion? Had not the same king dug up old grudges from his childhood days and found reasons to heckle and harass that obliged Lord Fulk to flee from Whittington?

Why? The answer was as simple as it was distressing. The king had deliberately unleashed a potentially explosive power struggle to distract his increasingly antagonist parliament from what was happening in his provinces on the other side of the English Channel.

Leon knew what would happen. The plots would multiply until those who sought to take Fulk FitzWarren's place would be overwhelmed. He also knew that the Brenigs were political animals. Intrigue was second nature to them.

He was no novice in deceit, but mayhap he was suspicious and uncharitable even to suspect Brenig treachery in housing him in this grand chamber—without ascertaining who he was—as he was suspicious and uncharitable to suspect Brenig treachery in permitting the heiress, with no guards, risking danger—

Only Brenna had faced no danger of alleged outlaws. The rescue, if rescue it could be called, was so easy as to be ridiculous.

Too easy.

There had been guards within call, and the boys Telyn and Tudur ready to call the alarm. He liked that stroke; he truly did. A fine jest, if it were not so reckless. Respectful. Convincing, if less in the province were amiss.

A brief flash of lightning chased the shadows. Thunder cracked close. Rain thumped down as if scattered by an enormous hand. The wind battered against the shutters, making the timber slats dance to its rhythm. He crossed the room, unlacing cuffs, collar, and side laces and hauled off shirt and tunic together, before throwing open the shutters. The wind gusted in through the slitted window, setting the candles fluttering wildly.

Too much, he thought, beginning to sway. Too much. The feeling of falling clung to him like a shroud. His head throbbed. He was having trouble focusing his eyes. He put his hand to his head. Abruptly the realization came that he had a lump on his skull the size of an egg.

Disposing his clothes on the peg against the wall, he stripped off his filthy breeches and reached out again for his shirt. He retrieved the amulet from its hiding place, and took it in his hand, feeling a warmth where it touched his palm, a sweet, sad warmth.

Memory, swift and involuntary: a dark night, a pale face out of which two eyes stared like living cinder, a vow. It was nostalgia, but he held it fast, and it sang to him of elvish dreams and memories. It took him back so vividly.

He'd had a dream of changing the world in his golden youth, when such things were possible…

And he'd gone all the way to the Holy Land.

But that was not far enough for his troubles, not far enough for safety from falsehood and deceit, his foster father's scheming, his own damnable stupidity—

He shook his head, and laughed angrily, giddily, to himself. He tucked the amulet into his weapon belt and stood in front of the slitted window, shivering in the wind that blew in out of the dark, in the hope that the damp air would clear his wits.

Brenna hurried along the corridor ahead of the servants, and wondered why she had left Aubrey so suddenly. Why was she so beset by doubts? Surely there was no harm in kissing her betrothed on the very eve of their marriage? She thought of the ceremony to take place on the Sabbath, and of how this storm would not be viewed as a particularly good omen…

There was an air of chill in the chamber as she entered, despite the cheerful fire burning on the hearth. His bulky shape was outlined by lightning from without and the contours of him shone where they caught the light.

She stood, stone-still. The light burnished his hair and accentuated the planes of his handsome face, transforming it for her into something splendid, something awesome. The perfect tapestry of one half of his face was a splendid foil to the tracery of livid white scars on the other cheek. The contrast was absolute.

It was not the face of a scholar or a seer; it was the battle-hardened face of a warrior, a man who had faced death and would not allow its dark promise to control him.

The face was dauntless—but the eyes were striking. Shielded by thick sable lashes, they were his best feature, eagle-keen and very clear. She'd liked their singular silvery color, so translucent they took color from lake or moss or stone.

The light shone, too, on the rest of him, bathing him in a nimbus of flame and making his bared skin gleam ruddy. He had removed his outer garments, and was wearing only his linen loincloth. She found it impossible not to stare, transfixed, listening to the wild beating of her heart.

He appeared incredibly beautiful, his shoulders wide, the skin of his chest stretched taut across his squared muscles. His abdomen was flat and without superfluous flesh. In the pulsing light, his massive torso looked as though it had bathed in iron dust. Even the down on his chest had a peculiar metal sheen. But his whole body was a map of injuries and hurts, old and new, and his arms were laced with myriad scars that served further proof he kept his livelihood by the sword. This was not, she thought, a man to cross.

The thunder grew louder. A gust of wind sent the lamps and candles flickering. It also restored her senses.

"You'll catch the death of cold with that damp wind!"

She went to the doorway and clapped her hands. A clutch of servants came in bearing a huge wooden tub, which they set in a corner behind a screen, away from the draught, and filled with successive pails of steaming water. Others appeared, carrying towels and fresh clothing, which they placed on a low table that stood close to the tub.

Leon went and stood by the fireside, warming the shivers and the aches of travel from his bones as he waited for the servants to finish their business and leave. With eyes that burned from exhaustion, he watched them all gather by the tub, and Brenna told them she would help him with his bath. She breezed past them to his side.

"If you'll just allow me—"

"Desist, woman!" Servants scattered. He barely noticed. "Stop that at once!" He brushed in vain at her helpful hands.

"What is wrong?"

A gasp sounded behind. Brenna clapped her hands, stifled the servants somewhat, and shooed them out.

"I'll not have a husband who scares the maids witless with all that grumpiness. Now if you'll be so kind—" She flung up her hands.

That brought him to a halt. His ears were going. Had he heard that? "Husband?"

She turned back and stood very close to him, but this time standing rigid, with her arms folded under her breasts. Fine tremors moved the tendrils of her hair, as if a qualm of fear shook her courage. "That is what I said." Her face was calm and as still as a brushed porcelain mask. Bland as if it were a foregone conclusion. As if none of it were uncertain.

"What brought that to mind?"

"You are always answering a question with another question!"

"Just a peculiar topic to bring up now," he said.

"Not at all. With all the political talk going on, 'tis natural to be thinking of the future, but we can discuss it later."

"You're crazy!"

"My father's word was reckless."

"Perhaps he was sparing in his praise."

She spoiled the exquisite mask by squinting through a dark waterfall of hair at him. "You are merely evil-tempered because you cannot bear the fact that you, my stalwart rescuer, have mislaid your armor." Her voice sparkled with hints of laughter.

"You carry on like a raucous crow."

Brenna flushed, but her eyes were steady. "And you have a temper like soured wine." A firm hand planted itself on his chest. "You will get a fever if you stand there naked much longer."

Leon stiffened, but her hand did not move. Her eyes
touched his chest, his flat stomach and hips and his...

He glanced down. His eyes grew very wide and still. His
heart jumped and started hammering. While he'd glowered
at her, she had industriously peeled off the linen undergar-
ment.

Brenna standing there dressed and he—

He felt his groin grow heavy as thick blood pooled in his
lower belly. His reaction must be blindingly obvious, he
thought. A cold feeling spread all down his back into his
legs. If a seasoned warrior reacted in this way, pity help her
poor silly young suitors. His teeth gritted. His lips peeled
back from his teeth.

"You need not stay."

"Do you want the maids to see you like this?" Her tone
was blank, void of cues, but her breast rose with each breath
and the way she avoided looking at him, as if her interest
in him were all his fault, was highly amusing. She gestured
to the water invitingly.

Leon bit back a retort. It would do no good. He could
think of nothing to say that would not make matters worse.
His body betrayed him. Surrender, for now, was the only
strategy.

Still frowning, he climbed in, yielding to the temptation
of a hot bath in a tub that was big enough to hold a man of
his great stature. The water was so hot his toes tingled. Gin-
gerly, he sat, glad of the debilitating heat of the water. He
let go a long breath and looked up from under his brows.

"Well, lady, for what do you wait?"

She slapped a big bar of brown soap into his hand. "Wash
yourself with this. I'll get some oil."

Brenna hurried to the carved chest, as if suddenly appalled
at her boldness. There was an awkward silence while she
unstopped a bottle and added a few drops of sweet-smelling
oil to the water.

Leon suspected she was rarely so tongue-tied; any girl
who looked like this one did would have learned at an early

age how to make the most of her assets. He rubbed his chin with both hands, feeling the stubble from several days' growth scratch the skin of his palms. No doubt he stank of sweat and grime and horse. He truly needed to bathe, and he could not deny it would be pleasant to have the woman tend him.

He held out the bar of soap. "Come, wash my back."

Her blush deepened. She pressed her hands together quickly, nervously. Bending over, she took the soap from his hand and rubbed it against a linen cloth. She touched him hesitantly, as if not sure of where she should begin or exactly what she should do. The hands were soft and gentle and the hot soapy water against his skin felt delicious. Her fingers traced the steel tendon that ran down the back of his neck to his spine. He felt the thick muscles of his back bunch at her touch.

"It's not too hot, is it?"

"No."

She moved her foot. Her knee was not far from his shoulder. The out-flung length of one leg. Her slender ankle and the pointed toe of her shoe. The innocence of her pose created the eroticism of the moment. Intensifying so that he felt the stirring inside himself. Not merely his groin. All over. He was suffused with longing. His manhood was stiff and quivering. As if it were his whole body.

"May I?" Her hands massaged his neck and the back of his head and the massive muscle that joined his head to his shoulders. She stroked his hair. Pain rushed up his temple, rang like hooves drumming clay. He could not help the small shudder that ran through him. She jerked her hand back. "You've got a lump on the side of your head the size of an egg!"

"I was a trifle careless," he said, keeping his voice light.

She pursed her lips, as if she wished she could say otherwise. "That may be true, but your hair still needs a wash," she said, her voice holding mild reproof.

He ducked down under the surface long enough to count

to twenty, and to want air. He broke surface again. For a heartbeat his eyes locked with hers.

"Do what you want. I won't stop you."

Brenna gnawed her lip, edged closer and let go a breath. "I will try not to hurt you."

He tipped his head back while she washed out his hair, combing through the snarls with gentle fingers, trying not to feel anything, remember anything, wonder anything.

"Close your eyes," she ordered, running a soapy finger over each eyelid. Her hands were light, moth-delicate, on his forehead. "Why do you shave your beard?"

"It makes me remember who I am, what I'm for. It keeps me from growing too proud."

"What a load of nonsense!"

"Then the truth it must be. It's hot. It's red. It itches," he mumbled.

Her laughter was sudden and heart-deep, a ripple of pure notes. "With golden hair and red beard, you'd look like a great marmalade cat."

"Another reason to shave!"

Brenna followed the contours of his wide shoulders down his arms, where the water glistened among red-gold hairs. He sighed and felt the tension ebbing out of him. He melted back against the rim of the tub. Steam rose, hanging in the air a moment before drifting upward. She added a few more drops of scent to the water, and the oil floated toward him in little round drops, coating his chest and belly. His muscles soaked in it, reveled in the heat.

Soft lips half parted, she lathered the thick mat on his chest vigorously, her hands small and light against the hard flesh. She slid her hands down his belly, through crisp tangles of gold. Her soapy hands circled lower and lower. Though he sighed with pleasure, Leon didn't think that was a good idea. Hot male need surged through his veins at her maddening touch. He asked himself if he was being seduced, or if she was...taking a stupid chance, if that was what was happening. He slid deeper into the tub, shielding his arousal slightly.

Slowly, gracefully as the fall of a feather, she moved to the end of the tub and motioned for a leg to come out. Ignoring his muffled protest, she leaned against the tub and began lathering it, sliding one finger along a deep scar hollow above the knee. His thigh shot jagged stabs and convulsed into shivering. He tried to relax his body, to go limp.

Brenna looked down, leaned back against her heels, shoving a lock of her black hair back over one shoulder. "Won't you even talk to me?" she said in a small voice.

"There is nothing to talk about."

"You mean, you have nothing to say to me."

Leon knew he had missed something there. She would not meet his eyes. She seemed strangely tense: a coiled spring. He thought that she was angry; but why should she be? She was female. There was no accounting for her moods.

"That is not at all what I meant."

"But it is!"

Leon frowned at her, wishing he knew what had happened. One moment she had been open and friendly; the next she exuded all the fire of a woman scorned. He rolled his eyes and sat up, sighing with exasperation.

"I will not play this game."

"I will not let you turn this back on me." There was an edge to her voice now. "You're the one who—"

"This is not the time—"

"Not the time? You must be joking! There is nothing more important for us to do."

For a moment things stayed as they were, balanced on a knife's edge of Brenna's temper and his nerves. Then he felt the anger unwind, slowly, into a quieter disturbance. A few more breaths. "Isn't there?"

Without warning, she poured a dipper of herb-scented water over his head. He swallowed hard, half choking, gulped air and outrage, blinked water from his eyes, and snapped two pungent words.

"Oh—you *are* annoyed—you have a tongue like an ox whip!" His first impulse was to upend her and apply a hand to her derriere. Then she grinned at him with disarming candor. "Forgive me, but I get carried away sometimes!"

Leon snorted and blew water from his mouth. "How dare you—" It came as a half shriek, so disgraceful that it shattered all his anger. Laughter rose to fill the void: breathless, helpless laughter that loosened all his bones and left him half choking.

Her own laughter died with his, but a smile lingered; her eyes danced. "'Tis a ritual to drown the fleas!"

"Blast your impudence!" He surged to his feet and flung hair out of his eyes in a spray of water. A shower of droplets flew in a great arc to land on her gown, the sodden fabric outlining her bosom, leaving little to his imagination. He reached for the linen she was holding, and snatched it 'round himself, splashing the floor as he stepped out.

"Perhaps it was rash—"

"Perhaps!"

"'Twas an outrageous liberty. Most men would be foaming at the mouth by now."

Leon didn't care. For one thing, a ragged spike of agony lanced through his skull. There was a buzzing like a swarm of bees inside his head. His vision was blurring again. He stood there, totally overwhelmed by it all.

"Oh, mercy! You are not well!" she said, and put a quick hand under his elbow to steady him as he swayed. Leon shook her off, steadying with an effort.

"It's nothing."

He stood there, not daring to move. Now his entire body convulsed. His flesh burned. He felt chills even in the midst of all this heat. His legs were turning to water. He tottered.

"Dizzy," he mumbled, his voice half drowned by a peal of thunder.

Brenna caught his arm, forcefully, this time. "Don't tax yourself! You're wasting energy arguing."

This time he let her lay hands on him, allowing her to draw him across the room, into the alcove that held the bed, though he would not sit. "God's breath, woman. 'Tis but a touch of wet fever, nothing more."

"Stuff and nonsense. That lump on your head has addled your brains."

He let out all his breath in one huff. "Don't fuss, woman. I've suffered worse blows than that charging at quintains."

"I trust you are correct, but hardly prudent. My good sense tells me that such a blow can be fatal if there is brain damage."

"'Tis but a bump."

"Even a bump can be fatal." Her voice was low, steady, unyielding.

"Would you have me dead?"

"Don't talk so! That lump on your head has addled your wits," Brenna blurted, then winced, as if regretting her words as soon as she had spoken them. "I—I am sorry. It is not my place to..."

"You need not apologize. I'm not offended, just tired."

The bed was in front of him. It looked vast and inviting. And perhaps it was imprudent and tempting his own ironclad resolve to test himself against that wide-eyed expression, the full lips, the midnight cloud of curls and swell of bosom so boldly designed to entice a man. What had the scriptures said about Eve tempting Adam with forbidden fruit? But then came a bewildering thought. If Adam had been in Eden with Brenna instead of Eve, he would not have minded being cast out of Paradise, not as long as she went with him!

"I can see that you are ill, very ill." Her reply rang out and yet was muted by the howl of the wind. "You belong in bed."

Why not? Why not? He rubbed his forehead, and gave up any notion he might have of resistance.

"I am not well, yes—" he managed finally. The last of his coherence was fleeing. "The heat...my head—"

"Sit," she told him now. "Easy now, take it easy."

She let him slide from her arm to sit on the bed. Cradling his head in her hands as if it were an egg, she lowered it onto the pillow. A grunt this time from him. He sprawled on his back, squinched his eyes shut, and he was only too glad to do so, weary as he was, his body racked by violent shivers. A dry towel was placed discreetly across his loins. A hand tangled in his hair, one finger stroking across his forehead repetitiously.

"Don't try to get up. You'll do yourself a lasting harm."

"Go away! Leave me alone!" he raged at her.

She did; and then he was sorry for the silence.

The hall thrummed with sound, for everyone in the hold ate in the great chamber. Fire crackled in the hearth and they all were gathered, young and old, with the warm air smelling as the hall always smelled, of wood chips and resins and leathers and furs and good cooking.

Brenna spared no glances for those who sat at the narrow trestle tables. Her attention was on the dais at the far end. Facing them all, Sir Edmund sat at the center of the high table, his sister the widowed Lady Alice at his left, his other sister the indomitable Lady Agnita at his right, thin and upright. The gray-clad priest sat elbow-to-elbow with the Lady Alice, and the harper sat with them. But many seats at the great table stayed vacant, the hall of a hold long at war, its male heirs decimated.

"Your pardon for my lateness, Grandfather."

Sated and drowsy from rich food and drink, Sir Edmund nodded over his cup. "We will forgive your lateness, Brenna, now that you grace our table with your beauty."

Brenna walked around the dais to settle beside her great-aunt. Lady Agnita flicked her gaze up from her trencher. "It seems your fine knight has declined to break bread with us."

"He rests. He has traveled hard."

"In my day, a knight could travel far and little notice it."

"Aye, but 'tis oft times said that things are not what they were."

Brenna looked away from her aunt and flicked a glance around the hall. Despite the weather, guests had arrived from near and far for the week-long marriage celebrations that were to include combat contests, sword fights, horse shows and displays by artisans and master craftsmen from every guild.

Sir Edmund called for more jugs of beer and cordial, and waved expansively to the gathered company. A gust whipped at the tapestries and sent the lamps and candles flickering, casting illusory warmth on gray stone walls. For a moment tapestries and banners blazed out above the tables. High in the sooty rafters, smoke from the great hearth eddied about like a manmade mist.

"So," Agnita said, turning to her. "Why do you look so forlorn, child?"

Brenna seized the moment to speak up. "Aunt, what is all this nonsense Elen tells me about Keith Kil Coed?"

Agnita shrugged. "Not much more than you already know." She lowered her voice. "Edmund's been set thoroughly on edge. He says that Keith will be arriving at Dinas Bran on the morrow. He hopes to convince you that he is a better proposition than Aubrey of Leeds."

Brenna gasped. If Grandy saw some seriousness in the matter...the complications were threatening to overwhelm her. "I cannot believe anyone would expect me to abandon my betrothed at the altar!"

"I realize that, child," Agnita replied, her expression serious. "But don't despair. Edmund is a wily old rooster."

"And Keith is overreaching his ambitions! Can't we stop him?"

"'Tis too late to stop him. He has already left Craignant and begun his journey here. We do not know what route he travels, so we must do as best we can." Was there a hint of warning in the soft, smooth tones?

Brenna had taken a wedge of cheese and begun to break it. It crumbled in her tensed fingers, falling unheeded to her trencher. "I pray that there is no trouble."

"Speaking of which," Sir Edmund said, leaning toward Brenna. "What is this I hear about the near mishap at the postern?"

Brenna shrugged. "Naught but a minor scuffle, Grandy. My knight did his duty well. The villains were caught."

"You try me sorely, Brenna, with your recklessness!"

"It is raining again," Lady Alice said unnecessarily: the sound of it on the horn windowpanes behind them was audible over the conversation in the hall.

"Maybe there's a reason." The priest bent and looked straight into Brenna's eyes, so that her heart beat a little faster. "Mayhap—someone—is responsible for the storms?"

A few audible murmurs traveled around the tables. She heard people mutter—*sorcery*...

"That is impossible, and I believe you may have the wit to realize that—" Brenna started to protest, but frowned and thought on it, on the rain, the unrelenting winds. Surely no one could control the weather? She stared down at her trencher of thick wheaten bread. "Mortals have no governance over the weather."

The priest frowned, hearing that. "A jest, if you please. Though this rain is most unseasonable and despite the Holy Father's decree, the hedge wizards sell their charms in the market and practice sinful acts in private."

"They need not be sorcerous."

"That is blasphemous."

This was a priest, Brenna told herself. A simple district priest. Why were folk so fearful of what they did not understand or what was different?

"Mayhap, Our Lord sends a second flood to show us His displeasure," she murmured.

The priest nodded piously. "In truth, 'tis a very great possibility."

Brenna gathered up a thick wedge of sheep-milk cheese and some bread. "Well, 'tis a pleasant conversation, but I fear it must end, or I shall never get to bed this night. I must be off. I will see you all on the morrow."

"Where to in such haste?" asked Sir Edmund.

A lie tempted Brenna. She rejected it and looked her grandfather in the eye. "For whatever it's worth, I'm off to prepare a potion and wish the rain on another region."

Sir Edmund scowled. "Wish a littler harder then."

Brenna tiptoed closer to the embroidered bed hangings.

"Aubrey!" she whispered under her breath. He made no sign. A prickly aura of awareness breathed over her skin, crisp and distinct as cold air.

Suddenly she was very much afraid...

She shivered and shook her head as thoughts uncalled-for ran like ice melt through her brain. Was he...was he unconscious? Was he...dead? Her doubt turned to sudden, over-mastering dread that urged her forward.

"Aubrey!" she said again, and finding herself close to him she bent and very lightly touched his shoulder. He moved then, and she almost gasped with relief.

"What—?" he said, lifting his head. He blinked, frowned, his nose a handspan from hers. His face was flushed and his lips a set line. Shadows slipped across his eyes as if things moved, troubled, in his memory.

"Drink this. 'Tis but a simple tisane to take away the headache and ease the fever." She cradled his head in her arms, feeling inside her a warmth that bordered on love. He made a sound between a sigh and a grunt, and obediently swallowed sips of the mixture. Carefully she relaxed her forearm, laying his head upon the pillow. "Now listen to me, I don't want you out of this bed except to use the chamber pot. Do you understand?"

His eyes closed. "Aye."

"Good." Raindrops spattered through the window slit, a sudden gust of storm. She went to close the shutters. "I'm going back downstairs. I have chores to do. You stay in bed, hear?"

"Aye." Faintly.

She forced a smile to her lips. "See that you do."

Darkness, and a scent of herbs, and a deep sense of peace pervaded the workshop. Brenna carefully set the lamp on a stand. Its feeble glow barely reached the walls of the herbarium. Neatly arranged on wooden shelves that ran up the wall, sat her herbs and powders and whatnots, each resting in small pottery jars. A large white dog rose from its place by the fireplace and ambled toward her, its tail swinging side to side.

"Hello, Flash," she said, giving the hound a pat on his head. "I am almost out of linctus. We must make a fresh brew."

She lit the pair of candles on the table. The wind gathered strength and the double candlelight leaped and jumped with the sudden draft. It gave her two overlapped shadows and made them waver about the stonework.

She winced. Evil weather...aye, the spring had been plagued by it, folk talked in the hall and villages about it. Tempers flared over insignificant things. Even the priest was uncertain. This was the way the world had become. But they were fortunate, for there were rumors of burnings at the mouth of the Dee, that very same sleepy river that rolled through their valley and made the crops grow, and made Dinas Bran the best and richest land on all the marches. And they still planned for next year, for planting crops, hoping for better rains from the mountains, hoping the winds would not come too late in the spring or the hail ruin the grain. These were familiar enemies, and they were forever.

This year was unusual, that was all, and there was one benefit from the rain: cooler weather this spring kept disease from running rampant. Aside from normal complaints, headaches and such, no one had been mortally sick.

Flash nuzzled her knee. "You want to go out *now*? Away

with you, then, though you won't like it much.'' The dog
leaned up against her leg, inviting a quick scratch behind
his ears, then trotted off into the dark, about his own necessities.

Brenna looked toward the tall slit window, toward the
night and still-brooding storm, wondering if she should
check on her betrothed. She had slipped upstairs several
times to look in on him, and found him dozing. Yawning,
she rubbed her eyes. She herself could do with a good
night's sleep. But medicines did not happen by magic. Nor
come out of moonfluff. And she was running low.

Tending the infirm, one could forget about amorous suitors, keep one's eyes on household matters, put liaisons and
intrigues out of one's mind and worry about the seamstress's
baby, who took colic; and Bronwen, from the inn, with a
knife cut from one of her customers. Bronwen feared scar-
ring, and wanted a mixture of the herbs and lard Brenna had
tested on her neighbor, the woodcutter's wife Margot, whose
scarlet smallpox weals had paled and vanished.

She picked up a bundle of dried herbs and thought of her
betrothed, his voice, his body. Having become better ac-
quainted with him, she was uncomfortably aware of his man-
liness, and of her own cravings. Her pulses raced and her
breasts almost ached with the memory of that moment when
she had been caught tightly against his naked chest.

Yet, in truth, he had seemed confused. She recalled his
smoldering gaze. It had been as if he were intent upon
searching out and reading every secret of her mind, but she
was sure he had no need to read her thoughts…

A sound in the night yanked Brenna from her thoughts.
She lifted her head in alarm. She listened through the thunder and rush of wind and rain. From the hall came a clat-
tering of metal, but quiet fell again below, leaving only the
rain.

She stretched the stiffness from her neck and back, found

a knife and cut a slice of bread and the end of the cheese...
Naturally, as if drawn back on a string, Flash appeared at
the doorway, dripping rainwater, tail wagging in hopes of
his share.

Chapter Four

Brenna stood in the corridor, her eyes fastened on the heavy leather curtain of the bedchamber and allowed a little wave of fatigue to claim her for a moment. She was truly tired; and she should take herself off to bed. But she knew she was hours away from sleep, that, even if she were to go to bed this instant, her mind would go on, until almost morning, worrying about the knight and whether he was all right. It would not take a moment to examine her rescuer, see that he was all right. Then, perhaps, she could sleep.

Unable to contain herself, she slid the curtain aside, crept to the side of the bed, and stared at the knight's silent form. He lay there with his eyes closed, but not in restful repose. Far from it.

Brenna checked the knight's throat pulse, and felt his flesh beneath her fingertips, hot and sweaty. He was breathing like a runner in a race; like a man smitten in his vitals.

She leaned close to him, rested her hand on his shoulder and let it travel down his body, pausing over his heart to feel the steady beating, then lower and lower still. His loins were cool and soft, but she felt a quickening in them as her fingers lingered.

"Can you hear me?"

He shifted a bit, but his eyes remained closed.

Her throat went tight. What was she to do now? Nothing, except to wait? And that had its own dangers. She picked up a wet cloth and lightly mopped his forehead with it. His eyes fluttered open. Had the cool cloth awakened him? she wondered. Or had it been the touch of her hand at the base of his belly a moment before?

He was staring at her.

"How do you feel?" she asked.

"A little better." He spoke very softly, so that she had to strain to hear him.

He glanced down at his nakedness. She saw the movement of his eyes and draped a strip of cloth that she had not yet moistened across his middle.

Hoarsely he said, "Am I dying?"

"I don't think so."

A little pause. A moistening of the lips.

A man screamed once—a single cry, ending in a short high screech.

"To arms! Attack! To arms!" In a single smooth shift, Leon grabbed her and rolled them both in one untidy heave off the bed. They fell with a thud on the floor, the knight twisting and falling in a protective sprawl across Brenna's body.

"Assassins!"

The sound lingered in the air, echoing, echoing... Then, faintly, faraway sound came ringing through the night's stillness, fading and repeating. Hollow, echoing, hideous screams.

Sprawled beneath him, Brenna tried to sit up. Unsuccessfully. He had very large hands, and those hands held fast, pinning her to the floor. By training or reflex he protected her.

"Ooo-oo Ooo..." A voice made a short trumpet-carried gasp and screamed, a piercing incoherent sound, as instantly cut short by silence...then she heard just a babble of distant confused cries. Her heart bounced into her throat and sank again.

Brenna was no stranger to summary justice. She had grown up with it. Occasionally its cost was life. But torture made her shamefully sick in the stomach.

An ember popped. The air hung too quiet, eerily still, sharpening the faint bell-like cries. Echoes of screaming mingled oddly with the reality of the quiet chamber air.

She squirmed, attempting to free herself. Ribs heaving, she kicked, a futile effort. Her body shuddered with the force of it.

"Let me up!"

"No!" he hissed, and covered her head with his shoulder, pinning her to the floor. Close, so close...

That was something. That was a great deal. It pushed away panic. Squashed as she was, with her head lodged somewhere near his belly button, Brenna smiled. He was a knight. Her own true knight.

"All right, but ease up. You're killing me."

He let go a little bit. Just a little. Brenna drew in breath.

"I'm getting you out of here."

He surged to his knees. Strong arms grabbed her slender body, and lifted her up past himself like so much sacking. Brenna braced herself as he lunged upward. She clung to his middle with one arm and both legs, gasping. Together they flailed, overbalanced, and fell onto the bed. She heard a shrill yell, muffled, in the dungeons. It was horrid, just horrid.

"I think it's the guards punishing the assailants," she gasped into the strong cords of his neck. She felt his body flinch silently against hers, an uncontrollable physical shiver.

"Do you know how many ways there are to kill a man?" His voice wavered oddly. The trembling did not cease.

Brenna shook her head.

"Good. Because I don't even know that myself."

The screams stopped.

His head fell forward. "Safe now," he slurred. "Stay."

The two of them lay there, wrapped about each other like braided pastry, but she was not about to move, not about to move even her hands, one on his shoulder, one on his forehead.

No movement in the chamber, no sound, while he succumbed to the fever. She wished she could get help. How often had she complained that Elen was an interfering old meddler? Now, she wished the maid would come.

As if conjured by magic, Elen appeared. She leaned close above them, holding a lamp. *"What...?"*

Brenna gasped, "Never mind. His weight has me pinned down. He has the fever. His skin...it burns—"

"He's still conscious?" Elen swung the lamp about, with a rustle of her robes, and set it on the table. The lamp shed a steady yellow glow upon the still figure, making of it a carven image. Brenna shivered with a sudden chill.

"Can you hear me? Can you move a little?"

He lifted heavy eyelids. "Don't know." His breath rasped.

"Ease your grip. Let me up."

He shifted his weight and Brenna rolled away, scrambling to her feet. Gold hearth lights prickled on his hair. His mouth made a thin line and sweat beaded his brow, but he had the shivers. She studied the glassy eyes that stared vacantly at the ceiling. Her heart lurched. Something wrong with the eyes, almost as if he were...

"Elen, do you know the examination Hippocrates gives to see if there is damage to the brain?"

The maidservant lifted her chin. "I do. You read it to me only last week."

"Well, then, don't stand there gawping. Give me a candle."

Elen lit a small wax candle and handed it curtly to Brenna, who knelt beside the bed, put up her empty hand to his face, and cupped her fingers lightly about his jaw.

"Look straight ahead, please. Don't close your eyes." She held the candle before his eyes. "Be very still, it's important."

He swallowed. "Don't like it."

"I know," she murmured. She flicked the candle away, brought it close again, flicked it away from each eye, peering at the left one. A chill went creeping down her back. "See that, Elen?"

Elen inclined her head. "The pupils open and close unevenly, and one remains wider than the other." She linked her hands over her waist garter. "What do you think?"

"Not a thing I can do, nor any herbalist. 'Tis caused by the head blow. Rest is the only cure. It will heal if he doesn't injure it again before it grows sound."

"So you can't do anything with simples for him?"

"Oh, we could compound cupflower drug for him, but that sometimes causes death. Willow powder will ease the fever."

Brenna touched his shoulder, trailing her fingers idly over his jaw, and went to her herbal chest. She always kept a few essential herbs and poultices upstairs in case she found the need for them…these herbals to open the veins, the hops to flush the poisons out, and the raw bean mash to counter the effects of poison. She reached into the container, found the leather bag, undid the drawstrings, and took out packets of herbs. Rosemary, juniper berries, dried roots, hyssop, onion blossoms and clover.

Where was the willow powder? Near the bottom, under a bunch of mallow stems, she found what she had been looking for. She shook the powder out of the packet and it barely covered the palm of her hand. Sweet heavens, there was so little of it! Why hadn't she dried more, filled up her whole bag when she had the chance? Too late now for regrets. There had to be enough here to break her knight's fever. Nothing else mattered.

If he died…

She pushed the thought aside, poured the powder back into the parchment packet, and reached over to the fireplace to give the inset crank of the hidden bellows a few turns. The flames roared up and the man jumped.

"No!" Hollow, echoing, a brief roar.

She all but ran to his side. He pushed himself up, blinked and stared at her with eyes that looked to be all pupil. A sigh fluttered through his pallid lips. His look of complete confusion frightened her.

The soft blossoming roar of a fire started. A large fire. Half in the shadow-ways there was a dimming, a dazzle of flame, the shouts of war, ghosts of battle swirling about them. Other things were there, too. Death was one.

For within the fire's very heart he discerned what could only be termed a female face, elemental, to be sure, its features shifting like currents, sliding away into shadow and reappearing slightly altered as if each heartbeat, each moment in time, brought it a new aspect. Suzanne. Had she returned for him, to finish that which remained undone?

Dreams crept upon him, which were Suzanne's proud self, burning pride and sometimes heartlessness. He felt more than memories. It was all lost in horror.

Tears came to his eyes, and a bitter taste to his mouth, the harsh sour tang of iron, pain and shame commingled. If he gave way to that past—

"No," he cried out loud, and the dream retreated, held at bay by a will as strong as forged iron.

He opened his eyes. Shadows gathered, stirring and urgent on this side and on that. His heart was still thundering. He could scarcely breathe. All the fire burned within.

He put his hand to his weapon belt that hung on the bedstead and touched the amulet, wishing now for the memories of that bright elf. He called her in his mind, and she came, with the scent of dried herbs and a vague sweet draft of air.

Gentle hands touched him. A halo of luxurious hair rimmed the face that bent above him, against the fire. Her face gleamed ivory pale, and she softly sang, which soothed and filled him with an uncommon serenity, lulling his senses.

He still clutched the amulet. Slim cool fingers pried his hand from it, eased his limbs, covered him with a downy peace in which the only pain was to his heart, an ache and a memory of loss.

"You've come on wings, angel of beauty..." He reached out his hand and Brenna took it. Her palm burned as if she'd grabbed a live coal. "I've been waiting all my life for you," he whispered in a voice so husky and low that she had to bend close to hear the words.

Low and thick, she said, "You should rest...you are feverish."

He turned his head. In a deep, soft voice, he murmured, "Angel of goodness! I want you near me."

Brenna watched the dancing, dipping span of his mouth smile. Something struggled in her chest, and came out in a hoarse sound, "Don't talk. You're not feeling well just now..."

His throat worked convulsively. He moaned and coughed. His skin shaded from red to gray to white, and the black pupils eclipsed the jewel-like brilliance of his eyes. His grip crushed her fingers. A moment later, his eyes rolled up and he went limp.

A dread settled on Brenna then.

She stood frozen until she realized his chest still rose and fell. She shifted her position until she was on her knees, and slipped her finger to the place on his wrist where veins lay next to the surface. The pulse throbbed beneath her fingertip as if the heart that drove it was going to burst.

"No!" she flamed. "You shall not have him, Death. Begone! You misjudge your time. Begone, I say. He is mine. By all the ancient runes, he is mine!"

A gust of wind blasted down the chimney throat, blew fire and cinders into the room. Shadows lurked and flickered about the edges of the room. The air was thick with roiling, dark disturbance. Had she inadvertently called down the old gods as the gossips said she could? Elen seemed to notice nothing, merely handed her a goblet of water, and found a cloth to wipe the sweat that beaded his brow and upper lip.

"Should I go get the priest to shrive him?"

"No!"

"Good men always die, especially from cracked heads."

In a milder tone Brenna said, "Not so. Rest and time are the only cures for a cracked head—I researched such injuries among the medical manuscripts when I was studying herbal remedies."

That's if he lived. Great round beads of sweat stood on his skin, but his lips were cracked and dry, and he was shaking all over. His breathing was shallow, labored, painful to hear. Was her knight dying? Fear slammed into her belly. He could not die. She adjusted a pillow under his head, and drew the covers over the supine form.

"Don't you been worrying, Elen. A bump like this wouldn't kill a healthy man—and this one is a fine specimen. He'll be all right once he gets some rest." She waved one hand. "You'll see. He'll be right as rain come morning."

"Would you like me to stay with him tonight?"

"No, thank you, Elen. Go and have your supper. I'll sit with him. If he wakes and needs me, I'll be here."

Elen sniffed indignantly. "Well, I hope you know if you need me...I'm there, too!" The maidservant tossed her veil in place with a flick of one hand. She turned and parted the door curtain and sailed out, dropping the heavily beaded leather with rather more force than necessary.

Brenna sat motionless, staring at her knight, with a dull ache inside. "'Tis tragic that you are injured just when I have need of you." She brushed stray hair from his forehead. "Sleep, my hawk. Heal."

Later, when Elen came to relieve her vigil so that she might rest, Brenna dismissed her with the promise that she would call her if need be. Elen lifted a brow, looked doubtful, and then left.

For hours Brenna knelt there watching him grow worse

and worse. The blood pulsed quickly through his neck and he seemed to be having trouble breathing. His lips were dry, and he was shaking all over. The fever seemed like a fire in his body; he yelled and thrashed as if trying to stamp it out. She rubbed her face. Her eyes felt full of grit. She wanted desperately to shut her eyes and sleep. Her knees were numb. She shifted her position from kneeling to sitting on the edge of the bed.

Tremors racked him. He was panting now, in short jerky gasps like a runner who had come to the end of his strength. She leaned over him and touched his cheek, traced the line of it, slid across the thick cords of his neck and brushed his sweat-dampened hair back behind his shoulder. Her fingers traced the muscles of his chest with feather softness.

Her heart skipped a beat, hope and misery tangled together. He looked impossibly vulnerable, lying all limp and... Her face went hot. Some thoughts were best left unthought.

"Don't die. I need you, my beloved knight."

If he heard her, he gave no reply. The tangle of bedcovers slid to the floor. Brenna crouched beside him and patiently adjusted them again about his bare shoulders. The touch burned her. She fed him the willow powder mixture, forcing it through his lips drop by drop.

"Quit fighting me!" she yelled, catching at his hands as he tried to push her away. "You can't die! Not yet!"

Which was foolish. His breath rattled in his throat. Anyone could see he was going to die before morning.

"Not yet!" She lay down beside him and stroked his hair, talked to him soothingly about whatever nonsense came into her mind. His left hand came to rest on the curve of her abdomen.

"Get well, my heart." She felt the fine tremor that went through his body, and repeated the words again and again, a slow litany that was nearly a song. She repeated them until the words were slurred, and her eyes were heavy, shutting.

Finally she gave up and let sleep claim her.

* * *

He was dead. He had died and gone to heaven.

Leon knew this was so for an angel nestled there, square upon his broad chest, her weight warm and silky upon his. This angel had dark hair and made soft snuffling sounds, a kind of divine snoring, but no matter, she was delightful and lissom and she smelled of spring blossoms, a delicate mixture of roses and sweet herbs.

Head burrowed beneath his chin, the angel lay atop him, the softness of her bosom crushed against his chest, a drift of hair against his ear, tickling his throat. From breast to belly to the tips of her toes, there was nowhere they did not touch.

Leon touched a velvety earlobe with the tip of his finger. Were angels soft and warm? Did they smell of herbs and flowers? Did they occasionally, as woodland nymphs, take on a mortal form? If so, did these changelings all have such delicate bones and silky flesh? He did not know the answers. It was not the sort of thing warrior monks and their confessors talked about.

He did know that it was a heady sensation.

Curled against him, she fitted into his arms perfectly, as if made especially for him. Perhaps it was his own personal angel, the guardian of his soul, the one that kept him out of harm's way? Poor little thing, he thought, she'd been busy over the years making sure he didn't throw his life away in some battle or other.

Now she was exhausted.

And no wonder.

Serving him, she served that terrible thing, war. The crusade had been long, long and bitter, and there was little glory in it. They named him in songs, called him Caer Llion the Ironheart, but what they sang as brave he remembered mostly as sand and heat and bloodshed. Battles, fierce and long, fought from the breaking of one day to the evening of the next, and himself tired and spattered with gore, his limbs turned leaden with the weight of armor, but alive.

Alive, because of his guardian angel. She had not left his side. She would not, this night.

He wrapped his arms around her strongly and tenderly, afraid she might fly off him at any minute. He rocked her gently and crooned soft, soothing words. She sighed, a pleased, dreamy sound, but did not waken. He felt the silkiness of her skin, and knew slide of muscle, smooth and taut beneath the soft fabric of her clothing, as she stirred and stretched.

Soft, feminine, mysterious.

Leon smiled and gathered the small exquisite creature closer, running his big hand across the flat plane of her shoulders and down the curve of her spine. The smile turned to a frown. There was something lacking. Something important.

"You've left your wings behind."

"I don't have any."

Impossible, he thought. All angels had wings. He folded her tightly to his chest as a mother might a lost child. He nestled his chin on top of her fragrant dark hair. He touched her cheek, the side of her neck, the hollow of her collarbone. He put his lips against her temple.

His heart sped and his breath grew tight. Without wings she was earthbound!

"It's all right, my angel. I'll take very, very good care of you." How odd my voice sounds! Leon thought. How hollow, how timbreless.

Perhaps he was not dead? Perhaps it was the fever? Many times during a bout of fever he'd woken in the darkness, beset by dreams that were all too real, haunted by nightmares that left him trembling and afraid.

No. This was different. This was special.

She smelled of feminine mysteries, of flowers and herbs, and his heart pounded against his ribs. Her hand rested on his hip. Her knee pressed on his knee and strained his thigh and he wished he could get her hand off before something else happened. He shifted a leg that throbbed.

Sheets whispered and slid. One arm came up, enfolded his head, stroking, a pass of her hand across his forehead, down his face.

"Shush." It was the word one used with a child.

A quick intake of breath, and he lay rigid. He didn't want to frighten her away. She might never return.

"Rest, my heart," she whispered, her eyelids fluttering. Her hand stroked his brow. "All is well. You are going to be all right. I am here."

I am here. The angel's voice was somehow familiar, an echo in his mind, rushing against his eardrums in time with the throbbing of his body. But he'd thought that too many times in his dreams. How many times had she come to him in the darkness of the night, her voice low and soothing, her touch granting the gift of solace and peace?

How many dreams?

Dreams of passion. Dreams of desperation. In those dreams, she'd come to him, lovely and naked, ivory and charcoal, but always ephemeral. It wasn't reasonable she assumed flesh now, when he wasn't sure if he were dead or alive, and the darkness of night hung like a black velvet curtain, containing them.

"Stay," he whispered.

The angel gave a delicious wriggle. Powerful sensations stirred. His heart skipped a beat. The rise and fall of her breasts tempted his hand, the scent of her inflamed him. She wriggled again. They stirred together like two leaves on a branch. Warmth suffused him. Erotic feelings ran up and down his body...

Hunger swept through him, a fierce surge of fire.

God, he couldn't stand it.

Too late, he tried to clear his mind of its wayward thoughts. It was all very clear suddenly what he wanted and what his body was doing on its own. His heart thudded along in heavy anticipation. Surely not. Not with an angel. Please God, that wasn't even a rational thought.

Couldn't stop it. Things just were. His heart raced, the

veins pounding in his throat. His breath came short. Hell, he thought. Dangerous to move. Lie still.

His eyes closed and he shuddered. Think nothing, do nothing. Lie still. Deep breath.

To touch her was heaven. To possess her...

His thoughts slammed against a wall. He wouldn't. He *couldn't*. Not after Whittington. Not after Suzanne.

So he lay still trying to be steadily stolid, and held her against him and maintained the good feeling as long as he dared, until she shifted, and woke.

Time must have passed. She squirmed a bit and lay still. He knew she was awake. Her arm had gone tense. Her breath came out raggedly. Her eyelashes fluttered. Slowly, ever so slowly, she lifted her head.

Candlelight picked out iridescent glints in her hair, glowed on her brow and cheek like rich cream, and coated gold on the soft flesh of her neck. Her head twisted so that she could see him more fully. Dark eyes—pretty eyes—didn't even flinch. She just looked, that was all.

"Hello!" His voice did not sound like his own.

"I—"

Entranced, Leon stared as the tip of the angel's tongue slid to moisten her full, rose-pink lips. She was so lovely. She was perfect. She was worth dying for.

"I've waited for you all my life."

"You are awake. I must go."

His heartbeat caught him. He wanted her. He needed her, and he meant to keep her near, for a while at least.

"No!" he said fiercely, gripping her arm.

"I have to attend to some things."

"Not yet. Stay with me."

"I cannot."

His mind was whirling with ten thousand questions, but only one escaped his lips. "You'd leave me on my own?"

"Is that so terrible?"

He nodded. "I don't want to lose you," he said thickly. He had not known until he had said it just how much it meant to him. As if they had a will of his own, his fingers began moving up her arm to her shoulder, then slowly tracing the delicate line of her collarbone. When they reached the neck of her gown, she drew in a sharp breath.

"This isn't wise..." She sighed and curled up away from him. She stared at him, a flash of her eyes across the starlight. He knew her from the lake, from the desert, from his heart. She had always been with him. She had saved him, guarded him, guided him, held the power of fate over him and now, finally, she had come to him in human form.

Half strangled by his thick throat, he said, "One night only." His voice was dry and harsh. His heart was pounding. He moistened his lips. What would he do if she chose to go? The thought made him light-headed. Hard to think. Which was bad. The words took a long time to form. "Is that too much to ask?"

Her eyes stared into his, dark as tarn pools.

Almost, but not quite, he smiled.

Almost, but not quite, she returned his smile.

She hardly seemed to breathe as his hand slid into her gown. She also turned very red, and he saw her eyes dilate and contract. Her mouth opened, and closed, as if she were trying to say something and could not decide what.

"As you wish, my warrior," she said softly. The words were like music. "You have me now, but I will have to go. In the morning. First thing."

Leon heard the answer. He felt the love. And he was content enough with that arrangement. "I understand, my angel. Show me the woman."

He drew her to him. They kissed, hungry for each other in this place where there were no boundaries, no strictures, no ties. Close, so very close. Bone sang to bone, blood to blood, his heart to hers, and his manhood grew hard. She was so close. So willing and so close!

"Everything's going to be all right. I promise."

His hand closed on her soft breast. A tremor went through her, and he felt the heat rising in her flesh. He closed his

eyes to concentrate on the feel of her. Nothing had ever felt
so soft. Flesh like sun-warmed silk. His fingers buried themselves in the cleft between her breasts and a spasm of desire
shook him.

They both heard cloth tear.

He opened startled eyes to find he had ripped her gown.
But she was not angry. She smiled, a slow, heavy-lidded
smile, tender and loving.

"Oh."

She let out a kind of moan, and put her head against his
chest. He felt the beating of her heart, like something trapped
in the flesh within his hand. She gasped again.

"I have such an ache in my belly, like hunger, only 'tis
sweeter, and farther down my body. What's happening to
me?"

Cuddled against her, Leon could feel how tense she was
and smiled to himself, felt a deep welling of sweetness of
unbearable intensity. He knew that she needed him now,
needed to have his body on and inside hers, as if that union
would make her complete. And he needed that, too.

"It's all right," he said in a ragged voice. "Believe me,
my dear, it's as scary for me as it is for you."

"You're just saying that!"

"No, it's true. I swear it on my heart. Feel." Taking her
hand, he placed it on his breast. Cautiously small firm fingers
tangled itself in the crisp hair that curled there.

"What happens now?"

"Just let yourself go. Do what feels best."

In one graceful gesture, she shrugged out of her gown and
let it fall to the floor. Her fingertips pressed at the contours
of his muscles, moving slowly, methodically as if she were
blind and learning the physical form of her charge. Veins of
pleasure raced down into his groin. He felt heat suffusing
his loins. Her hips lurched inward against him.

"Oh, oh, oh-hh…" Her head went back, her white throat
exposed, her long dark hair spilling wildly over him. She

sucked in her breath and looked at him as deer look at hounds, wary and distraught.

"I am afraid."

He said nothing.

Her breast heaved and little shudders rippled through her body. "You do love me, don't you?"

Leon kissed her breasts. "How could I not? You were made for me. Without you I should not be complete. I sense the same thing in you."

She put her face into the hollow of his shoulder. Her arms came around him. Her nails dug into the flesh of his back. "I've waited forever to hear you say that, because I love you, and only you. My lifemate. My blood and heart, my other half. Make me a woman, beloved. Please."

Unable to stop himself, he ran his hands down her incomparable body, his fingertips tracing the indentation of her spine, descending slowly. He felt her quiver and the skin of her buttocks raised in gooseflesh. After a time, she pried him gently from her, pushed him back down on the rumpled bed long enough to search his eyes with her own. Whatever she saw there, must have given her satisfaction. Her lips parted, and she smiled down at him as an angel might at a favorite mortal.

"Beloved?" The word was filled with hidden depths, promises of unearthly delights.

"Yes."

"This moment is very sweet to me," she whispered, her face close to his, pressing her mouth against his, pushing her warm body against his, as if wanting to give him her warmth, her passion, her love of life. He felt the heat rise between them, catching like tinder.

Soft hands touched him. Her flat palms made circles across his chest, nails flicking at his nipples. It was hard to breathe. It was hard to think. His mind was on fire, but it could not match the heat of his body. His heart was hammering and her hands did quiet, disturbing things that made his skin all too sensitive, the edge of pleasure—or intense discomfort. He was no longer sure which.

"Oh!" The exclamation forced out of her mouth as if with a blow. "It's so silky."

Her words were a spur, heightening his pleasure. Her touch was magical, unbearable. If she did not stop at once he would... He tried to push her hands away.

But her delighted hands at once continued exploring his body. Leon found he could not catch his breath and when he panted his exhalations seemed fiery. Desire, mindless and savage, clotting his throat making speech next to impossible. He could only gasp, "Keep going."

Her hips lifted and she stared into his face, her eyes huge and liquid, her hair in the semidarkness a shroud rich with promise, below which her breasts rose and fell with her rapid, shallow breathing.

"Oh-hh..." A sigh like a cloud riding high on warm wind and sunlight. She melted into him, her heat defining him, her hands testing the shape of him.

He tried very hard to be gentle, afraid he might hurt her. But she clenched his buttocks fiercely, rhythmically, as she slid up against him and back. His flesh felt hot as it moved against hers and she whimpered, pressing against him, her soft belly accepting the hungry rubbing of his manhood, her arms around him, her legs spreading, opening up like the petals of a fragrant flower, her sweet breath in his nostrils...

He pushed up against her and she cried out, frantic now for the union. "Now," she said to him. "Oh, now."

He began to move then, as demanding as she was.

Desire was soaring, fluttering and unbound. She felt warm and fluid. Her knees parted to receive him. He lost himself in her. He filled her with his flesh and touched her with his passion.

He lost all sense of time and space, as if he were displaced and rushing with the wind, and for that stolen time there was no fear, no guilt, no worry, no death. There was nothing but the raw sensation of pleasure and the release of something small but bright. Something almost like hope.

In another heartbeat she would be totally his. He could feel himself stretch her internally, and she quaked and kissed him as if she never wanted to let him go. Heat flooded through him. He was scorched, he was scalded. He felt his thickly muscled body give a warning shiver. There was an explosion in his senses, somewhere infinite, somewhere enchanting.

He felt something that had long frozen about his heart melt away, and he knew peace for the first time in years, a wholeness lost since Suzanne's death.

Chapter Five

As Brenna crossed the bailey to chapel for morning prayer, the castle walls rose above her gray with daylit mist. The storm had blown itself out. Soon the sun would rise and the day would be sunny and long and sweet. She hurried past the kitchens, which, at this hour, were warm and busy, with ale losing its chill beside the fire, and porridge warming on the top of the stove.

A high, soft sound drew her into the workroom and mews beyond the dry stores. Here, the hooded raptors rested on their perches; small russet falcons, large gray hawks, and, in solitary splendor, a great white eagle. The mews was deserted except for a page who slept on a bench nearby, a thin lad, pinch-faced. He lifted his head at her entrance and leaped up.

"Lady," he said.

"Hush. Go on sleeping. There is naught amiss."

Brenna's own falcon drowsed quietly. A fine golden falcon from the north, it was her grandfather's gift for her birth feast, a season past. It had been new-caught then; soon it would be ready for proving, that first, free hunt, when the bird must choose to come back to its tamer's hand or escape to freedom.

The bird was the exact shade of Aubrey's hair. She paused

to stroke the shimmering back with a gentle finger, and shifted her weight from one hip to the other, experimenting with the feel of her body.

It was a new body, a woman's body, with sinew and flesh informed as they had not been the day before and with pleasure newly awakened in her. She savored the moist sliding of tissue against tissue, and smiled secretly at the sense of weight and fullness in the bottom of her belly. Her slightest movement started the tension building again. She felt like a candle, a glowing white beeswax candle.

Aubrey of Leeds was the flame.

She closed her eyes, trying to remember the exact arrangement of the flecks of green in his hazel eyes. A scrape of toenails on stone brought her about sharply, winning a keen hiss from the falcon.

Flash bounded in on long legs, tongue lolling, his fringed tail waving joyously. Elen followed him.

"There you are, Brenna. I wondered where you had gone."

Brenna brushed off Flash's exuberant greeting. "I wanted to be alone, to think."

"How was the knight when you left?"

"Sleeping. The fever's broken." Brenna smoothed the crest of feathers attached to the falcon's hood; feathers the color of burnished gold, rising above soft leather dyed a deep and luminous green. Gold and green: green the color of her betrothed's eyes, gold no brighter than his hair.

Once she'd seen a stripling, his hair just that color, and he'd gone away, no one could say where. She had clung to the memory, wove fantasies about him, made him into a dream knight, impossibly heroic, and measured every other mortal man against that singular, infallible, perfect entity.

Now her dream had turned to reality. Her forever knight had come, Aubrey of Leeds, that tall man with his stern face and his bright eyes and his hair like the sun's own fire.

The chapel bell rang loud in the silence. "Morning mass is about to begin. Let us go."

Never willing to be far from her side, Flash bounded out the door. The mews erupted in a flurry of wings and fierce hawk screams. Only the eagle held still. The eagle, and Brenna's falcon, that tightened talons on the perch, gave an infinitesimal turning of the blinded head, uttered a contemptuous hiss and was silent.

A bell rang somewhere. A distant bell, muffled and indistinct. The sound of it filtered into Leon's sleep and woke him from a dream of bright little elves and ravishing angels.

He sat up in bed, his heart pounding. Something rattled and thumped somewhere, a rushing in his ears, a sound too crisp to be imaginary. How could so many people be so busy...and so loud...so early in the day?

The room was dimly illuminated by one squat oil lamp sitting high up on a ledge like a giant insect. There was a fire tamely burning in the hearth, amid a blasted scatter of chimney ash across the stones. In front of the fireplace was a stool with clothes draped over it. His eye searched the room, the dark outlines, knew it for what it was, a bedchamber. The walls weren't square, but curving, which meant this particular bedchamber was in a keep or tower.

He was not sure what he had expected. Nothing came to mind. Except his head ached, and he was alone, naked, in a bed he did not know. A moment of fright came back to him. He could not remember what he had been doing when he went to bed, other than that his brow hurt. He touched the temple that had been giving him misery, to find it was sore, but no longer acutely painful.

He lay back again and sought to recapture the warm calm of sleep, but he couldn't relax his mind, though the bed upon which he was lying was exquisitely comfortable, with a mattress of feathers. He stared at the shadowed beams above him.

They reminded him of his dreams, the angel, all midnight and moonlight, one of the heavenly hosts. And himself, who was earthen and coarse, and whose power was only that in his arm and his wits. It must have been a dream of some kind, a delusion of the fever... He wished no more such dreams, which tormented him with what he was and was not and could never be.

It was nearing dawn. The sky was growing light. Imperceptibly, the gloom softened. He lay there, eyes open, watching day break through the window slit. A chill predawn breeze stirred his hair.

He stared at the ceiling; at nothing. Things floated. It was a feeling of having traveled, far and somehow perilously, yet with no recollection of the journey. His thoughts skittered about at random, no idea what he was facing this day, no solid memory why he was here. He had a vague notion it was a tourney. Or was it to storm a stronghold?

What was bothering him?

Was he not Ironheart? One of the few honest men in a court increasingly corrupt and full of wicked men? The disciplined, tempered knight who inspired not awe or fear, but a fanatical loyalty among those who served him? The leader whose men would follow to the gates of hell and beyond? The legendary warlord who killed with deadly cold efficiency, and who could not be crippled by emotions?

But he was not a monster. There *was* some emotion left in him. He had feelings like other men, though he hid the gentler ones under a tough exterior. A skill he'd mastered and perfected over the years. To survive the body blow to his life. Just to go on. *To live.*

Something banged, sounding closer. Voices rang and echoed. Then a good deal of cursing, and another thump. Ignoring the throbbing in his temple, he cocked his head and listened, his body tense. Had it come from outside or from directly nearby?

The noise repeated itself. *Thump.*

He judged the sound. Changing of the guard.

A door shut downstairs, echoing. There was a commotion on the stairs. The very timbers of the turret creaked. He heard voices. Suddenly there was a sound that startled him.

A rattle sounded in the corridor, something metal bumped the corridor wall, where someone was walking.

He elbowed himself up and swung both his legs off the bed, reaching for his sword—which was not where it should be. In its place, a small chest stood open, and within it, he saw the tops of glass vials and herb bundles—a healer's kit.

Where was his blade? He stood up, heart pounding in his chest in perfect rhythm with the throbbing in his head. The stone floor struck cold through the rushes. He swore, two pungent words. He was naked, and he had no clothes and no sword.

Malediction! He hated to be without a weapon. He passed from swearing in French to English, and thence to Latin. Latin was a good language in which to swear.

Hushed whispers. Muffled indistinct.

"It's him?"

"Aye, he's the one. I told you he'd come."

What, Leon thought wildly, *am I hearing?* He listened. He listened very hard. And heard someone saying that accidents were easy. Words he did not like at all. They sounded like an ambush being arranged.

Dread spread through his gut. He felt his heart lurch in his chest. Sweet heavens! Who might have tracked him here? His neck hair stood on end.

He grabbed one of the iron pokers propped beside the fireplace and angled for the doorway, back to the wall, straining to hear. All was still. He stood, feet apart, in a fighting stance. It was easy to doubt his own senses, to wonder if he imagined those disembodied whispers. They came again, and this time there was no mistaking what was said, clear and harsh in his ear.

"Hush, hush, *hush!* Never say so."

"It only makes sense—" The voice died out, the words hanging in the air.

Someone with hurried fumbling fingers was unlatching the door cover. Leon's muscles went rigid, flattening his spine against stone. Metal rings rattled. A foot scuffed at the entrance. The blade of a dagger moved into his line of sight. His teeth bared; he took a single long step forward, poker poised.

The leather curtain swung abruptly inward. He had only a fleeting glimpse, a distracting splash of color, before his left wrist snapped outward.

A little gasp.

Leon felt a sudden, almost painful stab of horror. The metal circlet holding plain gauze flew off dark locks that spilled loosely down a slender back.

It was a woman!

In appalled disbelief, he watched the poker descend in a killing blow. In a wild attempt to divert his aim, he twisted his whole arm in a tight little arc, while he threw himself back on one leg away from her. Hard-pressed anger snapped and sang along his bones like overdrawn harp wires.

Leon struggled for breath. "Move!" The word was a roar, emanating from the very depths of his chest. The poker hit the wall with a mighty bang, then there was a thump and clatter as it fell to the floor.

Brenna's arm was seized in a viselike grip. She was shaken like a rat in a dog's jaws. She heard a snarl and Flash's deep bark. The room spun. Her head whirled and she saw two of everything, including Aubrey. And one Aubrey, particularly in his present mood, was more than sufficient.

"Drop it."

"Ease up, you're killing me!"

She tossed down the dagger with a clang of metal and flying hair. He threw her aside with one hand. Another chorus of barks. Her teeth rattled; she clenched her jaw and blinked rapidly to clear her vision. The two Aubreys merged into one who was turning away and rubbing his temple.

Flash stood in the doorway, barking his most unfriendly bark. Brenna signed him: come.

"Be still, Flash, be still. This is not an enemy." After a

brief moment, he subsided, and trotted to her side, fur raised along his spine, growling deep in his throat.

Running footsteps echoed down the corridor. Like a squirrel popping out of a tree, a pink-faced serving woman tossed aside the leather curtain.

"What on earth—is aught amiss?"

Brenna shook her head, clenching her jaw. "It's all right, Nesta." She trembled, a brief convulsion, then lifted a hand, palm upward, and motioned toward the door.

"As you will, but have a care, my lady." The maidservant hugged her arms about her, cast a glance at the tableau, bobbed once to Brenna, and vanished in a flurry of robes.

Her knight held himself rigid, his bearing contained, aloof. It was only when Flash snuffled at the dagger, that she saw those keen eyes flick to her face. Catching his hard expression, Brenna shivered inside. Had she meant so little to him?

"Flash...hush. That's a good fellow," she commanded. A cold nose touched her hand. She scratched the dog's ear. "Go on, now. Go lie down."

Flash growled again, a low sound rumbling up from his chest, and retreated to the center of the room, where he could keep a vigilant eye on her. Silence fell, and in that silence Brenna heard her pulse beating in her ears. She slowly inhaled a deep breath and then, with a long shuddering sigh, released it.

"So," she said, and glanced the knight's way, a quick shift of her eyes. "Such an uproar over a razor. After all the trouble I've had to find one! I had to scour the keep for it."

"How was I to know it was not an assassin's dagger?"

"Why must men be so *witless?*"

Leon flexed his hand, wiped at his eyes, only then feeling his heart come back to him. Even as he felt knots loosen inside his gut, he said, "Why must women be so *witty?* Did I hurt you?"

Brenna's eyes blinked, focused. She was having trouble catching her breath. Her heart was still hammering in her throat. Rather clumsily she patted her hair and her robe smooth again.

"I'm...all right." And, aside from a few stray hiccups, she was. "But, in truth, you did frighten me."

"I meant to." He could not find any trace of fear in her face. So he challenged her in turn. "Consider yourself fortunate you were not maimed—or worse. I take not kindly to fools who carry unsheathed weapons." His voice had an edge to it, a dangerous one.

"Not a very trusting sort, are you?"

Leon felt a painful tide of heat flow into his ears. Her expression was troubled. Perhaps she expected him to offer words to reassure her. His mouth felt as dry as if he had just trekked across a desert. "I don't like surprises."

An odd look passed across her face, quickly gone. She bent and picked up the gemmed circlet and veil. Rising graceful as a plume of smoke, she jammed them on her head. As their eyes met, she had the grace to blush a little.

"You're a horrid patient. Just horrid." Her voice smiled, and a spell seemed broken—or provoked.

Who was she? Her jet-black hair hung to her waist, and she wore a woolen gown, green and unadorned. It looked severely practical and faintly crumpled, and the cut was oddly archaic. She looked as if she had been working in the kitchen, for there was a smear of white powder on the bodice, but she did not have the manner of a servant. She was too confident.

From a small drawstring pouch attached to her waist girdle, she drew a parchment packet and tipped the powdered contents into a goblet. Although young for the role, it seemed she was a herbalist who knew the ways of medicine, he thought, which accounted for the chest of herbs and simples.

He drew in a breath and let it go slowly. No doubt about it. He'd fallen to a bout of fever. He'd been feeling nauseous and disoriented when he'd left Chirk. He'd put it down to guilt at leaving Thomas with a lame horse, for they'd taken no remounts with them when they'd departed Crewe.

The journey had been long and tedious, though Deso had kept a steady pace through the forest shadow, a panting rhythm of leather and metal and the beat of hooves. He couldn't remember much after passing a leper shortly after noon.

That had been yesterday. Or the day before. He pressed his fingers to his eyes. Hell, it might have been last week, for all he knew. The rest of that day sank down featureless in his memory. His mind was a blank.

Head high, the woman examined him with quick flicks of her eyes, sure sign of unease. She seemed strangely tense: a coiled spring. Her eyes gleamed with expressions of— what? Disappointment? Uncertainty? Powerful curiosity? Even a tinge of sexual attraction, maybe. But she appeared to be holding herself under tight control. She took a deep breath and breezed past him to the alcove.

"Standing about in a draft is dangerous. I would not have you in ill health. Here, sir."

A gust of cool air, a sheet from the bed, came whisking through the air and landed about his shoulders. There was a crispness to the fabric, the smell of new, clean cotton. Heat flushed his face as he wrapped it toga-like over his nakedness, and stepped to the window embrasure, from whence came the sounds and bustle of morning.

"You comfort me," he said under his breath.

His mind was a maelstrom of conflicting thoughts and memories, ideas and suspicions. He heard the sound of footsteps moving toward him, soft slippers against wood. Very lightly she touched his shoulder.

"See the hawk hunting? That means a good day." She jarred him from his dark thoughts, then stunned him with her familiarity. Quickly she leaned forward and pecked him on the cheek.

Leon did not move. His skin prickled and pounded where her lips touched, and his heart was beating as if he had been running. A scent hung close around him, vaguely familiar. Herbal, clean—feminine.

Dream images sliced across his mind, unsought, unwanted. Haunting visions of an oval face framed by a lustrous black mane intruded, filling him with heat and dread. A spell—she was casting a spell. He was dismayed for the moment and, recovering, made a stiff bow.

"Good morrow to you, too, lady."

"Are you all right now?" she whispered through a silver lilt and gurgle of laughter. Her coal-black eyes were expectant, half delighted, half frightened. Something about her eyes, the tiny pleat between her brows, was familiar. Maddeningly familiar.

"I am well enough."

For a moment all was silence. He got the feeling she was appraising him, looking for damage...or signs of repair. She let out a long, long sigh and put her hand up, brushed at his hair. He didn't stir. Cautiously a small, sure hand touched his face, urging his head to one side.

"The swelling's nearly gone. Good. Any pain?" The voice was gentle, barely a whisper.

Any pain? The question lingered in the cool morning air, as if the words blended naturally with the light breeze.

The proud planes of a haughty visage tugged at his memory. He looked into the wide dark eyes, trying to remember what was vaguely familiar about her. Something nagged him, though he couldn't pinpoint the problem.

"No," he said untruthfully.

She must have detected something in his expression. The dark eyes flashed up to that place that hurt him so, there, just at his temple. Licking her forefinger, she reached out and touched it and pressed gently. Pain startled him out of his stupor. He made the effort: he didn't actually clutch his head, but he flinched. To cover the movement, he pulled the sheet tighter around his middle.

"Well, you look terrible," she said forthrightly. She withdrew her hand and folded her fingers together. She scanned his face. Her eyebrows puckered. "Like carrion crow pickings."

He kept his teeth together. "Don't worry. That's my habitual expression."

She was not even insulted, let alone deterred.

"Then we'll have to find some way to change it. A touch of red-root salve, and some fresh bread and honey should do the trick. Or mayhap a bit of fun and laughter will make it less fiercesome," she said with unfeigned exuberance.

He folded his arms across his chest. "Then why do you tremble with fear?"

"It is not fear. I have this strange feeling I want to take care of you and make you laugh."

Her voice had taken on overtones, the words hanging vividly in the air. Glancing down he could see no guile in her look, only an intense, unbearable sincerity—so appalling and so unprecedented that a man was drawn to keep looking, wishing to be sure that it was truly there.

"Men take care of women. Women do not take care of men."

No longer playful, she regarded him pensively, her dark eyes steady. "Aye. Men fight, protect, lead and so on and so forth. But a woman keeps alive gentler emotions. She eases her man's way, comforts him and gives him refuge from the cares of the world."

Something utterly idiotic came to mind, so of course he said it, "And that is what you wish to do for me?"

She looked away from his intense stare, as if shy of a sudden, and regretting her impulsive words. Then, as quickly, she turned her glance back, a sideways motion from the corners of those dark eyes.

"Aye. I had thought—" Her voice fell away. She gave him an odd look and sighed. It was disconcerting. Her slim white throat was arched, her head with its thick, black hair thrown back as she gazed at him with emotion welling up—hope, it might be.

Leon's heart beat faster and faster. Night dreams were

disturbing. Day dreams were dangerous. He needed distraction. He sought it in jest. "Most women scream and run, no doubt thinking such an ugly brute must eat babies."

"You are not an ugly brute." Her voice was so gentle and strange he shivered at it.

"I am not handsome," he muttered, thinking she would now try to deceive him with hollow flattery.

"I did not say you were handsome." Her gaze touched his ruined cheek, his thick neck, his broad chest. His toes curled in the rushes when her glance lowered to skim his sheet-draped loins and legs. She lifted her head, stared straight at him. "Your face holds strength and inspires trust, but if you allow it to be knocked about so, you could well become ugly."

Peering down at her, Leon stared at her face, partly shielded by the gauze veil. Pink flowed through her cheeks, and her expression reminded him of his delectable, hungry, shy angel. He held out his right hand, on which he bore a golden ring worked with a seal. "Don't be absurd, woman, else you will make me laugh," he said, slightly unsettled by his thoughts.

Her brows met. "Perhaps we should discuss this."

She took his hand, rasping her fingers over his sword calluses and the whitened scars that crossed and recrossed his strong hands. She turned the ring to the light, looked at it closely, lifted dark eyes, as if she wanted to talk and had something boiling up inside her.

"Do you agree?"

He nodded once, not moving otherwise.

"Even so." She sighed again like a child, unselfconscious, candid. She looked innocent enough, but her skin was exceedingly pale and her eyes as black as sinfulness. There was just something about the pieces that didn't fit...

Brenna looked up at him from under her eyelids. A nimbus of gold seemed to outline him, he was so bright in the morning light. Just the sight of his big strong form caused a skip in her heartbeat. His name does not fit him, she thought. Aubrey was not strong enough for such a man. He's too splendid. All that raw force, no subtlety.

"You look different than I had imagined."

He lowered his eyes, and stared stupidly at the two hands, one small and fragile, the other large and battle-hardened. All his breath tangled in his throat. Became a ball of ice, of fire. Her touch could not have affected him more if she'd put a lighted brand to his fingertips.

He gathered his resolve in this as in other things. "And you," he said, withdrawing his hand. "You seem so familiar that I—"

Feeling a sudden rush of panic, Brenna retreated a step. She clutched a hand to her chest, willing her heart to stop beating so violently. He seemed not to recall their night of passion! Should she mention it? Would an outright challenge be best? Or nuance and equivocation? She was not usually so irresolute. But this was her betrothed!

"I must be blunt," she said abruptly, making up her mind to try a frontal assault. She held out one hand. "Aubrey, please. We must talk."

He slowly and deliberately stepped back. "You mistake me, lady. My name is not Aubrey."

It was like hearing the voice of a demon, so shocking in its intensity that Brenna felt the breath sucked from her as if all the air had been withdrawn from this place. Her gasp was audible. There was no longer a smile on her face. The rebuff was almost physical in its strength. She laced her fingers tightly together.

Leon for his part stood still. She gave him a distressed look, a little tightening of the jaw. "You are not Aubrey of Leeds?" Her voice had risen questioningly.

"No," he said, shaking his head. "I am not."

"What?"

She met his eyes with a shock like two blades clashing. She had frozen like a hunted doe. She did not so much as blink.

"I am not Aubrey of Leeds," Leon repeated, as if to a child.

She flinched, visibly, then smiled a tight, uncertain smile. Her mouth stayed open an instant. There was a wild flicker in her eyes. Her confusion was palpable. In an eyeblink, her self-possession began to fray about the edges. She seemed genuinely shaken. Part of him was surprised. The threat of harm had not shaken her composure, yet now she trembled.

Something tensed inside him. She leaned forward and stared at him, as though she were trying to read something there, he thought. Her eyes were dilated and intense, focused hard on him: all black pupil. She took in every line of his face from brow to chin. Her face worked, somewhere between desperation and grief. She drew in a shallow breath, and unclenched her hands. Her voice, like a whisper of dry reeds, murmured, "This will...will change everything!"

Leon stood there staring back at her like a beast pinioned under a witch's stare. He could not have moved if he had wished to. Whatever she read in his face, her expression altered—she looked as if she felt some grinding, internal pain, like a wounded animal. Her eyes were glazed, the glance unfocused and looking past him in a way that made him wonder if there was an insect on his ear; but then she looked away, swallowing.

In an attempt at levity, and in a thicker voice than normal, he said, "Does this mean I'm to be banished to the stables?"

"Oh, I didn't mean it like that..." The pink reached the rest of her face, and the frown stayed.

Brenna stood there, a large struggle going on inside herself, trying to gather the power of her wits to think. What to do? What to say? Chill tendrils of despair writhed in her belly. Perhaps she was too apprehensive, but the thought crossed her mind all might have been planned; that he might be an outlaw working with the assailants, or perhaps worse, mayhap some spy from Wrexham or way up on the Wirral, and the attack and rescue were no more than a strategy to infiltrate the keep.

No. It could not be. She was fighting herself, that was the problem.

"Then what do you mean?" It was that hawk's stare an instant. There was outrage in it.

"We are far from the road. You travel light, but then perhaps you have no wish to be found hereabouts—"

"I do not."

A frisson swept her; a combination of fear and something else unidentifiable, something between incredulity and panic. It was not what she thought. He did not mean what it seemed he meant. Did it?

She felt the charge of some powerful emotion that she refused to comprehend. What came out was ridiculously quiet compared to the uproar in her head.

"By what name does your family call you?" she managed, just above a whisper.

"Leon..." he began and hesitated, as if reluctant to give it, took a gulp, then offered it, like a gift. "Leon. My sisters call me Leon."

Brenna could not fully restrain a laugh over her relief that he had sisters. "Then so shall I—and you must call me Brenna." She looked at him a moment. "It is a shame you are not Aubrey."

"You do have a way with you of cutting right in along the bone, don't you?"

Brenna nodded her head sharply once.

"You were expecting him?"

"Sort of."

"Then I am sorry to have to be the bearer of bad news, my lady," Leon said in an odd flat tone. His face was impassive. "Aubrey of Leeds is no more."

Brenna was stunned. No, it could not be. He could not mean... "I don't understand."

"Aubrey of Leeds is dead."

"Dead! You are sure?"

"Aye."

"But how?"

Leon hesitated an instant, then said, "Felled by a lance at the tourney at Rouen. Snapped his neck."

Brenna waited to feel grief for the loss of her betrothed. A twinge of sadness came and went at the thought of a young man killed in the prime of life, but she did not know him, after all. She had only agreed to marry him because her knight had not come and because he paid the ridiculous bride-price she had insisted Grandy demand.

Now he was dead.

And she had slept with a stranger.

Nay, worse than that, she'd shared with him the intimacies only a husband should know!

She was trembling now, her stomach was a hard knot, and her hands shook. She feared the worst. It was almost punishment. Aubrey was dead, her dream knight committed to memory, her honor abandoned by this man. 'Twas as if the fever and the blow to his temple had somehow erased their night of shared passion from his mind.

She would not think the worst.

Maybe, just maybe, she was mistaken. For the alternative was too unbearable: dishonor…disgrace…

She shuddered just to think about it. She kept her eyes lowered, struggling with the tightness in her throat. Her tongue seemed to have trouble working.

"We were to be wed come the Sabbath."

Leon shivered, though it was not cold in the hearth-lit room. "I am so sorry…"

"I did not love him." She sighed. "But for his generosity alone he deserved to die in bed, full of years and honors."

She sighed again, and Leon resolutely kept his eyes on her face, not letting his gaze follow the rise and fall of her bosom. He ought not to be having lustful yearnings for a woman so recently bereaved. It was impossible—but true. She was standing so close that he was having trouble keeping his thoughts from wandering into forbidden territory. Her perfume was scenting his every breath, her mouth as soft and ripe as summer strawberries. He felt there was something about it he should remember.

The mouth had dimples at the corners, but they were part of the set of a determined jaw—sweet saints, he knew this face. He had lived with this face. It was the face in his dreams. Huge brown eyes, long ebony lashes; a trusting smile. Soft, full lips; lips he had loved, cherished. No, this was something else. Some other form of recognition.

What did this mean? How had it happened?

He was fascinated out of his good sense—so fascinated he almost missed what she was saying.

"If you are not Aubrey of Leeds, why did you risk your life for mine?" she asked, and her voice was strangely changed. It came thin and strained.

He breathed deeply once and turned his head slowly. He stared at her blankly a moment, then frowned. His hazel eyes carefully traced her face, then slid down to pin her breasts beneath her gown.

Brenna was aware of her flesh tightening over her body. She looked up into his eyes and saw something there that glittered and startled her and was, she very much hoped, desire. She felt a foolish surge of anticipation. He gave the appearance of a man haunted by memories. His expression was that of a man trying to remember something...

"I saved your life?"

She nodded, momentarily choked for words.

"Ah, lady, I'm always delighted to learn something new. So why aren't I convinced?"

The tone of voice was just short of a snarl. Brenna felt her soul dissolve within her. It hurt. It shouldn't, but it was truth, and the pain was overwhelming.

She turned her back on him and went back to the fireside and poured something from the steaming kettle into the goblet. Leon's eyes followed each movement of her slim back, the shift of her bodice and the pull of the fabric across her spine as she reached, bent and replaced the kettle.

Brenna caught her lower lip between her teeth. How could

she keep the pain bottled up within? Act as if nothing was wrong? Aware of tears pooling in her eyes, she placed the shaking tip of one finger at a drip running down the outside and scooped it back into the cup. She ached for reassurance that her suspicions were false. She had to speak.

"You are grumpy. Perhaps you didn't sleep well?"

"I slept unusually well. Is there any reason I should not have?"

Chapter Six

Fear condensed into certainty inside Brenna. It was as she had suspected! Her knight had no memory of the night past!

No memory of ridding her of her maidenhead!

He had clearly forgotten everything that had passed between them. The bitter truth branded deep into her brain. Fever and a wicked blow to the head had snatched his memory!

The hurt inside was cutting so deep that she thought it would kill her. It felt like a knife stabbing her. Her heart was beating so fast it seemed it might fly out of her chest or break into ten thousand pieces.

If only she could forget, as well.

"A second time I ask you."

She gave a little lift of her shoulder.

Leon hesitated, all too aware of her breasts as they rose and fell, then repeated curtly, "Is there any reason why I should have not slept well?"

That challenge was blunt. He heard the soft, ripping sound her breath made as it rushed out.

"No."

"Are you sure?"

There was no answer.

Brenna turned her gaze upon him. He stared back, his eyes

cold, his strong face set in serious lines so unlike the agreeable man she'd given her heart to.

Where to go from here?

Possibilities crowded her mind. Could she tell him of the night past? *Should* she tell him? she wondered. Such allegations were not uncommon. She could make any claim she liked, and how would he know? Her body became so taut it felt like it might snap. Uncertainty and despair were two rough hands wringing her heart. Perhaps this, perhaps that! 'Twas a problem of such unprecedented and unexpected dimensions that she could not think for a moment how to tackle it. All she felt was a desperate urge to cry.

"What is it?"

Brenna opened her mouth to speak, then thought better of it. He had softened somewhat, but she knew that aloofness of his could return. Intuition told her to say nothing. What would he do if she told him? Deny it? Claim 'twas naught but a dream? Or a recently bereaved and distraught girl's fancy? Any sane and sensible man would believe her mad or simply foolish or both.

Would this one be any different? Maybe. Maybe not. She did not know him well enough to tell. Was it worth the gamble? No, she could not take the risk. He must never, never know what had occurred during his fever. A night's stolen virtue was one thing, but if he did not remember...

A furtive, stupid thought sprang up, the first ghost of a plan shaping itself in her mind. A shiver racked through her. Her mouth grew dry. She bit her lip. No! Cast aside such idiocy! It would be a folly that could bring nothing but trouble, and well you know it, she told herself.

Brenna straightened her shoulders, attempting at least the image of composure. *Courage,* she said to herself as she turned to Leon, smiling—and yet her smile was not the carefree thing of a short while ago. Something trembled in her eye, at her lip: this smile was of joy and grief together.

"I would have you take this potion. It will ward off all manner of mischievous ills."

She came to Leon's side and handed him a cup of pungent-smelling liquid. He accepted the goblet, and swirled the fluid, sniffed it, dipped his tongue tip. It was bitter as gall. A sudden alert bloomed in his mind. He stiffened. A chill of misgiving knotted in his gut. A herbalist would know the berries and the roots, the edibles and the dyes...

And the poisons...

He felt the fine hair at the base of his neck stand rigid. In Pakenham, Geoffrey Ruffus had died, they said, of poison on the bottom of a wine cup. Three others of Fulk's closest friends had met with accidents. He had proved the case of Aubrey of Leeds, but not the connection of the assassin with Hubert de Risley—

A touch of renewed rage hit him. He should have killed Hubert when he had the chance. But then de Risley had been one of many, and the king had forbidden—

"Damn your impudence!"

Their gazes locked.

Stunned, Brenna froze where she stood. His angry stare had turned her to stone, like the gaze of that monster of the ancient tales, the basilisk. She was well aware of his unease. He was tense, shifting slightly. What is he trying to tell me? she asked herself. She drew a sharp breath, and said nothing at all as he swirled the liquid in the cup.

No, it could not be. He could not mean...

She went hot and jerked her glance away. "I don't understand," she said, her breath catching.

Her seeming obtuseness made Leon furious. Rage boiled up inside him. He felt his face burn. Understand? Did she take him for an idiot? He made a sound low in his throat.

"God's teeth, woman, are you trying to poison me?

Brenna gasped, taking a step backward. His words struck like a blow to the pit of her stomach. How cruel! How unfair! She ducked her head so that her hair swung across one shoulder.

Leon watched in fascination as the thick silky lashes brushed her smooth cheeks. She looked suddenly very uncertain and very young. Her fine hands locked together as if to stop their movement. Only the regular flaring of her nostrils and the tremble of her lips betrayed her unease. But she was not at a loss for words.

"You speak nonsense. You saved me from those awful creatures. It's my turn now."

Now it was he who found no words.

Saved me? From what? *Awful creatures?* Nice of her to fill in fever-blanked spots; yes, indeed, Leon thought. His shoulders squared. He wrapped his fingers tightly around the earthenware cup. What exactly had he done?

"That sounds like a fair exchange, but you still have not answered my question," he said through bared teeth.

Placing her hands on her hips, Brenna glared at the deluded man before her. "I would not deign to answer such a charge, you conceited, arrogant..." She groped for just the right word, and when none came forth, spat out, "...soldier! I would not waste my talents on such an ungrateful wretch!"

An odd look passed across Leon's face. "Believe me, I am not ungrateful, lady, just careful."

"That's not fair!" she cried. "Not fair at all. Where's your good sense? I know my doses. Trust me!"

"I do not care to put my life in jeopardy only to hear your lies—to be told I must trust you even as you admit that you *know your doses.*"

"Who made you that way?"

"And what do you mean by *that?*"

"Someone must have been awfully nasty to you to be so bitter," Brenna said, keeping her voice even. She folded her arms across her chest, lifting her chin. "Drink it. Don't worry. 'Tis safe. Your life is not in jeopardy. 'Tis naught but tea and herbs, with a little cordial to sweeten it and help the medicine go down. The herb is sour and bitter."

Face afire, Leon leaned back against the wall, cursing himself for seeing shadows where there probably were none. Fighting himself again. It was the only standard he knew.

"Then that answers the question." He swallowed the concoction, sip by nauseating sip, and though the tisane went a little strange on his tongue, there was nothing the matter with it. He watched her putting containers in a sack, scores of little jars, all over the table. And scattered powders and leaves and herbs.

"What are those?" he asked, more to make amends for his ungracious behavior than from any need to know.

She looked up and parted her lips in a smile, one that showed her even teeth, a magical thing to watch. She was incredibly lovely, he thought, graceful as a lark descending from the heart of the sun. Her skin was creamy, her lips full and sensual, holding the promise of paradise, of hot, melting passion. She knew just how to duck her chin and look sidelong from the corners of her eyes.

"Clove seeds for Nesta's son who's got a toothache," she said of one. Another jar went into the sack. "Feverfew for Widow Blunt's migraine. This packet's powdered ginger root. It eases wind pains in babies. There's been seven births in the village this spring, and two more due before the new moon. I look forward to these happenings."

Leon took a deep breath, trying to ignore the words swirling about him. Eons ago he'd waited for such an event—

Images rose, unbidden and unwanted in his mind. They flew at him, splintered and reformed. He stared blankly at her for a full moment, then frowned. She needed a child in her arms, nursing at her breasts. *His* child. A heat came to his face. Hell, what made him think such things? His heart slammed against his ribs. He had to stop this! Had to stop yearning for something he couldn't have. He set the cup down emptied, resisting the impulse to fling it at the wall.

"Who will care for you when it is your turn?"

"My turn?" Brenna reeled backward with a gasp. In a swift instinctive gesture, she put her hand over her womb as if to protect the life not yet cradled there. An odd feeling lanced through her, a hunger and a yearning that was unlike anything she had ever experienced. Of the many possibilities she had imagined, a baby had not been among them.

Brenna's heart filled her throat. Shaken by the emotion racing through her, she looked over to the alcove, blinked rapidly, and finally focused on the rumpled bed. Given what had happened between them there, reality was more compelling than any dream she'd ever had. But it was not so simple as that, it never could be. She shivered, trying to steady her nerves and heartbeat.

It will be all right. Everything will work out fine.

"I hadn't thought about it," she admitted. She raised her palms. "I've no idea. I guess I'll wait until..."

"Aye," he interrupted abruptly. "Or are there simples to prevent such things?" The question was as blunt as the heavy poker stashed against the fireplace. The cold iron tool looked softer than his narrowed eyes.

Brenna lifted her head and smiled serenely, in spite of the tremors shaking her insides. She swallowed and spoke quietly, calmly, as though gentleness and sweet reason were contagious. "There are things to stop unwanted pregnancies, if that is what you mean, but they are dangerous. I do not deal in such."

"I suppose you never spend time trying to make lead into gold, either." Leon heard his own words as though at a vast distance, an echo from a time when he could speak and touch and feel, a time when betrayal hadn't spread like black ice through his soul, freezing everything.

"I don't understand," she whispered.

"I'll just bet you don't."

The brusque tone of Leon's voice made Brenna flinch. She took one look at the hard line of his jaw and caught her lower lip between her teeth. The glare he gave her sent a quiver down her spine. She wanted to ask what she had done to make him look at her with such disfavor. Was it simply that she somehow reminded him of an unhappy past?

"In this valley, most folks are grateful for whatever the Good Lord sends along. Babies are just born, and they make the best of it for as long as they can until they either die or grow up," she said, smiling, encouraged by the fact that he hadn't taken her head off yet.

Leon didn't return the smile.

Her bright expression dimmed a little, but remnants of the smile lingered. "The miracle is that any survive at all."

"I know!" His hand slashed the air expressively. "Too often, they die!"

Suddenly nervous, Brenna swallowed again and added, "We have our future laid out in front of us. It isn't always as we perceive it or wish it to be."

Dark hair swung and the slight catch of breath brought each of his masculine senses to quivering alert. Leon swore under his breath at the frightened look she gave him, like a friendly little elf who was hurt at his coldness. Shrouded by dark memories, he had allowed his bitterness to escape. The lost look in her eyes was a silent remonstration for his testiness. He deserved it, and he knew it. He swallowed, but no ease came to his suddenly dry throat. He shrugged and sighed.

What good are regrets?

"There's truth in that," he said, concerned by her sudden pallor, wanting to fold her into his arms and give her comfort.

Comfort? he asked himself. Well, that, too, I suppose— among other things. Desire surged through him, shocking him with its speed and ferocity, hardening him in an aching need. After all these years, all these mistakes, the sensation swept back with unkind intensity.

He had learned that his greatest weakness was his bone-deep belief that a man should protect and cherish those who weren't as strong as himself, especially women and children. The weakest woman could manipulate the strongest man simply by using his protective instinct against him. That was what Suzanne had done. Repeatedly. After too much pain, he had finally realized that the more vulnerable a woman appeared, the greater was her ability to deceive him.

If the pain had gone all the way to the bone, so had the

lesson. It had been eight years since he had trusted any woman except his sisters. They were both a decade older than he was and had dedicated their lives to the church, exempting themselves from his general distrust of the female of the species.

Brenna fastened the straps of the casket. "I know," she said cheerily. "Which is why we sometimes must give destiny a hand and not leave it to our guardian angels."

For a large man, the knight moved in a flash. He gave the impression of a hunter fixed on prey as he straightened and, with two powerful strides, was standing close to her.

"Say that again," he demanded, his eyes instantly gleaming as he grabbed her wrist, staying her with a restrained strength that allowed no opposition. His thumb spanned her inner wrist, his fingers completely, possessively, circling her fine bones. "Say it just the way you did before."

"We must give destiny a hand," she said agreeably.

Leon dropped her wrist after the count of five heartbeats. Five too speedy heartbeats. Her dark eyes flared wide as they met his again and he was struck by a profound sense of déjà vu. Had he met this woman before? Impossible, and yet…

"What is it?"

Leon felt uncertain and vulnerable. What was the matter with him? He hadn't experienced anything this nerve-racking in years. Was he bewitched? That's what you'd like to think—but you know better, he told himself. He did know better. That was the trouble. He roused himself with difficulty.

"Nothing. Just the ghost of a memory."

Hope rose inside Brenna, unbidden. Was it possible that he longed for the woman of his fevers—herself? She tilted her head to the side, considering him, debating whether or not to make the first move. The morning light fell upon his face, catching his eyes, reflecting a rainbow of color. She looked into them and was at once lost.

The tiny hint of the idea that had nudged her earlier was now growing and forming. Her betrothed was dead. Unless she wanted to have Keith Kil Coed foisted on her, she had to find herself a husband. Fast.

And who better than Leon, her dream knight turned real?

For a moment she wondered if Grandy would consider him "worthy" enough, then decided she didn't care. She knew absolutely nothing about him, except that he had come when she needed him. She rarely ever made a mistake judging character. And she had had only good feelings about Leon—and what good feelings!

Her knees felt curiously liquid as she glided closer to him, and stared at the great expanse of his chest, not knowing quite what to say. He had wanted her in the night. He could be made to want her again.

Nothing is changed. Nothing.

A single tingle of apprehension trickled up her spine and disappeared as she berated her logical inner self. *Brenna, if you throw this golden opportunity away, I'll never forgive you.*

She raised her hand and skimmed a line down the middle of his broad chest, just to prove to herself she was not scared. Heat spread through her at the thought of his arms cradling her and his mouth exploring her own. She felt her control slipping and her heart thrusting against her breast. Her palm flattened over his rigid stomach.

He said nothing, but he didn't take his eyes off her. He must be a man accustomed to hiding his thoughts. A muscle rippled in his cheek and was still. The lines were harsh on his face. Something changed in his eyes. They were now a vivid green, their color swirling like polished malachite. They held her in place like a physical bond, rooting her to the spot.

She chewed on her lip, nervous and uncertain. But that look in his eyes was gone so quickly that she wondered if it had ever been there. The vague plan began to take definite shape in her fertile mind. Did she dare ask him? After all, he could only say no. She sucked in a deep breath.

"Leon…" was as far as she got.

Her breath came against his chest, and Leon could feel her heartbeat as if she were within him. Somewhere deep inside him he suspected that it was dangerous to allow himself this intoxication, to be this close to her, to involve himself in the form of magic he now believe she represented. On the other hand the challenge was irresistible. He lifted a hand, and his fingers were warm against her neck. For a moment their bodies froze, linked in the heat of desire.

Brenna was aware of the way her body pressed into him, molding across the hardness beneath his sheet. She could feel a warm glow starting in the tips of her toes and running all the way up to her flushed cheeks. A soft whimper escaped her lips. Tiny little knots began to curl deep within her. She ached to experience again that shattering, sensual passion that this man had awakened in her...

His fingers touched the swell of her bosom. Her body began to tremble. She could not breathe. The spark turned hot, glimmering. It burned her breast. A quiver began deep within her. This was as it had been last night. Now it was coming, the aching, the throbbing, growing with every breath.

As Brenna watched his mouth descend slowly, ever so slowly, her lips parted. *Kiss me...kiss me...* she willed. But already he had dropped his hand. The movement was sharp, abrupt; she felt his mental withdrawal as he backed away from her. She could almost feel the struggle going on inside him.

"My apologies, lady." His voice was hard.

The spell was broken. She felt the waves of shock undulate through her body and she turned safely away.

"Whatever for?" She was glad her voice didn't shake at all, and her hand trembled only slightly as she smoothed her hair.

Silence hung heavy as the seconds crawled by. His jaw was set in tight control. His eyes narrowed; his lips thinned. What that meant, she couldn't decide. He looked once at her. A deep searching look, a look that was almost a challenge. The long sable lashes swept down and up, leaving the hazel eyes more composed.

"Your pardon, lady. I am not at my best."

Brenna didn't pretend to misunderstand. Pain knifed through her heart. Shame for her own stubborn stupidness lumped in her throat. Keeping a distance between them, she looked straight at him and tried to hide her feelings under a joke.

"No, and you're in a foul mood," she chided gently. "*That* is something you should know."

Leon pursed his lips. Was he really that bad?

"Explain yourself!"

"Why, Leon, do I detect a spot of temper?" she asked sweetly.

Leon studied the pale face before him. Her eyes, dark as coffee, held his. Her face so calm, so sure, was directly in front of him, but he knew her words were merely a brave attempt to lighten the moment. He liked that. It showed she had spirit.

"Are you always so bold with your questions?"

"'Tis said I am. Cheer up, you'll get used to it." She smiled, showing him just a bit of her tiny white teeth. "Unless, of course, you are planning to turn tail and run."

"You said that, not me."

Brenna dared another glance his way. She admired the clean lines of his body, the length of thigh, his flat belly, the curve of his shoulders, his lips, the brightness of his luxuriant hair, tipped with nut-brown shadows. She focused on the clear eyes that changed with every mood. They held her like anchors, reminding her of the night past. She went hot and jerked her glance away.

"I—you remind me of someone. Have we met before?"

She glanced over her shoulder. "Yesterday." Their eyes met and held. They stared at each other for a pulsating moment, then she added, "At the postern gate."

Memory flooded. He remembered now where he was. Dinas Bran.

It had been a gray afternoon; he had been at the postern gate hoping for lodgings before the early dark, fighting off beggarly rogues. He had been a little unsteady on his feet, a little warmer than the air called for. But between that and this, nothing. It was as if a shutter had been locked and the lights within put out. "Ah, yes, the beggars."

"Not beggars, but escaped criminals, now secured and fettered in the dungeon awaiting the sheriff. I wish I could tell you—could show you—my thanks for what you did. I'll never forget. It was fine, the way you fought for me," she cried, her cheeks glowing with a suffusion of underlying crimson.

"It was nothing. No need to get sentimental."

"I'm so glad you've remembered!"

"I feel I *should*." He stressed the last word with an upward sweep of his head, a movement so quick and decided that his golden hair seemingly glinted with its own light.

"What an odd way to put it. As if—" Brenna frowned, working it out "—as if you didn't remember *yet*."

"Is that so strange?"

Brenna winced. She'd been far too quick to assume what his words implied. "Can you remember more of these things?" she persisted, not quite able to believe it.

"What more do I need to know?" he demanded, fierce head up, assertive nose jutting. "And for what kind of reason?"

"What kind of reason?" she repeated, playing for time. "Sir Edmund will want to give you thanks."

Edmund of Brenig. How many years was it since he had last seen Sir Edmund? Eight? Nine? He'd lost count. The old man would not recognize him, of course. Who would? But that did not matter. It was better so.

Leon rubbed his jaw. If there had been hot blood between the Brenigs and the family of FitzWarren, there were few left to carry on the feud. Sir Edmund had buried his wife, both his brothers-in-law, and all four of his sons, in somewhat less than fifteen years. Were thoughts of revenge

enough to keep a man alive? They hadn't been for Fulk
Riven.

"More importantly—" the dark eyes held his with a new
intensity "—the aunts will wish to meet you. It's not very
often we have a visitor so tall and strong, so handsome and
dashing."

Leon felt strangely pleased, but paused before answering,
unsure whether to be amused or annoyed by all this. After
all, he had a face that, of itself, would rival that of even the
most ferocious beast! What game was she playing? He took
a breath, adopted a careless stance.

"I guess I'll take that as a compliment, but I must be on
my way."

Brenna spread her hands helplessly. She felt a deal less
bright and merry than he could suspect, but she would have
died of shame and black affront before allowing him to
know it. She had been stupid already—that was as obvious
as the sunrise. Why not make a complete job of it?

"Must you go?"

Her smile was very sweet and just a little wistful, offering
him friendship and, perhaps, more than friendship. Leon
found her proximity intoxicating, and when she smiled at
him, the urge to kiss her was well nigh irresistible.

It was an awkward moment, and he resolutely kept his
eyes on her face, not letting his gaze follow the rise and fall
of her bosom. But he was having trouble keeping his
thoughts where they should be, for it was not his brain he
was heeding at the moment. At length he said, "Aye."

She looked up at him. "Why?"

Breath caught in Leon's throat and he swallowed. Her
regard was like scorching embers. He saw no pupil, no iris
beneath the long, ebony lashes, simply the swirling spirals
of a pure life force. She was unutterably different from any
of the women that he knew.

Leon was no superstitious fool. He supposed it was possible that such a thing as witches existed—though he had
never met one, and doubted he ever would. But never had

he felt such intensity from a woman before. Her dark eyes were searching into his soul, lighting all the little secret desires he had hidden in the darkness of his heart. It unnerved him.

"I have a duty," he said. His back was as stiff as his voice. "On my honor, I have to go and do it, if there is still time."

"Where is this duty?"

"Valle Crucis."

Again came the searching look of minutes earlier, only this time there was dismay at the heart of the scrutiny. Her small breasts rose and fell with her rapid breathing. She said, hoarse and low, "You go to join the monks?"

Leon moved his head in negation.

Her brows met, and she closed her eyes briefly. She looked still more uncertain, and her mouth wavered out of true for two whole seconds before straightening again.

"Then why do you go there?"

He gnawed on that for a moment. "To hunt for rats."

Wild thoughts and wilder hopes went to and fro within Brenna's mind. Perhaps he was a spy sent from the court? Or was he just like the other knights who, having heard the legends of Dinas Bran, came here seeking to find the Holy Grail? Just the mere thought worried her. Then common sense prevailed. No. He was no spy, nor common adventurer. He was first and foremost a knight. *Her* knight. She released her pent-up breath in a long gasp. "I thought perhaps—"

"You thought wrong," he said, and it sounded as if the words had been clipped short by a sword blade. Voice and manner should have stopped her, but she accepted no rebuff.

"I'll hear no more of it," she said. "You are no rat hunter, but a knight through and through." There was only the faintest suggestion of a twinkle in the way she glanced at him—a poor, watered version of the mischievous glint that normally would have accompanied such a challenge.

"It is kind of you to say so."

"I doubt if you will find it easy to understand, but I have never left this castle, except twice in my life to ride to a manor that lies two days' journey away." Brenna lowered her eyes. "Grandy is happy that I occupy myself without carp or complaint."

And why not? asked a small demon voice deep in her mind. She was a woman. Either she would accept her fate. Or—

Or. Leon.

Her throat ached with the effort of keeping back a cry. It had all been so simple, all her life mapped and ordained. A childhood of learning and preparation; and when she was a woman, her dream knight would come. She remembered how stubbornly she'd persisted in that faith. Her suitors had been a nuisance, but easy enough to turn away, until Grandy had offered her no choice but to accept Aubrey's proposal. Not even that betrothal could make her forget her special knight.

Until this one. It was not only a proud, high-nosed, deep-eyed face and a velvety-rich voice. It was the whole of him. He was unique. This one was hers to keep, and keep him she would. He was made to be her lover. A scant night with him had overcome her. A month...

Leon cleared his throat. "Go on," he said.

She did not look up. Her voice, when she spoke, was almost inaudible, as if she revealed a secret. "I relied on dreams. And then you came. I knew at once it was you!"

He fell back a pace. "You knew me?"

This time Brenna laughed out loud and struck her hands together. "Of course I knew you!" She gave him a glowing look. "How could I mistake you? I hadn't a notion of what to do, and you, like my chivalrous knight, came to my rescue. But you..."

She fell silent, but he did not speak. He was at a loss for what to say or do next. He did not understand her. He began to wonder if each of them was carrying on a one-sided conversation. Her eyes flickered away from his, and then returned, as if she was well aware of his unease.

"As soon as I saw you, I knew you were the one."

"The one?"

"I thought…" 'Twas foolish to hope that all of his memory would return. Just the mere notion had set her heart afluttering, and, the first sign of fracture, a wobble in her voice when she continued, "I don't want to say what I thought. 'Tis but a dream."

Leon grimaced. What could he reply? He knew all about dreams, but he had to deal in realities. Eight years he'd lived with reality, and thinking at every turn of half a score of ways a determined enemy could get at him. Still, she was not to blame for the situation nor for the beauty that unsettled him so. *And Deso needs a day's rest,* he told himself. *It is not bad thing to linger here a day. But no longer than that,* he resolved.

"I daresay I can stay one day more, but I must be more presentable if I am to I meet your family."

Brenna's eyes darted about. At the familiar chamber; at the furs flung upon the floor; at the casket of precious herbs and simples. The razor lay upon the table, strange among the quills and parchment, the little pots of ink and sand, the bronze ewer and dipper. A man's razor, deadly sharp, designed to expose rather than conceal. It gave a clean face, a defined face.

"Well, of course you do! I'm not so lacking in wits that I do not understand you are at a disadvantage and can hardly feel comfortable in a state of undress. Why don't you try these out for fit?"

She indicated a folded bundle on a shelf, and did not look again until he stood before her fully clad. She held out his weapon belt, which she'd unearthed from beneath some embroidered cushions.

Leon fastened it, and when he looked up again he saw the razor in her hand and a gleam in her eye. He braced himself and looked her over once, all too aware of the thick pounding of his pulse. "What in the name of the saints are you doing?"

"I've never shaved a man before. It could be entertaining."

"You jest, surely?"

"You tell me." He had almost seen the dimples. The look was in her eyes.

"No offense, but I don't fancy having my throat cut."

She lifted her chin a notch, defiant. "I think you exaggerate the danger. My hand is steady. I could shave your face smooth as a woman's."

Leon eyed her, knowing pride when he saw it; unwillingly his lips twitched. She was turning out to be a clever adversary, fully able to call a bluff. What she didn't have in muscle, she did have in sheer guts. So he kept his exasperation in check and said, "I prefer the hand of experience."

"Look at it this way. You're helping someone gain valuable experience."

"One I can do without."

"Coward."

"Certainly not. Simply prudent."

"Which only makes the expectations that much higher."

"I know my limits."

"Undoubtedly," she returned with a chuckle. "Still, I'm a quick learner and another scar or two will not be remarked upon." She smiled wickedly, as if she knew something he didn't. "This could be an experience for both of us."

He pounced; Brenna eluded him with animal ease, then startled him speechless by setting the dagger in his hand and saying, "Take it. Keep it. Aunt Agnita says there's a whetstone and mirror somewhere. I'll go fetch them." She took a large breath. "Come in, Nesta."

A stir drew his glance to the doorway. The pink-faced serving woman carried in a tray of food dishes, set it down on the table, bobbed once, and scurried out the door.

"Hungry?"

"I could devour a horse and chariot and chase the driver

halfway to York,'' Leon said gravely, and she stared a moment before her eyes widened and she giggled.

"I had to ask, hadn't I? Very well, if there is a horse and chariot in the cookhouse, you shall have it for supper. For now, honeycakes must suffice.''

Chapter Seven

Brenna ran up the spiral stairs leading to the tower where her grandfather spent much of his time, and at the little landing outside the turret, rapped at the rough wooden door, not at all expecting an answer.

Her mind had been, and still was, reviewing the entire comedy of errors over and over again from its inauspicious beginning to its uncomfortable end. She had to speak with Grandy, appeal to him, make him understand that her life had been forever altered, tell him of her knight, lusty and intriguing, and of the sweet passion he aroused.

No, that was impossible. She must keep that part out of it. That was her secret, hers alone. For what would happen if she informed him she was no longer a virgin and that Leon was the man responsible? Would her grandfather even believe her?

It seemed so incredible that she could hardly believe it herself! After all, Grandy had waited in vain for her to find a suitor to her liking. Had she not spurned every offer until, in desperation, he had ordered her to accept one?

And if Grandy did believe her, what would he do? Slaughter the man responsible? Kill her, as well? The first contingency was far more likely than the second. He would be hard-pressed to hold himself in check and would not insult her with either pity or sympathy. Sir Edmund was old. He had pains in his joints and his scars when it rained, but time had not tempered his volatile disposition. Knowing her grandfather, she knew he would be so angry he would be capable of any iniquity and all manner of mischief possible.

She did not want to confront Grandy. There was so much temptation to do nothing. He would be ill-tempered on being woken from the daylight sleep natural to a man who spent his nights peering at the stars, examining, measuring and scrawling illegible marks in ink on charts and parchment.

But she dared not leave the matter unsettled. She dared not. If she did not face him now, it may well be too late. And mayhap the rain had not allowed his observations last night. So it chanced he was not abed as he was accustomed to at this hour but was up and about, and already his own tale-bearers had gotten to him first. Her heart beat hard at the very thought.

Brenna swallowed, and listened. Hearing nothing from inside, she lifted the latch and let herself in. Simply in opening the door to admit herself she loosed a gust of wind that dislodged a half score of parchments inside.

"Bother!" Sir Edmund was at his worktable, having just slapped a measuring rod down to pin an array of parchments across the table surface.

Brenna gently closed the door.

"What is it, child? Is something amiss?"

She looked up and saw her grandfather watching her with an expression that she labored to decipher: greeting and the merest inexplicable touch of apprehension—as if she disturbed him.

"Nothing," she said, not wanting to alarm him. "I merely wish to speak with you about a...delicate matter."

Face and manner shifted and stilled again. He wiped his shaved quill carefully, put it down. "I do think we need to have a talk, Brenna."

"Yes, Grandy." Feeling vaguely guilty, though she hadn't a clue why she should, Brenna groped for something to say. But there was no need to dissemble, for Sir Edmund began speaking.

"I don't wish to criticize you, my dear, but I'm not—" Sir Edmund hesitated. "I'm not pleased with yesterday's debacle."

Brenna pasted as bright a smile on her face as she could muster. "No harm was done, all the same."

"I will not prevent you from the things you do. I want only to point out the risks you take. In the future, I shall expect better from you, Brenna. Do you understand?"

"It is about that…"

"Edmund!" Lady Alice burst into the room, her face flushed with exertion. "Urgent news! You'll never guess what has happened," she gasped, her breathing labored.

"Go on."

"I have just come from speaking with Nesta." Alice sucked in audible breaths. "It seems the young lord is an imposter!"

Sir Edmund's gaze flashed past Brenna to Alice and immediately returned to Brenna. His eyes narrowed.

"Are you aware of this?"

Brenna turned away, unable to face her grandfather's probing stare. She had never been able to lie to him. What could she say? "I'm not sure what Nesta thinks she knows, but Leon is not an imposter. He is simply not Aubrey of Leeds."

"Nesta says Aubrey of Leeds is dead!" Lady Alice took a deep breath. "What will happen now, brother?"

There was quiet for a moment between them. Sir Edmund's expression was inscrutable as he composed a rattling stack of parchments and cleared a small space on his huge chart table. Then his head lifted, his eyes riveted Brenna to the spot, and she stood perfectly still, forgetting even to breathe.

"Keith Kil Coed has asked for reconsideration of his offer should anything happen to prevent your marriage to Aubrey of Leeds."

"Are you trying to push me into marrying *him?* I won't do it, not under *any* circumstances," Brenna insisted.

At her side, Lady Alice heaved a great sigh.

"You were to wed on the Sabbath. The arrangements have been made. Nothing will be changed but the groom." Gone were his pleasing tones. He folded his arms in front of him.

"No!" Brenna said stubbornly. "Did you not hear? I don't wish to marry Keith."

Sir Edmund glowered at her from beneath heavy brows. "I appeal to your common sense, Brenna. Have you any idea of the cost of these celebrations? Have you?"

Brenna said nothing; she felt fairly certain that despite the questions she wasn't expected to give an answer. She was right.

"I think not! Two chests of silver! Your own weight!"

Brenna opened her mouth to say something, closed it, and shrugged.

Sir Edmund reached out a hand for a quill pen. Then he seemed to change his mind. He let it lie. He drummed his fingers on the table, setting the parchments fluttering and the ink pot reeling. He swore and grabbed for it, knocking awry a stack of parchments. They slid across the table, one of them bumped into the ink pot. It spun in a furious circle, spewing a black lake across a stack of parchments, and then slid off the table and fell to the floor, spilling more ink across the rushes.

Sir Edmund swore again, more heated words this time, and stamped. His foot hit a fallen stylus. He roared a pungent string of oaths suited to the battlefield.

"Brother, really," said Alice faintly. "There's no need for such language."

Brenna bent to retrieve the ink pot. She did not know what to say, so she simply stood there while Sir Edmund took the ink pot from her, stoppered it and used a rag to mop up the spilled ink.

"I understand this is sudden, Brenna," he said at last, his

attention returning to her. "Think on it. We can talk about it later."

Brenna leaned against the wall with a small sound of misery. She was sure that her spirits had never been lower in her life. Maybe it was a combination of doubt, lack of sleep and too much excitement, but it suddenly seemed that her life was out of control.

"I don't need to think it over," she said tiredly.

"Things will not be as difficult as you think, Brenna. Dinas Bran will continue to be your home. You'll not have to take yourself to a strange and perhaps hostile household." Allowing her time to digest his words, Sir Edmund removed a scroll and unrolled it. He tapped it with a gnarled finger. "With this compromise, I attempt to make at least one of your dreams come true, a man that you can admire and glory in. Keith is a fine young fellow. I wish we had a hundred of him."

Brenna breathed deep, to steady herself. "Kil Coed is handsome enough, but I mislike his ways."

"I don't know why you say that. He's strong. He has a stout arm and fast reflexes. He has no equal on the field, and few enough off it. He fights in every little skirmish and cattle raid, and he outfights everyone."

"That's perfectly true."

Sir Edmund shook his head, looking perplexed. "I don't understand you, Brenna. Keith is lordly. He is proud. He is handsome. What more do you want?"

"A kind man. Keith is cruel. Last summer, when his favorite hound was gored by a wild boar, he ordered the dog destroyed, because in its pain it snapped at him."

"Flash?"

"Aye. If you recall his right hind leg was badly torn in the hunt, but it seemed wrong to me to destroy the dog if a little rest and good care would set him to rights."

Sir Edmund exhaled an exasperated breath. "Just so. Though 'twould seem a hasty decision rather than a cruel one."

"If a man mistreats a dog that loves him, what will he do to a woman who scorns him?"

"Don't argue, Brenna. I have been more than fair about this in the past. I allowed you time to choose whom you would wed."

Brenna kept her voice level with an effort of will, so level that it was flat. "And I chose Aubrey of Leeds!"

"Who is dead!" Sir Edmund's deep-set eyes raked her face.

Brenna bowed her head slightly in acknowledgment. "I have already conceded once on this matter, Grandy. Never again. I will wed," she said, speaking with great care, "when I find a man I can love. Pure and simple."

Sir Edmund's face began to turn red. "I was hoping that you'd look favorably upon Keith when he arrives, that you'd come to your senses—given up this fantasy nonsense."

"I'm sorry, Grandy, but I have my reasons."

"I'm running out of patience, Brenna. You will wed on the Sabbath. End of story." Sir Edmund was shouting at her now. He snapped his lips together with a visible effort, and continued quietly, "Be reasonable, child."

"I am being reasonable!"

"You know what concerns us."

"The marauders in the west?"

He nodded his agreement. "Which is why, by fair means or foul, Keith must—" He broke off. For once Brenna could see his tongue had led him further than he liked to go. She led him to the end of it.

"You want me to marry Keith Kil Coed so that you can manipulate him. Your motives are not pure at all!"

Sir Edmund was totally taken off guard, although he hid his turmoil well. "What choice do I have?"

There was no argument Brenna could make to that sad truth. Politics would take precedence over any emotional tie. But she had to try. It was her life that was at stake!

"If I didn't think I'd be cutting my nose that it might

spite my face, I should put a curse on every man in the kingdom.''

Alarm registered on her aunt's face. ''Hush, Brenna. Such words will brand you a witch!''

''Whatever it may be, it will be better that I ponder it now than after I have pledged myself,'' Brenna said balefully. ''And it would be a fantastic revenge if I could do it!''

''Calm down, Brenna, calm down.'' Alice was looking at her as if she were losing her mind. ''You are working yourself into a state. This is not like you.''

Brenna realized that she was well on the way to frightening her aunt. With an effort, she swallowed emotion and summoned some steadiness.

''Your fears are groundless, Aunt,'' she said with forced cheerfulness. ''I would not have wished Aubrey of Leeds dead, and would have wed him because I was too weak to withstand Grandy's command. But he is dead, and I am again beset.''

''We cannot always order events as we wish.''

Brenna stared at her grandfather. Grandy was clearly distressed, fussing about, putting charts into stacks. What could she say or do to persuade him to abandon the nuptials? She opened her mouth. And shut it. For she knew he would not be moved.

The nuptials must go ahead.

Brenna felt a shiver in her bones. She could not do a thing about that, but if she took the given situation and turned it to her advantage, then Grandy had no weapon to use. It was up to her to take the initiative. She was fighting for everything that mattered to her. She could try. Why not?

''If I must wed, then I will choose for myself. It is fortunate my knight is already at Dinas Bran.''

Leon…

Leon had rescued her from her own folly, and he had saved her. On impulse, out of instinct, call it what she might. The fact remained that, from that moment, their fates were joined.

"Indeed?" Sir Edmund's glance was pointed. "And who would that be?"

"His name is Leon. He is big and strong. I swear he could lift a wagon with one hand!"

"That is a little extravagant," Sir Edmund judged sourly. "The name is unfamiliar to me. No doubt he's poor and landless. It's out of the question."

"Nay. I have no doubt he is a great knight, all dauntless honor and dashing courage. 'Twas he who brought word of poor Aubrey's demise."

"That is hardly sound logic," Sir Edmund said irritably, shoving aside all fruitless argument. "The fellow may have intervened and saved some unpleasantness, but that is all I will grant you. Forget the rest."

That was a refuge. She snatched at it. "Leon saved my life. I do not forget it, nor shall I."

Sir Edmund's brows met. "Our troubles haven't yet come under the tale-spinners' ridicule, Brenna, and it is not my intention that they should." He stopped, grimacing. Suddenly he seemed immeasurably weary, and she could see what it cost him to go on. "Very well, I will put no obstacles in your way if you really want to go through with this. You may choose as you will. But remember you know Keith Kil Coed. He has my blessing. This newcomer you do not know at all."

He returned to his seat and opened a scroll. She was dismissed.

Leon rested his elbows on the broad stone window slit and leaned into the open air, crisp and sharp with wood smoke. From this angle only a sliver of bleached-blue sky could be seen, with scattered ribbons of high wispy cloud.

A shadow passed over him and he looked up. There was a rush of air whispering and the dry rattle of feathers. Several ravens landed on the ledge. He broke a piece of honey-cake and gave it to them, provoking battle, beating wings and stabbing beaks.

For a moment he watched the ravens. Their plumage flashed with the same iridescence as Brenna's hair, evoking an assemblage of hazy images in his mind...

Memories, long buried beneath carefully woven cobwebs, reappeared, thrusting into his consciousness...the years went reeling back and back. He saw himself again as a brash squire, beside himself with joy at accompanying the FitzWarren entourage to bid farewell to the Crusader army, proudly watching a parade of lavish, glittering armor that had seemed endless.

It came as memory comes, swift, piercing and all at once. It had been at Dinas Bran that he had been enchanted by the dark-eyed elf. He had even taken a vow to return and wed her. How could he have forgotten?

After all, he had carried her token these past fourteen years! He sought after the leather cord he had slipped about his neck and the embroidered pouch fastened there, holding to it with both hands, shivering at the flood of memories...

...of moonlight and the silhouette of merlons across skin so smooth it shone like water on marble. The dampness of his palm, which he had anxiously wiped on the end of his tunic. The scrap of torn lace that dangled from the elf's night rail. Above all, the way those candid, forgiving eyes had seemed to looked into his heart and seen nothing unworthy of that sunburst smile of approval.

No, elf was wrong. She was a woman now. Brenna. His own special guardian. And when he thought of her, as he had once done fiercely, passionately, a hundred times a day, and did even now, especially after one of the painfully sensual dreams that still haunted him, he always thought of her as a woman.

Now he returned as promised, but even if it had not been to suit himself but to please his foster father, he had not kept his vow but had married another. Brenna's pledge had been broken, also, for though she was not wed, she had been betrothed.

"No," he whispered. He hardly knew what he denied. He

tucked the amulet within his collar, tied the laces that concealed it at his throat. It was fortunate that Brenna did not either recognize the foolish boy he had been or remember his even more foolish vow. Her silence had been absolute.

He swung his arms, easing the tension in his shoulders, and startled the ravens who took flight in a great upward beating of wings against the sky.

Now something else stirred. A creeping feeling went down his neck. He spun toward the soft, unexpected sound. As he turned, his right hand went to his left side, fingers grasping for the sword that wasn't there.

He listened. Listened hard. Nothing to hear but the noises from the courtyard below and, off on the edge of hearing, the hiss and rustle of the birch forest that grew to the north.

Leon slowly turned around to observe the entire chamber. Nothing at all. Utter stillness. What was it that caused that discordant note? There was no one else there—the room was empty. And everything was in its place.

But no, not quite.

The candle flames in the sconces swayed. Shadows moved. The uneasy feeling grew. His hand ached, yearning for its lost weapon. He fixed his whole being on a tapestry at the other side of the room.

The heavy fabric stirred. A thin hand appeared from behind the wall-hanging. The sheltering tapestry fell away and a hidden stairwell beyond was revealed, at the top of which stood three small boys.

Leon narrowed his eyes. His hand relaxed. He felt his breath go out of him in a hiss.

"How come you here?" The question hung in the air with a menace that was almost tangible. He misliked the idea of secret passages. He would make it his business to find out more about this one.

The boys glanced at one another. The tallest stepped forward, a single pace only. He carried a heavy scabbard, carefully tucked under one arm.

"We came by the passage so the guards wouldn't see us,"

he said in a thin voice, reedy with nerves. He looked into Leon's eyes and hastily away. "Us stable boys aren't allowed on the upper floors. We thought of waiting for our brother Telyn, who has a permit, but it's rather—" he paused, taking a breath "—a delicate matter."

"Don't worry, I'll not harm you and I'm not about to call the guards," Leon said quietly, moving forward. "Your name, young sir?"

The boy gave Leon another quick look and swallowed. "I am Tudur. And these are my brothers, Tassaud and Taffy."

"What have you there?"

Tudur met his gaze squarely, but his face was ashen; freckles stood out appallingly plain, blots like dust on his skin. Slowly, cautiously as a red buck testing unsure ground, he approached Leon.

"Your sword, sir. We thought you might need it," he said, and held out the scabbard.

Leon took the sheathed blade, and studied its hilt and pommel for several long, thoughtful moments before sliding it out. 'Twas his own sword, an excellent weapon, well balanced, properly weighted, with good keen edges that were parallel almost to the tip, and it was as sharp as the cutting edges. He raised the sword in his right hand, and saluted the empty air in a flourish of edges—more for the boys' benefit than to test the sword.

"Where did you find this?"

Tudur flung up his head, his brown eyes round with startlement. "Why 'twas on the destrier, along with the saddle sack." He indicated the sturdy leather satchel Tassaud was clutching.

Leon took the sack, noting the metal clasp had not been tampered with. "I feared them lost for good. I am beholden to you, young sirs. How can I reward you?"

A mound of honeycakes remained on the plate, the first of the new day's baking. The watered wine was bland enough for youngsters to sample, a whole flask of it. There was fruit and new cream and a handful of sticky sweets.

Taffy's bright brown-gold eyes sparked with wide-eyed interest at the feast and he elbowed Tudur in the ribs, but it seemed his brother had more important things on his mind.

"Lady Brenna thought, that is, if it's not inconvenient, sir, seeing as you have no squire or pages with you, that I could be your squire and Tassaud and Taffy your pages," Tudur finished shyly, but with head erect and shoulders squared.

Leon looked at the sword, and then at Tudur, long and deeply. "You're a slender fellow, with not much meat on your bones. You're not up to swinging a sword yet."

Tudur nodded agreement, but when he looked at Leon, his brown eyes were ablaze. "But I will be soon."

Leon returned the nod. "Yes, soon," he said gruffly.

Certainly the lad possessed the grit it took to become a knight, probably the aggression and recklessness, too, but the price of such molding came high. His own training seemed far behind him now. He was a different person than the young, idealistic boy who'd gone to learn his trade at Whittington so many years before. There was hope, then, and dreams and the thrill of achievement.

All that he could see in Tudur's face.

"I will think on this."

It was then that he got an idea. An evil, wonderful idea. Brenna wanted him to stay. Why not? This was his opportunity to learn the secrets of Dinas Bran at no risk to himself. And...more and more dangerous a thought...if there was something sinister, considering the position he was in, it did make sense to take precautions. And even if it was bad...and even if he couldn't accept it...he'd at least know the truth.

It would be days before Rodney caught up with Thomas at Chirk and they tracked him here, and he could use a servant or two to send messages and suchlike. In the meantime, the youngest lad was near to dying for the taste of a sweetmeat.

He gathered up his scabbard and buckled it on, then spun the sword into its sheath, and said in his mildest, laziest voice, "It's a good thing cook sent up extra cakes. Come, sit with me, you three, and share the feast."

They settled themselves at the table and laughed, counting the cakes out, one for each and one over. "You take it," Taffy said to Leon.

"No, you."

Taffy grinned and bit into the confection.

Leon allowed them a few minutes to wolf down the honeycakes, then spoke briskly. "About the passage..."

Gossip had run through the hall all evening and it had had twins by morning, so Nesta reported. And mostly it was true what the gossip was saying, simply that there had been a ruckus at the postern gate, several churls had been arrested—and a new and startling tale. One that traveled as all such tales must, swifter than fire through a dry field. 'Twas said Brenna had declared her betrothed dead, and that she harkened after a rascally beggar.

Elen came in search of Brenna to refute the wilder elaborations on that report. She would scold her for such nonsense.

And Brenna would laugh low in her throat and do something outrageous such as...agree?

"For once, the gossip is true."

"What are you saying?" Eyes wide, Elen stared at Brenna.

Brenna drew a deep, shuddering breath. "Do try not to look so horrified, Elen. That knight in my father's chamber is not Aubrey of Leeds."

"Brenna! Sir Edmund must be informed at once!"

"He knows! That wretched Nesta must have glued her ear to the door, and then she ran to Lady Alice to spill what she'd overheard—that Aubrey of Leeds is dead—and, of course, my aunt had no hesitation in relaying the news to Grandy."

"Aubrey of Leeds is dead?"

"Aye."

"Then who is yonder fair knight?"

"If all were right and just in this world, the golden-haired knight in my father's chamber would be the love match I've thought on these past fourteen years."

"You're not on about that again?"

"I told you I promised my knight I'd wait forever."

"The word of a child."

"The word of Brenna of Brenig—which I broke!"

Truth. It burned. *I promised. My first promise. I would wait forever for you to come and claim me. I broke it.*

Elen set her hands on her ample hips. "Brenna, you were but four years old! Fourteen years is a long time. He's probably forgotten the incident. If he even remembers you, it will not be as a woman who kept her word, it will be as a child who swore a child's heedless oath, more threat than promise. I'll wager it means nothing to him."

Brenna sighed and spread a square of cloth on the table. "You're probably right, Elen. There are times when I truly wish I could turn men into frogs!"

"Be sensible."

"I am being sensible. Eminently sensible. I believe this knight—" She picked up a bronze mirror, cradled it in her hand and held it so that it caught the light, neither brown nor gray nor green, but a mingling of all three, like Leon's eyes. What I thought was only a dream, she thought. You are the reality. One corner of her mouth quirked up, as she added in a carefree tone, "—comes to Dinas Bran for a purpose, even if he doesn't know it himself."

"How so?"

"How? Do you ask how? Is it not plain?" Her voice sparkled with hints of laughter.

"You have that cat-in-the-cream look, Brenna. What mischief have you in mind this time?"

She gave a little laugh. "No mischief, Elen, a good deed."

"This isn't a game, Brenna. For your own safety—"

"This is deadly serious."

Elen threw up her hands. "I am not quick of wit. Be clear."

"Now that Aubrey is dead, things are different."

"How so?"

"Grandy insists the nuptials go ahead. It is not my pleasure to wed Kil Coed, and I find Leon to my favor."

And what favor! From the first moment she'd seen him, she had known he was the one. From the first time he had touched her, she had known the wonder.

And the longing.

She had felt his incredible strength.

And her own weakness against it...

The memory of her night in his arms haunted her. Rather than ending her hunger for him, it had made it worse, like trying to douse a fire with oil. Another thought haunted her, too. What if he discovered her deception?

"You mean then to enmesh him?"

"Nay." Brenna placed the mirror on the cloth. "To rescue me from the attentions of such as Keith Kil Coed! Nobody in their right mind would want to be married to that creature."

"There are many maids would think otherwise and would snap at such an offer. Keith is very handsome."

"Aye. I'll grant you that, and any clever woman could outwit him—so long as she catered to his conceit and temper."

"But you think this newcomer a better proposition?"

"There is something different in Leon. Not merely his clothes, which are fine and well made, but in his assurance. He is a person accustomed to the ways of strength and power—a good match, I think. I have found nothing about him to dissuade me."

"Are you saying—"

"The wedding feast is prepared, the priest is here, Grandy

has withdrawn his opposition and, once he has had time to consider the matter, he will welcome Leon most heartily.''

"Of course he will! He'll also give him a handsome reward, something splendid—a brooch, a hound, one of his best hawks. But, oh, dear! Not his beloved granddaughter!''

"Why not?''

"A wandering landless knight, come in for a free meal and a bed! What sort of match is that?''

Brenna swallowed hard. "The best! Leon goes his way alone and in that solitude and freedom is his strength. He's never lived here, so he hasn't got any feuds of his own in Wales. Don't you see?''

"There is much goodness and honesty and generosity in you, Brenna. If you would add prudence to these, you will surely reconsider offering a base-born churl such regard. Don't give your enemies any more substance to talk about!''

"Indeed not, Elen. His manners are good, and his speech exact. It stands to reason, this is no base-born churl.'' Brenna tied the cloth into a neat package. "Would I consider him otherwise?''

"Are you saying that the end justifies the means?''

"No, but—''

Flash came suddenly to her from beneath the table, pressing his great head against her leg. Brenna idly scratched the hound's ears. The news would be all over the castle by now, and as far as the village by noon, she was certain. She did not have much time.

"What I would offer this man is not a life of privilege, but a life of service. Any dowry I bring him is a land in danger. I would have time to have his consent before he senses the poison in the bait.''

"Brenna.'' Elen spoke quietly, but her tone was like a slap. "'Tis time you were married, but this is not the right way to set about it. We know nothing about him.''

Suddenly, Brenna was very much afraid...that she did *not* have it right, that loving this knight was too dangerous for all of them, that defying her grandfather might foul up something the old man had planned—

Or Keith Kil Coed, finding out about it, intervening—

She shrugged her doubts away. What she needed was time to get everything properly arranged. Her heart hammered away in her in the realization that she had the only opportunity this very morning! How to convince him?

Sir, she would say to Leon—or should she address him as "my lord"?—I am in most need of a knight, for I fear my grandfather himself has...

...Bid? Commanded? Commanded was far stronger, and she could get immediately to; My aunts would not ask your help for fear of reprisal, but I ask it—

Then Leon would say, What exactly do you want me to do? Sir knight, she would say, I am in deep and dangerous trouble. If you would help a maiden in distress... Sir knight, if only you'd do something...if you *could* do something...

She had no more doubts. It was the best way.

Let the men do what they wanted, play their little games. In the meantime she would initiate some action even she might not be able to stop. But at least she would have tried.

"Aubrey is dead. Leon saved me from those villains. He is our guest and welcome to all that the hall holds. I would offer him no less than what would be offered a man of rank."

"And what will you offer him?"

"The chance to be my husband." It was a whisper, barely louder than the wind among the reeds of the river.

Elen clicked her tongue. "Silly child! 'Tis an absurdity. A desperation. What if—"

"Ifs count for nothing. Leon will accept. I know he will!"

They were both very still then, regarding each other unwaveringly in the clear, sparking light. They both knew the risks. They both knew there'd be a price to pay.

At last Elen sighed, and put up her hands.

"Ah, be easy, child. Don't look so scared. I'm not going to scold you! I've been young myself."

"Fine," Brenna returned, feigning nonchalance. She picked up the cloth bundle. "And I thank you for your concern, Elen, but I'll act as I think right."

"I hope you'll not regret this one day. Promises come back like ghosts to haunt—"

"No. I'll regret nothing. Whatever happens. This oath I will keep."

Elen dropped her arms and made a face. "I will say naught further on the subject. Just be careful, Brenna."

Chapter Eight

Brenna burst into the chamber, the shaggy white hound hard at her heels. Her arms were filled with packages.

"Sorry to keep you waiting, Leon." She moved forward in an apologetic rush. "I wasn't too long, was I? I've got all sorts of good things," she said, hastily placing the packages on top of a carved chest.

The dog snuffled the air and studied Leon with its strange-colored eyes, milky-white as clouds. Brenna clicked fingers and Flash slunk away quietly to the door and lay down, nose on feet.

Leon leaned back and stretched his booted feet out under the table. "You look all flustered."

Brenna's head snapped around. She flung out an arm. Her bottom jiggled and her veil flung and she looked furious and—quite enchanting.

"And why wouldn't I? I've almost had enough of this weather. I'll be glad when it improves."

"It hasn't rained all morning."

She inhaled a deep, impatient breath and bent over to pick up one of the packages. "It can't rain all the time!"

Beneath the fabric of the robe she wore, he could see the rounded upsweep of her breasts. Lust flooded him. It seemed to him that the womanly curves would fit his hands perfectly. Saints above, what was wrong with him? The world was full of beautiful women. The fever had obviously taken its toll of his sanity if he saw one woman endowed with tempting curves and could not make himself stop wanting to…

It was just excessive male urges, or perhaps eight years of abstinence finally taking its toll. Nothing he couldn't handle. What was she saying?

"…being confined indoors makes for bickering, all the time, and everyone looks to me for answers—the steward challenges the cost of food, the cook protests the scullions are lazy, the priest chatters that rain can be conjured out of nothing, the servants eavesdrop and make intrigue, and they all come to me for counsel—what a lot of clacking mouths!"

Leon folded his arms across his chest. He thought of several crushing comments and promptly discarded them. "Then you shouldn't be so damned perfect," he said instead.

Brenna considered that, standing, staring, with her hands still clutching the package. If Leon was to become intimately involved, she felt she owed him the truth. It might work if she could put a taste of amusement into the words. He might laugh. She had seen the quick light of humor in his eyes more than once. He did have a sense of humor. If she made a joke of it, surely he would smile. She sucked in a deep breath.

"Please don't be deceived. I'm no paragon. I am afraid I'm possessed by a terrible temper."

"That is merely a bend or two in your perfection."

She bit her lip, unsure if he was teasing her. He didn't look as if he was, but how could she really tell? She shook her head. "Not so. At times my patience runs short, and I am inclined to air my own views on all manner of things, and can prove most stubborn about it."

A faint flicker of amusement touched his expression. "I think you are too harsh, or mayhap 'tis your sense of humor that seems strange to others less disposed to merriment."

He was making a jest! She could risk breathing again! She gave him a sunny smile. Conspiratorially she said, "I'm the family radical. The rest are terribly stuffy. Except my outrageous great-aunt Agnita—she's just odd. They tell me I take after her."

Leon leaned forward, planting his elbows on the table. His mouth crooked slightly at one corner. "Why don't you finish showing me your bounty before we get off the path with a list of your faults."

That reminded her of her mission. "I've got a splendid whetstone and mirror!" She busied herself with unpacking these items, holding them up for Leon to admire. That was when she realized that he had moved out of the chair he'd been lounging in and was now standing beside her.

"You are very kind, but I no longer need them," he pointed out gently. That jolted her. Her eyes flew to his face.

Brenna gasped and took a step backward. It was the first time since entering the chamber that she'd looked at him closely. A part of her realized his cheeks were completely free of the golden fuzz they had worn earlier, while her brain sought to adjust to the shock of seeing that strong jaw scraped shining smooth.

"Oh, you've already shaved!" There was the smallest of pauses before she asked, "How?"

Leon heard the tenseness in her voice and understood it. He indicated the leather satchel set against the chair. "My own things were returned to me."

"Returned to you?" Brenna repeated. Her voice was husky, and she hoped it betrayed nothing of the uneasiness she felt. She glanced at Leon and then at the satchel.

The dark brows raised in curious question, wariness and wonderment competing for a place in her expression. His attention stayed on her profile. She looked a good deal set aback, perhaps turning all the implications of that over in her mind a second time.

Leon smiled. He couldn't help it. "Aye. By three brothers with great ambitions to become knights," he murmured candidly. "I told them I'd consider it," he said, deliberately sounding as if he were repressing a groan. "Though, why I'd want three extra mouths to feed, I don't know."

"Oh," Brenna said. Feeling simultaneously relieved and guilty, she relaxed slightly. It all made sense. All except one small matter. There was something more, she knew, and it was ill-omened, but she couldn't get her scattered thoughts to focus. She bent her head and fiddled with the mirror to cover her confusion. She sought for something to say, some way to broach the subject she wanted to discuss, but now was not the moment, and she could think of nothing else.

"If I do take them on, it must be for a damn good reason." The deep voice went flat and brooding.

Brenna stared up into his face, turning crimson, feeling mortification paralyze every muscle and bone. His eyes flickered as a hawk's will, veiling just perceptibly. Her mouth opened and then shut, fishlike, and no words came out.

When she bit her lower lip, Leon saw her teeth press into the softness. Her lips were a strawberry-red that caught the flush of her cheeks and echoed it. She was so close that he could see the beat of her pulse on the delicate curve of her throat, and he caught a pleasant waft of lavender, which seemed new and familiar at the same time. For one wild moment he thought— But no, surely not, it wasn't possible...

"Tudur and his brothers are orphans," she said stiffly. "A place in the retinue of a knight would give them the security of a place in the world, a chance to better themselves."

Leon frowned down at her upturned face. Her cheeks remained pink and he wondered whether to speak or remain silent. He decided he would have to say something since she had encouraged Tudur and his brothers to seek him out.

"It was kind of you to concern yourself with the lads, but the reality is so much different than the dream. Minstrels paint bold and glorious word pictures of knights, but they do not sing the truth. A knight's life is not one of daring deeds and maidens rescued. It is one of discomfort and futility,'' he said, his tone faintly bitter, faintly weary.

Brenna heaved a great sigh. "Another illusion shattered. I'm sorry, Leon. It was thoughtless of me to encourage the boys so.''

"No, just soft-hearted.''

Brenna tried to smile. Something in his eyes made her think that he was angry. She chewed on her lip, nervous and uncertain. But that look in his eyes was gone so quickly that she wondered if it had ever been there.

Had she imagined it?

She had to stop this!

"And here I was thinking you were the soft-hearted one. Secretly, behind the grim facade.''

Brenna paced in a fretful circle, made a little shrug, and her mood changed. Dark lashes swept over dark eyes and lifted again, restoring an intimate moment. She smiled at him, such a smile as held friendship and mockery at once.

"Knights don't come like raindrops, and neither does a good set of armor." She unwrapped the largest of her bundles. "I'm sorry it's not new, but it's not bad. And there's a helm to go with it! Look." She held up a bundle of chain mail.

Leon reached out one hand and tapped his fingertips on the armor. It made a small metallic click as his nails struck the rings of mail-mesh so fine it represented almost a year of someone's life, making the rings and then weaving them into a clinging, lustrous fabric of steel. Not the sort of thing one found laying about a keep, unused, waiting to be discovered and gifted to a wandering vagabond.

His lips quirked. "Pretty enough."

Brenna flushed, as if sensing his sarcasm. She paused for a moment, a strange look coming into her eyes, then drew a breath and went back to business. "Most of this came from my father's estate. I found a gambeson, too—padded with real goat's wool. Here, feel it." She held it out.

Leon admired the quality to gratify her, the twinkle in her dark eyes being more than worth the effort. A smile played around his mouth. "This would have been handy yesterday."

"You've a right to remind me of my foolishness. I would in your place. It was a brave thing you did, against such odds."

"Anybody would—"

"No, only a man not afraid to take risks." Her voice wavered oddly. There was a silence that went on and on. Extended out to forever and beyond. Then she broke it. Said, flatly, clearly, without emotion, "I have need of such a man."

A jolt ran through him. *Need* was such a seductive, dangerous word. He heard the word not only with his ears, but in some deeper place, the marrow of his bones and the corners of his spirit. The thought having been uttered, it settled in the back of his mind like a single grain of sand, impossible to ignore and its implications too awful to contemplate. His way was chosen for him and he could not go back.

"Greatly obliged," he said with sarcasm. Voice and manner should have stopped her, but she accepted no rebuff.

"Doubtless everyone in the castle has heard of your prowess by now. But it will not make Grandy change his mind. That he should even consider such a thing…!"

"What thing?"

A quiver of the lids as she lowered her eyes. "I thought at first you were Aubrey of Leeds…then, when I knew you were not…I'd hoped that you had come…so that I need not…" She paused to lick her lips. "It is very inconvenient and disagreeable, but now that Grandy has discovered Aubrey is dead, he has decreed that, come the Sabbath, I will still be wed."

Leon stiffened his back, keeping his eyes full on her face. "You're serious, aren't you?"

"Aye."

She lifted her eyes and they stared at one another. Where

was the trap? Leon could sense there was one, and yet he could not see it. He stood unmoving, but the cords in his neck drew taut as cables. A shadowy memory appeared. Another time, another place. A terrible image of Suzanne, eyes wide, frantic—desperate. He had to clear his throat before he could talk.

"Is there no way out of it?"

Brenna shook her head vehemently. "I have no choice in the matter. Much though he loves me, Grandy loves his demesne more. He would never destroy it for my sake."

"Yet he will give it as a gift to your husband?"

"If he proves worthy of them."

"By his existence he is worthy. Save only for the keep of Chester, Dinas Bran is the strongest holding in the northern marches, nor has it ever been taken. It is a rare prize."

"Aye, and I am the heir, but cursed to be a female. For this sin, I am to be willed away like a horse or a dog or a package, to be forever the property of some stranger," Brenna said, hoarse and low.

"What are you suggesting?" he asked brusquely, his tone a shield against revealing tender emotions.

With a kind of stark clarity Brenna realized she had to act. She looked straight in his eyes with all the directness of a born soldier. "That I have thought of a way to spoil their scheme."

"And that is?" he asked, not yet caught up with her leaping thought. Her eyes caught his, held. "What is it that you want?"

"I want freedom, that has nothing to do with marriage!"

Leon bent a little nearer to her. "Tell me, Brenna of Brenig, what is your idea of freedom?"

"Freedom is when the spirit's desires are unhampered by material obstacles."

"In that case, women can never be free, for they have to depend upon men for nearly everything that they really want."

"I see you are going to make me say that I don't really

want freedom.'' Brenna smiled now. ''But I would have a say in who shares my bed!''

''You wish to pick your man?''

''I would have as my husband one I can trust.'' She paused, as if thinking out exactly what to say. ''I hope that you'll consider what I'm about to ask of you, but I'll not badger you. I'm in dreadful earnest—don't say anything please, just yet. I don't want you to do something that you dislike, and I'll not blame you or hold hard feelings if you decide to say nay.''

''Does anyone ever tell you nay?''

''Often,'' she retorted, an underlying flush of color in her cheeks.

''It would be hard to refuse such a charming maid anything.''

''Keep quiet and listen to me! You are not hot of head, but a cool, determined fighter. You have honor in yourself. I know you well enough for that. You are the kind of man who is a success in whatever he undertakes. It is your destiny.''

The low voice throbbed in his brain. She stood before him, slim, straight, so vitally alive, her dark eyes begging him to deny the charge. In his bosom was a strange warm glow. It had been many moons since any woman had clung so obstinately to a belief in him, regardless of the facts, with that unshakeable faith that went to the heart of life. But this girl—this girl with the wild-rose color, the sweetness vividly in her smile, the wonder of youth in every glance and gesture—believed in him and continued to believe in him in spite of his churlish attitude.

''Go on.''

Brenna's face was hot. She tried to laugh, to make her words as light as she could ever have wished them to be. ''Leon, will you...do you want to—'' There she stopped. The blood suffused her cheeks as she thought of how fast she talked, and of how bold her words might sound. She held her breath for a few seconds and then rushed into the question that was hovering in her mind. "Will you be my husband?"

Leon's tongue had gone abruptly dry inside his mouth, so that the words refused to leave it. Why not? He had promised, after all. He swallowed hard. God, there was a spell on him.

The moment seemed to stretch out painfully, and still he could not speak. He realized she was holding her breath. Waiting. Her fingers were clasped so tight he could see the whites of her knuckle bones. She wanted him to say yes. There was still doubt, but a little flick of warmth softened the coldness settled like snowmelt in his middle. *Why not try it?* he told himself. *What do I have to lose?*

"I would be honored," he said.

She smiled, her face blazing into vivid life. Then it happened. With a soft gurgling note, halfway between laughter and a sob, she skipped forward and hurled herself upon him, fastening her arms about his neck.

"You will? You're not just playing games with me? You'll really, really marry me?"

"I'll really, really marry you."

Leon hesitated, perhaps the space of two breaths, but it seemed forever. He drew a deep breath and let it go. Gently, ever so gently, he untangled himself.

"We must not be precipitate."

"Precipitate—" It was a dumb echo.

He cleared his throat. "I need speak to Sir Edmund, before we…" He could find no more words.

Brenna felt herself suffuse with color. He was right. The proprieties must be observed. She should have known better. She managed an uncertain smile.

"If you insist," she said, a faint, diffident voice, determined to remain dignified. Given what had happened between them before, she thought *that* a priority. "I shall take you to meet my grandfather, but first you must have your hair trimmed. Please sit down." She indicated the empty chair in front of the table.

Leon sat to keep the tremor in his legs from betraying him. This time he would stay in complete control of the situation. His emotions and poise would remain unruffled. That decision was made before Brenna brandished the dagger in the air. A man's dagger, deadly sharp.

"Take care," he said, and though he kept the abrupt snap from his voice, the echo of it was very plain.

"Be still! Else I'll trim an ear instead of your hair!"

He turned in a violent movement, and thumped the table with his foot. "Why must it be trimmed at all?"

For a moment the blade was motionless. Brenna struggled with the wild tangle of his heavy mane. It was as outrageous as its bearer's mood; it curled with abandon, and it had a life of its own, a will to escape her fingers and run wild to his shoulders. "Lucifer himself was not crowned with such splendor! Surely 'tis made of sunlight and magic?"

"Mmm," he grunted, as if it were a ridiculous statement. But he held himself motionless as a fawn in a thicket.

"You must meet the Brenigs as a knight, not all shaggy-haired like a pilgrim or a street hawker."

"Do I look like something the pantry cat hauled in?"

Brenna inclined her head a degree, then realized he could not see the movement. "Worse," she said. "More like a stable cat after a shameless night and some torn fur."

Freeing one hand from his hair, she raised the blade. One deft stroke, two, three. His hair pooled like gold about her feet. Her hand stilled.

"I would have the court ladies argue like street women over you—and know that you're mine."

He laughed sharply at that quip, tilting his head to give her a clear view of the flawed half of his face. The skin was sun-browned, the scars pale, shiny as melted wax, though it was clear the damage had been inflicted long ago. But rather than making him ugly, they increased the fierceness of his appearance, as if he were a Celtic chieftain ribboned with crude facial tattoos.

She drew a stray wisp of hair from in front of one eye with her first two fingers. "'Tis like warm, sweet honey."

"Stable muck! That's two pieces of flattery out of you at one sitting." He hesitated a breath. "Are strangers always so welcome here?"

Brenna set her dagger upon the dresser, alien against the bundles of quills and rolls of parchment, the little bottles of ink, the brushes and combs and ointments. She went to the window embrasure and gazed into the distance.

"Mostly. Grandy wields his lordship well enough. The barons respect him. But he grows old and would spend more time looking at his stars than keeping the border at peace. He hopes my husband will assume that role."

"Is there no man hereabouts eager to do so?"

She flushed, a shell-pink flag fluttering in her cheeks. "None. Or rather, none on whom both Sir Edmund and I would agree. If Grandy has his way, it would be Keith Kil Coed."

Leon's neck hair lifted. "Kil Coed?"

"Aye, do you know of him?"

He remembered Keith, their youth bonded in antipathy, a mutual distrust that stemmed from a relationship with the same woman. He remembered Suzanne, so complex, strong-willed, incandescent, saddled with her father's ambition and his legacy, an estate built on blood, influence and vigor. An impossibly beautiful woman who had so improbably fallen in love with him. Now he felt one step closer to the riddle's end.

"Only that he's formidable."

"He has dwelt among the marcher people all his life. He is one of their own, and he is strong and sincere. Grandy favors him. He sees you as a foreigner and an interloper, an upstart, a presumptuous stranger."

"Is he so wrong?"

Brenna turned and looked at him. Clothed in perfectly tailored hose, a tunic and tabard, the power and strength of his body were obvious still, leashed for this moment only.

She thought of the great lion of the mountains, that was most deadly when it seemed most quiet. She leaned back against the window ledge, and studied his face. A ghost flash across time and space. He looked nothing like the boy he had never truly been. No, not with this forbidding exterior. A long time it had been since that day on the battlements. Long enough to forget.

If a lifetime was long enough.

"Don't be absurd." Her words came in a rush. "No doubt there has been one reason then another to keep you away, to postpone your return to Dinas Bran. But you have come back. Like the boy on the battlements promised. Though you've changed since then."

Brenna stared into those piercing hazel eyes, like shards of ice, and thought he was about to deny it. But then he spoke and all the ice turned to running water and rainbows.

"No doubt," he said with a wry smile. "You've changed a little, too, definitely for the better, though." Those keen eyes touched on the rise of her breasts and she felt herself blushing. "I was beginning to wonder if you'd forgotten. You were very young when you swore on my hand that you would wait for me."

"I thought *you* had forgotten," she said. "With so much to think of...a world to conquer—"

"When I was a boy, my modest ambitions seemed the most splendid things. Now..." Leon spoke absently, his thoughts centering upon their proximity and their seclusion in the bedchamber. Her loveliness took his breath away. She stood naturally, but the window ledge pressed against the small of her back, arching her rib cage. Her breasts. It was a beauty enhanced by her unconsciousness of it.

She came to stand before him. "It is said, the heart has reasons the mind cannot know." A whisper, a caress, a warmth, as, stretching up, she kissed him on the cheek, a kiss feather-light and honey-sweet.

Leon stood quite still and silent, aware of the beat of his heart, the rushing of his blood through his veins and arteries, the accelerated pulse. He stared down at her, his gaze fixed upon her upturned face, upon her full, inviting mouth. Her eyes were so full of promise. He felt a shock of recognition. The look was very familiar, as if he'd seen it many times before. But it was like a vague memory, deeply buried, that won't come clear. He felt strongly that he had gazed longingly into those eyes before, and yet...he couldn't have. He tried to blame imagination stirred by an errant hope for what he thought he read in her face. Something savage and primitive in him snarled that he wanted to be the *only* man for her.

"Do you kiss all men thus?"

Drawing back, she began to laugh, the merrier for that her cheeks had caught fire. "Indeed, you flatter me."

"I have an unfortunate flaw, my lady. I tend to speak my mind. You must forgive me, and grant me the answer to my question."

She flushed hotly again. "If you would know, I must admit to a dearth of kisses. I have, however, suffered a deluge of stomach-churning poetry—all in the name of love."

Leon felt as if ants walked up and down his spine and on his arms, and felt his heart beating fit to burst. He bowed his head until his eyes were hid. Love and war, he thought—what else is there? Love is the more dangerous of the two. His course was the easy way. Brawn and might on the battlefield.

Drawing a shaking breath, he lifted his gaze back to her face. She smiled slightly and he felt his knees go weak. It was intoxicating to be the object of her attention. His fever had served him far better than he had any right to expect. Or perhaps it was luck, or fate. Or God. Hell, forget the impropriety of it all, he told himself. Have you come this far to turn back now?

So he abandoned himself. He set his hands on her shoulders and kissed her on the lips. The tenderness of her mouth on his was shattering. His entire body shook and trembled, his heart thudding in his chest, his palms damp. His blood raced molten with magic from his head down to his thighs. His breath grew ragged, and feelings began to rise up from the depths of him; deep, primordial feelings, engulfing him, overcoming him.

He had never felt this way before. The shock that ran through the body had nothing to do with logic. Mad fragmentary thoughts raced through his mind. This was what it was to fall in love. The certainty, sure and absolute. *This was made for me. This is the other half of myself.*

"Enough!"

They drew apart in the same instant, with the same feral wariness. Half of one another, half of the one who had come into the room. A woman it was—a wizened crone, with broad squint folds around her eyes and wings of white streaking back from her temples to disappear beneath an old-fashioned wimple. Her eyes flicked from one to the other. She looked more closely at Leon's face and frowned a little. "You be Brenna's knight?"

Leon gathered himself together at a good speed, considering the shocks of the past few minutes. "Aye."

"Edmund sent word to do something—I don't know what exactly, except he thinks I can make Brenna see sense when no one else can." She drew a long breath, and Leon held his. She turned to him and whispered, "My brother is in a terrible tantrum—he has the temper of a grass fire, you know."

"My great-aunt, Lady Agnita," Brenna said, smiling through set teeth. "She is very candid and sometimes quite forgetful, so please forgive her odd behavior."

"Brenna," said the lady Agnita, "it were well for you to remember that I am no longer a passionate young girl to be carried away by carnal desires, but an old woman permitted the odd delusion. You do not have that luxury. You may be my brother's grandchild, and heir to Brenig, but there is the safety of Dinas Bran to ensure, and how—"

"I know, Aunt, I *know!*" Brenna interrupted before the gates of this domestic flood could open any further. "You lectured me on just this subject more than ten, no, nine days ago!''

"So recently, Brenna?'' Lady Agnita said, her voice laced with the deceptive acid sweetness of unripe fruit. She smiled a small smile that crossed her face like the beat of a bird's wing, but bleary or not, that glint of humor was not so swiftly stifled that Leon failed to see it. ''Then it is time to suffer another.''

Brenna looked at him, and her lips trembled as she valiantly restrained only God knew what sort of remark. Leon had the impression that she was holding herself together with a supreme effort of will. He glanced back and forth between the two of them, unsure whether to be amused or annoyed.

The lady Agnita set her hands on her hips and her head to one side, veil rustling. ''Edmund is anxious, with increasing good cause. You have most urgently to wed to dash the hopes of assorted nobles and eligible bachelors. Such a marriage will place Dinas Bran out of reach of any of the baronies. He fears this fellow is a conniving rogue and counsels caution.'' Agnita's dark eyes met his for a long moment. They were very bright and sharp, missing nothing. She heaved a great sigh. ''Perhaps Edmund is right. Where did you find him, in a kennel?''

"It's all right, Aunt. You're being rude to a hero, and inconsiderate besides.''

"Since when is this person a hero?''

"Since there were assassins at the postern gate yesterday. Ask Telyn, I'm sure he'd be eloquent.''

A wrinkled translucent finger rose and touched his jaw. Her finger was cold. Leon remained composed, as if at ease, but his body tensed.

"Interesting. I heard these outsiders were savages who didn't wash and ran about in raw goat hides, stealing things.''

"Aunt, that's enough. Don't insult our guest. He's both bathed and shaved!''

Lady Agnita touched a tendril of golden hair. "I can see that. From what Edmund told me I expected to see some unkempt churl, but you seem reasonably civilized, young man." Her gaunt hand dusted lightly up the side of his face, all pared clean, skin stretched taut. It was a gesture just short of insult, and just short of a caress. "What lovely skin. Such a nice, even color—pity about those scars."

"The scars add a certain…character, don't you think?"

The lady Agnita clapped fragile hands that seemed to be delicately fashioned from old parchment. "You *are* a philosopher." She grinned so suddenly that Leon blinked. He could not help himself. It was Brenna's smile. Impulsively, he reached out, put his hand over hers.

"You are too kind."

"It's not only your fine character that endears you to Brenna."

Leon's breath hissed sharply. That was wickedly wonderful, like racing the lightning or dancing on blades. His teeth were sharper still, bared in a grin, more broadly this time than before.

"Not to mention your splendid smile. And that cleft in your chin…ah!"

"Is that all?" Leon asked.

"Just so, but Edmund is in a frenzy lest as a young woman of such high passions Brenna might accept the hand of an improper suitor, and live to regret her choice," Agnita said, and this time she no longer sounded like someone being deliberately vague for dramatic effect. She smiled at Brenna in a conspiratorial way. "Tell me, child, about his other skills."

Brenna's face tilted downward, and she flushed. "He can hold his own with most—and more than that, I should think," she said, hoarse and low.

"It looks, grandniece of mine, as though you've got whatever wish you *didn't* speak aloud."

Brenna stared at her hands, refusing to look up. "That's what the old tales say that you should do."

"You young fool! They also say, Have a care what you ask for—you may get it."

Leon lifted an eyebrow at that. He wondered just exactly it was Brenna *had* asked for and from whom she had asked it. Then he realized with a sudden, nasty shiver of apprehension that there were many stories, about a people who knew the arts of magic, who lived here long, long ago, and who fled under the hills, never to be seen again.

Brenna flung up her head. "He comes where he is needed."

"Aye. A real knight, like my poor lost Arthur." Agnita's tongue caressed the name and she sighed; then she smiled. "A man of honor. I'm satisfied he's not after the cup Arthur brought back from Jerusalem."

Leon had heard lurid tales of a silver chalice encrusted with emeralds and rubies said to have been found and hidden at Dinas Bran, but there'd been not the least bit of proof, no witnesses, no testimony, no evidence of truth, and he'd no more thought it true than any other logical man would have. He turned toward Brenna. His lips were twitching with ill-suppressed humor.

"Dare I guess...the *Holy Grail?*"

This sally displeased the old woman. "Aye. Knights come all the time, nodding like fools and laughing when they see it, saying it has no value, and that it's a miracle no one has strangled me," Agnita said crossly. "It's enough to make a person feel like a doddering old woman, when I'm nothing of the kind!"

"They're unkind, lady, but what your Arthur brought home couldn't be the Grail."

"Why not?" she asked, arching white eyebrows.

"It's not been found—and if it had, the priests would have taken it to Rome."

Brenna nodded. "That's what I told Aunt. And the Grail that the Crusaders went looking for was a splendid thing, wasn't it?"

"Aye. A silver chalice."

"Well, Jesus of Nazareth was by all accounts a poor man. I believe the Grail was of practical value. Do you really think he would have been drinking out of a silver chalice?"

Leon shook his head. "Let me understand this. Are you saying you know where the Holy Grail is?"

The lady Agnita stabbed a finger in the air. "Precisely."

"You could take me there?"

"Oh, certainly, but is it proper?"

"Indisputably," Leon said, straight-faced.

"Aunt, you always say you can't remember where the cup was hid—not since that knight from Canterbury sought to wed me and wanted it as part of my dowry gift."

"Do I?" Agnita said in a rather uncertain tone. Her fingers flailed the air. "Well, I have such a faulty memory, and I'm afraid I've had to conceal the thing so many times that I've completely mislaid it." Her hand fumbled out, gripped his arm.

Leon dropped his arm around her shoulders, squeezed tightly. "Don't fret. We'll continue this discussion over dinner and a tankard of ale," he said hastily, glancing at Brenna.

"Quite so." Lady Agnita nodded. Her hands came together again. "You will leave here and go and talk to Edmund, before he grows tired of waiting and does something he'll regret?"

Leon inclined his head slightly. "As you wish."

Lady Agnita grinned suddenly and touched his hand. There was warmth in her eyes. "The Grail rests secure. Not so Sir Edmund's temper. Go with Brenna."

Chapter Nine

Sir Edmund frowned. He'd stomped about and made loud noises, until Agnita agreed to speak with Brenna. In that tactic, Edmund thought, he had his best chance to bring Brenna to heel. But no sooner was he settled to working on an intricate celestial calculation, than Brenna was at the door again with a young man in tow. A young man, moreover, who looked so ferocious that he dropped his goose quill and made a blot over two hours' work. He sighed audibly.

"Brenna, my child…just exactly *what* are you trying to do? Besides make certain that Dinas Bran is a fool's delight? This fellow looks like he'd slit someone's throat for a good price."

Leon stood rigid. Never—never in all his life…

The man's hair was white as winter snow, and the skin was lined and tanned like old leather, but the dark eyes were still bright and alert. It shocked him how much Sir Edmund had aged, but that imposing presence was no less formidable.

"You need not make a face like a sour crabbed apple, Grandy, I have not yet introduced Leon to you." Though Brenna's face was pink, her voice remained steady.

Shaking his head at her, Sir Edmund frowned. He was, Leon reckoned, on the edge of a black rage. There was an ugly promise in the way the old man looked at him that made his skin prickle. His face was flinty, the lines on his face as deep as ravines. He glowered at Leon from under his bristly white eyebrows, his lipless mouth pressed so tightly shut that it all but disappeared and his hooked nose and bearded chin came close to meeting in the middle.

"Watch whom you're calling names, saucy child. I'm not of a mind to be inconvenienced by this fellow."

A dreadful suspicion had begun to steal over Leon that the old man recognized him, for clearly the keen intellect was not blunted by age. Then he relaxed. Of course the old man would have forgotten him; it had been so long ago. Leon took a deep breath and wondered if he should even think about answering. He gave a little lift of his shoulder.

"You hardly need trouble yourself, sir. I do not think there is overmuch to say."

"By the gods, he's got a tongue on him! A temper, too. What do you do for sport? Trade insults with dragons?" Sir Edmund was well aware that he had insulted the young man, but he did so without malice, to test the temper and bearing of Brenna's knight errant. He was not disappointed with the fellow's reply.

"Only if they insult me first."

"I wasn't insulting. I was admiring. I do not count you lightly, young man, with the ease you bear that blade. Cold iron weighs heavy."

A hand settled on Leon's sleeve. It was warm and strong, yet it trembled. He opened his mouth to say something, glanced down, saw Brenna's expression, and closed it again with a snap of teeth. She looked on the verge of tears. His anger left him as quickly as it came, and he was dismayed to find another, stronger emotion inside him. He swallowed and struggled, then he inclined his head a degree, with proper grace and courtesy.

"Sir, you honor me," he said lightly, coolly, but he smiled a white wolf smile. "How may I serve you?"

Sir Edmund laughed harshly at such bold words. It was

not, precisely, what he had expected the fellow to say. He'd half expected him to turn curtly away and leave, but he only stood full of stiff pride and suppressed anger. Brenna could do worse.

"Very good, young man! Your manners are prettier than mine."

"Interesting—if true."

"Very true. You bear watching. Brenna thinks critically of every knight, every lord's son, every potential husband in the entire population. This sudden infatuation is beyond my comprehension. With what cunning trick did you manage it?"

There was little for Leon to do but raise his eyebrows at that, so he did. At least he raised the right one, in a deliberate, understated gesture of interrogation that he used when listening to the inadequate excuses of an erring vassal. With luck, even an irate castellan would balk. He was not disappointed.

"Very well, forget that question. But answer me another one." Sir Edmund gave him a long stare. "You come to Dinas Bran without invitation. You travel alone, and few do so without great cause, or so early in the year. Why?"

A bubble of panic rose to Brenna's throat. Her family was a bit much for an outsider to handle. If Sir Edmund continued in this nasty manner, giving Leon a scold fit for a groom, then Leon would surely have second ideas about acquiring such kin!

"The road is open, as it is to all travelers, and I had farther to go than most."

Sir Edmund sucked in his breath. He looked at Leon, mouth flattened. The fellow was quick of wit, not easy to rattle. It was time to test Brenna. He shook his head and said, "Brenna, this fellow has no beard! What sort of man is he? There is no place in the marches for the gentle man or for the weakling."

Brenna was outraged. Leon was neither. She had counted scars on the broad and corded chest, on his hands and face.

Every man had scars; they were his pride, the badge of his manhood. Leon had an uncommon throng of them. In her mind, she saw his face dappled in sunset glow, unhesitatingly taking on four opponents, knew that, if anything, he underplayed his prowess. She wet her lips with her tongue, and blurted, "Grandy, Leon routed my attackers, unarmed and alone!"

Leon shrugged. "It pleased me at the time."

"We are beholden to you, sir. Brenna is precious to us. Do you understand me?" Reaching to the pouch on his belt, he brought forth a small draw-cord purse.

"Clearly, Sir Edmund. Quite clearly."

Sir Edmund took a ring from the purse and held it out to Leon. "Will you accept this as a gift from me? It is not costly, but it may serve to remind you of a good deed done."

Leon waved it away and hesitated, not sure how his next suggestion would be received. He was still mistrustful; his own experiences dictated caution, but Sir Edmund's fierce concern for his granddaughter's welfare was reassuring, as was Brenna's air of blithe confidence. She stood silently beside him. He could hear her quiet breathing, the gentle pressure of her hand on his arm.

"Come along, young man, speak. I won't bite you, unless I don't like what you say!"

Leon breathed out through his nose and swore great inward oaths, though outwardly he was calm, seeing clearly just how ironic was the present situation. "I really am not so bad as I daresay I appear—or as you think me."

"Maybe I'm old, or maybe I'm slow, or maybe I'm just missing something," Sir Edmund said at last. "Permit me to make clear my position. I did not summon you. I hope you leave as quickly as possible. Your presence here disturbs me. The thought that friends of yours will follow disturbs me."

"And that's all?" asked Leon, not satisfied with the reply. He stood in his accustomed stance, legs well apart, shoulders back, sword heavy at his hip, his mind digging into the prob-

lem, thinking of border lords at each other's throats, the
mandated marriage, asking himself whether bribery, diversion
or main force was the appropriate answer to fools.
Thoughts and images floated 'round in his head. He'd begun
thinking differently since this morning, his thoughts a mixture
of guilt and a small wave of uncertainty.

"That's enough," said Sir Edmund, and his voice was
not one inviting questions or quibbles. He stared at Leon
sourly. "I keep thinking that I've met you before, young
man, from some feast or other. Though—" he looked pointedly
at Brenna "—your previous visit to Dinas Bran was
somewhat less obvious than this one, or I would not have
forgotten. What are you called?"

Leon met Sir Edmund's stare. It was dark, still, watchful,
waiting. He hoped the secrecy would hold up. And that Sir
Edmund would ask no questions—nor come to any sudden
recognitions. He had already abandoned all thoughts of identifying
himself as Fulk FitzWarren's foster son. It was not
a deceit, just a precaution. No need to invite trouble, and if
any did remember him, he would handle that issue when it
arose.

Distraction always kept people off guard and from remembering
a face, and a small breach of truth was better
than a major one of manners, he thought. "I do not know.
Perhaps it might be true. Perhaps you once saw me differently,"
he said. This much at least was certain. To give his
own name was a risk, for was it not almost as notable as
his flaxen hair? Sometimes one gambled. He made a reckless
cast. "I am Caer Llion," he named himself. "Of goodly
strength and skill."

"Caer Llion. A bold name, and Welsh. How came you
by it?"

"I was born in the south."

"I'll make it worth your while to go back there, if you
will go away right now."

"I appreciate your directness, Sir Edmund. I hope you'll
appreciate mine. The answer is no."

"Name your price."

Bait and trap. Leon avoided the familiar ploy with practiced ease. "I'm not a tax collector, Sir Edmund. I'm not interested in your coin."

"If you don't want coin, what do you want?" Sir Edmund demanded. The edge of cold anger lingered in his voice.

Leon tilted his head and studied the old man, just to let him know he knew a raised stake when he heard one. "I didn't come here looking for trouble or to challenge or be challenged, whatever you may think. I merely lost my way." A smile played around his mouth. "But I can defend myself, as you know."

Brenna's breath shortened. She put a restraining grip on his arm. Beneath her hand, the flesh was as rigid as a lance shaft, muscle clenched against bone. She shook her head at him, her eyes pleading, expectant. "Not yet, I think—" their eyes met, held "—I wouldn't want you to break our agreement before we put the contract in writing," she whispered, softly as falling silk.

Leon found the touch of her hand both reassuring and disturbing. An odd excitement quivered in him, a tangle of lust and chagrin, and he felt his traitorous body harden. He shifted to relieve the discomfort of his body.

"I won't," he whispered back.

"Grandy, it would please me," she said, "if it pleased you, to meet me halfway in this."

"It's easy to act on impulse, Brenna, and much harder to think about what the consequences might be," Sir Edmund said in a low and level voice. He shook his head. "But the consequences will show up sooner or later, and then you must deal with them."

"I love him," said Brenna, her voice no louder than a leaf dropping on moss. That surprised Leon, brought a frown to his brow and almost a warmth to his heart. He gave her a look sidelong to see if she was jesting. She refused to meet his gaze, standing stiff as a sentinel.

"Love is a compelling reason." Sir Edmund spoke in

soft, cold, incisive tones. "If, indeed, what you're feeling is love. But one doesn't find love in one moment, one kiss. You don't even know this fellow."

Brenna's breath hissed between her teeth, a slow shuddering. She answered him in a whisper, saying, "That doesn't mean I can't love him!"

"You love only the novelty he has brought."

Sir Edmund stared at Caer Llion. A bold fellow in truth, cool, unruffled, with brazen eyes not lowering before his own, touched with something very like amusement. They refused to be stared down. A lion cub indeed. Sir Edmund's own gaze slid aside first, and he told himself he was weary of this foolishness.

There was a small silence, then Leon said, "Answer me one question, sir, just for the sake of curiosity."

"Ask—though you won't get the answer if I don't like the question," growled Sir Edmund.

"What sort of man *would* you want Brenna to marry?"

Sir Edmund considered Leon thoughtfully. Then he looked into Brenna's eyes for a long moment, as if speaking, though no words were exchanged. "Show me your hands," he said suddenly.

Leon held them out to him, palms upward. A line of tough calluses adorned the palms, and his fingers bore the rough marks of shield strap, sword and rein. The old man took them in his, turned them over, pushed back the oversleeves and examined the long, scarred forearms. This time, when Sir Edmund looked at him, there was a new respect in the castellan's eyes.

"These were not acquired in the spectator's stand, nor are they the hands of a knave."

"Little difference between a knight and a knave save the clothes on their backs."

"You are quick, I give you that." Sir Edmund looked sharply at Leon, who had a sudden conviction that the old man knew perfectly well who he was. He told himself he was imagining things—probably that stare of supposed recognition had been only short-sightedness. "That was a brave act, yester eve. If the ring is not to your liking, what do you ask in exchange?"

"As to that, Sir Edmund, I have my reward, but I will tell you something else. I earn my bread by the strength of my arm and the skin of my teeth, by my wits and some good sense. *What* I am I will not argue with you, but I mean no harm to you or yours."

"Then forgive me for asking—why *are* you here?"

Just the touch of a hand, reaching out. Leon looked down at Brenna, the perfect oval of her face. Her river-dark eyes were like whirlpools spinning him down. The eyes closed for an instant, a universe blotted out. Then they flew open. Her eyes were perfectly enormous now.

Don't do this to yourself, he thought. His reason told him she was a temptation to lure his soul to damnation, that he'd had enough of damsels in distress to last any man ten lifetimes. But his spirit filled him with visions of that shadowy dream, of a lissom form, of erotic, heady pleasure, of a joy that might be his.

And there was the other promise, unspoken but assuredly certain. He would be bound to this place, to this irascible old man, taking up the burden of castellan, in charge of the province the king least trusted—and he knew the history of the man, the bloody necessities, the cruel certainties. He shivered. Marriage to Brenna made that duty *his*.

She was looking at him now, head tilted, eyes wide, waiting for an answer. The bland innocence in her gaze made him decidedly suspicious. She *knew* the duty that was set on him. She did not know he'd been down that road before and knew where it led.

A strange feeling went through Leon's heart then, as if he had heard a spell uttered. Had she detected a hint of the old torment within him? Dire thought. Chilling thought. A tremor ran through him. Did this woman know him better than he knew her? He did not like that, because it meant he was not in control.

He almost found it in him to refuse. But he must not let his misgivings cloud his judgment. His mind ruled him now, his iron will. And he, Caer Llion, had lived past the savage hungers of his youth. He had spent eight long years accumulating his great fortune, which now, finally, could buy nothing that he wanted, nothing to still his aching need: a home. A wife. Sons...

Leon looked down at her, searching the flawless face. The skin was perfectly drawn, not a line, not a blemish marred its satin surface. She stood quite still, and he felt compelled to reach out and touch the face to assure himself it was indeed flesh and blood, warm and pliant, that he was not staring at some fantastically conceived and crafted mask.

Her lashes dipped for an instant and her lips parted as if she were about to say something. Then her lids rose. The lustrous dark eyes stared back at him. Her slim hand moved and she placed it over his. And she managed somehow to turn that simple gesture into a tender caress.

Leon felt a tremendous jolt, as if he were joining battle, and his heart thudded. He dropped his hand. Suzanne had smiled so, been warm to his kisses before the marriage. He did not like what he was thinking. It was unsettling. But to ask...to trust—

Did he have a choice?

He would be fair. This game must be played out, wherever it leads, he thought, for at least afterward I'll know, I'll know—

He cleared his throat and, in a self-conscious tone of voice, like a youth reciting before his tutor, said, "Sir Edmund, I...I have the honor to ask permission...to ask for the hand of your granddaughter in marriage."

Silence hung heavy for a long moment. For the first time in her life, Brenna saw her grandfather completely nonplussed. He opened his mouth like a fish, then closed it again without any sound coming out. "It doesn't seem right, somehow," grumbled Sir Edmund, as if feeling flustered.

Brenna smiled to herself. From long experience, she knew

that when Grandy reached the stage of grumbling to himself in his beard, then willing or not he would grant whatever foolish request she troubled him with, and not grudge it to her. Her grandfather's voice jolted her out of her complacency.

"Brenna tended you last night. Have you dishonored her behind my back?" he asked angrily.

Brenna's heart suddenly ricocheted against the walls of her chest. She could almost taste her apprehension.

"I have not." The ice in Leon's voice could have frozen hot coals.

"She said she loves you." Sir Edmund made it an accusation. "Did you put her up to it? If you've compromised her and then forced her to prate about some affection between you to gain my approval—"

"I have forced her to nothing, Sir Edmund. Nor will I ever," Leon interrupted bitterly.

"Then why on earth would she say she loves you?"

"I confess I am as much at a loss as yourself. Perhaps you should ask her."

"Are you in love with her?"

Brenna pressed her hands together and held her breath in the long pause that followed. *Say yes,* she begged Leon silently.

He felt both bemused and flustered. In his eight and twenty years he had shared little of himself with anyone. He did have some friends, good men, but true intimacy seemed impossible for him. Now in Brenna he found someone able to break past previously unbreachable defenses. She smiled and his spirit leaped. No, it wasn't that way, he amended silently to himself. She hadn't broken past anything. She simply found the door waiting for her to open.

He said it. No, not him. 'Twas a stranger inside his head that whispered. "It's quite possible that I am."

Sir Edmund's breath caught in his chest, and a smile moved beneath his mustache before he hid it behind his hand. It was the look in Brenna's eyes as she gazed at Caer

Llion. He had seen such a look in a young woman's eyes before: in the eyes of her grandmother, when he first met her and knew that they had both fallen in love.

That same look had never left his gentle Morganna's eyes, not since that first time, but had only softened and gentled during the passing of years. It had been there almost fifty summers later when her black hair had turned white and he'd knelt by their bed and cried while the priest had shrived her. He was silent for a while. When he finally spoke, his voice had changed its timbre. The words, the tone, were deceptively gentle.

"Well, it just so happens that—" Sir Edmund smiled again and this time did not trouble to hide it "—there is a position here at Dinas Bran for a knight who knows the meaning of defense."

Leon gazed into the onyx eyes and was not fooled. "You have made no objections, sir, so I take it I am..." Leon pulled himself up short and grinned crookedly. "I am to wed Brenna on the Sabbath?"

Sir Edmund looked long and hard at Leon. "Aye. We'll discuss marriage settlements later," he said gruffly. "As for you, Brenna, I'll tell you bluntly, I have ruined enough good parchment on your account today. I hope not to see you again until supper."

The tone fact-of-the-matter, the conversation ended.

Rising to her tiptoes, Brenna pirouetted along the recently buffed and polished off-white stone tiles of the passageway. She was as delicate as a butterfly, thought Leon, and when she moved she seemed to float like a bird on a current of fragrant air. The scent of lavender and herb oils drifted after her.

"Tomorrow is the hunt. The day after, there's to be a fair. There will be great merrymaking, with singing and dancing and jugglers and trinkets to buy from peddlers and tinkers— oh, and some jousting. The next day is the Sabbath."

He watched his intended bride, feelings of tenderness, bewilderment and exasperation joining the melee of other emotions churning within him. She was beautiful, bright and dainty, with a light in her eyes that seemed mirth just about to break forth. He was entranced, delighted—and dismayed, because he very well remembered the past.

Brenna stilled. She caught Leon's eye and he smiled gently. There was strength in his face—and kindness. She spun back to his side. "Come, let us take advantage of the weather and get ourselves a breath of fresh air."

Leon gathered himself to say nay. When she smiles like that, her enthusiasm is hard to ignore, he thought, and found himself bowing low, mute, obedient. Went as, and where he was commanded.

The sun was well up and the keep about its daily business when Brenna led Leon down the gravel path past a noisy carpenter shop and the ringing forge of a smithy. Further along, a cooper worked on a barrel, and a thin man in a dark green tunic peered out from the doorway of what appeared to be a cabinetmaker's shop. From the alley between the workshops and the long storehouses came shrill screams that denoted the hawk mews, and, spanning that, a series of arches.

Leon understood the planning in this seeming architectural disorder. The narrow ways and bends would fracture a large invading army, provide a cover for defenders; battlements could sling stones and hot tar on invaders, slits house archers.

The stables were in the rear of the keep, a separate building with a tile roof and swept clay floors that smelled more of straw and horses than manure, though there were long rows of stalls, where more than three dozen horses were champing their morning fodder. Several clucks and cheeps indicated chickens were located somewhere nearby, although Leon saw none.

The stallion was delighted to see him and made a thorough fuss as he ran a hand over its ears, along the splendid arch of its neck, and stroked the long silken forelock.

Tudur, Tassaud and Taffy were there, too, helping their brother, Telyn, groom a frisky red mare. Brenna touched the quivering muzzle. "This is Seren," she said.

The boys were full of questions such as, What happened to a knight's horse if he got killed in battle? and How long would they have to practice with wooden swords before they got the real thing? Would they would get to go all the way to France to see the king? Why were the black bitch's pups all liver-spotted? Until at last the horses were saddled and they could escape the endless interrogation.

They rode down the lanes and across the bailey. The iron portcullis was hoisted and the two heavy oaken gates, strapped with metal, stood open, guarded by four armsmen on foot.

Only a score or so of armsmen? Four gate guards? The gatekeeper, in a chain-mail vest and cowl, hardly seemed to notice them from where he sat on a high stool with his legs propped up on the crossbar of the open gate.

Dinas Bran was one of the original Welsh border posts. It was surely built well enough to withstand anything, including the centuries. Constructed of good ten-times-hammered iron, its welds could hold an elephant. So why was security at the gate so lax? He made a mental note to himself to consider that question later, and continued with his examination.

"Security stinks," Leon growled, glaring about. "Too much stuff all over the walls. A raider's paradise."

"Your problem is you're too suspicious. No, don't tell me, I can already hear the lecture!" Brenna reined up and called to the guards. "Edgar, we'll not be above two hours."

One of them nodded back. "By God's good grace, my lady."

Brenna jerked her head in a quick nod, then urged her mount through the gates. Iron-shod hooves clattered on old cobbles, echoing across the courtyard as the charger followed her.

Deso snorted and bucked with high spirits when Leon rode him through the gatehouse and down to the river meadow beyond the looming gray walls. White puffy clouds dotted the green-blue sky overhead, but to the east the clouds were darker and thicker, with the sheeting gray beneath that spoke of rain.

Slackening the reins, he let the horse have its head and they thundered along the dark band of water at a hard gallop. When the first exuberance had flown like sparks from Deso's hooves, Leon steadied him to a canter, then eased him down to a swinging walk.

Brenna drew her mare shoulder to shoulder with the stallion. The rushing wind had whipped the two thick braids that hung to her waist. Strands of hair that had escaped from the braids blew softly across her face.

For a time, they rode without speaking, seeing only a handful of people, a carter with barrels of something driving his wagon toward the castle, a boy struggling with a braying donkey overladen with firewood, and two children herding geese.

Leon turned in the saddle. From this angle the vast bulwarks reared up sheer as cliffs, defiant and formidable—they were far enough away to overlook the stark masonry patched with moss and ivy and thick tufts of weed.

"There are woods ahead, which the king wanted cut down, but Grandy lodged strong protest, because there's lots of game for hunting and because of the village woodcutters. Grandy has undertaken to keep the law there himself."

They rounded the hill where the road forked. To the left were expansive fields dotted with a few cattle sheds, a shanty for the herdsman and, farther on, the hunting forest. They took the right-hand choice, and that led them to a wooden bridge where a marker stone stood, a pillar beside the bridgehead with the Brenig mark on it. Another such post, this one of wood, stood just the other side where the ground fell away in steep, rocky slopes down to the broken banks of the Dee. They rode across the planks and startled a flight of ravens from their brigandage in the furrowed barley field beyond.

The stone marker defined the point the road left the demesne's ward. The neatly cultivated fields just the other side of the bridge belonged to the village. Down the rock-strewn slope, the stream rushed and gurgled. Several villeins were wading up to their hips in the murky water, catching frogs for the cookhouse.

Brenna swung down from the palfrey, as lithe as a boy, hampered as she was by all those skirts. He'd have broken his neck. No wonder men wore breeches!

"See the tree at the edge of the bank?" She picked up the hem of her gown and held it clear of the ground, tucking it into her wide leather belt, in the fashion of the village women when they worked in the fields. She turned quickly. "I will race you," she said, and ran.

Leon ignored the unseemly display, which exposed two slender white legs very high up to the thighs. Brenna had a faculty for adding the unexpected, the ridiculous, that tempted a man even in the heat of temper to burst out in laughter. When she was halfway to the tree, he began the chase, his long legs covering the ground easily.

Brenna looked over her shoulder, saw he was gaining ground, was not an arm's length away and whirled, running wildly, without caution, her breath coming fast and heavy. She tripped and swerved, off balance. Then the breath was near taken from her as he threw a strong arm around her waist, lifting her from the ground, still running, not even hesitating when he took on the added burden of her weight.

Things waved around. It was a long way to the ground, and his shoulder jolted into her belly. She half closed her eyes. Her arms were banging against a broad sword belt. The hilt winked silver lights up at her. He set her down in a flurry of skirts and she touched the tree, triumphant.

"I won!"

"Won? You did not even finish the race!"

Brenna could not keep the glee inside herself. "I touched the tree first, therefore I won!"

"That is a deceit." He laughed softly, as if to himself. He bent and picked up the veil that had fallen from her head. The sun on his golden hair shone like a haze of fire. "I don't suppose you know how to play chess?"

"Some." She took the veil, holding it against her chest. "But don't be afraid, even if I *wish* to win, I'm careful what I wager on chance and overthrow."

Leon burst into laughter, the first time he had really laughed in a long time. "What a shame," he finally managed to say. "The stakes are what make the game interesting."

Brenna's guileless, open countenance broke into a wide grin as she said easily, "Well, in that case, I shall have to think of something unusual," and they both laughed together.

She continued, "Seat yourself on those dry roots, and I'll get us the refreshment Tudur was kind enough to pack."

A gust of wind whistled through Leon's hair, and a roll of thunder rumbled across the hills. He sat on a fallen bough, his back against the tree, heedless of the wind. His thoughts were absorbed with Brenna—of that face alive with hints of both virginity and hoyden mischief—a crown of dark hair, mirth dancing in the eyes, lurking about the edges of the mouth...

Sir Edmund's maiden granddaughter and only offspring, a bid for peace, an end of the old rivalry—of those things and the confusion in his mind. The presence last night ran through his thoughts like an escaping dream. Had he dreamed it, thus at the edge of sleep? Was it a memory, or had it truly happened?

That it fled recollection troubled him.

There came a noise that caught him with his thoughts drifting. He rubbed his eyes and his face. The horses were quiet, but their movements spoke. They swished their tails.

One stamped. Another snapped at a fly. Brenna unhooked a wine flagon that hung from the palfrey's cantle. She walked toward him, small and sleek, with an unmistakably feminine grace, and handed him a dull metal goblet.

Leon fingers tingled. Strange. It was warm. Mayhap because it had been in the saddle sack resting against the mare's warm haunches, he thought. But its warmth spread in fat, pleasurable waves through his body. And it was a strange color. Bronze, but greener. "This feels magical."

She frowned. "Nonsense. 'Tis but a mug the stablehands use."

He held up a hand. "Sorry. No magic, then. No doubt there is a perfectly good scientific explanation for the sensation."

She glanced up, dark eyes wary and quizzical. "Sensation?"

Another roll of thunder cascaded across the valley, and the wind whistled, gusting enough that Leon looked to the east and squinted. "The sort a man gets when his blood runs hot because of a maid."

Taking the empty goblet from his hand, Brenna set it aside. "The same thing ails me. 'Tis as if my blood runs hot."

Thank God for that. At least there was one fixed point in the spiral of doubt that had begun to engulf him. Leon gathered her into his arms. She nestled against him. The scent of her body sang to him. Odd memories floated into his head.

Brenna felt the tension creep through his frame. She peered up at him from beneath her lashes. "Do you like me at all?" She spoke her thought, unsoftened and unadorned, then nearly held her breath in apprehension of his answer.

"I do think I like you far better than I thought I would." A ghost of a laugh shook him. He pulled her closer. "Perhaps a fair amount better. I find you—"

"If you say beautiful I shall like you much less, sir." She smiled and traced the outline of his lips with her fingertip.

"A whole lot less." Her low, seductive tone reminded him of another's, but he could not remember whose.

"I was about to say, remarkable. Outrageous. Amazing. Gentle. Gracious. Intelligent. A good match for my own admirable qualities, not least among which they tell me are my looks and my intellect." He kissed her neck and felt her shiver in response.

"You *are* outrageous."

"So my accusers say."

There were the very ghosts of dimples at the corners of her mouth—an attempt at restraint.

"I am accounted," he said, unwilling to be defeated by a maiden, "a fellow of good repute. Not quarrelsome. Not meddlesome."

"My aunts say I am forward. Impulsive. Given to pranks and flights of fancy."

"A grievous fault."

Her eyes went wide. "I am," she said, "faithful to my promises, chaste—not modest, however."

"I could be faithful. I abhor chastity. I cannot manage modesty."

The dimples did appear.

"You tease me. Wretched man."

"It's hard. Mayhap it'll come easier with practice."

More thunder, closer, rolled out of the east. Overhead the sky was covered, except for the western horizon, with dark clouds. Deso had had enough of thistle tops and stood feet braced and head up, sniffing the wind. Seren, too, stamped and snorted with ears up, rolling her eyes at the thunder.

"Best we be getting back to shelter." He swung her into his arms and carried her to the palfrey.

Chapter Ten

The great hall was far from empty: it was full of men-at-arms, retainers, their servants, their women, a priest tonsured and haughty, a jester or two, a flock of babbling courtiers, a thin surly scattering of thanes and the odd, restless page.

The uproar muted abruptly as they came in. A wind seemed to pass through the hall: a long sigh. All over the room, the gay chatter died. The silence started in waves moving out from where they stood, until one by one all in the hall had become aware of them, and turned to stare quite boldly.

Three paces only had they taken toward the high table where Sir Edmund waited, before his name was called.

"Caer Llion!" Leon's arm stiffened under Brenna's hand. He stopped, pivoted in midstride, and faced the man who hailed him. "What do you do here?"

She looked up to see a tall, dark-haired man coming toward them, lean and elegant, shoulders drawn back arrogantly. He stopped a body's length in front of them, his hands at his waist, his fingers playing with the short dagger that was attached to his belt by a silver chain. For a brief moment the two men looked at each other intently and she could feel the tension in the air between them. The stranger bowed a little to Leon, deeper by a faint degree to her.

Brenna nodded in return and darted Leon a glance. Their eyes held fast an instant. His face was so grim, she laid a staying hand on his arm. What now? Her throat went tight.

Leon inclined his own head not a fraction more than was polite, and said smoothly, "As you see, Hubert, I escort my lady to table."

"Demoiselle." The knight gave her formal greeting. There was arrogance in his face, in the aquiline nose and firm chin, and the narrow, piercing black eyes. "Hubert de Risley, at your service." He cleared his throat. "Caer Llion and I have long been acquaintances."

"Then you are welcome to Dinas Bran, sir."

Hubert strolled away from them and joined a group of young nobles. Leon's eyes glinted upon them all, and flickered around the circle of faces. The faces were all northern faces, like a gathering of black eagles. Their eyes watched; they waited. He could taste their hatred, cold and cruel, like blood and iron.

Leon bowed and advanced down the long hall. His back was erect, his chin up. At his side, Brenna matched his bearing and steadiness.

A ripple of whispers broke out behind them.

"By the saints, a face like that would chase all the devils out of hell."

"By God's blood, whoever he is—he's a dangerous fellow!"

"He brings no men of his own, not even a squire."

"A great destrier with a saddle bound and bossed in silver and a richly embroidered saddlecloth is lodged in the stables."

"Look at those scars. By the finger bone of Saint Stephen, I wouldn't like to meet that one on the battlefield..."

"Or in the bedchamber..."

"Brenna will soon pluck his tail feathers..."

"This is no witless lover but a Christian knight, not one in fear of his soul..."

Brenna's face felt hot, but she smiled at them, slowly,

carefully. Went on smiling until the corners of her mouth hurt. And she carried her head high as she walked with measured tread beside Leon toward Sir Edmund who stood at the far end of the hall beside the dais.

The trumpet sounded. Leon bowed on one knee, his neck bent so that Brenna saw only the thick hair on his head. Beneath huge chain-anchored circles of oil-filled lamps, which lent their own odd pungency to the war of perfumes and the aroma of foods waiting, it burned with metallic gold highlights.

He raised his head, drew a breath. The gathered assembly watched him in silence. He met Sir Edmund's stare. It was dark, still, watchful, waiting. They shared a long look. Sir Edmund inclined his white head, and Leon fancied warmth in his narrow eyes, at least approval of his granddaughter's choice.

"Caer Llion," he said in a ringing voice, and laid a hand over his heart. "Pledged spouse to Brenna."

A sigh ran through the hall, then shouts of approval rang out. Brenna stirred at his left side, her robes rustling, in the silence near the high table. She extended her hand, touching his shoulder to make a gesture for the crowd.

"Rise, beloved knight." She voiced the customary salutation, her voice calm, unruffled.

"Come, sit by me, share the honor of the feast."

Sir Edmund's hand clasped his and set him to the right of the center, in a seat but little lower. The heir's place. Eyes glittered; voices murmured. Not in twice seven years had that chair been filled. This done, Sir Edmund took his own place at the head of the high table, indicating the others join him.

"Make haste. I'm as hungry as a winter pig."

Leon felt his heart more than fill; he felt it loosen from its habitually guarded state. He looked about him in surprised satisfaction, became aware of Brenna's sheer delight, and met Hubert's frown from across the room.

"Looks like the cooks have done us proud." Lady Agnita sat down beside Sir Edmund.

"Looks like." Someone agreed. The woman, he assumed, was Sir Edmund's other sister, Alice, a timid-looking creature with gaunt hollows beneath her cheekbones.

There was a little silence. Then all the guests crowded forward at once toward the long oaken tables covered with white cloths and groaning with food. Platters of venison garnished with herbs and crackling bits of fat, dishes of capon and ham, bowls of stewed field peas, and great wheels of bread were stacked in the middle of the tables. At each place an eating utensil had been placed, and between each a trencher, so it could be shared by each two guests.

Brenna settled down beside Leon to share a trencher, so close his shoulder almost touched her own. Her stomach gave a tiny little flip that became a definite flutter when his sleeve brushed hers. Certainly it was not something for her to go breathless over. But she was. Breathless. Even as she wondered if Leon felt the same, she discarded the idea. He was so composed in his scrutiny of the tables and their occupants that it made her response to his closeness a feminine foolishness.

"Try the wine," Brenna said. "It is brewed from dandelions, and prevents stomach complaints. I made it last summer."

Leon picked up his goblet with a nod and took a deep swallow. It tasted somewhat tart to a tongue accustomed to wine from the finest grapes.

"It is very refreshing," he said, since some acknowledgment of the virtues seemed called for.

Lady Agnita smiled. "How have you found the marches?"

Leon got the message. "It seems a pleasant land, and some have been most hospitable."

The meal drew to a close. They lingered over a dish of nuts and raisins, and the hounds nosed between the trestles for scraps. The door of the hall flew open. A figure filled it.

Leon's blood ran cold from heart to clenched fist. "So," he said softly, as if to himself. "It begins."

Keith Kil Coed strode through the tables, resplendent in blue and silver. Tall even for a northerner and broad with it, he towered above the seated nobles. He stalked to the dais and halted before it. "Your pardon for my lateness, Sir Edmund. The weather kept me longer than I had looked for."

The ruggedness and harshness of his features seemed to reflect the atmosphere of Wales itself, Leon thought. Indeed, he had the undeniable marks of nobility about him—the full brindled beard, battle-bent nose, regal brow, and deep-set eyes of a Cambrian warrior—not the refined bearing or imperious features of the clean-shaven Norman gentry, yet nonetheless the agile poise of a chief, rough-hewn yet proud.

"Sit then, and enjoy the feast."

As if for the first time, Keith's eyes found Leon's. Stopped; widened. A naked devil looked out of his eyes before he lowered his lids but he failed to keep the iron out of his voice.

"What, Sir Edmund! A guest at high table? You do him great honor." His eyes narrowed; his lips thinned. "Is not that seat reserved for Aubrey of Leeds?"

"Aubrey is dead."

"Then shouldn't we be mourning instead of feasting?"

"Caer Llion came with the news and offered himself in Aubrey's stead. Brenna has accepted. They will wed on the Sabbath."

Keith gave Leon a sudden sidelong glance. "Dinas Bran is a rich prize for an ambitious wanderer." His fists clenched on his sword hilt; his face set, expressionless. He stood too still, spoke too softly, coolly, without welcome. "Aren't you going to greet your brethren, Caer Llion?"

Brenna's cup crashed to the table, splattering her with ale.

She did not even notice. Could she have heard right? she thought wildly.

"Brethren? Hardly."

"I can claim that, Caer Llion."

"That's an honor too great for me to affirm."

Brenna started a little as the edge of a blade made a long, harsh scraping sound as it slid from its scabbard. It suggested to her more than any words could have done, that there might be more to this conversation and more to this acquaintance than had seemed at first likely.

"I do not lie." Keith's voice had turned hard and controlled again.

"Is it courtesy that brings you here? Or need? Or simple goodwill?"

"Shall we leave off playing, Caer Llion? Courtesy's a word I don't know the meaning of, northern savage that I am. Need... The day I need the likes of you, my dear brother-in-law, you can be sure I'm in dire straits."

Brother-in-law? Brenna felt the hairs on the back of her neck stand on end. Her jaw tensed, and she felt her stomach lurch, then sink to the pit of her abdomen as if she'd just been stabbed. This was not happening, she thought. Leon could not be married! He was to wed her on the Sabbath!

"Then," Leon said levelly, "it must be goodwill."

"I thought we'd got rid of you. I don't know how you dare show that face in the north again."

"Do not say dare, sir. Dare is not a word to be used to a knight."

Keith laughed, not a pleasant laugh, but pained and boding ill for Leon. "Who would have thought you'd come back? Why are you here?"

"Should you be the only one to gamble fate and fame and fortune on the wind from the north?"

"I am a Welshman. What is your claim?"

"None. I am an outsider," Leon replied, never taking his eyes from Keith's. His shoulders flexed. "And worse. I am the king's justiciar."

Keith laughed. He was laughing too much and too freely. Yes, Brenna thought; there was a scent of wine on him, and something else, sharp, acrid. Hate? Fear? He laughed again, but his eyes glittered beneath the lowered lids.

"Well won again, kinsman. You do our house great honor. You do the devil's work."

"Why, Kil Coed, you have almost a southern wit."

"Truly? I hadn't noticed."

Leon spread his hands. "If you live with polecats, you tend not to notice the stink."

Brenna glanced up at Keith. He was standing very still. Then slowly and deliberately, he uttered the Gaelic word for swine, the most obscene of several curses. And he let out a great breath.

She knew.

She knew by the intent look in his eyes, Keith was about to say something. And it was *bad*.

"It is the price you pay, Ironheart."

Ironheart. The single word flashed through Brenna's mind. They had heard stories of that famed knight. The harper sang how he'd unseated twenty men at a tourney and that in Palestine, in the wars there, he could hack a man or his horse in half with one blow and that the enemy fled before him or surrendered at once.

There were also darker tales, of his marriage to the exquisite Suzanne Kil Coed when he was but a lad. 'Twas evidently a true love match, for with her death in childbirth only five months after the marriage, he went near insane with grief. Rumor had it that his pain was so great he'd made a vow never to wed again and had gone off to fight the Saracens.

"Ironheart." She tested it upon her tongue. *This* was Ironheart! Her dream knight was Ironheart, the most dreaded man in all Christendom!

"The game is well worth the price."

The tension in the hall had risen until it was all but visible.

Sir Edmund stirred at her left hand. He rose suddenly, nearly oversetting his chair.

"Enough," he said, low and harsh. "I will not have you coming to blows in my hall."

"Blows, Sir Edmund? I was but exchanging courtesies with my late sister's husband. I see she left her mark on you, Caer Llion."

Leon's eyes glittered, but his voice was level. "Let be, kinsman, I am in no mood to quarrel—unless you challenge this offer?"

"A marriageable granddaughter, a wandering Crusader—ah, knight. Sir Edmund sees the ravens gathering—knows he cannot command his own barons, who are more apt to war with each other over the lovely Brenna's hand—so, ah, aye, he offers you Brenna with no more than a wedding and an heir-getting. Who would not leap at such an opportunity?"

"Your logic escapes me."

"Sir Edmund is an honest and doting man, as I hear, fond of his sisters, fond of his only grandchild, but with his lords chafing at the bit, and wanting peace in his old age. He sees his demesne foundering for want of an heir—and, if he had such, he needs no alliance with his enemy of long standing. I'm certain he desires no FitzWarren kin in his granddaughter's bed. Besides, he'd put to death any babe with features such as yours." One finger flicked out to gesture at Leon's face.

Leon said politely, "Few try me in the game of insult."

"No one calls me a coward." Keith emphasized the word. "We settle this with a joust. One-to-one. Winner takes all that the loser possesses or claims to possess."

In the distant corner of his mind, Leon knew that he should decline, but Keith's sneering contempt and his own wounded fury were too potent to be rationalized. He felt his lips snarl back. "I always honor the challenges of weak opponents."

"Good. Let our skills be matched two days hence on the

field of honor. Be there. If you are not, I will come after you.''

Leon glared. ''No tricks, Kil Coed.''

''No tricks,'' Keith conceded, but his eyes danced.

Leon left him with a bow and a glance of deep distrust. ''I accept polite defeat. You will taste it at the tourney.''

Leon had not arrived at his chamber above two minutes when Brenna came bursting after him in a high fit of temper.

''You cannot be serious. You cannot do this. You dare not do this.''

''I can, and I can, and I dare,'' Leon said softly, deeply regretting this poor beginning. She was furious with him, and he didn't know which of several things she was mad at.

''You might lose.''

Leon gave a shrug. ''Small chance of that.''

''You would jeopardize your life, our happiness, on the tourney field! That is not the behavior I want in a husband!''

''It is a matter of honor.''

Her mouth opened, her head came up. Her eyes watered. Her chin quivered. ''Honor! What honor is there in accepting such a foolish challenge?''

''There's honor in fighting.''

''There's also honor in not fighting.''

''Honor is something you defend. Sometimes intentionally, sometimes even when it isn't at issue.''

''I want a live husband, not a dead hero!''

''I am a soldier. I gamble swiftly with death.''

''You two should be brothers. You hate each other too absolutely to be anything else!''

''I don't hate him.'' Leon said it as if he believed it. ''Keith's mistaken, 'tis all. Maybe one day he'll accept the truth.''

Brenna gripped his arm, pulling him about. ''Are you really as arrogant as that, or are you simple? Men like Keith don't back down.''

''They can be persuaded to step sidewise.''

"And the moon will dance the sword dance, and the sun will shine all night!"

Leon shook his head. "Your heart is good, Brenna, but I'm afraid you're still too young to understand the lure of power," he said. "Keith lusts after Dinas Bran. He wants it all—the estates, the title—mayhap even you. He'll never have it. But I won't kill him—not intentionally, at least. That I promise."

Brenna's eyes met his. As he looked into them, he again had the feeling that he had done so before. A picture flashed through his mind...those black eyes gazing down at him with an expression of longing and desire...and then the picture was gone, leaving him strangely unsettled and tense.

"You know who I am." It was not a question.

"Caer Llion."

"Caer Llion, but most call me Ironheart, for that is the name by which I am known."

"By now most of the castle knows it. The servants have ears and tongues, and you have not denied it."

Which made him the villain in the case.

"I didn't lie to you," he said. "I simply did not reveal the truth."

"Leon..." Whatever Brenna was going to say, she stopped, then just took on a hurt look. He did not know why. Not exactly. He guessed he'd been unfair, and he'd burst the bubble of false trust. "Why did you..." she started to ask.

But she didn't finish that, either. She just stared at him, confused, hurt, and looked upset with him, or the situation, or something maybe he'd led her to think. He couldn't tell. Maybe it was even real, but he'd thought that before. It wasn't reasonable it could be true now, when he didn't even know her, except she'd enchanted him as a child and that she liked lavender and honeycakes and was lots of fun.

Still, she was not a woman, he had thought, who would use tears. But she turned away in the best tragic style and wiped at her eyes furiously. He was angry, then, seeing her set upon him with such common tactics.

"I'm sorry," he said. He meant it. "I was delighted by your acceptance and now—" Devastated by your coldness, he could finish in courtly fashion. But it would be a mistake to enter that ground with this woman, he thought, because she would not quickly abandon the matter he set between them. "Now," he said, with utter honesty, "I see that you have reservations that did not at all enter our previous negotiations. I swear I shall keep my word. I am sad if you think badly of me. Common sense constrains that. So…you are not obliged to accept my suit."

"Forgive me," she said. "I had not intended to do this." She stayed with her back turned. Wiped at her eyes. "You could have trusted me. Told me yourself. Not let me find out in front of a hall full of people."

She hit right on it, and the lump in his throat wouldn't go away. He was scared of that little, little step she was asking, to trust, to love, everything he'd tried to give away, too long, too desperately, until he'd learned strong people didn't want it and weak ones drank you dry.

But he'd hurt Brenna. God's teeth, it wasn't fair of her to be mad—*he* was mad, and hurt, that she was mad.

"It is not in me to trust," he said coldly. He felt more than angry. He felt rejected, the ground giving way under his feet; a man stung in his personal hopes, answering in temper. "This is hard for me to…I was married once, to Keith's sister, Suzanne. If not your love, Brenna, at least I hope to win your good regard. I never wished to imply anything else."

Brenna looked slowly around at him, and turned and stared at him as if she by no means believed it. The fact that he wanted her pleased her enormously. She considered the serious set of his face and the determination that gleamed in his eyes. She didn't know what regard should look like, but she supposed that at a time like this it was important that the man be serious and determined.

One settled for half, if there was no hope of the whole.

Whatever Leon expected her to say, it was not to change the subject completely. "What was Suzanne like?"

For some reason her words stunned him. He didn't understand how or why, but they did. His frown deepened so that two vertical lines appeared between his eyes. His hand went to his face. He brought it down sharply and clasped it behind him, scowling down the proud arch of his nose.

"She was beautiful," he said, thinking how incredibly hard *those* words were, even when you didn't mean them.

Brenna heard the raw scrape of grief in his voice. His face was rigid. She dared not ask more, for fear of breaking the wound wide open. She thought that she ought to have said nothing at all, but she was never skilled at keeping quiet. She exhaled sharply.

Leon wondered what she had thought of saying, and realized he had held his breath. Did she know? Did she suspect? He had no idea. He wasn't about to ask her, either, not when she seemed to have settled down a bit.

"May I kiss you?" she asked.

Leon said nothing. Neither did he move away from her. She took his silence for assent. Softly her lips met his. It was a brief, delicate kiss, warm and tender. His arms came up, embraced her. She pushed him back, hands on his shoulders.

"What's wrong?" he asked. His voice seemed thick and strange.

"Nothing," she said. There was nothing at all to her voice. "You don't think you can trust me yet. I'll show you how wrong you are. But no more secrets, Leon. I can't stand that."

His heart jumped and started hammering. "There *is* something...I haven't told you, but I can't just...it happened a long time ago."

Brenna smiled at him. Her eyes were liquid, dark as midnight. A finger came up to touch his lips. "No. You don't trust me, yet. But I'll lay you a wager, Leon. Before this year is out, you'll trust me. You'll do it willingly, and you'll do it gladly, without the least regret.''

Leon rubbed his cheek as if the scar pained him. ''I could only do that if I loved you more than life itself.''

''I know that,'' Brenna said lightly but not in jest. ''What will you lay on it?''

''My soul.'' Leon smiled through set teeth. ''And you? What stakes can you offer?''

''Why, anything. Anything at all.''

''What? How are you going to manage that?''

Her face exploded with laughter. ''Don't ask questions. You be there in chapel on the Sabbath and I'll be there. Just trust me.''

He wanted to trust her, he wanted so much to trust her, and that was the most dangerous thing....

It was a dazzling morning, all sign of rain having been swept from the sky and the air brisk and keen. The hunt was gathering, with guests and grooms mixed with horses, hounds and a handful of agile pigeons. Confusion reigned for a moment in the small yard. The commotion caught Brenna by surprise, making her heart beat faster. Colors and edges seemed both bright and unreal this morning. The steward, Robert, was shouting at the grooms. The milkmaid was flirting with a knot of squires.

They were mounting in the larger courtyard when Keith jerked his beast's neck and sent it crashing into Leon's charger. Both the stallions reared, bared their teeth, whistled. Leon hauled on the reins and Deso snorted and came back down on all four hooves.

Brenna looked at Keith, then at Leon. Leon had been in the midst of settling in his saddle when his stallion reared. She was glad to see it had not ruffled his balance at all, he was nicely set in the saddle. He backed Deso away from the other charger.

''Well, Caer Llion,'' Keith drawled. ''Glad to see you're

ready for the hunt, and still as good a rider as you ever were.''

Leon glanced at Brenna, who made a warning sign to him to restrain himself. He picked up the triangular shield, slid his left arm through the handle, gripped it with his fist.

Malice prevailed. He said, in elaborately polite court dialect, ''I wish I could say it of you, Keith. You should know better than to spook anything trained by me. Surely you must remember what little you did learn.''

The formal French was impeccably scathing. Keith looked startled. He edged his mount back ten paces. ''Please excuse me, my beast needs the exercise.'' He made a big circle well clear of Deso, nodded to Brenna, and went off.

A slow smile started on Leon's face, as if he found the whole thing amusing. Brenna settled back in her saddle pleased to see Leon hook Keith like a fish. But she couldn't help but wonder why Keith was so intent on baiting Leon.

''A skittish morning,'' she ventured to say.

''So it seems.''

''I'm not convinced this is a good idea,'' she murmured.

Around them, other members of the hunt were mounting, cursing the hounds that barked and wandered about the courtyard. One of the hounds was nipping at the horses' hooves and was wreaking havoc among the mounting riders. Hubert de Risley angled his steed through the suddenly boisterous assembly until he was alongside Keith. She saw them talking in low tones before they joined the main company.

''Watch those fellows,'' she said fiercely. ''They are up to no good.''

When Leon glanced around, no one seemed to be looking exactly at him. One of the huntsmen passed around a wineskin. Keith took a monstrous slug from it, swaggering in his saddle.

''You don't mind if I don't take your word for it…at least not yet.''

''I think you provoked him too far, Leon.''

''*I?* I provoked?''

"Yes. Keith looks as if he's had a hard night."

"I wouldn't have guessed. He seems to be in fine form."

"Just watch him carefully. I haven't the faintest notion what he's up to, but it's bad."

"Do I have eyes in the back of my head?"

One of the huntsmen near them turned in his saddle. He was of middle years, with gray-streaked hair and a neat clipped beard; he was also cut across the nose with an old white sword mark. He was from Rhewl, come for the oath-swearing. "Keith's pushing it, drinking away his sensibility. He's very good for this area, of course, and loyal as a burr, but it would be stupid to take some wound just for the follies of that young bull."

Brenna grimaced. "Alain—"

Leon lifted one hand. "It's good to see a man who's loyal. It's also good to see one speaks his mind and stand up for the real virtues. Who are you?"

"Alain of Rhewl. I was at Acre with Brenna's father, Tristan. I'll keep an eye on Keith." He smiled, looking modest and embarrassed. "If you need anything on the hunt, or after, call on me."

"Thank you. I will."

Alain nodded and turned his beast and rode sedately away to take his position in line.

Brenna touched heel to Seren's side; the mare danced forward, head up. "Alain retired from the Hospitalers to straighten out his properties—he was a fierce fighter and got captured at Antioch. He was released on a private ransom given to some of Richard's men, after nearly dying of starvation."

"A good man to have on your side."

The line of riders finally began, in a straggling formation, to leave the courtyard. With hounds in the lead they rode out the iron-barred gates, gate guards standing to sharp attention to salute them.

"My lord is magnanimous today."

Leon met Brenna's bright mirthful gaze and laughed. "My lady is full of compliments."

"Does that please you?"

Leon drew a deep breath. "It sings in me." He spread his arms wide, which, by more than chance, was the signal for the hunt to begin.

Above the shouts, the thud of hooves and rattle of weapons, a hunting horn blared a single sustained note, and then the hunt charged forward in a roar of motion. The horses sprang forward. The huntsmen roared.

Horses whinnied, clods of soil were flung from pounding hooves, and the smell of excitement filled the air as they began the downward course...numerous enough for an armed venture rather than a ride for pleasure.

Whooping and yelling, the riders pursued a wild pig. It was an old male, with long tusks and small eyes. Consigned to a solitary existence, it roamed the countryside, eating acorns and tender roots. There had been nothing on its small blank mind but food until the hunters flushed it from its tranquility.

Two or three young hellions spurred after it, baying like hounds on the scent, but the boar was lean and leggy, very quick. It started to run, then twisted and doubled back, trying to get past the riders. Its eyes glittered with viciousness, and it made huffing sounds through its snout.

"Circle behind him!"

Leon threw one of his spears, but the shaft glanced off the boar's tough hide. The pig changed direction. It hurtled past its pursuers, heading toward a slight hummock where a stand of oak trees loomed and below which the land fell away toward a patch of bog. The riders were hard behind it, shouting to each other and laughing, but they had to skirt the bog and the boar beat them to the woods. They could hear it crashing through the young growth along the edge.

The dogs plunged after it, snapping and barking. A half dozen of the hunt decided to pursue the animal. If they could get close enough, they might still manage a lucky spear throw into ear or eye.

"Stay here!" Leon ordered Brenna and the other women. "This could be dangerous."

The riders were forced to dismount as no horse could penetrate the thicket. When they burst into it, they found no undergrowth marred the heart of the oak stand, and the hunters were able to encircle their quarry. Leon and Keith, rivalries forgotten in the excitement of the moment, were trying to keep the boar between them until one could get a clear throw at it. The boar was so enraged by now that its grunts turned into squeals of anger.

Lowering its head, it charged.

Keith dodged. Tusks sharper than knives missed him by inches. The boar wheeled in a tight circle and immediately charged again. Keith hurled his spear, a wild throw that missed the pig but flew directly at Leon.

There was no warning whatsoever. Leon heard nothing until the shout. A hoarse, "Blood of the Martyrs!" that seemed to fill the copse like thunder.

Alain of Rhewl hurled himself, striking Leon with his own body in the instant before the spear hit home. The two of them fell together as the animal rushed past. Leon had only a fleeting glimpse of the weapon before it thudded into an oak immediately behind where he had been standing.

Men drew back a little, swords ready; the quivering spear was still wedged in the tree beside him. The boar spun around and came a third time, straight at its two most vulnerable tormenters.

Leon rolled to his feet in one motion and flung a dagger. The swine, heading toward him, took it in the eye. Its forelegs collapsed after a few faltering steps. Squealing, the wild pig plowed its murderous tusks into the soft earth as it fell.

A whoop and a howl heralded the boar's demise. It was loud in the spreading silence. Ears strained; breathing quietened.

"That spear missed killing me by a whisker. Have you gone stark mad, Keith?"

"I am so sorry…"

"Yes," Leon said coldly, "so am I. Pity there's no proof 'twas not a wild throw."

Keith turned and stumbled out of the clearing. Brenna came running up then, clutched at Leon's elbow.

"Leon! Are you all right? Alain?"

Shaking his head to clear it, Alain sat up. Seeing Brenna's worried face looking down at him, he forced a shaky laugh. "Aye. Though I'm not so sure about those lads of yours."

Leon glanced 'round. The squires had drawn themselves into a line at his back, and their eyes were bright and hard. All his sternness melted; he loosed his rare and splendid smile.

"Put those swords away, boys." He leaned down and offered Alain his hand. "That was a mad thing to do, Alain."

"Mad," Alain agreed, panting. "I thought you were hit."

"I thought I was, too. Most ingenious and classic—it nearly worked. Pity Keith is such an abominable marksman."

They looked at each other and began to laugh.

Chapter Eleven

The village, as any other, had its square: wide enough and varied enough to rouse even Leon's respect. For once it was not raining. The wind blew softly, bringing with it familiar smells and sounds: a stall with a reek of beer and spiced wine about it; a clamor of men and the odd shriek of a woman's laughter; someone singing, the clatter of a drum, the sudden sweetness of a flute.

The Blue Boar was a small public house, no more than a booth, to the side of the village green. So small it was that its patrons were obliged to seat themselves on stools in the square outside. When Leon and Brenna arrived, there was already a crowd gathered, enjoying the brief sunshine.

One of the regular patrons espied her and called, "Lady Brenna! I knew you'd be comin' along this way. I've been waiting."

Ambrose One-Eye was truly ancient. A veteran of the Second Crusade, he was a great teller of tales. With a few drinks under his belt, he would spin and weave wonderful sagas of magic and drama and suspense such as legends are made on.

"Young Bronwen gave me something especially for you." Ambrose One-Eye leaned down and, from beneath his seat, produced a posy, a pretty thing of daisies, pinks, primrose, hyssop and tiny meadow flowers.

Brenna's eyes widened in delight. She thanked him with a kiss on his weathered cheek. "I'll carry them on the Sabbath."

"I wish you well, young sir. Brenna will make a fine wife. See you make her happy."

"I will," Leon said stoutly.

"I'll hold you to that. My hands shake from too many years and too much ale, but they can still hold a sword."

"I see you drink wisely," Leon remarked, pointing to the old man's tankard. "A pint of ale keeps you hale. A draft of wine makes a man pine."

"All men drink wisely when they first begin. It's later on they run into trouble."

"You speak like a man of some experience."

"Seeing as I'm probably thrice your age, you may well be right, young fellow."

A dark-haired youth of some twenty summers came, stone cider jug in hand, to sit on the bench opposite the old man.

"Is your name Ambrose One-Eye by any chance? I thought it must be! Then you're the fellow who started the legend that the Holy Grail was brought to Wales?"

"'Tis no legend, me lad, but the honest truth, though as you can see, fate has thrust me among the ignorant." The old man's grin showed toothless gums.

Raising the pitcher to his lips, the youth took several hard gulps. "Tell us then, old man. Tell us your tale."

"Aye," Ambrose One-Eye said, glancing at the company gathered outside the taproom. He got to his feet, fumbling for a coin. "But my throat is bone dry. I canna tell a tale with a tongue that is thirsty as the desert sand."

The young man laughed, head thrown back, dark hair rippling over his collar. "Drink up, Ambrose One-Eye, and I'll buy you another. A man with a drink in his hand tells a better tale than one without."

"There is a desert directly to the north of Jerusalem, a

dry, peeling, curling desert, like a plain of shattered yellow pottery. We met the Saracens there. They came down from the dunes—they came screaming—I was wounded. I don't know how long I lay there in those dun-colored sands. I was weak from the terrible injuries I'd received and stricken with death chills. Then I saw a silver cup floating in the sandy air, and I heard a voice tell me, *Drink of my cup. Drink and live.*''

Leon's heart slammed against the wall of his chest. There was that legend again. Everyone seemed to have something to add to it.

''Northern lies.''

''Plain truth. The moment the cup touched my lips, a spasm shook me. As I drank a liquor of cold fire, a radiance shone. From out of that blinding light appeared the figure of Our Lord Jesus Christ—and I knew at once that it was the very cup from which Jesus had drunk at the Last Supper.''

Leon glanced at Brenna. And there she was, utterly still, all rapt attention, listening to the drunken old man's ramblings with every appearance of belief. Her face shone.

''The old man's tale is intriguing, is it not?'' he whispered.

''I've heard it dozens of times and it still enthralls me,'' she whispered back.

''You say you saw Our Savior?'' someone asked.

''No. I saw only the Grail and the tongues of flame wagging in the air about Him. He cried, 'Whom doth the Grail serve?' Then it was over. The Grail was gone. The flames and the luminous clouds were gone. I wept. I was not worthy to behold such a miracle, to feel the warmth of the Presence, to smell the fragrance of heaven. Why did He choose me if I was not worthy? It has puzzled me for nigh on three-score years.''

He ran out of wind and words alike and lost the thread of his thoughts altogether. Murmurs ruffled through the throng.

"'Whom doth the Grail serve?' There's a minstrel's song in this, old man. Have another drink."

Ambrose One-Eye drank again, wiping his mouth on the back of his hand. Behind aged eyes, wise with years, wicked with memory, the story shaped itself, and the loose tongue fumbled for the words.

"When I came to myself, I was with the Hospitalers at Tyre. They told me Arthur of Rhuddlan had found me, tended my wounds, and taken me there. I told my tale to others. Some believed me, but most laughed, not having seen the miracle themselves. Arthur tried to convince me that the Lord had merely sent me a dream to blot out the sufferings of my long and grievous illness."

"This Arthur was Lady Agnita's husband?"

"Aye. When my lord Arthur left Palestine, he could see that, though my body was mended, my mind was still weak, so he brought me to Wales with him."

"And the cup?" someone cried out.

"The cup?"

"Aye. The one you've been telling us about while you drank the ale we paid for!"

Ambrose One-Eye gave Leon a bright glance from under his single eye, and elaborately tapped his forehead. "I am befuddled by the ale." He paused, his voice trailing off into an old man's quiver. "I cannot recall, other than that it will be found by a lad with a white-eyed dog."

As one might expect, Leon thought, the listeners were not pleased.

"Is he dim?"

"Senile old fool, morelike. Go get someone else to buy your ale, old man, and tell your lies to them."

"Pay them no heed, Ambrose," Brenna implored in a low voice. "Come, Leon and I will take you to your daughter, Bronwen."

The village was full of knights, some merely lounging about, others gambling with dice, others chatting or quarreling, still others quite visibly drunk for so early in the day. Villagers and villeins were there, too, enjoying the fair. There was laughter, now, and good humor, but not quite free good humor: Leon marked that; and the conversation was on the weather and how the rains hung on longer than in other years, and how it delayed the spring planting, which would mean a late harvest, and if the frosts came early, there'd be a shortage of food next winter.

It informed him, it was interesting, yet the barons and the locals were easing their way carefully through harmless subjects, and the looks that flew from himself to Brenna and from Brenna to himself were not always happy looks.

"Bold as brass," someone said as they strolled through the streets.

"Hush!" another warned fiercely. "Ears can hear."

"And so they should! Why, I've heard tell—"

One changed knife hands to make a sign over his heart, hasty and afraid. The others looked afraid, too, and backed away, all to the other side of the passageway.

Brenna edged her way through the press of people. She knew what they had heard. Everyone was hearing it. She glanced sideways. Leon bared his teeth in a feral grin, the light flickering through his ruffled hair as he walked. His hand caressed the hilt of his sword.

"Murdered the betrothed, he did, or so they say."

"When they're not saying that he saved Keith Kil Coed's life."

"Saved it! Why, Keith lured the young lord away from the hunt and actually tried to—"

"Be a good thing if he had. A foreigner come to wed our Brenna. At least Keith's a proper northerner." The speaker was as hairy as he was big, with tousled black locks and a bristling blue-black beard. He looked down at Leon from his intimidating great height, and his voice was disdainful when he boomed loudly, "This is pure stable muck with a piecrust on it!"

"Who threatens me?" Leon wanted to know.

"I am Edgar, Captain of the Gate."

Leon frowned. "Is there not a gate to guard?"

Edgar's teeth gleamed. "D'you think we've insulted him, then, m'lady?"

Leon casually shifted his balance. He smiled amiably at the captain of the gate. "I pray you think of your mother and that you are not her only son."

Brenna caught at his elbow. "Leon, this is Grandy's own captain!"

"Bluster, no more," he growled under his breath for her ears alone. More collected now, he thought perhaps he did go too far, and 'twould be wise to stop. To go on might please this intense fellow, and might even do some good; but truth still went begging, and judgment should come more slowly. He forced a grin for Brenna's sake.

"Seems you're a bit of a hothead," he said loudly.

"It's a knack I've got," the captain said, shrugging.

"Oh—" Leon would have brushed it off, made some careless answer, but somehow that wouldn't do for Brenna. She always seemed to look closer at him than anyone ever had, close enough to know bluster or the smallest lie. His grin faded to honesty. "Me, too. I've no quarrel with that. But it must be tempered with caution and courage to make a good soldier."

They looked at each other in a silence of impasse. The captain sighed, lifted a low-lidded, hooded gaze, and drew away. He frowned and tangled his fingers into his beard.

"I must go," he mumbled uncomfortably. "I'm meeting my sergeant down by the river. We practice for the jousting."

Leon did not speak until Edgar had disappeared into the crowd. "It is just as well that I should know the truth, and know who is against me and who is not. That man truly resents having me around."

"Oh, I dispute that. Why would anyone resent you?" Brenna tried to smile, but it turned upside down. "I mean it. You are all that Dinas Bran needs and I want."

Leon flushed. "What you want and what the locals want are two different things. Locals don't like outsiders coming to live with them, mayhap change the way things are done."

"It's worse than I thought," Brenna confided, her throat tight. "I doubt there is anything to be feared at the moment, but it is best we do have some caution," she whispered.

"Prudent counsel. Let's out of here."

She lifted her hand to his chin, turning his head to her, looking into his face. Sudden tears burned behind her eyes. "I can't bear for them to think ill of you. I want everyone to love you as I do."

Leon tried to speak, couldn't, and hugged her instead, and held on to her until he could trust his voice. "Don't fret. They will have other things to think about. The jousting, for instance, that should keep *everyone's* attention, and the wedding—"

Brenna laughed and led him deeper into the maze of tents and stalls and booths. "Where may I take you? Would you like to watch the wrestling matches? Or would you like to wander down to the horse fair? Well, where shall we go?"

She smiled at him.

He smiled at her.

"I know an excellent sitting-out place if my lady will deign to accompany me," he said. "A corner where we can see without being seen—always an advantage, you will allow."

"You seem to know this place rather well," she observed as she suffered him to lead her away.

He smiled shrewdly. "A wise general always studies his ground," he said.

The chosen corner certainly had the advantage of privacy. It was an alcove at the end of one of the long narrow passages with which the village abounded. There an elm tree grew in a tiny flagged courtyard, and a bench was set under it.

Brenna chuckled. "Oh, Aunt Alice would be shocked if she heard about this—no one else in sight."

Her woolen gown was very fine, and when Leon sat beside her he caught the sweet, earthy pungence of her skin mixed with subtle hints of herbs and lavender. She was the essence of female: bright mystery, clothed in beauty.

Leon stared down at the delicate fingers entwined in his. Odd memories kept floating into his head. Disturbing. Arousing.

The heat crawled up his face. His feelings for Brenna had been veering between passion and protection, between wanting to take care of her and take her to bed. His emotions were complicated now by a great surge of tenderness, a sentiment he'd had little experience with.

"I feel like a refugee," he said.

"No, you have found sanctuary." She sounded very sincere. Those lovely dark eyes did not waver, her gaze as trusting and innocent as a fawn's.

He reached out and touched her soft cheek, and ran a single finger along the line of her jaw. She closed her eyes, her lips parting temptingly. His fingers slid from her cheek, came to rest upon her throat. She smiled without opening her eyes, a dimple flashing.

Leon put his hand on her shoulder and drew it down, slow and caressing, down along her sleeve to her wrist. She had to hold her breath to stop from sighing, and she was suddenly aware of every inch of skin, tingling, aching.

"I've never met anyone like you."

The timbre of his voice caused a melting sensation between her thighs. It reminded her of their night together. She wanted to run her hands over him, to savor all the texture of his tawny hair with her palms and fingertips, to taste his lips, his cheeks, his eyelashes, his shoulders, to trace every velvet shadow on his body with the tip of her tongue...

Her breath came out in an audible rush when she opened her eyes once more. "That makes us even. I've never met anyone like you, either."

Her voice was too husky, but Brenna was helpless to change it. Something in Leon's eyes was making her blood shimmer wildly through her body, leaving chaos in its wake. Motionless, she waited for him to say something. She saw the sudden expansion of his pupils, heard the intake of his breath, sensed the hot leap of his blood. His mouth came down over hers. The taste of him swept through her, making her tremble.

It took an immense amount of willpower for Leon to end the kiss. He held her tightly, fiercely, while he fought for breath, for control, for the discipline of mind and body that he had learned at such great cost and had taken for granted for so many years. He forced himself to loosen his arms from around Brenna.

"Leon? What's wrong?"

Leon saw the yearning and the uncertainty in Brenna's wide dark eyes, and let out his breath in an explosive hiss. He came to his feet in a lithe rush.

"Nothing. I'm hungry. Are you?" His voice was too deep, too thick, telling of the heavy running of his blood.

"Hungry?" Brenna blinked. "Yes. I'm…hungry."

"There slinks the southern dog. The gall of the man! Walking in and expecting to be honored so."

"Aye, this used to be a pretty good place for company, but it's going off sadly by the look of things."

Leon had been offending no one. He'd found himself loitering by a stall spilling over with gaudy silks, contemplating a bit of frippery and the girl to whom he would give it. A cold feeling spread all down his back into his legs. His eyes flicked once toward the voice, and his lips peeled back from his teeth.

"Leon," Brenna hissed, "don't do that! You'll scare everyone—and I want them to hold you in high regard!"

"Too bad! Do them good to see the truth!"

"It's also another way to alienate them."

"Saint Charity is dead and her daughter Clemency is ailing."

Brenna placed a warning hand on his arm, and stood mute at his side. They had come full circle of the village and were again outside the Blue Boar. One or two knights were there lounging on benches under an awning and already well into their cups.

"Do you know what Ironheart'll do when he's lord of the northern marches? He'll command all the lords to shave their beards and make them swear to serve him as slaves serve their masters," Keith Kil Coed judged sourly.

"Except that he wouldn't," one said, refilling his cup, "and that's why he'll accept our fealty and leave us free to govern our own lands as we choose—as does Sir Edmund."

They were men divided by old loyalties, Leon thought, and men still divided by their opinions, not all of which he had heard. And more than that had risen to trouble him. He had judged the temper of the village itself as one thing—but he judged the temper of the barons as another. It was far more complex a weave, and shot through with betrayals and old jealousies; and it did not give him comfort at all in what he had heard.

Far past caution, Keith snorted. "Shall I bow to that interloper? Shall I forget what Ironheart did to my sister? By all the saints and the powers below, I will not! I will kill him first." His hand fell to his dagger.

He keeps using that title today, mused Leon. Trying to needle me, I have no doubt. It's working, too. He edged a pace to one side and fixed himself into an easy stance. However, his muscles were taut, like coiled springs, ready to leap into action. He shrugged.

"Don't press me too far, Kil Coed. Have a care for your neck. I am not immune."

Someone cried out loud. Leon pushed Brenna behind him. She spun, eyes wide and fixed. Dropping into a crouch, Keith wove patterns in the air with his dagger. The weapon was a live thing. Leon's weight shifted forward onto the balls of his feet. Old tactics, and effective, he thought. Separate the enemy from his allies; surround him and conquer.

"Don't be a fool, Kil Coed." Leon stood, hands loose, watching Keith. Without tensing or raising his voice, Leon knew how it would be. All three knights were looking at him. Something deep stirred in him.

Keith made a lunge at Leon who twitched aside. Where his heart had been, a black blade clove the air.

Leon murmured softly, "What am I, then? Your practice stroke?"

"Do you know how many men have taken this test, Ironheart? And how many passed it?"

The blade flashed so close to Leon's cheek that surely it was shaven anew. He laughed sharp and fierce, a supreme gesture of contempt and success. "Tell me. I do not know."

Keith cursed him. He lunged again, and this time Leon blocked it, his hand closed hard upon the knight's wrist. The dagger fell, Brenna after it, snatching it, wheeling about, cat-quick, cat-fluid. Hubert de Risley, at one side, sounded as if he was swearing seriously and at risk of his soul, under his breath.

"There is little need of this, Keith. We meet on the morrow, so let be today." Now the thing was done, Leon felt the coiled violence go slack in him. He released Keith's wrist.

"Clear out, the lot of you. Go sober up. On the morrow I take up Kil Coed's challenge and you will renew all fealties."

"Imagine that! On bended knee before the great Ironheart." Hubert de Risley licked a spot of ale off his lips and smiled.

Leon knew Keith Kil Coed's weak spots, and he knew how to exploit them. It came down to one thing in the end. It always had. What he wanted, he intended to have.

"As I live and breathe, I'll not lower myself so."

A massive form lunged at him. Leon wheeled, slamming into the big knight. Air exploded from his lungs; he fell backward. Keith virtually flew away from him, crashing sprawled on the stone floor beside the well—mainly because Leon used the slick mud and the force of his own wild off-balance swing against him.

The force of Keith's fall caused the well handle to spin out of control, sending the big wooden bucket to the bottom with a splash. Keith surged to his feet, stepped back as he gathered himself to renew his struggle.

Brenna shouted, "No! I forbid this!"

It was Keith who answered her. A sound only as he toppled backward into the well, a low sigh that reverberated from the damp stones to the water below, so that all that could be heard by the breathless spectators was a soggy splash, an echo, melancholy as the song of a wild bird.

Someone raced over and began to turn the winch, to bring up the bucket to which Keith was clinging. For a moment he hung there gasping. Then he muttered sullenly, groggily scrambled to his feet, and went off holding his grimed hands away from his sides. Since his clothes were ruined, it was a futile effort.

Hubert de Risley's rasping voice interrupted. "Four men tried to assassinate Kil Coed, and came under his sword for it. None of them lived." He made a sharp hand gesture at Keith. "There's good reason for you to be trembling in your skin."

Leon raked his face with a swift cold look. He said, "Any other good advice, Hubert?"

Hubert de Risley's chin lifted a degree. "Caer Llion, my friend stands in sore need of tending. Have I your leave?"

A kind of awe settled over the bystanders. It took a breath, then an effervescent murmuring commenced. Leon glanced around at the younger men, who were tittering behind their hands. The senior men muttered, knotting into fierce little groups with rumpled brows, jabbing fingers punctuating their talk as odds were given and bets taken.

As expected, Leon sighed to himself. It was invariably necessary to fight or outbluff the local tyrant whenever he took on a new position. What made it worse this time was that the resident bully had been Suzanne's brother and Brenna's likely lover.

"They won't forget that little stunt," Brenna said.

"That was the whole point. I meant them to be impressed. That's the language they understand."

All through the lower hall the household staff, with mops and buckets, fought back the thin gloss of mud the traffic brought from the courtyard. Brenna met Keith coming down the hall, while on her way to her workshop with a basket of old bread.

"Brenna, don't do it. There must be any number of ways to break the contract. Caer Llion's visage alone—"

"I'm not concerned with his face," Brenna said sharply.

"Who doesn't flinch when they look at him?"

"*Stop it,* Keith. You're being ridiculous."

"Give me that." Very coolly, he relieved her of her burden.

She did not answer or make response of any sort to his greeting. She walked along the corridor and into the workshop with leaden feet. The smile had died utterly from her face.

He followed her with the utmost composure, and placed the basket on one of the shelves. But there was no lack of resolution about her when she turned to face him.

Abruptly she spoke, in her voice a ring of something that was almost ferocity. "Keith, why don't you just go away quietly, accept things as they are?"

He raised his eyebrows slightly without replying.

But Brenna was not to be so silenced. Her hands fastened with determination upon the front of his surcoat. "You face me, Keith Kil Coed," she said. "And answer me honestly. Why do you plan such mischief against my chosen husband?"

"To settle old scores."

"There is no need to tread over old quarrels—what is

done is done and we should concern ourselves with what lies ahead.''

"A noble sentiment but one which I am not quite prepared to look upon. I'll leave you to your sulfurous magic.''

"You'll go nowhere till I've done with you.''

He stood motionless, suffering her restraining hands, a smile upon his lips. "As I've told you many a time, Brenna, I am very much at your service.''

"Keith,'' she said, and her voice quivered, "if there's any honest feeling in you, if you are capable of a single spark of affection, of allegiance, you'll turn around right now and go back to Craignant.''

"That so? I thought you seemed mightily pleased to see me. Caer Llion will betray you as he betrayed Suzanne.''

"That is most unkind.''

"Unkind? *Unkind?* Caer Llion has all he can ask for. All his ambitions are fulfilled, overlord of a great estate, new vassals to do his bidding, and a pretty wife to pleasure his bed. But I—I have had the entire prize snatched from my hands.''

"You never had it,'' she pointed out serenely.

"I did before you cast me aside for another. Then he died. I heard the news, I was overjoyed. And now Ironheart comes and claims all. And leaves me with nothing. Nothing.''

She spread her hands. "Keith, be reasonable. I never gave you any encouragement, or any indication your offer would be accepted.''

"Nothing," he repeated with vicious softness.

"Why do you hate Leon?'' Brenna asked. "What has he done to you?''

"He was born,'' Keith said bluntly. His knuckles grayed as he gripped his sword hilt. "Of all the errors of my life, the greatest was to allow Suzanne to go to Whittington as companion to Hawyse FitzWarren. She was my twin sister, and she was pure gold. And Caer Llion killed her.''

Brenna felt her face drain of color. No, she thought angrily, eyes stinging and dazed. Dread mounted. Outrage drove it back. Her faith in Leon was no mere thistledown to be so lightly scattered.

"That is not true! Suzanne died in childbirth, and the infant three days later. Aunt Alice told me so!"

"Only because her heart was broken." His eyes challenged hers. "Do recall that Ironheart could do to you what he did to his wife—betray your trust with forsworn promises."

"Keith," she said with sudden passionate urgency, "do not cause havoc in the marches. Caer Llion has honor. He has the king's blessing. Swear fealty and return to Craignant. Keep the peace."

"Ah, no," said Keith. "You won't turn me back now. It was too late for that when I saw him seated in your father's chair, acknowledged heir to Dinas Bran."

"Keith, you hold my happiness between your hands. Don't pursue this feud."

There fell a silence. Brenna clasped her hands and strove to compose herself. She wondered what was passing through his mind as he stood there, staring straight before him. Had she managed to reach his heart? she wondered. She had always believed that after his own savage fashion he loved her.

"I have to," he said slowly, his dark eyes fixed on hers. "Haven't you ever had to do things, been forced to do them?"

"I try to stay true to myself, if that's what you mean," she confessed to him, and he smiled most sweetly at her.

"You're so bloody good, Brenna. Always on the straight and narrow. Well, it's not the way the world is working."

A sudden trembling took her lower lip. "Just wish me happy, Keith," she whispered. "Please."

He sighed, drew her into his arms, and kissed the top of her head. "I do, Brenna. I do. You know how much I do."

At first Leon thought his ears tricked him. No one walked for pleasure beneath these dim trees, so whoever it was meant no good. He crouched low behind a thicket, and gestured for Brenna to be still.

He put his hand on the hilt of his sword. At least—and the realization came to him in a comforting rush like the warmth of a fire on a winter's day—he was rather better armed than he had been the last time something untoward began to happen. The weapon was a reassuring weight in his hand.

Brenna trembled, a sudden spasm, and knelt on the damp ground, hooded falcon motionless upon her wrist, and willed the bird to be silent. Her shoulders braced, the muscles taut between them; her free hand closed in a fist over the jesses. The falcon neither moved nor uttered a sound.

They had ridden to the woods, dismounted near the edge of the forest and tethered the horses, intending to trial Brenna's young falcon on the blackbirds that seemed to infest every branch. The air was full of their cries, yet there was another sound, more sinister, the shuffling of feet in the undergrowth.

The dim air stirred and thickened. Someone paced on the other side of the clearing. A deep and familiar voice said, "Sir Edmund usually has good reasons for this kind of thing, Hubert, you know that. You're restless as a child."

"I merely pray we're not facing some new disaster!"

"Brenna's marriage is first priority."

"So he summons us all and lets us sit waiting. He must have a good reason, yes, certainly. Keith, some of the barons have got very tedious lately. It's time you shook them up a bit."

"Get me to do your dirty work? Shame, Hubert."

"Sir Edmund's lot has been snubbing me lately, and spreading the most astounding rumors about me."

"The place is full of rumors now the demise of Aubrey of Leeds has become known. He was a tolerable choice—your insistence on his execution may not have been wise, Hubert, particularly as the alternative is Caer Llion."

At Brenna's sudden intake of breath, Leon's hand tightened on her arm. He gave her a sharp glance. She had a worried look. So, he reckoned, had he. Slowly he relaxed his fingers.

"How was I to know he'd come here? Or that Brenna would fall into his lap on his very first day? How neat that was!"

"What are we going to do about him, Hubert?"

"Is there any question about that? I have to get rid of him."

"Get rid? How? What do you mean?"

"Get him out of the marches, is what I mean. Move him along, send him on his way. See to it that he uses up his time here without finding out anything about us."

"So you don't want me to do anything at all?"

"Have you suddenly turned coward?"

"No, Hubert. Maybe I'm tempted, more than a little. Is that so surprising, that the idea should cross my mind? But the risks! I don't linger in closing traps. That clan gathering at the hunt was enough, to say nothing of the debacle outside the Blue Boar."

"That fellow is a menace to us all. Perhaps a fortunate accident could occur. It would make things easier."

"That is trickery."

"No trickery, Keith—but the Good Lord's wondrous will. A simple accident—say, a nasty fall on wet steps?"

"I don't like it. There is little I would put out of my scope, but killing by stealth, no. Besides, there'd be rumors run riot if he slipped on the steps outside, and no end of trouble for us all."

"Caer Llion is an expert horseman and his mount is too well trained, or I might suggest a horse might startle this very afternoon with fatal result."

"Some would question the sudden misfortune that terminated two of Brenna's betrothals."

Brenna shuddered. She looked up into eyes as cold and bleak as a winter moon. Could what Keith had said be true?

"Do you think he could have guessed? Is there any proof that the lance—"

"Of course not, or Caer Llion would have me in irons in the lowest dungeon this moment," Keith's voice snapped. "He didn't get to be king's justiciar by being a fool. Which is why it must be aboveboard. I must defeat him fair and square."

"They do say there is not a man alive who can best you!"

"As sure as the sun will rise tomorrow, there is a man better than me," Keith said, very low, "But don't worry, my lord. I will have my revenge and I'm not the yielding kind."

"Good. I'll take care of this, then. I just wanted you to know what was happening. Let us away from this benighted place."

Brenna gripped Leon's arm. "You know what this means? Hubert de Risley is egging Keith on! He goaded him into coming here. This may be his very own trap, all nicely baited. Don't fall into it," she whispered.

"I can't renege now. The game is too well begun. I have to play it out."

"Even to your death?"

"Or Kil Coed's."

"Or both." Brenna let him go. "Stupid, obstinate man. Why am I arguing with you? Go ahead then. Kill yourself. You'll be comfortably dead, and you won't have to face what comes after."

That stung Leon, but not enough. "If God wills it, so be it. But I'll do all I can to forestall it. Can that content you?"

It would have to. He would yield no further than that.

Chapter Twelve

The jousting was to be held in the broad grazing pasture below the castle, bounded by the river to the west and a small wood to the south. All agreed that a rough-surfaced gray pillar stone standing alone in a field, like a giant's accusing finger pointed at the sky, should form the northern boundary. No man other than a druid would touch a standing stone, memorial to a vanished race of unknown powers.

To either side of the lists an enclosure of withy screens had been erected close to the center of the first field where the fighters could claim sanctuary if they were in difficulty or needed to take respite. This did not please the villagers, who derived income from those fertile, long-tilled fields, which in turn thrived on the sweepings of the castle's stables. And at this time of year, there was seed corn to riddle, arable to plow, and the lambing—the season would not wait for something so trivial as a tourney. But it was Brenna's special day, so all was forgiven.

In the third hour after noon, all but the most determined feasters streamed down from castle and village to the fields about it, gathering for the joust: games of strength and skill, war games and peace games, foot races and mounted races and contests between lords on their warhorses. Most of all, they came to witness the bout between Keith Kil Coed and Caer Llion.

As Brenna approached the jousting area with a pitcher of water, she saw a raven strutting along the top of the reeds. The bird turned its head and looked directly at her. She smiled at such a good omen. It boded well for the future.

"Vincent, I want a word with you."

Hubert de Risley's voice grabbed Brenna's attention. Perhaps it was premonition, perhaps instinct, but she felt a foreboding and pressed herself closer against the screen, as if she could sink into the reeds and thus hide herself.

"Sir Hubert, I beg your forgiveness, but I have been unable to find the vessel." It was a frightened, pleading voice.

"Vincent, I have heard enough. I do not want excuses. I want that cup. Find it."

Brenna's mind whirled. What could be the meaning of this? She remembered Vincent, Sir Hubert's foxy-faced squire, a thin miserable man. She inhaled deeply, held the breath, then slowly exhaled. The voices, accompanied by footfalls, came closer.

"I am trusting you. No one must be aware of what you do. No one must see you enter the enclosure." Hubert de Risley's voice was hushed. "Drop this into the water container. Do you understand, Vincent?"

The footfalls ceased. The curve of the screen, and the long afternoon shadows, still hid her from the two men. She shuddered in her place of concealment. Her breath came in shallow scoops, if at all.

"Aye, my lord. I understand."

"This is in case the lance fails to find its target. I'll not be thwarted a third time."

"Once is strange, twice is coincidence, but three times is becoming a habit," the squire said in his high thin voice.

"Your opinion was not invited, Vincent. Just follow my orders."

"Aye, my lord."

One step. Two steps. Again Brenna shivered. The dangerous moment passed, and they moved on.

So that's how the cowards are going to play it. Poison Leon! Kill her beloved knight? Not if she had anything to do with it! Brenna was already running toward the withy screen entrance.

"Leon! Leon! Are you all right?"

He gave her a surprised look.

"Why not?"

"Drink nothing! Eat nothing! Not unless I have tasted it first!" Her urgency was as compelling as it was daunting. He gave her a long peculiar look. She had no idea what was going on in his mind. Her own was in turmoil.

"Tassaud! Taffy! Collect every drinking bowl and vessel, every container of ale, water, and wine. Pour their contents to the ground. Tell all the grooms, squires and pages to call the sheriff if they see Hubert de Risley's squire lurking. Call him anyway! Mind you do it, and hurry!"

"This is our first mission of mercy," said Taffy, his chubby and rather droll face all aglow with eager anticipation at the mere suggestion. "Consider it done!"

"What are you waiting for then, you dolt!" Tassaud snapped, and grabbed his hand. With his spare hand, Taffy hitched up his trousers, which were in danger of sliding around his ankles, and loped off behind his brother.

"Tudur! You go up to the bailey. Have the steward fetch a fresh supply of everything and have the servants bring clean cups. Off you go. Run all the way." By the time the words were out of her mouth, the boy was heading for the keep, a blur of elbows and knees and youthful enthusiasm. "Someone's slipped something into the drinks," she called after him. "Tell Master Clifford that from me, if you will, else he may think we've all gone mad."

"I assume you have grounds for these allegations?" Leon asked.

"You can safely assume that," Brenna said grimly. "I

have to tell you, Leon, that I do not care much for the company you keep!''

"Anything else?" His eyes narrowed. The searching intensity of his glance made Brenna shiver.

"I would tell you more if I could. Later, I hope I can. Till then, I must ask you to trust me." She turned away abruptly, too worried to allow herself to speak. Her panic shocked Brenna. Normally she was the last one to lose control, but normally she wouldn't have the threat of having a man murdered before her very eyes. And not just any man. A man she had taken one look at and gone to with the absolute certainty of water running downhill to the waiting river.

A man who thought trusting a woman was like trusting the devil himself.

Leon watched Brenna, not taking his eyes from her until she disappeared beyond the withy screen. Her absence left a humming stillness around him like a pause in the wind. And although the grooms were jabbering excitedly around him, their voices were distant echoes.

A last test of Deso's saddle cinch, a judicious tightening, by his own bare hand, trusting not even Telyn's offer to settle his equipment. Then he put on the right-hand gauntlet, set his hand in the shield grip and his foot in the stirrup, still judging the girth as it took his armored weight. Deso took him up in good order, but with a little shiver and a pricking up of the ears. The stallion was fresh and eager.

Leon took a lance from Telyn and trotted Deso to the far end of the designated tilting ground. The ground was sodden, but not mushy, the conditions underfoot a little less than ideal. He tugged the stallion's creamy ears in encouragement. Deso snorted and gathered himself, small quivers of excitement rippling through his body.

The Steward of the Lists came up to the viewing platform where the noble guests were seated, and bowed before Sir Edmund, ready to start the joust. Below the platform crowded a couple hundred local folk, come to see the action.

"Grandy!" Brenna hastened up beside her grandfather. "A word with you, Grandy..."

"Not now, Brenna. Not now."

"Grandy, I want you to stop the tourney!"

"Silence!" Sir Edmund beckoned to the Steward of the Lists, who was hovering nearby. "Is the ground fit to hold the joust?"

"I fear so."

A lifetime with Sir Edmund had taught Brenna the futility of gaining his attention at such a time, so she took her seat. She leaned forward, hands clasped, eyes fixed on Leon. Meanwhile the people waited, as all the banners hung limp in a momentary want of breeze, then snapped and thumped with a wayward gust. The silence hung still, and there was a collective intake of breath.

"Caer Llion is wearing my old helmet, I see, and the silk surcoat that he wears carries the Brenig colors...I must say, I am curious as to what happened to his own effects."

Keith rose in his stirrups and waved his lance in the air. He filled his lungs and his huge voice bellowed forth.

"I hereby declare a joust between myself and Caer Llion. Single combat. Let all bear witness that this be a fair fight— to the yielding or to the death!"

"Fool," Leon said, tugging his left hand into a gauntlet. He drew out the embroidered pouch that held a torn scrap of lace, looked at it as he had done a thousand times before. He held it up on its leather thong for the people to see.

"In honor of my lady, I accept the challenge!"

The crowd roared. A roar to get on with the spectacle.

He closed his fingers over the amulet, returning it to nest against his chest. He had taken part in many a tournament. All for sport. This time he faced a man who meant to kill him, and to meet him in single combat in front of Brenna was doubly daunting.

Keith was at the far edge of the jousting barrier, beside the druid's standing stone. A huge raven was perched on it. Unblinking, it regarded him with a predator's glare. Keith brandished his weapon, and yelled at it. He flung the sword into the air, spinning up, up, bird and man watching it together, until it dropped and he caught it with a deft turn of his wrist just in front of the pillar stone. The raven did not move until the sword was back in Keith's hand. Then it opened its wings. Their cold shadow fell across his upturned face as it flew away.

"It's sorry I am I didn't kill you!" Keith called after it.

Deso snorted and bunched his haunches, wanting to be free of the pressure of the bit. Leon held the stallion steady between his knees, tightened his grip on lance and shield, and bowed his head to the herald's glance. He was as ready as he ever would be.

At the other end of the tilt, Kil Coed turned his bay and, without warning, drove in his spurs and hurtled across the ground at a thundering gallop.

"Caer Llion!" he bellowed, the sound a muffled boom emerging through the vent holds in his jousting helm.

At once the starting horn was sounded, but too late.

The crowd roared even louder.

Even as Deso responded, Leon knew that Keith had gained the first advantage, his impetus that much greater. If the lance should strike true, then Leon would be either hurled from his saddle or skewered like a fowl on a spit.

The ground shook to the thunder of destrier hooves.

Leon braced himself, aware as always in this instant before collision of being both mortal and terribly alive. Kil Coed's shield was coming toward him, a Griffin blazing white. He centered his lance. Keith's lance raked off his shield and his own met Keith's shield with a thunder crack and a shock that went up his arm. A howl went up from the onlookers as his lance bent and exploded in splinters.

Both knights recoiled in their saddles, but both kept their seats. Both inspected their shields and threw them away. The horses fetched up, stamping and blowing in their impatience.

Brenna half rose in her seat. She knew her face was bloodless. She feared she might be going to faint, though she never had before.

"Now this is worth watching!" said the lady Agnita, nearby.

"They are well matched, truly," said Hubert de Risley, but his brows flattened.

"I had thought Keith Kil Coed a man of honor," remarked Sir Edmund. His hand come down lightly, caressingly, on the arm of his chair, and began to stroke it. The threat of violence hung in the air, all the more telling for it being so understated.

The two knights cantered back to their own ends, and took a second lance each. And again, with new shields, crouching behind them, they set off toward each other, power against power, heavily bearing down as they met...

And the lance of one caught the shield of the other off center, and slid harmlessly...but Leon's lance shattered, and he laughed, the laugh echoing within his helmet. He was laughing still when Keith turned his foaming steed, nostrils flaring, eyes glittering.

For the third and last time the horses checked up at the end of the lists, and each knight took a fresh lance.

Brenna drew a deep breath and tried to still the trembling of her knees as she reseated herself. She closed her eyes, her hands clenched. She felt as if she had swayed in her seat. He would be killed. She knew it.

She opened her eyes again. Leon did not look as if he feared the outcome. He even raised his lance and saluted. Hard though Keith fought him, his armor shone unmarred, his plume unruffled. His cream-pale stallion looked newly groomed; he sat in the saddle as if he had been born there, light, easy, breathing without effort.

Leon reined Deso in short and turned to face Kil Coed face-on. He hefted his heavy lance, finding the right balance, feeling the stallion beneath him bunched, muscles ready to spring. He guided the stallion with knee and thigh, trusting the animal's trained obedience under him.

The two knights were off again, crouching low, their dented shields covering their bodies, the plumes floating from their helms...they would meet exactly in the center.

Brenna held her breath.

At the last moment Leon snapped erect in the stirrups and flung the lance with a curse and a prayer. It sang through empty air. He steadied his shield shoulder, took the blow without mishap as Keith's lance shattered on his shield.

Cursing, Keith cast the stump aside. Sawing at the reins, he pulled his horse to a standstill and jumped down. He ripped his sword from its leather bindings and let out a battle cry.

Even as his own lance buried itself in the churned-up earth, Leon was kicking free of the stirrups. He leaped to the ground, landed awkwardly, staggered, regained his balance.

Keith spun the heavy sword, slicing great arcs through the air as he swung his blade down with astonishing power, mocking Leon with his laughter.

"I'm going to prick your guts open wide, Caer Llion."

"Then cut the lather and get on with it," Leon said, drawing his own sword.

He rolled his weight forward onto the balls of his feet as Keith let out a loud curse and lunged. The familiar ring of steel rent the air. Swords clash, disengaged, and clashed again.

"There! And there," whispered Brenna, more to herself than to anyone close by. Her eyes shone. Her breath was held...and released as Leon swooped...and struck and ducked...and dodged another great blow.

Blade grated off blade.

Keith gave ground, half turned away from Leon to give more momentum to his swing and brought his sword around with enough force to cut a man in two. His laugh was as hard and harsh as a raven's cry and Leon drew it into himself like a breath.

Leap, slash, jump back...weight forward, thrust...

sidestep... Leon narrowed his lids, his mind a recitation of
sword drills. Then Keith bellowed and lunged like a crazed
bull, and Leon staggered before the blow, back and back.
Hot pain pulsed and ricocheted around his skull. Pain to save
his life, to summon his battle fury.

"Christ have mercy!" gasped Brenna, clinging to Sir Edmund's arm.

"He's a king's champion!"

"I know...only...oh, Grandy!"

Keith mock saluted Leon with his sword. "How's your
head, Caer Llion?"

Leon shrugged. "You were lucky." He set his feet, balanced on them, alert, pain locked tight in a small closet in
his mind. He would not be slow again. Keith had bad habits
as a swordsman. When he lowered his shield—

Keith lashed out with an overhand chop at Leon's head.
Easily blocked this time. Then with a quick flip of his
weapon, Leon thrust his sword tip at an exposed part of
Keith's leg. He was rewarded with a gratifying splotch of
blood on Keith's chausses.

There was a sudden furious clambering for better vantage
points. The crowd was a roiling gallery of faces that jumped
here and there out of the shadows of awnings into the dazzling sunlight, and here and there white teeth flashed, and
eyes winked, and encompassing the spectacle was an un-
abated roaring clamor.

But Leon's focus fell away from these and narrowed to
the two glowering slits hovering before him and the slanting
point of metal. His ears were acutely attuned to the grunts
and snarls jerking in Keith's throat. His feet moved in a
terrible dance, his eyes seeking the moment of weakness,
the uncertain glint in his opponent's eyes, waiting for the
opening to strike. Now the fool tried the same again.

Leon's shield came up flat overhead as his sword lashed
out too quickly to be deflected, and connected with Keith's
helmet hard enough to dent the iron. Keith dropped his

sword. His eyes went dull, lost focus. He sank to his knees, pawing the helmet from his head.

Leon unslung the shield from his aching left arm, set it on the ground, and leaned over the fallen man.

"Yield," he snarled.

"Never," Keith panted.

"Yield," Leon repeated.

"Never!"

Leon lifted his sword, the point reaching for Keith's unguarded eyes. A hiss of steel accompanied that into silence.

A terrible hush lay over the people who watched.

Red color zoomed in on Leon and his vision blurred. One thrust of the sword, and Kil Coed would be his, blood and soul. It was sweet, that prospect. He brought his arm back, farther...

"No!" Brenna spoke calmly and clearly. "Thou shalt not kill."

Leon could not have heard her; he was too far away for that. But he lowered his sword till the point was resting on his offhand boot. So he stood until Keith struggled to his feet.

"I should've killed you a long time ago."

"Why not now?"

"Promises come home to roost. I promised Brenna I'd not kill you intentionally."

"But *I* made no such promise."

Leon tightened his grip on his sword hilt. Keith shifted his stance, holding his own blade in readiness.

Leon drew in a deep breath and let it out slowly. "I don't want to kill you and you don't want to be dead," he told Keith.

"And I don't seem able to kill you," the other admitted.

Leon permitted himself to smile. "It's an interesting situation, known in chess as a stalemate."

They exchanged one more long look, then Keith handed his sword to the man who had defeated him...and limped away down the length of the field leaving his destrier for the victor.

The next sound Leon heard was the thundering of a horse's hooves. The spectators roared. His helm swivelled in the direction of the ruckus.

It was Hubert de Risley, astride his black destrier.

Squires set forth. Hubert swung the flail around his head, threatening the boys, his stallion plunging close.

Leon heard the jink of chain, the whistle of iron swinging through air. There was no time for him to think, to plan, to escape. The warhorse was upon him. Reflex took over. He ducked and rolled, and a massive wedge of metal cleft the air where his head had just been. Rolling up onto his feet, he flung himself over sideways to escape the flaying hooves.

Then Deso thundered toward the melee. He threw up his head and uttered a stallion neigh of challenge. With teeth and hooves, he attacked the black so savagely, it fled before him.

Leon gave a whistle, shrill, commanding. As if something pulled heavily on his reins, the great stallion came to a snorting halt. Then there was a jarring jolt as Hubert's destrier stumbled, and Hubert was sailing through the air, landing in the churned-up mud, spread-eagled and dazed.

From behind the withy screens a whole mob of knights and grooms raced onto the tourney field. And the crowd stamped and shouted till it seemed the keep itself would blow away.

Leon slanted a look at the gallery.

Brenna was on her feet. By her side, Sir Edmund stood smiling, with a tinge of color in his sunken cheeks. Beyond them Agnita, with tears on her face, laughed and clapped her hands. Alice ran 'round her chair and caught her sister up in her arms.

Men gathered up Hubert and roughly bore him to Leon, who stood, composed, and watching Sir Edmund. The castellan stood silent, giving away nothing of what he thought, but he was not frowning. Brenna stood near him, pale and shaken. Leon wished he could go to her, hold her and assure her, but there was work to be done.

And it was not all a victory. Keith Kil Coed would take this exceedingly hard, and become not less but more set on challenges. And a man might take on one challenge, but not challenge after challenge, all hired by Hubert de Risley's gold...if they were at all willing to contest on the field, and not in some dark stairway. He put nothing past Hubert.

"I weary of you, Hubert. You incited this. Any man who impugns the honor of myself or Brenna or Sir Edmund or his household will be accounted a traitor. You have bedeviled me, you have insinuated, insulted, inveigled and imposed on my goodwill too long!"

He had the satisfaction of seeing stark fear seep through the self-importance of Hubert, before the cold reckoning crept into him that getting rid of Hubert de Risley would only shift leadership to another fool exactly like him. And it would unsettle the known factions in this district.

He sighed. "I won't destroy the very laws I've worked on so hard for so many years, for so little reward. Especially not so publicly! So I will not kill you, Hubert."

Warily, Hubert rose to his feet and dusted himself down.

"You will leave this place and never return," Leon said fiercely, sheathing his sword. "Give him and his servants safe conduct to the open road."

The steward's expression grew truculent. "He belongs in the dungeon."

"Do it!" Leon removed his helmet. He drew a deep breath and let it go. "I advise you to go, and go now, before the sun sets!"

Hubert de Risley hesitated, perhaps the space of two breaths, but it seemed forever. Then he bent his head in scant courtesy, backed, bowed, turned and left, in strictest propriety.

Leon was leading Deso to the stables when he heard an odd sound, a sharp cry, cut off too soon. The alley was empty, already claimed by evening shadows. But the stable door was ajar and as he approached it, there was a thud and another muffled cry. Quickening his step, Leon pushed open the door.

A bundle of hay had been dumped on to the floor, a bucket overturned. Against one stall, a man had Tudur pinned against the wall, one hand clamped over his mouth, the other trying to restrain the boy as he sought to get a grip on his belt. The assailant's back was to the door, and he was so intent upon subduing Tudur that he'd not yet realized they were no longer alone.

Leon was reaching for his sword hilt when his gaze fell upon a sack of muck, half full, by a stall. Snatching it up, he was upon the man before he could sense his danger, yanking the sack down over his head and shoulders. Blinded and choking, the man released Tudur and reeled backward. Before he was able to free himself of the sack, Leon kneed him in the groin and he went down, writhing on flagstones at Leon's feet.

Tudur had sagged against the wall, gasping for breath. His cap was gone, his hair in wild disarray, his face and tunic streaked with stable muck. But he recovered with remarkable speed. He kicked the prostrate man in the ribs, called him a slimy toad, and kicked him again.

Leon drew his sword and leveled it at the man's heaving chest, then reached down and jerked off the sack. 'Twas Hubert de Risley's squire, Vincent. He moaned in pain and pawed at his eyes, blinking and gasping and then cowering at the sight of that menacing blade.

"I'll fetch a rope, sir. We can tie him up."

"Did he get anything?"

"No."

Leon glared at the cringing man. An accusation of attempted robbery was not easy to prove, and Hubert de Risley was getting ready to depart. "Begone, join your master. If I ever see you again, I'll geld you with a dull blade!"

He prodded Vincent to his feet with the point of his

sword, and within moments, shoved the man through the stable door and out into the lane. He thrust his sword into its scabbard.

"Have you any idea why this fellow attacked you?"

"No." Tudur fumbled at his waist. A small drawstring pouch dangled from his belt. From it he withdrew a dull metal cup. "But I think this has something to do with it."

Leon looked at the cup and thought it the same one he and Brenna had shared on their first outing. It wasn't much, a smallish sphere with the top sliced off and the inside hollowed out. Even if it were solid gold, it wasn't big enough to warrant Hubert de Risley's singleminded pursuit. And any fool could see it wasn't gold. 'Twas not even valuable. Then he remembered the peculiar warmth of the cup in his hands, the strange images it evoked.

"Where did you get it?"

"I found it."

"Where?"

"In the secret passage."

"Put it away. I'll see if I can find out who put it there and who owns it. In the meanwhile, take care."

Leon rested one foot on the iron grill before the hearth, and turned his boot toe this way and that as he gave thought to the situation. One measured one's gains by one's losses. His engagement with Keith Kil Coed and surprise encounter with Hubert de Risley told him a number of things, none of them good. Loyalties had obviously changed; friendships were set aside as a result.

They were not Sir Edmund's friends, Leon thought, and yet they each desperately sought closeness to the castellan, each seeking any chance to outdo his neighbors. They feared Leon because Brenna loved him. And Brenna...oh, greatly did they fear her influence.

And Brenna? Men might make a sign against magic, denying the evil thought, but she was no sorceress, able to turn lead into gold. She had only the Brenig birthright, and that was precarious.

He ought, he knew, to fear and resent them. To be making plans for—if not their death, their removal. And that might happen, it might well happen, both Keith Kil Coed and Hubert de Risley having set themselves in an impossible position with the king's authority. There had already been disrespect of the king's justiciar, at very least.

But he was no woolly-headed idealist, and he had to ask himself how the other barons would swing. Right now they were wavering between the king's ambassador and the Welsh pretender, Llewelyn ap Lorwerth.

A soft knock interrupted his thoughts. He crossed the room and pulled aside the leather curtain. Brenna stood there. Merely seeing her cheered him like a potent draught. Hers was a beauty the minstrels often sang of. The knowledge that she would soon be his by the laws of both king and God was a heady one.

Brenna's eyes fixed on the weal at his temple. Already the flesh was swollen. Discoloration mottled the skin. Then she noticed his torn, bloody shirt.

"You are wounded! No one said you were wounded!"

"'Tis but a scratch."

"A scratch? A scratch you call it? Scratches do not soak a shirt in blood. You stand before me bleeding like a stuck pig and say ''tis but a scratch'?" She could not bear the frantic note in her voice, but she could not seem to shut up. "And how many blows can a man sustain to his head before he becomes a fool?"

"Don't panic, Brenna. My head is hard, and my wound is not serious. The blade but scored my rib."

"I do not panic." Her voice did not sound like her own. She struggled to keep it steady. "I am a healer. A most sensible woman. Now, let me help you out of that garment so I can inspect the injury for myself."

Shaking with the fear she battled, she helped strip him of his shirt, but as she began to dab some of the blood away, she realized it was not as bad as she had feared. The wound was not deep and 'twas clean, though not pleasant to see.

"It might have been worse." He winced and grunted. "My mistake. I was too impatient."

"You great fool," she said, her voice rising. She took a deep breath. "You stay right there! I'm going to…to fetch some balm!"

Without pausing, she flung the leather curtain aside, slammed it back behind her, and stood there panting. She twisted the cloth between her fingers. Her stomach felt a little queasy.

"Some betony salve and the softest bandages you can find," she ordered a passing servant. "Be quick!"

Calmer now, she reentered the chamber. She swallowed down a great lump in her throat and went forward. She knelt at a chest and pulled out her sewing equipment.

"It requires a stitch or two," she said. Her voice went to a croak and died. She bit her lip, took another deep breath, and laid out needle and thread.

"I'm ready. Do you want me to remain standing?"

"It would be easier to treat you that way." She didn't think she had the nerve for this, and truly, every muscle in her body seemed wobbly. Her teeth actually chattered. Then habit took over. Her fingers worked steadily, quite independent of her. She had not lost her touch. He made a muffled sound. She glanced up. "Are you all right?"

He nodded briefly, once.

"Don't worry," she said quietly. "I've sewn up far worse wounds than this."

A wholly foolish sense of comfort shot through Leon. She looked so incredibly kind and compassionate and generous, he thought. The kind of woman who would be faithful and true. Not the sort who would ever indulge in a clandestine affair. Not the kind who would betray and dissemble.

This woman was nothing like Suzanne.

The way she was fussing about like a broody hen, assuring him that she would look after him, was making him dizzy. The scent of her hair, of woman, filled his nostrils. She squirmed and breathed deep, trembling. The sound made him think of soft feminine sighs and passion in the night. His whole body responded. Heat suffused him. He did not move. He couldn't.

The salve came in a covered jar. Brenna slowly opened the lid and he sniffed the yellowish unguent, and recoiled; its pungency made his eyes water.

"Goose grease and betony," she said quietly, dipping a slender finger in the ointment. "It smells dreadful, but it works—makes the wound heal clean. Brace yourself. This will sting."

"Stop nattering. Just do it." He jerked when the paste touched the wound. She covered it with care, and picked up a binding cloth.

"Stand still."

"What else would I do?" he ground through his teeth. "Tie it 'round and be done."

Men. They hated to reveal that anything hurt, she thought. At another time, it might have been a challenge but now... Securing the binding, Brenna's hands were gentler than her tongue. "You listen to me, Caer Llion. Luck won't always run in your favor. Keep this up and you'll get yourself killed!"

"Maybe I will." He reached over and cupped her face in his hands, ignoring the sharp twinge in his wound.

"Murder was planned. They will try again. Next time someone might slip toadstools into your soup. Or mayhap—"

His mouth came down over hers, ending the husky flow of words that were like tiny tongues of fire licking over him. His arms shifted subtly, both molding and supporting her body, stroking her over his hard length, telling her without a word how perfectly they fit together, hard against soft, male and female, hunger and fulfillment.

He let go and stepped back.

"We'll talk about it. Tomorrow, not tonight."

"I could stay," she whispered.

"Nay, I can wait one more day."

"A day will not make a great deal of difference."

She gave him a shocked look, halfway offended, he thought, in her young pride. And he gave her a little smile, seeing her standing there somewhat confused and worried-looking.

"Maybe I'm twice a fool to deny myself, but I would start our lives together tomorrow, the way they should be. I'm more than fond of you, if you haven't figured that out, and I would have you come to me a virgin on our wedding night. Understand?"

She nodded, bit her lip and broke into tears. She hugged him and held on to him a long, long time.

And he held her like a brother and rocked her until he felt his own reactions grow not at all brotherly and out of control again. He set her back by the arms. "You had better go," he said steadily, with only the faintest hint of breathlessness.

Brenna was utterly still for a moment. Then she bit her lip and ran right past him out the door.

Damn, and damn, and damn.

A man, Leon told himself, ought to have better sense.

Chapter Thirteen

The joyous ringing of the chapel bells startled the hapless ravens from the turret roof and they took flight in a great upward beating of wings. Brenna's hand trembled as Sir Edmund led her down the aisle. The altar was straight ahead and Leon was waiting, his face, the unmarred side, like a white marble image in this smoky region of incense burners, lamps and candles.

Every pew was packed, occupied by guests, the villagers, the estate workers and anyone who could be spared from the castle itself, all people she had known ever since she was a child. Aunt Alice and Aunt Agnita were in the very front row, Elen and Nesta farther back, along with Master Clifford and Edgar. Ambrose One-Eye was there, as was his daughter Bronwen, and Margot with her woodcutter husband, Giles. So, too, were Telyn, Tudur, Tassaud and Taffy. She smiled at them as she passed.

On her grandfather's arm she reached the top of the aisle. The bells, having rung out their chorus, left a numb silence and the last ravens had fled. The priest asked who gave the woman in marriage and who took her. Grandy released her arm and she took Leon's.

She looked up at Leon. What did this ceremony mean to him? she thought. He had agreed to all Grandy's demands, but was he wanting a wife merely to provide a son? To wed her and bed her, get her with child and then go off to war? Dismay and an overwhelming dread that he desired from her no more than that mingled, twisting in her heart.

Leon's pulse quickened as he cast a glance at Brenna standing next to him. A circle of thin gold crowned her head, but her dark hair had been allowed to remain free and was woven with the tiny wildflowers of spring. She carried the nosegay that Ambrose One-Eye's daughter had given her.

"If anyone objects to this marriage, let him now step forward and speak or forever hold his peace."

Brenna waited with the slightest tinge of anxiety, her heart pounding painfully against her rib cage. No one spoke. The priest continued with the ceremony.

She glanced at Leon. His eyes were hard and green-flecked; his face stern. She felt as if in a dream. Only his fingers were warm and real entwined with hers. Then suddenly he caught her glance. He smiled, and hesitantly she smiled back.

"A year did you say?" he whispered unexpectedly.

Brenna swallowed. It was her wager of trust that he meant. Her heart lifted with unexpected hope. A smile trembled on her mouth. "Willing and gladly—without regret."

He nodded. Suddenly she knew all would be well.

The priest's question was answered. "With full heart I take this man as my own true husband."

Leon met her gleaming eyes. Fire sparked through his body and centered in his loins. He slowly let out the breath he'd been holding and repeated the vows with steady certainty. He took her hand and slid the heavy gold-and-ruby signet ring from his little finger onto the third finger of her left hand.

As they moved back to the courtyard in procession, the villagers crowded around them. Now the children were throwing flower petals and sundry grains over them, and they called, "Good luck, m'lady" and "May you have every happiness!"

But not all were so pleased. Edgar glared at Leon. In a savage undertone, he said, "Take care of her, Caer Llion. Or you shall answer to me."

She felt the tiny quiver that went through Leon's arm, as if he might have clenched and unclenched his hand. "Of course."

The captain of the gate stepped back, and Aunt Alice kissed her on the cheek, with a warm smile. "Be happy, my dear," she said too loudly.

Ever indiscreet, Aunt Agnita added her congratulations in her own inimitable way. "Who knows, perhaps within the year there will be an heir to bring joy to the hall?"

The idea made Brenna's lips curve upward. She looked up at Leon's face and saw the pain there—and cold, hard pride, too, as he stared straight ahead, as if remote from the proceedings. Was he thinking of his dead wife and child? Only his solid warmth, so close as they went down the pathway, made him seem with her at all. Behind them, Sir Edmund, arm-in-arm with his sisters, talked cheerfully of the breakfast awaiting them.

The trestles bore their burden of food well. There was salmon, fresh from the Dee, in a creamy sauce; pasties of mutton and leeks. Freshly baked bread with honey stood next to white round cheeses. For sweets, there were pastries rich with butter and honey and as crisp as honeycombs, and lime tarts, and little cakes made of rose petals and orange blossoms, a conserve of ground almonds, and fat bowls of thick cream.

Festivities and food abounded in the courtyard as well as in the hall, not to mention the kettles of venison stew set up in the lower town square, offering meat to any bringer of a bowl and supper and a trencher of bread to those who had none, on the castellan's largesse.

There were many who raised their cups and drank to their health. Cheer spread throughout the keep, audible through the windows above the tumult outside: there were cheers, there were toasts, there was moderate tipsiness. Several of the servants were a little the worse for ale, but they all seemed very happy.

To the high table they brought a fair supply of festive braided bread thickly topped with poppy seed, intricate constructions that were almost too delightful to eat. When Leon told her so, Brenna laughed and showed him how to unbraid the bread as they ate it, and how one braiding meant prosperity and how another meant long life, and how one was for a good harvest and why they baked a whole apple into one kind of bread.

"So's there's plenty all year long," she said.

"And does it make it sure?" was his question. It seemed to him it was a good start, at least, even if it behoved of old ways.

Brenna unbraided a bit of poppy bread and wrapped it about a bit of ham and gave it to him. "Sure as anything in this world," she said.

When they had finished eating, she took his hand and led the way across the hall to an alcove with a tall, horn-paned window that was set ajar to catch the breeze. The half light of afternoon, muted, hazy, filtering, dimly illuminated the area. The window looked down, he saw, upon the roofs of the town below the wall, shadowed angles of black slates and chimneys.

There was a great bonfire lit in the square. Huge bundles of sticks were flung on until the fire mounted and plumes arose to mass into a haze of smoke smudging the sky. Cheers and merriment broke out on every hand for no reason that he could see except the tossing of sheafs on the bonfire.

"What are those bundles?" he asked Brenna beneath the noise and the cheering.

"Our sins," she said. "And the bad things we've done. All going into the fire, my lord."

"Mine, too?" What a notion! Get rid of the past and start afresh!

"Such sins as you have, Leon, which by me are few. Certainly not compared to some I could speak of."

She was wrong in that, Leon thought. "There is a saying, Brenna, about a fool's taking the trouble to lay sticks on the devil's fire."

"Truth is, I don't know about the burning, but the ale flows freely, and the music cures the heart."

It was the longest day of his life, Leon thought. Would the sun *never* go down? He kept looking at the sky and finding it still light. Would the twilight never come, when he could bear Brenna away to their private chamber? He dared not press harder with his thoughts. So he sang to the endless music on the harps, and the jugs and cups went 'round, and they sang some more. Then there were more entertainments: tumblers and conjurers and dancers.

Brenna sat quietly, unaware of the noise and the many people around her. She was busy thinking of the night to come.

I would have you come to me a virgin.

What should she do? What could she say? After what had gone before, she was at a loss. Should she pretend that none of it had happened? Or should she set him straight?

Heart racing, Brenna searched her mind for a way to delay and prepare for the confrontation. At best, she thought—get control of herself enough to think whether telling him the whole story was the thing to do. At worst, delay the inevitable moment.

"What is it?" he asked suddenly.

Brenna looked up at him in startlement. Her heart went thump. "I beg your pardon?"

"Why do you frown? I'd hoped you were enjoying yourself."

"Was I frowning?" Brenna made an effort to lighten her expression. "I can't imagine why. Of course I'm enjoying myself."

"Good. I like it when you smile."

She tilted her head and gave a small laugh. That was the best she could do, she thought. Leon took her cue. He began to talk and drink. To talk about the people who attended their wedding feast; to talk about the river and fishing, mountains and cattle, woodcutting and farming. Her goblet never seemed empty, and she wondered if her husband was filling it deliberately. Did he sense her nervousness and seek to abate it by dulling her wits?

Then it was nearly evening and the twilight turned the evening mist to jewel tones. They slipped unnoticed from the feast—or perhaps by common consent the celebrants chose *not* to attend to their leaving—and flew to the second level that housed the bedchambers.

The silence seemed to stretch after the leather curtain was drawn behind them. Leon made no move toward her. Instead he took a waxed straw from the holder and carried fire from the watch candle and lit the three wall candles.

Brenna walked across the oaken floor, her skirts making a muted rustle as she leaned against the window slit and peered out. Rippling fingers of crisp air cooled her flushed cheeks and she caught sight of the river, a narrow silver ribbon under the shifting moon.

I would have you come to me a virgin.

Yet it seemed late for this claim. She ran over the alternatives in her mind, again and again, but nothing changed. So she turned and began to remove her headpiece with an enforced calm deliberation.

A lock of her hair fell free of the loose pinning. She lifted her hand to tuck the curl back into place, and caught Leon watching her. For a second—for just a heartbeat—she thought he was going to cross the space that separated them, reach out and touch her. Something unfamiliar pulsed in her veins. Anticipation? Excitement? Then, abruptly, he stopped and she could breathe again.

"I have a confession to make." She let out the air in a rush. She shoved the hair out of her face and smiled a little.

Leon frowned, wondering what she was getting at. Her cheeks were faintly pink. Something was wrong. His heart did a curious little half beat at a cold shadow of memory, a forerunner of the betrayal he both feared and expected.

"I should have told you before, but the moment was never right." She made another small and peculiar laugh. "This is hard for me to…"

He stood and looked at her. What secret was she about to reveal? That she was with child? No! Not Brenna! He could not be betrayed twice. The very thought of it made him freeze inside. He waited. Tension surged in him. He was reduced, finally, to asking outright, "Are you trying to tell me you are with child?"

She put her fist to her mouth and shook her head.

He grasped her upper arms. Was he fated to make all the same mistakes, until the same end came?

"Then it must be that you are not a virgin?" He heard himself ask it, and the words rang in the air like a hammer of iron.

She only looked at him, her eyes wide and dark.

The look he gave Brenna almost frightened her. Those clear eyes saw everything, like a hawk, intense and hunter-sure. Dangerous. The same look gleamed in his eyes. Emotion colored them. There was a primitive flare to his nostrils that she had never seen. His anger was a tangible thing, bunched in his jaw, stored in the strong cords of his neck. The grip of his fingers on her arms was painful. Brenna could almost feel the bruises forming.

A small panic wrenched her midsection and caused her heart to beat a little faster. In her lifetime, she'd never seen a truly enraged male, nor fallen prey to one. *I will not let him frighten me,* she promised herself. She kept her eyes resolutely on his face. He blinked twice, as though trying to place another image over hers.

She cleared her throat, fearing his next move. "You're the only man I've ever loved."

Leon's own throat tightened with a suppressed moan at the surprise and pain tearing through him. Somehow he hadn't expected Brenna to lie. Not to him. Not about another man.

There was a terrible violence inside him. He wanted to tighten his hands about her throat and choke her. His was a knight's well-used body, one honed by years of practice with sword and lance, and years of combat. Her vulnerability seemed enormous, her stillness beneath his hand an act of infinite trust.

Small. Delicate. Like the life of a small bird within his palms. With his fingers, he could crush the life out of her. That was not what he wanted. What he wanted... God, what he wanted...

"I will not accept dishonor—yours or mine."

"Leon! Of what do you accuse me?"

The words were not registering. The voice echoed in the hollow space between seeing and knowing. It was *her* voice. Somehow she was down there, amidst the mayhem, inside the otherwise silent vision. *Her* voice called his name.

Stop me, he thought. *Don't let me.* He could not remove his hand; could not speak. No sound came out of his mouth when he moved his lips. He drew himself up the last possible fraction. Anger was dangerous. He took a shallow breath, stretching his neck to fight it.

"I know my limits. An annulment can be arranged." He spoke without expression; it was the only way he could maintain control of his raw emotions. He released his grip on her arms and clenched his hands, looking at his knuckles. He flexed his fingers, and pressed his elbows tight against his ribs. Control, he thought fiercely.

Brenna looked up at him. A distinct shiver began at the base of her spine and worked upward.

"You can't run away just because one thing isn't right. Anyway, you can't have an annulment. You promised only this morning *until death us do part.*"

It was not, precisely, what Leon had expected her to say, and for the first time he detected a note of alarm in her voice. Up until this moment she had been almost unnaturally calm.

"I just unwed you!"

"Then kill me!" she cried, hysterically defiant. "If you won't pay my price, kill me!"

"What price?" he snapped, almost spitting the words out in an attempt to stem the pain he had vowed never to feel.

"A year. You promised me a year. I trust you to keep your word. As a man of honor!"

That bit of perversity caught at Leon's emotions and brought a wry smile to his face. She always seemed to have that effect. It was a challenge, a gauntlet thrown down to cover what had gone before. She had demanded a year, and she dared him to accept her still. He had a debt of honor, and he would have to acquit it.

Of all times!

Everything or nothing. Brenna met his gaze. The anguish he saw there made his heart ache despite his effort to hold himself aloof.

"Well, I don't have to go," he said, somewhat lamely. "I could give you a year if that's what you want."

"I want...I want you to love me just a little bit." She sniffed then, and he looked down and saw her crying. "I apologize for marrying you. I apologize for the inconvenience. It's just that I love you so much I thought you'd have to love me back."

"Curse you! A year isn't enough. You'll haunt me all my life—you and your damned witching eyes," he said, teeth clenched.

"There is no need for blasphemy. And you are being unreasonable. I have never betrayed you," Brenna said, as if willing him to understand. Then, before he could say anything, she added, "Not from the first, since I was but a child showing off, and you were a great lump of a boy and afraid of heights."

Though her voice was steady, there was still something of candlelight swimming in her eyes, and a faint fluttery wistfulness in her mouth; that sweet and curving mouth. Why bring that up now? Something kept nagging at Leon just beneath the threshold of conscious thought, telling him that all was *not* as it seemed.

"You don't believe me?"

"I think you would like me to."

"Someone has hurt you badly, my love, to make you so suspicious." Strong emotion trembled in her voice. He stared down at her, his face bleak and still as a winter sky. His green eyes searched her own. "I think we should talk now."

Leon scowled at her. Brenna suspected that beneath that calm exterior there was a frenzy of emotion.

"About what?"

"Anything. Everything." She laid a hand over his heart. "I need to know what happened. You need to know what happened. Then we can pick up the pieces and go on."

Leon cursed once, savagely, then he leaned against the wall by the bed and folded his arms and looked at the floor. He stood silent, unable to speak. It was beyond him; he could not reveal his hurts, they were buried too deep. He had no words to describe what Brenna meant to him. Nor could he describe his hunger to hold her warmth and laughter within his arms.

This was not working, Brenna thought, wishing with all her heart she had never stirred the pot. But it was too late now, and only drastic action would change the course that events had taken. It wasn't jealousy. Well, mayhap just a bit, but that wasn't it. Why would he suspect she carried another man's child? *Think*, she told herself. What is wrong with Leon?

A deep breath. A moment's consideration.

"What is it that you wear 'round your neck?" she asked.

For the briefest instant, unease flashed across his face, but just as quickly, his expression changed to one of calm. "A token given to me by a lass to remember her by. The amulet must be forever about my neck to shield me."

She gave him an odd look, and she turned as if to hide

her hurt. A fragile hope hit him in the gut. His searching gaze rested on her. "Don't," he said softly.

"What?"

"Don't look away from me. If you're going to fight, at least have the courage to look at me."

Brenna took a long breath and obeyed. She laced her fingers together and looked at Leon and felt as though she were being torn apart. He remained in silence a long time. At last he spoke, in a whisper she could hardly hear. "A scrap of lace given by that elf on the battlements."

She stared at him, digesting the implications of what he was saying. Then she laughed, a rich musical sound, full of warmth.

"Oh, Leon. You kept it all these years!" That thought cheered her immensely. She heard herself ask, although in actual fact her head was whirling, "What of the guardian angel?"

That was not the question he was prepared for, either—or it was the earnestness of which confounded him. He closed his eyes. But he could not stop his thoughts.

In his mind, so far away, the tented camps, the endless desert sand. There all was bustle, an incessant movement of men and horses, industrious as a colony of ants, and himself like a caged beast trying to exorcise the past by extravagant feats of valor. What honors he had won! He had always imagined his angel looking over his shoulder with great attentiveness as he executed these bold deeds—as if she would be interested in such foolish things! It had been a way of keeping sane, having his angel walking beside him, a real presence in his world. And at night—

Do not think, do not think of that; don't think, don't think, do not think of it.

Never sure what had been real and what his contorted fantasy. He had dreamed and remembered, uncertain which was which. There was too much pain and misery in those dreams and memories, tangled and confused with pleasure.

"A figment of my imagination only."

The huskiness of Leon's deep voice made Brenna's heartbeat quicken. She came to stand in front of him.

"Have you proven that? There are imagined magic, that is illusion, and real magic. The two should not be confused. It could be a real person, one whose love for you transcends all barriers, even those of time and space."

Leon gave her a look to see if she was jesting. In the faint light she was a shadow, save for her eyes and her small hands.

"I cannot be so enchanted. Even when I yearn to be."

Then quietly, shyly, tentatively, hopefully, Brenna said, "Shall I tell you, then?"

He gave a wave of his hand, beyond talking for the moment. His breath seemed stopped up in his throat.

With an effort, Brenna kept her face straight for her mouth threatened to betray her. "Indulge me for only a moment, then I will tell you. Will you let me kiss you, Leon? I would dearly like to do so."

He felt a sense of panic, like finding himself poised on the edge of a fatal drop. But the step was easy. Very easy. He had learned that at the edge of combat, of judgments, of skirmishes. When there were no choices, one moved, that was all.

"Is this another test?"

"Sort of. I should like to set you a riddle. Just sit on the bed here. Keep your hands at your sides. Now close your eyes. Tight. And keep them closed until I tell you."

Leon shrugged, and did as he was bidden. Then she kissed him on his lips in a shy, inexpert and maidenly way, but most deliciously. Heat rushed through him. It made him quite dizzy. Gentle hands ran from his chest to his waist, and lower, moving over him, making him tighten with desire. He could hardly breathe for the violence of the need hammering through him. If he had not been holding to the bed, he might actually have rocked from side to side.

"Leon." She spoke his name in a whisper as soft and as warm as the night wind. The roving hands unfastened the ties of his breeches, tugging them down until she had the freedom of his body. His breath came in with an odd, rippling sound. When she touched him, the breath he did have trickled out in a groan that sounded as though it had been torn from his soul.

"Brenna, I..." His throat closed in a rush of sensual awareness. The temptation she offered was dizzying, almost overwhelming. A shudder of anticipation and need rippled over him. Brenna made a soft sound at the back of her throat. He waited for her to speak. Instead, she took his mouth again and kissed him, a slow sensual teasing, her body brushing his on a regular sort of movement and for even a longer time until darkness swam in the back of his brain. She tasted like the wine they had drunk. Deep and drowning. Intoxicating.

The torment increased. Her fingertips traced the length of him gently. He couldn't prevent a hoarse gasp. His nostrils flared, drinking in the smell of her. It was a scent he remembered as *hers*. Now he smelled like it, and tasted it in the back of his throat. It was like stepping into the sun, a blazing joy transforming him as surely as pain once had. Then he remembered his dream again, and his breath caught. His whole body went still.

He heard a rustling sound, sensed Brenna's gown sliding to the floor, and shuddered heavily. There was another pause, and he waited for another kiss, but now she said, "Open your eyes."

When he opened his eyes she was standing naked in front of him, full-breasted and narrow-waisted. Visible under a curled mat of fine hair, which was almost a mist of dark smoke, was the wild plum of her sex. Her black hair flowed proudly behind her, almost to her hips. He was breathing too fast, too hard, but he didn't care. Brenna was breathing as quickly as he was.

"I think we can say with certainty that you liked kissing me."

He asked himself if he was being seduced, or if she was...taking a stupid chance, if that was what was happening. But if Brenna wanted to end this up with bed, he could agree with that. It had been a long time, she was highly desirable, and there were limits. Leon sighed. He had tried, but he couldn't give her up. He couldn't. I'm a fool. I know it, he thought, but I can't stop wanting her.

"You could say that." He was glad to hear that his words only quivered a tiny bit.

"Could you tell the kisses apart?" The flush of her cheeks had suffused her whole face, and her eyes were bright.

"There's a difference?"

"Too right, there's a difference. It was I who kissed you first. But who was she who kissed you next?"

At that, he did rock upon the bed. He was bespelled.

And he remembered then, upon that thought of miracles—or of witchcraft. "It was *you*."

Sighing deeply, Leon pulled her onto his lap and nuzzled her hair. "You've had me tied up in knots," he murmured roughly against the pulse in her throat, nibbling on her earlobe. "I should have recognized the smell, the taste. You are unique. No woman tastes like you…will ever taste like you."

"Want to taste me again?"

Then he kissed her hungrily, as though time could wait until he'd had his fill of loving her. He lifted her high then, placing his warm face against her breasts. Delicate cords deep within her reacted instantly by tightening until she ached.

"Leon…" she whispered as desire began to rise, enveloping her.

His body tensed against hers. Leon's hands pressed her closer. His lips touched hers, but as he rolled onto his injured side, he winced from pain.

"Lie still," Brenna whispered. "Let me do the work."

He felt her warmth when she leaned over him, kissing his neck. She trembled from the brush of his hands against her breasts. Floating. Flowing. Pain stopped. So did time.

Her hands and lips were a potent, delirious persuasion to

think of nothing else at all and hold himself as long as he could manage.

"What of Suzanne?"

"Suzanne?"

The bedside candle, aromatic with herbs, broke a waxen dam at its crest and sent a puddle down the candlestick and down again to the catch-pan beneath it. The puddle glowed like Brenna's skin, pale, damp, flawless. Naked, she sat next to him on the bed, her legs curled under her.

"Keith's sister, whom you loved so well, that drove you near mad with grief when she died. *That* Suzanne."

"Explaining everything settles nothing."

"It helps to give sorrow words. The grief that does not speak harms the troubled heart, and makes it break." Brenna sighed, stretched, and began absently stroking the fine growth of silky hair on her husband's bare forearm.

This woman could drive him mad, Leon thought. She was nothing if not persistent. "What do you want to know?"

Brenna tilted her head. "Everything. Wade through the bad, my love, get it off your chest."

He made a harsh, inarticulate grunt, scrubbed wearily at his face. "You misread me sorely, Brenna, if you think I bore that woman any love or that she cared for me. I married her to please my foster father, not myself. I was a green young squire not yet twenty, she some five years more. She *said* she loved me, but I never once bedded her. I did not know until after the ceremony that she was with child by another."

"Who was?"

"I don't know. She never said. When she was dying, she said she hated me, and was pleased to die for she could not bear me near her, that no woman could bear my ugliness." His hand came up toward the scars that she no longer noticed.

Those wretched scars and everything that went with them. She pulled him close again, a warm, hard hug that smelled of wood smoke and flowers. "Never again," she said fiercely. Her voice caught, and he knew she was crying.

He let her hold him against her and hid his face against her soft breast and heard himself say, "I've had a hard time trusting women after that. I kept suspecting that anybody who showed an interest in me was really trying to take advantage of me." He bit his lip. "I didn't believe I could be special enough to any woman that she'd never look at another man. But I swear that I won't doubt you again. Word of honor."

She came around him, wrapped him tight, held him close. She felt his shoulders heave gently. Grief and guilt would linger, anger would return, but the great storm had passed.

"You should have told me about this before. It helps me understand a lot of things."

"That's why I'm telling you now. You can see why I harbor such horror of falseness and deceit. From now on, there won't be any secrets between us."

She took a fistful of hair and hugged him tighter and shook her head. He heard her sniffing back tears. She touched his face, the marred side.

"Hell with the scars! Wear them like a banner. Like a challenge. You survived that. You're not ordinary. You look beautiful. Hear?"

"Don't be silly. Men aren't supposed to look beautiful," he whispered huskily against her throat. "Take my word. I'm not beautiful, not in any way."

"Yes, you are, beautiful to me." There was thunder in her eyes, and a trace of tears.

"Maybe something has rubbed off you onto me," he whispered, kissing her soft stomach and each breast. Leon muffled a chuckle that changed into a groan when she jabbed him in the ribs. "Really, Brenna. You hurt me."

"Really?" she asked sweetly, then jabbed him again.

"Do you wish to turn a minor wound into a fatal one?"

Desire shot through her as he explored her breasts very

slowly, very thoroughly. "If you're not feeling up to it, my lord!"

"You wouldn't be so bold if I had my full strength."

Brenna suddenly realized Leon's free hand was between her thighs. One long finger pressed intimately against her. She trembled wildly as he found her moist heat with his fingertip.

"Oh...Leon," she returned in a broken whisper. "I love your hands on me. I love your body. I love—"

But Leon's mouth was over hers, sealing off the words. Brenna strained against him, then arched, bringing Leon's harsh breathing closer to her ear. Something went wild inside her, an insatiable urge to make him feel what he had done to her and the way blood sang through her veins. She took him in as deeply as she could, and smiled when he gasped her name.

Leon's company came at last, rain-damp, as a murky sunset stained the sky, with his men in their ranks behind Sir Rodney and his banners flying. Leon and Brenna met them in the courtyard.

"I came as soon as I got your message."

Sir Rodney wore his black hair cropped close to his square skull, erased at the temples by a lifetime of wearing a helmet. His black eyes glowered at all who met his steely gaze.

The sounds of footfalls upon the ground signalled a servant's arrival. "Sorry to intrude, my lady, but the lady Alice would like you to join her in the kitchen."

Brenna gifted Rodney with a warm smile and kissed Leon on the cheek. "I will see you at dinner."

He hugged her tight, kissed her again, and she headed toward the kitchen. Leon and Rodney walked together toward the stables. Rodney cleared his throat in a significant, edgy manner. He was a brave man, and a solid and fearless captain. Long years of discipline and campaigning had schooled him well. Nothing rattled him on the field; he remained cool, kept his temper and his wits.

"You've got something on your mind. Out with it."

Rodney's words came in a rush. "We've known each other—what?—seven years. In all that time I've never known you to show the least bit of interest in women—I mean, interest in marriage, at least. Now, out of nowhere you suddenly write and announce that you've gotten married! I mean, she's certainly a beauty, but you've known—"

"I've known no one, nothing like Brenna," Leon interrupted. He stopped his captain with a restraining hand to Rodney's arm. "I don't know whether someone like you can understand, Rodney, but she's seen *inside* me. She's seen all there is to see, the bad I've done, and felt the things that I've only hinted at to you, and she loves me anyway." He took a deep breath. "You will never know what that means."

"What do you mean, *someone like me?*"

"Look, you're the best friend—perhaps the only real friend—I've ever known, but when it comes to women… you have no…consideration. You're charming, you're attentive, you're persistent, and when the lady in question wakes up in your bed, you're gone, a new conquest in sight. Why some woman's brother or father hasn't run a sword through you… When it comes to you and women, Rodney, you are not very constant."

"And you are?"

"As constant as water running downhill."

"I wish you well, Leon. I truly do. But I still have my reservations about this headlong flight into matrimony."

Chapter Fourteen

Brenna lay on the bed in the darkness, listening to the wind as it rattled the shutters. She'd scarcely seen Leon in the past two days, not since his men had arrived. Typical of him, she thought. It was less than a month since they had been wed. Now he's so involved in securing every track by which their enemies might come down the hills or from which new enemies might arrive at their backs that the days were not long enough.

The shutters rattled again. Mayhap that was a bad omen? Fear filled her, a tumbling down of old beliefs, thoughts of ancient stones, recollections of ill legends and human hate.

She felt a warmth seep into her as she dismissed those thoughts and thought instead of Leon. They were one flesh and she was glad. It was day's end and she drew her image of him around her like a quilt, feeling his strength enter her flesh, her bones, as she imagined him caressing her back, his hot mouth over hers....

Leon eased the leather curtain shut behind him. The chamber was dim, the night lamp burning with its shaded flame flickering in a waft of air. Flash surged up in his niche, eyes glittering, his body a shadow of alarm, recognized Leon and subsided slowly.

"Are you awake?" Parting the bed curtain, Leon sat down with a bounce. His fingers swirled dark seal fur nap until it shone in the gauze-filtered light. Gold hearth lights prickled on his hair.

"If I wasn't before, I am now."

"You are happy?" he whispered in her ear.

"I am happy," she murmured, rubbing her cheek against his chin. He looked away while his hand stirred the nap on the furs.

"I need to get out of these clothes."

Brenna smiled. "I hope you do."

"You're impossible." His voice broke on the last word; he held her tighter, heart racing, face hidden in her heavy hair.

Magic. Leon's mind drifted across the word. *Sheer magic.* He rolled over and gently ran his fingers over her hot cheeks. Then all thought faded.

Brenna sat in one of the carved wooden chairs. It was nice sitting across the table sharing a meal with Leon. She finished buttering a slice of bread and spread it with raspberry jam.

Leon took a piece, ate it. He sat down and stretched his long legs before him. Shafts of gold light spread from the long narrow window, slid across the thick straw rushes, and sparkled on silver in his robe. Backlit, only the curly tip edges of his hair shone in the cheery sunbeam.

A cold nose touched his hand. He gave the cur a piece of crust. The dog swallowed it in one gulp, its tail thumping against the floor.

"Flash! No begging!" Brenna clicked her fingers. Flash retreated to the doorway, cast a white eye back at her, then shook himself and ambled outside. She frowned a little. "No matter how I try, Flash still retains bad habits acquired as a pup."

"As the twig is bent so shall the tree grow."

"Flash is not a tree!"

"It's hard to teach an old dog new tricks."

A sheer sigh of exasperation escaped her. "Flash is smart. He'll discover for himself that where there is kindness and love there is no need to beg."

She rose and took the fragments of his breakfast and the end of the loaf for good measure. Each day, she fed the ravens that roosted on the battlements. "It's better this goes to the ravens."

It was as she gathered the last scraps that a man came into the hall. He stood, coif cap in hand, revealing a thatch of unruly dark hair. "What is it, Brian?"

"'Tis Margot, my lady. Her pains have started before her time. The midwife has gone to the next village. I wonder if you would come and aid her? My brother is fair worried. This is their first, and firsts can be tricky."

"Go back and tell Giles I am coming. I will gather my things. Lucky it is that I collected some raspberry leaves only yesterday."

"Raspberry leaves?" Leon muttered.

Brenna turned 'round. "They help with the birth pangs."

Leon frowned. "Brenna, I would have you take a guard with you, when you leave the security of these walls."

"Married not a moon and you are fencing me in with rules?"

"I do not impose restrictions for arbitrary reasons."

Brenna was about to protest when she caught sight of Leon's face. "No, you're being reasonable. Eminently reasonable."

"What news have you?" Leon asked Rodney who had just ridden in from an inspection of outlying villages.

"The villagers report strangers in the district. We came across three mounted riders, but when they saw us, they turned westward and made a hasty retreat."

"I suspect they were checking our defenses. If they had intended serious provocation, they wouldn't have left so easily. But I think we can expect to see more of them soon, and with more deadly intent. I wouldn't like to think so, but I wouldn't be surprised. We're going to have to be very vigilant from now on.''

"You have been too lenient, and let your enemies gain courage from your forbearance.''

"You jest, Rodney. Am I not known as Ironheart?''

"Aye. But your enemies' heads still rest on their shoulders and not on pikes upon the gates.''

"I prefer my friends close and enemies even closer. Better to know your enemy. Keep him alive, else another will spring up in his place.''

"Remember that Hubert de Risley was the purveyor of lies to the king,'' Rodney said, "and I would not begin to imagine the fervent imagination of Keith Kil Coed. Or the scope of his lying tongue.''

"Not all imaginings. He had substance on which to practice, Rodney. And I myself did not scotch any rumors or mischief. If anything, I aided them by my silence.''

"There were ever other provocations, other reasons for hostility.''

"If we have the northern marches opposed, that slaughter will go on. We must have the barons united and not split the marches in bitter division. We must have no more fighting to give Llewelyn ap Lorwerth a foothold in our lands.''

It would not, however, go amiss to be prepared, he insisted to himself…it was a disorganized enemy, a small effort, if war came early and moved quickly.

"But Keith is your brother-in-law. Things can be resolved.''

Leon let go a heavy breath. "There is no great love, now, in our brotherhood, but guilt, that we have, each of us, each for failing Suzanne, I suspect. Someday I must make peace with him, but until then, we must guard ourselves against treachery, constrain traffic in and out of the keep.''

"Have you explained that point to Brenna?''

"Aye. She does not yet see reason. Better dissension now than Brenna become bait. That…that, I cannot allow.''

* * *

"A boy." Margot smiled down at the swaddled baby in her arms. "But of course Giles and I knew it would be."

Brenna gazed at the infant with his fuzz of dark hair and tiny petal-like face. The sight of him stirred her loins and churned her stomach. "He is beautiful," she heard herself say.

An unexpected longing clutched her heart. Her whole spirit ached to give Leon a child. Soon. She hoped it would be soon. She knew he loved the little ones; his eyes followed those who played around the castle. And there were three new pages come to rattle about the keep and bounce off the walls and furnishings.

The sky was the color of pewter and clogged with clouds. But there was some brightness to be found high on the battlements. This place, failing all others, gave Brenna a staying place for her heart, her imaginings, her wishing—her outright magic if ever such thing resided in her...she watched a few of the ravens who had lighted on the parapet, pursuing their business with their odd gait, feathers ruffling in the wind.

Leon came in search of Brenna, as he often did, if only to catch a smile, or mayhap a kiss or two. Afterward, he had to go to talk to one of the tenants about some missing sheep.

The ravens fluttered and crowded one another to reach the bread. He saw a flutter of sunlit wings, a noisy, silly congregation on the stone ledge. The sun shone on their backs, touched iridescent blue on the black plumage of the greediest one, who looked at him with a wise, round eye, and then with no hint of shame bullied a smaller bird from the ledge to reach a piece of bread. Leon watched their antics with a smile.

The raven, having eaten the last scrap, dropped onto the walkway near Brenna's feet. It seemed to be hurt; it was flopping around in a peculiar way. She reached out and tried to catch it, but it hopped awkwardly just out of her reach, tempting her to try again. Its plight seemed real; its movements were comical. Brenna made another grab for the bird; it stayed just out of her reach. She laughed out loud.

Leon grinned. "Seems as if you've found a pet."

"Well," Brenna admitted in a rush of confidence, "more like she found me. 'Twas very strange."

"How strange? What was the manner of it?"

"I was drinking from a rill, and of a sudden I *knew,* clear and sharp, that someone was watching me. And there was the raven by the single oak, bold as you please. As if…it knew me. 'Tis a good omen."

"It is?"

"Aye. Dinas Bran once was called Crow Castle, and 'tis said that while the ravens nest here, there will always be children playing in the corridors. The ravens are here, but the children are in short supply."

Leon glanced at her, and she felt herself flushing. As their eyes met, she felt that simmering sexual excitement that his nearness aroused in her.

"Did the woodcutter's child live?"

Brenna nodded. "A son—a fine son. 'Twas not an arduous birth. Both mother and child are well. Giles is most proud."

"Come here."

It was a whisper she was not even certain he had uttered yet it seemed at once as soft and as harsh as the wind coming in off the mountains.

She came into his arms. "Do you love me, Leon?"

"It is possible to search for love and find it. More often, I think, love finds us when we're not even searching. Like your raven, love has found us, Brenna. We cannot turn it away."

With Brenna nestled in his arms, the clean-washed scent of her hair filling his nostrils, the living warmth of her against him, the softness of her skin under his hand—these things made him want to believe what he said, and he did. With all his heart he believed it. They kissed then, and with the touching of their lips he knew that she believed it, too.

* * *

Brenna sat at her weaving. She glanced up at Leon standing by the window. There was a dull ache in her chest. Soon he would be leaving—he had told her so that morning.

"Shall you be absent long?"

"As long as my business needs. I have to mete out judgment on some stolen sheep, and see the sheriff about some taxes, and there is the matter of a relic that needs to be delivered to the abbey. I will be gone two days, mayhap three."

Brenna's strong hands did not falter, feeding out thread, pulling the shuttle across. "Go. Remember I love you and come back to me soon. I will be here waiting."

"You sound disgruntled, Brenna. I thought you managed fairly well with your healing and good works."

"I do, but sometimes I long for adventure."

"I like your attitude, but it can be risky."

"He who risks nothing is nothing. Only a person who risks is free."

"But not safe. You're safe here, Brenna."

"Unless Hubert de Risley or Keith Kil Coed, or one of their henchmen attack directly," she said quietly.

"They won't—don't dare anything *directly*."

She looked at Leon. He was prowling back and forth in front of the window. She could well believe the barons feared to attack Leon directly, as fierce as his face was at that moment. She wouldn't have wanted to fight him, the way he looked.

"What are you working on?"

"Curiosity plucked the goose," she whispered, veil ruffling.

He crossed the room to her and bent, picking up a small garment. "Baby clothes?"

"No harm in getting started on them well ahead of time. Though if you're likely to be away so much, what chance will there be to conceive?"

"Oh, Brenna, my love. I'm not going far." He laughed

shakily. "Only to Valle Crucis and back. Three days at most. When I return, we will try again. Many times."

She encircled his neck with her arms, drew him close and kissed him. "That is so that you will remember who it is that waits for you." She kissed him again. "That is to spur you to your task." Then, putting her hands on either side of his head, she pressed her lips to his in a long, passionate kiss. "And that is to hasten your return."

"Lady," he replied when he could breathe once more, "if you kiss me again I will not be able to leave."

Her laughter was full and free. She hugged him tightly to her, then pushed him away. "Off with you then, my love. Go this very instant, for I would have you return all the sooner."

With Leon's departure, everyone seemed ill at ease. The aunts decided they were bound for bed early, and Sir Edmund was in a mood. He only muttered at Brenna when she went to talk to him and waved his fingers, which meant go away, he was busy. He had been scraping parchments and had just scraped part of one he wanted by accident. He was not on his best humor on that account, so Brenna took herself off to her chamber.

She went to the fireplace, poked up the embers, and swung the kettle over. While she was doing it, the servants let in one of Leon's young pages, a grave-faced boy with a sealed note for her. Presentiment hanging over her, she took the paper and unfolded it.

It said, in a hasty hand, *My dear, meet me by Goblin Brook. Tell no one. Do not fail me.*

Brenna sent the page, who still waited, for Tudur. By the time he arrived, she was ready. Flash met the young squire at the doorway, excited and turning around in circles.

"Flash," she said, "we have to tie him."

It was betrayal. She took a strip of leather, tied one end to the table leg, got down on one knee and fixed the other end to Flash's collar. She ruffled the dog's ears.

"Stay, mind the fort," she said. After which she got up, and went with Tudur into the hidden passage. Barking pursued them down the stairs, its echo resounding off the stone walls.

Just after noon they reached Goblin Brook. The sky was dotted with gray-bottomed clouds that occasionally sent patterns of shadow wandering the rugged hillsides. Near a spur of forest, they dismounted and tethered the horses. There was no sign of Leon so they decided to eat a meal on the slope.

Tudur sliced two thin slivers of yellow cheese and handed one to Brenna. They ate silently for a time. While Tudur packed away the remnants, Brenna decided to fill the waterskin at the brook that lay at the base of the slope among the tight tangles of blackthorn and elder.

Tudur untethered the horses and fastened the saddlebags. He felt the need to relieve himself, and wandered into a little wood. His mount took it into its head to follow him. The red mare whickered. She cast an anxious eye back at Brenna, then followed Tudur's gelding.

Brenna sang softly to herself as she went happily about her task. Then she became aware of the sound of horses. She straightened and listened to the approach of the riders as they crashed through the undergrowth, calling harsh cries to one another.

Tudur moved deeper into the heart of the wood and scanned around for a suitably dense bush behind which to squat. The smells of early spring assailed his senses: the bare but renewing earth, the fragrant flush of leaf-grow, the damp bark and the suggestion of rain upon the breeze. The black boughs overhead formed a curious pattern against the pewter sky and he fancied he heard his name called, but the sound was lost under the noise of birdsong, and he paid no heed to it.

Brenna saw the riders bearing down upon her. They were not Leon's men.

"Tudur!" she called. She shot a look over at the thicket, but neither the boy nor the horses were anywhere in sight. She was glad that at least Tudur would make good his escape.

There was no time for fear, only action, and she gathered up her skirts in her hands and ran. She ran as fast as her legs would take her; over bracken and a fallen log. The men were gaining on her. She risked a glance backward and could see their shadowy forms looming close. She stumbled. Branches tore her hair and face, snagged and broke against her legs. She splashed into the stream.

The birds had fled. They had wings. She had none. She could only stay and face her attackers. Her pursuers were only feet away. One of them had his sword drawn.

"Go no farther, lady," the head rider warned. As he spoke, he motioned to his men to surround her. Brenna waited in the middle of the stream as she was encircled by seven men. All now had their swords drawn.

Brenna tensed to leap. Too late. Strong arms locked about her, dragging her back. One of her flailing fists caught the fellow flush on the mouth, her knuckles twisting at the last instant so that her gold-and-ruby ring—the one Leon had given her as a bride gift—scored lengthwise across his lower lip, tearing through the tender flesh. Blood spouted in red ribbons.

He leaped back. His breath shot like an explosion.

"Take her down and bind her."

Arms crushed around her. Overpowered and half smothered against a massive chest, she continued to struggle, squirming and kicking. Hands pulled cruelly at her legs and body, some lingering unnecessarily over her breasts and thighs. She was pulled down and carried to the bank, where she was thrown hard to the ground. Her forehead split open as it hit a rock. The smell of wet dead leaves and earth assailed her nostrils.

"She's a pretty one," said the man who appeared to be in charge.

"Aye, and she's well filled out under that cloak," commented one of the others who had just handled her. Brenna struggled to sit up. Her head throbbed and she heard a rushing in her ears. The men sheathed their swords and were looking to their leader.

"Don't seem to have no cup, though."

"That's cost us ten silvers."

"This here little prize should be worth that."

Brenna put a hand to her aching forehead. It felt sticky. All her senses seemed to be enveloped in a curtain of heavy wool, dulling her hearing, blurring her sight, depriving her of feeling.

A breath of something passed through Leon. He *felt* it. It seemed…it seemed something very like Brenna's presence brushed the edges of his mind, so vivid a touch he could imagine her riding at his side.

After Suzanne, he had never found it difficult to control himself where women were concerned. Brenna was different. He wanted her more, not less, each time. It was just as well he was going to Valle Crucis. He needed distance from Brenna's fire, distance and the coolness of mind to remember that a woman didn't have to be spoiled to manipulate a man. She simply had to be clever enough to allow him to deceive himself.

Suzanne was the same age then as Brenna is now, he thought. She gave no emotional satisfaction. For each pleasure she offered, Suzanne exacted full payment, her preoccupation with her own difficulties so total that sometimes Leon felt as if he were only a bystander. Suzanne took.

Brenna, he thought to himself with a leap of anticipation. Brenna gave.

She gave to all. The young, the old, the ill.

There was an incandescent honesty about her.

Ever since he'd returned to Dinas Bran and met Brenna, the world had taken upon itself a weird coating of unreality. Perhaps it was because he wanted so badly to escape his own fate for just a little longer. Forget war and all its hatreds. Learn to live in peace with one's neighbors. Peace. A dream. An ideal. A word.

Whom doth the Grail serve?

The thought came on him like a lightning stroke, stopped his breath and robbed him of clear thought. He had hated the Saracens who had slaughtered men of his, but that was war. He had not been fond of assassins whose heads had graced the fortress gates of Whittington, but that was political, and they had been Fulk's men, following a king's orders.

He looked at his hands, resting joined across the pommel, studied the sword scars on his knuckles. The scents of dried lavender and woodsmoke drifted wraithlike through his awareness. Again, something like an invisible hand, light as thistledown, touched him.

"Leon!"

He cast a look over his shoulder and began to turn Deso about on the road. Had anything happened at all? Could that timeless instant have been all in his imagination?

But something flickered across his sight, an uncertain touch like the light through leaves, like a brush of spider silk across the nape of his neck. He looked about again just as a raven left a tree ahead of him and dropped to the road, for no cause that he could tell. It fell into a puddle, making a plume, and it was gone, without a trace.

He turned Deso full circle.

"Brenna?"

Flash scrambled to his feet and surged to greet Leon, nudging at his hands. Flash was here. Brenna never went anywhere without the faithful hound. He stroked its ears.

"Brenna? Do you hear me? Answer."

There was no response. The silence was stifling, leaving Leon's pulse hammering in his ears—his heart pounding. He strode into the chamber and peered into the sleeping alcove. Empty. He had expected no less.

The chill gripped and twisted in his gut. Even his brain felt cold. He felt the blood pumping in the veins of his neck. He should have known. He should have thought. He should have—

"Where?" was his first conscious thought, and the dog cast a glance at the far wall, and that seemed his answer. He turned, called Flash to heel, and stayed for nothing else.

Leon ran. Servants scattered like mice along his route, finding niches that took them aside from the course of confrontation. Guards at the stairs came to attention. The hall showed vacant. And in not many moments he was in the stables yelling for his horse, his helmet and his shield.

"Thomas, get to the training yard and fetch Sir Rodney fast as you can. Tell him to follow with three squads. Then go to Sir Edmund and tell him not to worry. Don't dally now."

Men ran. Sir Edmund's captain arrived, saw the tenor of things and asked no questions of him, nor did a thing but stand to the side. In moments Leon was outside, hand on the pommel of his warhorse. Without touching the stirrup he vaulted into the saddle, jerked his long sword into a more comfortable position, caught the helmet tossed to him and slung it over his saddle bow.

"What will you do?" spoke the captain standing by the doorway.

Leon met the fellow's eyes levelly. His composure was an iron lid clamped tight over something that glowed hot beneath. The captain saw something there that matched his own mood.

"Find Brenna. I swear by this," he said, laying his hand on his pendant. "I swear by this emblem and by the Holy Grail that I will not return alive without her."

"I'm with you."

There was no demure. Leon but put up his coif and donned his helm. The captain took a throwing ax from Telyn, tossed it once and jammed the weapon into his belt.

One-handed, managing Deso with his knees and with his shield hand holding the reins, Leon tightened the last two buckles on his side as he went.

"God go with you, then, sir," said Telyn.

"He might," spat Leon, sinking spurs into the stallion's sides, though there was no need. Deso did not need spurs; for love he would race the wind. "But 'tis certain the devil will."

He was away, in a shower of sparks where his horse's metal hooves struck the stone. Then three other riders overtook him in his breakneck flight: Edgar, Sir Edmund's own captain, came up, and two more guardsmen came with him. Others would follow, he knew, but he had no time to wait. Time was vital. He had to find Brenna before it was too late.

When they arrived at the king's highway, he heard the dry rattle of feathers overhead and looked up to see a bird flying above him, going in the same direction. It circled and dropped lower.

The wind blew, scudding ripples over the narrow Dee. Across the timber bridge, and the horses broke into a gallop. They rode through the street with a clatter of iron-shod hooves echoing back and forth off the houses and off the high and low walls of the town. Villagers watched curiously from their opened doors, and came out onto their steps or stared down from the upper windows.

Leon looked at the hill line before him, turned his head, squinting for any movements in the dense green blots of oak scrub they passed. Nothing.

Wings clapped. A bird erupted from the brushes. A single feather fell, a black arrow, spiraling to snag on Leon's gauntlet. The charger fretted, ears flat, eye rolling. Leon glanced up to see a raven sitting on the stump of a tree watching him.

A glossy black raven, like the bird on the battlements.

Leon's breath hissed between his teeth. The answer to prayers, it might be. Yes, it just might be Brenna's raven. He didn't believe in chance. He didn't believe in coinci-

dence. He certainly didn't believe in wizardry and magic.
Sometimes he didn't even believe in the power of prayer.
But, somehow, sometime, his beliefs had been challenged.

He set his tapered shield and soothed the restive stallion
with crooning sounds. Of its own accord, his hand raised
infinitesimally, as if to take a falcon upon it. The raven
swooped and settled there, motionless, eyes glittering. Very
slowly he lowered his arm.

He would let Brenna's love and faith be his guide.

A ridge loomed in front of them, then. Horseshoe Pass.
The riders halted. The scuffed leaf-strewn slope marked the
signs of a struggle. Flash ran back and forth, sniffing at the
brushes and nosing at the ground.

"My lord!"

Now who was that?

"My lord, quick!" It was Tudur, running hard, dashing
straight into the water. He floundered across the stream, and
scrambled to a gasping halt before Leon, wet to the thighs.
"They had her before I knew, and when I went to give
chase, the mare would not..." His breath came fast and
heavy, half in pain, half in anger.

"Easy, catch some breath." Leon steadied him.

"Mounted men, and armed. They took Brenna."

"What armed men?" Leon's voice was as cold as ice.

"I'm not sure, sir. They had no colors."

"How many?"

"Seven. I think they wanted the cup." Tudur held out the
small vessel that seemed to be causing so much trouble.

Leon took it, feeling its warm mystery. He felt as if he
were caught in a dream, and yet he was intensely alert, aware
of every flicker of sound or movement. Light in his hand, it
held the weight of worlds. The bird's beak clashed; its wings
stretched. With a sigh, he returned the cup to Tudur.

"I want you to get rid of this," he said.

Tudur blinked. He fondled it lovingly, like a wild animal
he had befriended and was about to set free. "You want me
to hide it?"

"No, I don't want it hidden. I want it to be lost. No one—not me or you or anyone—must find it. We're not ready for the Holy Grail," Leon said softly, his voice lowered almost to a whisper. "None of us. Maybe in a thousand years, people will know how to handle something so wonderful. But not now. See to it."

Flash returned to Leon and flopped down, panting, at his feet. In his jaws, he carried a fragment of fabric.

Brenna's mantle.

Then nothing moved. Time stopped. Only the sound of the wind blowing through the trees.

"Caer Llion?" The captain peered at him with concern.

Vision blurred in and out of focus. Leon crouched and ran his fingers over the wool. Even before he raised his hand to his face, he knew what it was: blood. Sticky, nearly dry, less than an hour old.

"Where does this road lead?"

"On to Moelfierna, and by way of Carrig-y-beg to Corwen."

"Moelfierna! Hubert de Risley!"

"They can't have got far," Leon reasoned. "If we ride hard, we should overtake them."

To hell with that. Think now, think today.

"If they went directly to Moelfierna, riding as fast as they should have been, they'll be inside the walls by sunset."

"My lord." Edgar glanced at the leaden sky. "The weather is with us. We know where they are headed, and Anslem here knows a shortcut." His bleak northern visage lighted up. "Show us, lad."

The huge young man smoothed a muddy patch at his feet, and squatted to map the wet earth with a dagger point: a straight line for the road that ran west to Corwen, a curving snake for the River Dee crossing it at Abernarfon.

Leon hunkered down over the rough map.

"The river curves as it follows the valley. The ford here—" Anslem pointed with the dagger "—it has a stony bottom. The water's less than knee-deep, fifty paces bank to bank. We can cut across behind the hills."

"The lead's too great. We can't close it in the time we have. We'll never overtake them," said the soldier nearest Leon.

Anslem straightened. He kept his eyes on the mud map. "I've traversed this country many times, sir," the big northerner mused. "And I know all the tracks and trails. 'Tis the best chance we have of catching them."

"Are you sure?"

"Yes," said Anslem with utter conviction.

Leon weighed the odds. The king's highway was the easier route and the faster, but Anslem knew the land and was confident in his predictions. Once barricaded within his fortress, Hubert de Risley could hold fast for as long as he chose. Leon shivered beneath his cloak. Follow your instincts, he told himself. Think what's to do, nothing else. What's first, then next. Keep thinking on that, not the ball of sick in your stomach.

"We can but try," Leon's voice rasped. He grasped the bridle and put foot to stirrup. "I merely pray we're not too late."

It was a succession of hills after that, tree-crowned, rocky and rough, the white-water river running through; and far away on both sides the tooth-white, tooth-sharp mountains. The ford was a brisk jog across, the brushy sides of the road offered no surprises more than a flight of startled birds and the occasional fox or scuttling hare, invisible but for a whisk of gray.

The raven kept pace with the riders. Sometimes it landed on the road ahead and strutted along the edges until they swept past. Again it perched on tree limbs, or leaped into the sky to make a dark slash across the empty air. Occasionally it flew ahead and disappeared, as if urging them to hasten.

The vale narrowed before them. There at last beyond doubting was the black gorge and the loom of Moelflerna against the western sky; a sky near purple and reefed by clouds of wet gray wool ready to wring out drenching rain.

"Ride!" cried Leon. "Moelflerna is before us."

Aye, like the very keep of hell, black gullet, black crag, black castle. And the last of the gullet was the tongue, and that was a path against one sheer wall, for the other dropped away to a precipice and far below a cold gleam of water; and this eagle's track reared steeply to the narrow iron-barred gate. Truly Moelflerna could never be taken, for there was not even space for three men abreast to assail its walls, and the cliff that edged the path melted into the very crag of the castle.

Nearer; almost on them...

Deso hurled himself up the steep ledge with all his strength and power, the bridle foam-flecked. Twenty yards or so of space between the somber, looming towers, aligned, and the wall of the stronghold. The gates were still open. Groups bunched above each tower. The walkways behind the parapets were swarming with men. Arrows and spears fell about them, and Leon saw inner walls and a paved court and people thronging, and the gates swinging shut. The portcullis came down, a great rattling and clamor of iron.

They were too late.

Chapter Fifteen

The thump of axes attempting the hinges and fittings of the gates filled the air. A man went down, an arrow through his arm, and they carried him away to safety. Above them towered the gray cliff, abrupt and sheer as the very walls of the fortress that crowned its summit.

Leon sucked in his breath. Of all that terrible race, this must be the worst, with arrows raining and life pouring away and one misstep the road to certain death. One of the defenders, twisting, fell back from the wall. Another ran along the parapet, a torch in his hand. Smoke flowed from behind him. Other fellows carrying bundles of flaming sticks ran toward the tower.

"We can do nothing as long as we remain here. Just as they can do nothing against us." Leon lifted a hand toward the fortress, black and immense above them. "On such a narrow path, twenty men might hold against a thousand. No one can win in such a position. Therefore, since they cannot move, we must."

"There is another way to reach the gate." A black-helmed veteran spoke. "It is not such a way by which a company can go, but sufficient to enable a single person to slip into the castle."

"Are you certain?" Leon let air hiss through his teeth.

"Certain!" echoed the soldier; and he smiled. "I was born here. And I climbed the cliffs as a lad. In quest of an eagle's nest I more than once reached the little plateau that thrusts out under the very wall of Moelflerna on the southern side. To enter the castle from there, all that would be needed would be a rope and an anchoring device, for the wall is low just there—not more than twelve feet high."

A moment Leon paused, considering. The idea was good, if one had the head for heights.

"All right," he said. His voice sounded oddly harsh. "Only one question, where do I go?"

"There, do you see, sir? There and there and there."

There was indeed, if one looked carefully, a narrow goat path disappearing into thornbushes and scrub. Beyond that the great jagged mass of the peak, the fortress, Moelflerna itself. Above, the afternoon rain had descended from the mountains in towers of purple thunderheads, but they had not yet begun to release their cargo.

"Our thanks, soldier. Alain, rope and a grappling hook. Rodney, continue the assault on the gate."

"You have counted the cost of failure?"

Hesitation or doubt he had none. He could not wait. He had to move. He had to do what he could to save Brenna.

"It needs no counting. It is plain enough. Show me the way, soldier."

The worst danger was the danger of this climb. The ground was nowhere level, being all aclutter of boulders and rocks. By comparison, the rest—the scaling of the castle wall, the stabbing of a sentry or two, and the opening of the gate—were safe and simple matters. Here, however, a false step, a misgiving even, or a moment of giddiness, such as might well beset him, must plunge him down to instant death. But he could not trust this task to another, and he was far beyond any care for his own safety.

Encumbered though he was by shield and sword, rope and anchor, at first the ascent was easy, and he was able to go forward swiftly, weaving from one foothold to another among brush rooted in the stone; soon, however, the precipice grew more abrupt, the footholds became scantier, and in places failed almost entirely.

Halfway up, his groping hands met hard rock. Stone dug into his sides, his surcoat seemed to catch on some projection. He twisted with panic force, felt the fabric tear and give, felt himself slip. He looked sideways and down into the awful depths below him. Instantly he stopped dead. He shuddered involuntarily, and clung to the rock.

After a few seconds he found a purchase with his feet, began to force himself up over black rocks in whose deep shadows lay the last white aprons of unmelted snow from the winter. Up he climbed, a few painful inches at a time, another moment of seeming immobility. Then he managed to get one knee over the lip of a ledge, found a better foothold. Breathing shallowly, he felt tiny needles of cold sweat prickle his forehead under the mail cowl.

He made a careful effort to remember his training, to regain his calm, to breath properly. There was a ledge above him, breast-high. He pushed himself up, got a knee over and crawled another foot. He could not fail Brenna.

Grimly, step by step, he began to climb. The hillside was deathly silent. The only sound was the rasp of his breath, the shuffling of his feet against stone, and the hammering of his heart. In stillness was death, in retreat destruction; in terror, damnation, he thought. He blinked, frowned. And burst upward in a flood of memory, a torrent of panic terror.

He shut the thought out with all his will, flooding the levels of his mind with everything of Brenna he could remember. Merriment, laughter, lovemaking, gaiety and joy and lightness.

Slowly, carefully, he made the ascent. At the top he looked at the blank wall carefully. He uncoiled the rope from his body, stood back and swung the grappling hook a moment, taking aim, then hurled it upward. It soared above the wall, and fell beyond, between two merlons, then thudded against the masonry. A crack in the stone, a black line in the fading light. He pulled gently at the rope. The hooks held.

He wiped sweat out of his eyes. He hadn't sweated so much in the desert before battle.

Hauling himself up hand over hand, his feet against the masonry, he came swiftly to the top of the wall, and knelt there, peering down into the courtyard. All was silent.

Big dollops of cold rain began to fall as he loosed the hooks from the crevice in which they had fastened. He flung them wide, the rope with them, and sent them hurtling over the precipice, that there might be no evidence of his coming. Then he dropped softly down upon the parapet, exulting to realize that he had made it, and that he was within the fortress.

The pounding of the axes below continued. A moment he paused, considering. He moved forward swiftly and gained a flight of stone steps that wound down into the inner bailey. This he descended, and so reached the quadrangle. He slid along the shadowed wall like a pike in a stream, swiftly, silently, until he reached the barbican.

The air carried a tang of fire. Smoke was rising from somewhere within the keep. At first a thin, shadowy wisp in the air, it blackened and thickened into a huge dark column. He looked up and saw the tall figure of Hubert de Risley on the ramparts. He drew in deep breaths of the tainted air.

Where was Brenna?

A quick shove of the shoulder and he had the crossbar lifted before any were aware of his presence. A lever thrown and the portcullis began to lift. The gate thrust open behind him just as Hubert's men came at him like a swarm of bees.

He thrust his shield right against the faces of men coming at him in desperate defense. One he flung back with a shove of the shield alone and the man beside him engaged that one; the other won the edge of his sword. He spared a quick glance. 'Twas Alain of Rhewl. For the moment he and Alain were battling a knot of enemy alone, and then Rodney turned up beside him, shield up, sword advanced.

Blades rang.

Leon hewed mightily. His arm flailed with a fierce and violent motion. His blade streamed scarlet ribbons.

From both the right and left, Leon could hear the ringing of swords, the clash of metal on shields. Men from Dinas Bran, their eyes wild in their helmets, struggled through the melee, sweeping aside the defenders like dried leaves before a tempest.

"We cannot hold them!" cried a man.

Leon had reached the wooden steps to the keep and begun to ascend them. He looked back. No one was close to him. He scanned the melee. The square churned and writhed with the fight. The sound was a booming, featureless roar—like that of blood racing through the ears. On the east, and nearer the center portions of the wall, the tower was aflame. Some men leaped from it. There was no sign of Hubert de Risley.

Men were now running in every direction. Released from their pens, the horses were running about the courtyard, adding to the confusion. Those who were able were trying to contain the damage. Someone organized a line of servants to throw water on the fires or beat them with cloth and leather, but flames kept leaping out in new places. The fire had a will of its own. Sparks ignited the roof of the keep.

There was the snap of a cable, its vibrations carried even to the steps. There were shouts. A movement sped past, like a puff of breath passing his ear. A great cauldron of oil, its oil now ignited, crashed beneath the tower and flooded the courtyard behind him. Smoke rolled through the air; black and thick. He was separated from his men who stopped at this wall of flame some forty feet in width.

He waved to Rodney, made retreating gestures.

"Back! Back! Withdraw!" He raised his voice. "*It's over*. We've won. *You've* won."

His captain lifted his sword to him in salute.

Despair and panic thickened in Leon's chest. The blaze that roared through the passages and up the stairwells consumed the keep, undaunted by the rain sweeping out of the mountains.

Brenna! Where was his Brenna?

Brenna slammed hard against the door jamb, trying to retreat. Her shoes were ruined and would have to be resewn. They'd not carry her far. Her woolen gown was sodden to the knees and her linen undershift clung to her legs, making movement difficult.

Think. Help yourself. You don't want to die today.

Fear jolted her stomach. If she ever got out of this alive, she'd never be so stupid again.

There was a terrible ruckus at the gate.

Leon!

Smoke belched from above, choking, acrid, stinging her eyes and nose, forcing the air out of her lungs. It was a place of death.

The door gave. She flew down the corridor, reached the servants' stairwell and, edging quietly down the squeaky stairs, lurched out into the scullery.

"Leon!"

No answer. Stupid to call out. Leon was not here. Stupid to have gone out in the first place, but how was she to know the note was false? A crash of iron. Horses screaming. Brenna's heart missed another beat; if she were frightened once more today, she'd not live out her span.

"Leon...help me!"

Brenna's voice! Like an animal, Leon sprang, all senses bright and humming. He ran toward it, desperately squinting past the flames, straining to see through the nightmare fire, and then he felt something inside him slowly give way, terrible and slow and inevitable like a bridge cracking over a crevasse.

She's still alive. It was the only thought that registered in his mind as he took the stairs two at a time.

Brenna heard footsteps, felt them through the floor. Hubert was coming back!

No! She began to tremble. She had to force herself to breathe.

She wrenched herself free of her paralysis and looked around for a weapon. Heavy footsteps thudded on the floorboards.

Leon bolted into the main hall, heard a clatter from the scullery and rushed through the open door. Then the air blasted from his lungs, and he shot forward, falling to his knees. He jerked around, and saw his wife rearing over him, a long-handled bed-warming pan in her fist.

"Brenna!" Leon breathed. The hard lines of his shoulders went suddenly lax, and he leaned back on his heels. Her fright did not leave her, and she clutched the copper pan handle even tighter. "It's me. Leon!" he rasped. "You are safe."

"Leon?" It really was Leon in front of her, though she had to touch him to believe it. With a great sob, Brenna threw herself onto him. She gripped his shoulders hard, feeling the solid muscle and bone beneath the chain mail.

Leon felt the floodgates opening inside him, felt his vulnerability to Brenna and did not shy away from it. He embraced it. He felt his heart nearly burst and it seemed as if the bars of iron that had encased it for so long cracked and fell apart.

He knelt there for a moment, then rose to his feet, the narrow rectangle of pain in the center of his back throbbing as the shock wore off. A ragged smile crossed his lips.

"You certainly know how to strike a blow."

He gently stood Brenna upright and helped to balance her, for her legs wobbled. Her hands clung like burrs to wool.

"Are you all right? I can't see you very well."

"Bruised—some little gashes. Nothing like you, I'm sure."

"Did he…"

No! She shook her head violently.

"Even so, this is too much. He dies for this."

He turned his head, slowly, feeling a stabbing in his right shoulder, and the dull aching throbs in his left. His right thigh hurt, and he looked down. The links were unbroken. A bruise from the flat of a blade?

"He left, to look for Tudur, to find the cup."

He could hear the buckling and crackling of the ceiling. The smoke was intensifying around them, seething and stinging the skin like a beating with twig brooms. He could not delay himself further. He let out a pent breath.

"Let's get out of here."

Still she clung to him. Setting his jaw, he scooped her up like a sack of meal and headed for the nearest exit.

Depthless darkness lay below, but the walkway was sturdy and intact, the fire not having reached this part of the keep. He set Brenna down beside him, and leaned on the wooden rail.

"Come," he said. His voice sounded oddly harsh.

Then suddenly there was a great rushing noise. A great stone column came crashing down, demolishing the wooden rail in its downward flight. He straightened, but his boot heels slipped in the flakes of gray that sprayed the platform.

"Watch," Brenna cried in a harsh echo of his own tones.

He felt himself falling toward the walkway edge, toward the depths. Red haze still blurred his sight. But Brenna was in the way, face white as cloth, white hands spreading like wings. She caught his arm.

"Trust me!" she screamed. Somehow she spun around, using his own motion to wrench him sideways, redirecting him with all the grace of a warrior; his boots swung over space and stumbled back onto solid footing. For a moment they swayed together in the center of the walkway, his limbs clutched to her in animal panic.

The fire roared to the roof and collapsed into embers. Slowly he relaxed. He gripped Brenna's shoulder and brushed some flakes from her hair. He drew in three deep rapid breaths, feeling his armor heave as he breathed.

"Thank you." His voice had become a thread. He could not muster more than that.

Brenna smiled an odd slow smile. "Well, I am your guardian angel after all, though I'm sure you would've figured out something without my help."

"You needn't flatter me to save my dented pride. I'm quite glad enough that you are safe. I hardly care about the rest."

Her hand fumbled out, gripped his arm. "I've had quite enough adventure, Leon. I want to go home."

Leon dropped his arm around her shoulders, squeezed tightly. "If I haven't told you before, remind me to tell you I love you."

Tudur sat on a flat stone, the wind riffling through the sparse grass and sighing among the bare rocks as he gazed at a snowcapped mountain top far in the distance. He stared up at a sky the color of slate. Overhead, black against lead-colored cloud, the birds were gathering. They were ravens—first one, then another wheeling overhead...three...four, circles against low clouds, not slow and searching but tight and purposeful.

His confidence was dwindling fast. What was he but a half-grown boy with ideas above his station? He wasn't cut out for adventuring. Heroes never got themselves into the muddle he had, losing their damsel in distress, or if they did, they went right on after the villains and fetched her back.

Like Ironheart.

Only he wasn't Ironheart. He was Tudur, and cursed with a worthless cup that everyone seemed to think was worth killing for. He wished he'd never found it, or when he did, that he'd left it gathering dust.

After the shock of Brenna's abduction and Caer Llion's uncompromising order to be rid of the cup, he'd wandered, dazed, wondering what to do with it, until he came upon the ritual ring of standing stones. He felt eerily that he'd slipped into limbo, that beyond the circle of stones no world existed anywhere. The stones loomed, rough-hewn sentinels that kept their secrets.

The moment he set foot in the ring of stones, he could feel ancient power flowing like an invisible river around the hilltop, which was an eddy in the ever-streaming current. The feeling of being surrounded by swirling forces, of being picked up and carried off on the relentless waves of this unseen power, nearly took his breath. 'Twas strange. And frightening.

He tossed the tarnished cup that seemed to have caused so much trouble into the air and caught it, and wondered again what to do with it. No matter where he hid it, he at least would know where it was, and he would be forever plagued by those wanting its magical properties.

But he did not like to think about that.

He looked up at the circling ravens. Two were descending, flapping down to set themselves on a standing stone where someone long ago had carved strange symbols into living rock. He could see their eyes, black and hard as polished coal. Waiting. Smart birds, they always knew when something was dead or close to it. He hoped it wasn't him they were waiting for.

On this magical spot where the Druids once practiced their ancient rites, it was easy to believe the things whispered before the firelight, the tales and scraps of tales men passed to their children for a hundred generations and more: one-eyed giants in halls of stone; goddesses who transformed themselves into owls to haunt the night on soft, silent wings; water maids who lured the unwary to rapturous death beneath the waves; enchanted hills where captured heroes slept the centuries away; invisible islands where gods cavorted in the twilight of never-ending summer...

In the unnatural silence, 'twas easy to believe the unbelievable there among the circle of stones.

Then he heard it—a sound to make him leap to his feet and listen; a rhythmic drumming in the earth, a clear, resonant echo rolling over the land.

Tudur ran to the edge of the ancient sacred site. The drumming he heard was the iron-clad hooves of a great black
destrier striking the hard stony track. The rider pounded up
the twisting path at full gallop, a sword in his hand. Not a
big man but bulky with iron, ring mail from shoulders to
knees. His helmet was gone, and Tudur could see 'twas Sir
Hubert.

"I want that cup, boy!"

"Come and get it!"

Stupid bravado. He'd never escape, too far to cover, the
rider already leaning out of the saddle to slash—

What to do?

Tudur picked up a rock the size of his fist and hurled it.
The animal reared, startled, while the rider fought to keep
his seat. Tudur hurled another rock at the man. It struck him
on the forehead, and he toppled off his horse. The fallen
man got to his feet and staggered toward Tudur, his sword
flashing. The boy took aim again, but missed. The fellow
came at him with a menacing grin on his face, tossing his
sword to his left hand and pulling out a short dagger.

And then the ravens appeared. They came until the sky
was black with them and their shadow blocked out even the
light of the waning sun.

Hubert de Risley staggered erect. Talons clawed at him,
wings rushed up about his head; beaks thrust into his face,
beating him back. He struck against them, wildly yet with a
fixed half-mad purpose. The thing in his eyes, the surging
darkness, the sudden light, came almost near enough to
name.

The ravens screamed a hoarse refrain; the beating of their
wings flattened the grass tufts. They came for the cup. They
soared away and dispersed.

By slow degrees Tudur's mind cleared. The sky was
empty of birds. Close by him, almost at his feet, lay what
they had discarded. The man neither moved nor uttered a
sound. One eye stared blindly at the sky; the other was lost
in a rush of scarlet.

Tudur dropped to his knees beside Hubert de Risley. With the hem of his tunic he tried to staunch the flood. He could not see Hubert's eye. It was all blood.

Inconceivably living still, but something was stamped deep in Hubert as image and letters on the sides of a coin. Not the black birds, not black at all, but a young squire whose pale face Hubert dimly recognized.

"I am lucky. God...did not wish me to die today—"

"Lie still."

The boy hurriedly blessed himself and prayed, teeth chattering, before his image faded, leaving him to darkness.

For Hubert de Risley, who, in blind arrogance, had once sent a half-pagan prayer to God that he might see his end in time to prepare, realized his wish was granted. He would have all the time he needed to prepare himself, years to see his end coming slowly, but only in his mind's eye. He would be sightless, every moment of it.

The valley of the Dee was hidden in a thin mist. Shapes moved within it, now all but invisible, now clear to see: farm folk on errands that could not wait for a clear sky, a milkmaid or two trudging toward warmth and dry feet. Once there had been a woodcart, and once a gaggle of geese.

This was mounted company, drab in the rain. There were ten of them. No banner floated over them; whatever badges they bore lay hidden under dark cloaks. Their mounts moved swiftly enough, but the beasts' necks were low with weariness.

The foremost was glistening red in the rain, and it alone seemed to run easily. It bore no rider.

"Elen, fetch Agnita."

Elen was as quick as aged legs could carry her.

Sir Edmund had already reached the stair to the gate.

The riders clattered under the carven arch. One by one, wearily, they dismounted. Sir Rodney took a limp bundle from Leon, who was last to leave his mount's back. Leon retrieved the soft form from his captain, arguing when Sir Rodney would have taken the burden from him, and gathered it close against his breast. 'Twas Brenna. She lay still as a thing born dead.

"She's dead?"

Sir Edmund sounded ineffably old, ineffably weary.

"It is all right, sir. She is safe. Asleep only." He suffered Sir Edmund to embrace them both, standing back when the old man would let him and saying, "Why, you're as wet as we are! Were you up in your eagle's roost watching for us?"

"Yes." Sir Edmund held him at arm's length. A tremor of weariness had come into the old man's mouth, and more wrinkles than usual mapped the territory around his eyes. He trembled on the verge of collapse. "Where did you find her?"

"Moelflerna."

"Where is de Risley?"

"Valle Crucis."

"Dead?"

"No. He saw the error of his ways, metaphorically speaking. He has surrendered his fief and joined the monks to reflect on the wrongs he has done."

"Tell me."

Leon's face did not change. "Later. For now be satisfied that Hubert de Risley has been sufficiently punished by an authority greater than mine. He will trouble us no more."

Brenna stirred in his arms, shivered and sneezed.

"By your leave, Sir Edmund, Brenna must be tended to."

If Sir Edmund recognized the evasion, he saw the truth in it. He smiled, a thousand wrinkles gathering about his eyes. "You also, my son. I shall speak with you when you are dry and rested."

High in the sky, small white clouds scudded before the strong wind from the southwest. Their shadows raced across the bright green of new grass, across the strong rich brown of plow furrows, the heavy horse teams drawing slow lines across the springtime fields. In between the sun shone, hot and welcome.

Leon smiled at Rodney with a sudden rush of confidence. "You should marry, Rodney. Bachelor knights have their place, but a family..."

The intimacy surprised Rodney. *He means it.* This iron-hearted man who rationed his trust like a miser, who held few in high regard, had fallen in love. For himself the thought of marriage might not be new though dusty from lack of use in ten years when he'd been settled as the wind.

"I am a younger son. I have no lands. Naught save proven courage, loyalty and—" he gestured at his mail and sword "—an entirely portable estate."

Leon stared out over the fields. "The borders are secure and the marches settled. I could use some peace myself."

"There are good folk here and no mistake. I feel comfortable with them."

"It is not definite, but our hopes are high that my lady carries a child. The king has sent word that his natural daughter, Joan, is to wed Llewelyn ap Lorwerth, and bids me find a castellan for Moelflerna. The post is yours now." He turned back to Rodney. "Hubert has a sister. Judith. As I recall, she is Brenna's age and most winsome. You could do worse than pay her court."

The old woman hugged her shawl about her, bony hands clenched on the edges. Beneath her veil, her hair was gray and trailed about her face, which was a map of years.

"The wound he received in the tourney. It has all festered beneath," she said in a faint, harsh voice. "He asks that you come."

Silence. A long pause...

Opening doors, raised voices, a shuffle of feet, said that the conference of Leon and Sir Edmund had broken up.

"I will see what I can do," Brenna said.

* * *

A stir drew Leon's glance upward. Brenna stood in the
doorway, holding her chest of herbs and simples. "There is
a rumor that Keith Kil Coed is sick, and that it is feared he
may not live."

"It is no more than he deserves." The voice was a
weapon, filling the air, inescapable.

Her brows met. Her jaw thrust forward. "You have no
reason to refuse him assistance."

"He may not have been at Moelflerna, but he sent that
note. He would have trapped us both, me to my death, you
to a fate worse than death."

"Who are you to judge this man?"

"I am the king's justiciar. He plotted treason. For that
alone he deserves to die."

She scowled, stubborn. "He is your kin."

Leon whirled in a white rage, his fist clenched. "He is
my enemy."

"It is time to set grudges aside in the interest of the
marches and the people."

"Oh, what would I give if...if—"

"If and if and if! Do you hear yourself?" She said hotly,
"If cannot change *is.*"

"Nothing is changed, Brenna." When his voice had
stilled, his heart beat hard, and not only with anger.

"We must all bear our failures to the grave," she said
sadly. All expression had vanished from her face, but the
black eyes were blazing. He felt a large struggle going on
inside himself. He could deny her, be rid of Kil Coed with
the mere might of his will, and turn all his high words to
the croaking of carrion birds—and lose her in the process.

Leon made himself meet that unmeetable gaze. "His hurt
was small, and he is strong. There are other healers. Let one
of them go."

"Leon, this is your chance to cast aside old hatreds," she
said quite calmly, but her face shone with her faith in him.

"Keith needs a healer, and quickly. He's at your mercy. Would I ask you otherwise? Will you come with me?"

"I am mad," he said. "But I am not a murderer. Not even when I can see—" A shudder racked him. There was only one answer for him, though he would have wished it otherwise. Honor kept things simple. He drew a deep breath. "Let's go to Craignant, and may God preserve us all."

White puffy clouds scudded out of the north and across the gray-blue sky, occasionally obscuring the midmorning sun. They rode down from the hills into a wooded valley. The entrance to the lower bailey was defended by a timber palisade flanked by two wooden towers. A guard emerged from the base of one of these to challenge Leon, his hands firm on the haft of his spear.

"Halt and state your business," he declared sullenly.

"Where is Keith Kil Coed?" Leon's voice echoed in the quiet of the yard. There was some little hesitation, and then the spear slanted down.

"You'll get no joy out of him. He's dying."

"So I've been told."

The guard moved forward then, with a clatter of metal and a heavy step. "He's in the lower hall."

Leon and Brenna rode into the bailey that was occupied by a mass of store sheds and stables, ramshackle dwellings, animal pens and service structures. The steward met them and took them to Keith's chamber.

"So you've come to gloat over me." Keith's voice sounded reedy, frail.

Leon stared down at his archenemy, horrified to see him reduced to mere bones under the yellowish, taut skin, his eyes sunken into cavernous hollows. "No."

Brenna moved close to his side. "Keith! Old scores will not serve here!"

"I don't have the cup, if that's what you're after."

"We're not. In any case, the cup's gone."

Keith looked up with the staring eyes of a startled animal. "Gone? Where did it go?"

"Only the wild birds know that," Brenna said. Keith sighed. "Still, we may find it again." Leon glanced at her sharply. "At the next millennium, perhaps a man with a pure heart will find it and there will be peace and happiness," she added with a smile.

"Why are you here?"

"Humanity," Leon said, as if that explained it all. "If anyone can cure you, Brenna can."

Brenna dropped to her knees beside Keith. Setting her jaw, she stooped and drew the covers from his swollen leg. "Can you move your foot? Wiggle the toes?"

Keith moved his foot carefully. Toes moved. "Hurts."

"The damage is severe. If the rotten flesh is not taken away now, the contagion will spread throughout your body and you will be dead within two days, perhaps less."

"Then let me die," Keith panted. "Shrive me and let me die."

"You are too strong just to be shriven and released," Leon said, leaning over him again.

Keith swore at him then, a blasphemy that caused Brenna to suck in her breath and widen her eyes. Leon, however, absorbed the curse without so much as a flicker. He had heard the same and worse a hundred times over and knew that they were part of a fighting man's armor, the bravado that concealed fear. The thing that surprised Leon most was that he cared. He didn't know why. Was there some point of honor in this?

"Swear no more oaths to anyone if you are wise. If you wish my advice, I give you it in this one thing. I can heal you."

"You can?"

"Aye. I'm certain so—if you'll mend your manners. If you can change that, I'm sure I can."

"Ha, what makes you think I will survive you cutting my

leg off?'' Keith demanded with a mirthless baring of his teeth.

"I have no intention of removing your leg. I have a more powerful magic than mere butchery, but first you must recant your sins.''

"What do you intend?''

"A poultice, one I make myself—for the horses.''

"Vincent tells me... Vincent tells me how you make your medicines. How you have your little jars...your little jars with the old bread, the fermented cheese—how you cured the smith with a salve of herbs and mouldy bread...''

"It cures infections. It can't cure stupidity, Keith, it can't cure hate!''

"Do the horses generally live?''

"Aye.''

He had to choose between a chance of life—an altered life—or certain death. It was the decision of a cornered man with a precipice at his back. Was his pride worth his life? He crossed himself listlessly.

"Shrive me,'' he said, without taking his eyes off her face, ''and then do your worst.''

Chapter Sixteen

The year had come full circle. Much had been done during that time. Much remained still to be done. But whatever the trials and anxieties of keeping peace in the northern marches, it seemed as though some benign spirit was keeping watch over Dinas Bran and its people. There was a sense of warm unity; an optimism at work that boded well for the future.

Leon had the feeling, new every day, that his life was rather astonishing, and that many great and marvelous gifts had been bestowed upon him. Problems were nothing; he welcomed them; for he felt with utter certainty that he could overcome them all. And at the heart of this feeling of his, giving him this special faith, was the love that had grown between him and Brenna. As soon as he finished this report to the king, he would go find her, and bask in her gentle radiance.

Leon heard horses come and go on the cobbles outside, heard voices raised in argument. He frowned and continued with his work. A discreet knocking sounded from the carved panels of the map room door.

''My lord,'' Thomas interrupted his message writing. The pen had dried in midthought. *Public acceptance,* he had been about to write, before he forgot his phrase. But the ink failed and made only a sketchy line. "My lord, Keith Kil Coed is on his way, and requests audience."

"Damn him," he said, dropping his quill.

He could deny Keith. He could always arrest Keith on no more than his displeasure. But he had to ask himself whether that would solve anything, and Keith had the support of many of the northern lords, and a bitter grievance, which for cold policy he could not disregard.

There was consternation in the hall, a thump and clatter of guards and weapons. Even a lord did not burst through into the map room uninvited. Leon heard footsteps, felt them through the floor. He glanced up, all senses bright and humming, capped the ink and sat back in his chair. It was Keith Kil Coed trailing an outcry of armed guards.

Keith was not wearing his armor, just a tunic of tan-colored linen, and although his sword still hung at his hip, the belt of the weapon tunic hung loose as a monk's girdle. His beard was neatly trimmed, his hair combed, and despite the war-ravaged face, he looked almost respectable.

Leon waved a hand, permitted the intrusion, and the guards retreated. Keith shut the door in their faces, turned to him, visage grim. "I must speak with you."

"You tread where you have no welcome. Be about your business." Leon leaned forward, his tone of a sudden invested with a deadly menace.

Keith paused for two breaths, and his shoulders fell. "Caer Llion, I come in peace."

"Peace? You'll have to do better than that! Why have you come?"

"You ask what has brought me. Two matters, both urgent." He looked like a man screwing up his courage for a desperate statement. "For the first, I came to ask forgiveness."

"Forgiveness?" Leon echoed, his brows knitting, his brain a whorl of speculation, of considering and connecting. Decisions, strategy, and maneuvering of armies, he could make with a clear head and strong confidence. He had done all that, and it weighed very little on his mind. But this was unexpected. He slammed his palm on a stack of parchments.

"Forgive what?"

"Oh, I was mad! Mad!"

Leon considered him a moment in silence. "Well, it is over and done with," he said shortly.

"You forgive me?" Keith said, as if he could not believe his ears.

A bee sailed through the window slit and the hum of its wings was the only sound that disturbed a stillness that was becoming unnatural. At last Leon spoke.

"Why not? Pray God take no offense if I help His will along just a little. That, at least, husbandry has taught me."

Leon was prepared to see Kil Coed's surprise, but he was quite unprepared for the manner in which his benevolence was to be received.

Keith drew his sword and pointed the hilt toward him, signifying his allegiance. "This hand, this steel, this heart, are yours to command as you will."

Leon pushed back his chair on that, and rose. He spoke in soft, cold, incisive tones. "You wish to serve me? I may give you liegeman honor, titles, even wealth—and my enemies may give you a horrible death." He looked into Keith's eyes. "A death as slow and as awful as you could possibly devise, Kil Coed. If I am pulled down...consider your worst nightmare. Hast ever known torture, Keith? Or seen the heads of your enemies set on pikes?"

For a moment Keith stared at him. One did not dissemble to this man, this strength. "No, my lord."

"I'll keep no hound nor horse nor man I can't trust. As for you, men do not desert me twice. Would you extend such trust? If you were me?"

"I am in earnest. I know the history of your line—and my own, Caer Llion. I know what happens when foul charges are laid, when lies become truth, when friends fall out, and when a throne changes ruler—vengeance and death." Then, in a slow, careful choice of words, he said,

"Because you do not give *your* enemies such bad deaths...I came to you. You have honor in yourself."

Leon had not expected that. He said roughly, "And what of Suzanne and this vendetta you have pursued for nigh on eight years?"

"That is the second reason for my visit, but before I speak, I must know. Did you care for Suzanne at all?"

Leon's expression changed. In the gentlest imaginable tone he said, "I did care about her. When we first married, I wanted her. But she...well, she cared for another. She was four months gone with another's child when we wed."

Fulk FitzWarren had made all the arrangements and sought out Leon, asking him to take his lady's companion to wife. And he had never questioned his duty to his foster father and Whittington, not then, not now, and not in all the years in between. A man did what he must, always. Marrying Suzanne was merely another duty.

"I now know the truth."

"The truth?"

"About your marriage with my sister."

Leon made a harsh inarticulate grunt, scrubbed wearily at his face. "And what is that?"

Keith's face twisted. "If you recall, I was away doing service with Richard when you wed Suzanne. I thought you had failed her. She was the other part of me, you see, and we always knew when the other hurt. I was vulnerable when Hubert fed me his lies."

"How do you know they were lies?"

"I made visit to Hubert who has gone to Valle Crucis to take vows of chastity, obedience and poverty. He has repented his past sins."

"That is good. He does well, too. Considering."

"For all his faults—I grew up in his fosterage before I went to Whittington—he is not an evil man."

Leon grunted skeptically. "For myself, I see him well past contrition but yet a league from good intent."

"Hubert was one thing once, another now. He's at God's

beck every minute. There's not the room for hatred. Which
is why he confessed…'' Keith hesitated. And that meant it
was very objectionable. ''…'twas he who failed Suzanne.
He was the father of her babe.''

''Hubert!''

''You didn't *know?*''

''I never guessed.'' He was silent awhile. This had been
a day of surprises. ''I was such a young fool.''

''Did she hurt you that much, Caer Llion?''

''She had her pride. That haughty silk-and-iron-clad pride.
She used what wiles she had to ensure her babe was not
born bastard.'' Then he dismissed the topic with the disdain
it deserved. ''And Brenna?''

''Brenna?'' Was it a shudder he saw? Had the man sen-
sibilities and scruples after all? ''She is a fine woman, and
any man would be proud to have her as wife. 'Tis unfortunate for the rest of us that she has loved but one man in her
life.''

''We will never speak of this again.''

Keith's eyes met his, locked and held.

''I have changed, Caer Llion. The miracle has changed
me. I lust as much as ever. Horror of horrors—I have even
desired Brenna herself. But I have locked my desires inside
my heart. I will not sin again. I have learned to fear the
Lord.''

The sun was lowering and the evening mist rising in the
valley. Wood pigeons were winging to their nests, and ravens swooped and dived through the still, light-filled air. The
clang of a distant cow bell came dreamily through the silence.

Leon made his way toward the doorway at the base of the
tower within the keep. There was no lock, only an iron latch
that squeaked as he lifted it. The circular stairs were narrow
and steep, and the steps barely wide enough for one boot,
even at the outside end. The gray stone walls were polished
smooth by years of shoulders passing.

He took the stairs carefully. A misstep would mean a long bounce downward. At the top, he lifted the hammered wrought-iron latch, which also squeaked, and stepped out onto the parapet with its chest-high crenellated walls.

Brenna lifted her head and folded back her white veil. Strands of dark hair floated on the breeze, fine as spiderwebs. She stretched out her hand without turning, and took his hand in hers.

"I hope I didn't disturb you."

"Of course not."

"I came out to get a breath of fresh air. And what have you been doing?"

"I have been...waiting."

"Waiting—" he said.

"Yes, waiting," she said. "Waiting, Leon, waiting!" Then she laughed, the sound liquid silver on the evening air. Drawing her arm through his, she pulled him to the stone edge of the battlements. The sun was setting behind a veil of cloud; the wind promising rain before dawn. "Will you *look* at this day? Let God put on a kirtle of rose and purple and soft gold about the sun on such a day and watch the sun turn its head with compliments."

"Like a gift of gold to a bride."

"We stood here a long while ago."

"Four and ten years."

"It seems like yesterday."

"A man doesn't prove himself in one day or one night, it's the years that show the truth," he said after what she decided was a muffled chuckle.

"You know, Leon...I was just thinking. That promise you made... It has been well kept, but—" Brenna looked up and gave him a wan, shy smile "—if you do yearn to begone somewhere...I freely give you leave. I would miss you. Whatever I said before, I would miss you dreadfully. Still, I keep my promises, too."

He looked down at her with a tranquil face, from which the green flecks in his eyes shone like spring leaves. A flicker that was scarcely a smile crossed his face. "You do, yes. And now you mention it, I might just give the matter some thought. Thank you for the suggestion, Brenna. I will indeed give it some thought."

This is where I belong, Leon thought exultantly. It is a world here, all I'd ever want. He was truly enjoying being wed to Brenna, and he looked forward to treating her to the lifetime of love that she richly deserved.

"Well? You have that look that says you've thought about it, and you aren't about to answer unless someone hammers it out of you. Out with it. I'm not like Suzanne, and I won't let you hide your thoughts until we can't talk at all."

"Well..." Leon fingered his chin, then swallowed, and committed himself beyond recall. "Of course, I will wait until the child is born. And the one after that. And the one after that. After they are grown and wed, I could go abroad for...oh, no more than a short journey, to be back in time for the first grandchild. Yes, I might do that."

"That sounds like you'll be staying for quite some time, my lord."

He picked her up and whirled her around and around.

"Forever and ever and ever."

*　*　*　*　*

Travel to the British Isles
and behold the romance and
adventure within the pages of these
Harlequin Historicals® novels

ON SALE JANUARY 2002

MY LADY'S TRUST
by **Julia Justiss**
(Regency England, 1812)
A society lady fakes her own death and discovers
true love with an eligible earl!

DRAGON'S DOWER
by **Catherine Archer**
(Medieval England, 1200)
Book #1 of *The Brotherhood of the Dragon* series
By the king's decree a brave knight must marry
the daughter of his fiercest foe....

ON SALE FEBRUARY 2002

HIS LADY FAIR
by **Margo Maguire**
(Medieval England, 1429)
A world-weary spy becomes embroiled in intrigue—
and forbidden passion!

 Harlequin Historicals®
Historical Romantic Adventure!

 Visit us at www.eHarlequin.com HHMED22

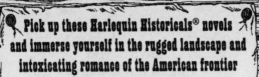

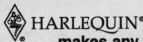

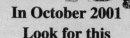

In October 2001
Look for this
New York Times bestselling author

BARBARA DELINSKY

in

Bronze Mystique

The only men in Sasha's life lived between the covers of her bestselling romances. She wrote about passionate, loving heroes, but no such man existed...til Doug Donohue rescued Sasha the night her motorcycle crashed.

AND award-winning Harlequin Intrigue author

GAYLE WILSON

in

Secrets in Silence

This fantastic 2-in-1 collection will be on sale October 2001.

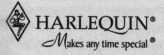

HARLEQUIN®
Makes any time special®